Whom Gods Would Destroy

An Occult History of the First World War

Part III: Armageddon

By Tyler Kimball

Whom Gods Would Destroy, Part III

WHOM GODS WOULD DESTROY, Part III: Armageddon

Preceded by

Part I: The Architects of Hell

and

Part II: Archangel

Cover art derived from Percy John Derf Smith's "Death Forbids" and "Death Intoxicated", plates from the 1921 etching series *Dance of Death* (Part I), "Lenin, der Günstling," by Karl Czerpien, published in Swiss magazine *Nebelspalter* #46, Nov. 15, 1919, under Chief Editor Paul Altheer (Part II), and George Paul LeRoux's *1918, or The Last Communique* (Part III). Back art taken from "At the End of the War to End All Wars," Illustration from *Die Muskete* magazine, 1918.

This manuscript has been prepared in Garamond, 12 point, with the title set in Manorly.

First Edition
All rights reserved.
Copyright © 2023 by Tyler Kimball
This book may not be reproduced in whole or in part by any means without permission.

Print ISBN: 978-1-0881-6548-5

Whom Gods Would Destroy, Part III

Book III: Armageddon

"The war for giants is over. The war of pygmies began."
- Winston Churchill.

Into the Ether

Presaging, and perhaps influencing, the Philadelphia Experiment hoax of the mid 20th century, rumors circled in the dying days of the war that famed inventor Thomas Alva Edison rendered vessels invisible to both submarines and the naked eye. The master of electricity had also mastered the electron, which, in the two decades following J.J. Thomson's isolation of that particle from cathode rays, seemed to be the source of potential magic. The truth of the matter seems to lie in the ambiguity of the word *ether*.

As part of a series of nearly fifty research projects conducted aboard the *USS Sachem*, Edison worked on an oleum cloud shell to disguise ships on the water, a chemical alternative to dazzle camouflage. Oleum is also known as fuming sulfuric acid, often used as a way to safely transport the acid in a solid state as it is easily reconstituted into a vapor by steam conduits. The chemical is sometimes confused with *oleum dulci vitrioli*, "sweet oil of vitriol," or ether. And ether was, in the context of invisibility and optics, usually the luminiferous ether, the now obsolete concept that light waves must propagate through a semi-physical medium instead of a true vacuum. In this theoretical framework, manipulation of this ether could create areas of darkness or, with more precision, render objects invisible.

So it was all a game of telephone, appropriately enough.

Edison's chemical tests bled into early experiments in diffused lighting camouflage, a technique that would not be revived until World War II, with the Royal Canadian Navy's corvette cloaking tests and America's Yehudi lights. The later story of the Philadelphia Experiment likewise features the detail that the *USS Eldridge* was surrounded by flashing lights and a greenish fog – apart from that slick, sci-fi green, this matches' eye-witness descriptions of Edison's experiments[1]. There may also be some conflation with inventor T. Townsend Brown's fruitless work on antigravity aboard the US Naval Research Laboratory yacht *Caroline*.

In the wake of the 7 May 1915 sinking of the *Lusitania*, Edison

[1] Vallée, Jacques F. (1994) "Anatomy of a Hoax: The Philadelphia Experiment Fifty Years Later." *Journal of Scientific Exploration* Volume 8, Number 1, p. 47-71

discussed his hopes for increased defense funding and massive research laboratories with *the New York Times*. This sounds rather mundane today, but this fusion of civilian business and military-industrial resources was unprecedented in America, before eventually replacing the nation in the mid-20th century.

Edison's primary concern had been America's reliance on foreign chemical supplies, particular rubber (he previously researched the development of synthetic alternatives at his Fort Myers lab), German dyes, and the phenolic resins used in phonographs, usually imported from Britain. He repurposed his Silver Lake facilities towards the production of phenol and its derivatives in September of 1914. It was during his research on phenol production that he found that it could be nitrated into picric acid, and then into ammonium picrate, a component of explosive artillery shells; other phenol derivatives included the plastic Bakelite, and the salicylic acid found in Aspirin. Edison's forethought kept Bayer supplied throughout the war, but he was reluctant to put his ammonium picrate supplies to military use, declaring that he only wanted to produce defensive tools.

The article showed a decisive shift towards active participation in the war effort, and inspired Secretary of the Navy Josephus Daniels, and his assistant, Franklin Delano Roosevelt, to reach out to Edison to deal with the U-boat menace, with Roosevelt pushing, rather presciently, for swift-boat technology. By July 1915, Edison and Daniels organized a multidisciplinary technocratic advisory board with strong connections to academia, corporate research, and all branches of the military, with open and rather transparent civilian outreach. Edison was appointed president of this Naval Consulting Board on October 7th. Unfortunately, he found the Allies unwilling or unable to share detailed data on submarine warfare, and his own government unwilling to fund his ambitious projects. Still, this was Thomas Edison, who, for all the criticism leveled at him, was a brilliant organizer of engineering and scientific minds. He was a force multiplier; if one allowed him to headhunt and lead geniuses, he would deliver some of the most productive years of his subordinates' lives.

By 1917, he could feel the pressure rising; the US was almost certainly going to fully mobilize within months, and he was feeling his age as he entered his 70s. Frustrated by the lack of government funding on research he was specifically asked to carry out, Edison moved to the naval station at Sandy Hook, New Jersey, and took up residence aboard the USS *Sachem*, a yacht formerly known as *SP-192*.

"Echo-location" technology was Edison's primary concern, a field rapidly developing from meteorologist L.F. Richardson's search for the *Titanic*. In 1914, the Canadian Reginald Fessenden of the Submarine Signal Company of Boston demonstrated depth sounding and underwater signaling via Morse code on the Grand Banks of Newfoundland. His 500 Hz oscillator could detect the submerged portion of icebergs with enough regularity and efficiency to begin deployment on Canadian-built submarines.

Background channels led to communication between Edison and Ernest Rutherford, the father of nuclear science. Rutherford had been researching sonar technology since 1915 using water tanks at Manchester University, and prototypes were already under construction by his team. Newfoundlander Robert William Boyle, who he had previously taught at McGill University, now worked alongside Rutherford on the Board of Inventions and Research. Rutherford also corresponded with Dr. Albert Beaumont Wood's team at the Admiralty Experimental Station at Parkeston Quay. In what must have been the single busiest year for any scientist in history, Rutherford secretly traveled to the United States to discuss the idea with American researchers, then returned to England and induced the first artificial nuclear reaction by bombarding nitrogen nuclei with alpha particles[2], before overseeing the fitting of these "ASDIC" sonar systems to His Majesty's fleet.

After his meeting with Rutherford, Edison's yacht undertook a secretive circuit around the Eastern Seaboard, making frequent stops at its major ports. The need for mobility and interest in underwater detection was spurred by, of all things, acts of "amphibious airship" sabotage conducted along America's shorelines.

On July 30th, 1916 at Black Tom Island, New Jersey, thirty-four

---

[2] Rutherford, E. (1919). "Collision of α particles with light atoms. IV. An anomalous effect in nitrogen". The London, Edinburgh, and Dublin Philosophical Magazine and Journal of Science. Series 6. 37 (222): 581–587.

boxcars carrying a thousand short tons[3] of munition earmarked for the Russian Empire exploded. Despite causing only three deaths, the blast was audible as far away as Philadelphia and inflicted over $22 million in damages, including busted windows in several New York boroughs and structural shock to the Statue of Liberty. It would go down as the largest act of World War One-era sabotage and the second most destructive wartime explosion in North America before the atomic bomb. The most striking detail of the whole affair was that multiple witnesses spotted a silvery airplane-like vessel hovering over Black Tom Island just before the detonation. On 9 September 1916, a strange airplane with a powerful searchlight scanned Wilson, North Carolina[4], and appeared to drop something near a Merck pharmaceutical facility.

At 2:30 AM on April 14, 1917, three night watchmen from the 6th Massachusetts National Guard's Company L spotted an unidentified flying object on the mouth of the Pascataqua River. The men were stationed near the Portsmouth Naval Shipyard as a deterrent to German sabotage, and reacted with unusual force for witnesses of the unknown, firing on the craft as it descended towards the water[5]. The vessel briefly hovered near a bridge, before diving into the river, where it appeared to continue out to sea. Similar amphibious airships with green lights were sighted along the northeastern seaboard in the first two months of 1916, associated with the destruction of munitions and chemical plants. These included some forty buildings in Philadelphia, Dupont factories in Gibbstown and Carney's Point[6], New Jersey and Wilmington, Delaware.

On 11 January 1917 fire destroyed over a million Russia-bound artillery shells housed in the Kingsland munitions factory in Brooklyn, New York, with lights or dark, blimp-like objects seen descending into the East River. In April, over a hundred workers, many of them children, perished in the arson of Eddystone, Pennsylvania's Hercules Powder Company.

While unconnected to a direct attack, all the way back in July of 1915, an inexplicably fast "spycraft" with scanning blue lights seemed to

---

[3] 907,184.74 kilograms
[4] *Charlotte Observer*. 10 September 1916.
[5] Hall, Michael David. *UFO's - A Century of Sightings*. Galder Press. 1999, p. 14.
[6] *The New York Times*. 10 January 1916. Vol. LXV No. 21,170.

map out portions of the Florida East Coast Railway and the military aeronautical station at Pensacola before heading into the Everglades[7]. Furthermore, there was renewed interest in two British cases. The *Formidable*-class (*London* sub-class) pre-dreadnought battleship HMS *Bulwark* exploded at 7:50 am on November 26, 1914 while moored at Kethole Reach's Number 17 buoy in the estuary of the River Medway. Only twelve of her 750 crew members survived, mostly because they had been blown out of an open hatch in Number 1 mess deck amidships, by what Able Seaman Stephen Marshall described as "a colossal draught." Marshall was thrown so high that he could see the ship's masts shaking. Witnesses on nearby battleships reported at least two detonations. A naval court of inquiry held that *Bulwark*'s crew stored ammunition in the precarious cross-passageways between their guns, and that the volatile cordite charges overheated when stored next to a boiler room bulkhead. Still, many in the navy and many more civilians suspected German sabotage, especially after the minelayer *Princess Irene* blew up in May 1915 in the same anchorage, though the highly explosive sea mines lining her deck may have had something to do with the explosion. The explosions of the *HMS Natal* at Cromarty Firth in December and the *HMS Vanguard* on July 9, 1917 were a bit harder to explain, but chalked up to the detonation of inferior cordite shells.

Witnesses on the shore and aboard the vessel claimed to have seen a U-boat in the water at the time of the *HMS Bulwark*'s loss, despite the high location of the blast and the confirmed lack of any German submarine activity in the area at the time. Likewise, no German ever claimed responsibility for sabotaging any of the lost ships. Similarly, an unknown aerial vehicle was seen at Cromarty Firth the night of the *Natal*'s loss and the night before the explosion of the *Vanguard*. A Chatham dockyard ordnance fitter who had worked on all four vessels was investigated, but it was likely a coincidence – harbor maintenance workers move between docked ships frequently, and they had no reason to suspect him otherwise[8].

However, concern over airship raids disappeared with a clear cut

---

[7] *Miami Herald*. 27 July 1915.
[8] Konstam, Angus. *Ghost Ships: Tales of Abandoned, Doomed, and Haunted Vessels*. (Globe Pequot, 2007) pp. 33-35

case of German sabotage in March. Munitions barges exploded at the US Naval Yard at Mare Island, California, killing six and injuring dozens. Authorities investigating the incident arrested a German naval officer named Lothar Witzke after deciphering a coded message sewn into his left jacket sleeve as he attempted to cross the Mexican border at Nogales, Arizona under the assumed identity of "Pablo Waberski," a Russo-American traveler inexplicably swept up in the Mexican-American Border War[9]. The US sentenced him to death with information from double-agents within his organization[10]. He tenuously connected his arson attacks to Kurt Jahnke, the North American chief of Imperial German Naval Intelligence. Jahnke's sabotage stratagem attempted to distract Americans from the European War by stirring up tension between the US and Mexico. He has been tied to the 1915 Huerta coup, Pancho Villa's raids, the Zimmermann Telegram, and tangentially to other acts of sabotage such as 1915's Vanceboro Bridge bombing. He would later be blamed for masterminding "agent provocateurs" and the training of Mexican troops in the lead-up to the Battle of Ambos Nogales on 27 August 1918, but the conflict might easily have been rooted in nothing but American and Mexican antagonism.

Previously, on 30 May 1915, a Russian-bound powder barge in

---

[9] Kahn, David, *The Reader of Gentleman's Mail: Herbert O. Yardley and the Birth of American Codebreaking.* (Yale University Press, 2006)

[10] Witzke's sentence would later be commuted to life at Leavenworth Prison after a series of nearly-successful escape attempts and a valiant effort in rescuing inmates after a boiler room explosion. Why nobody suspected him of deliberately causing the explosion is unknown. He would be released into German custody on April 23, 1923. His date of death is unknown. Lothar Witzke had started the war as a Imperial German Naval lieutenant on the *SMS Dresden*, which was sunk after intense harassment activities in the shipping lanes of the Americas. Witzke survived the sinking with a broken leg, and was arrested and detained in Chile. He escaped from captivity in 1916 and assumed a fake name and the identity of a sailor. In this disguise, he reached San Francisco in May aboard the *S.S. Calusa* and reported to German Consul General von Bopp. Through Von Bopp, he joined up with Kurt Jahnke, after which he engaged in the above activities (in addition to the Mare Island Incident, he claimed involvement with the Black Tom sabotage, though due to his location and means, this seems highly unlikely).

Elliott Bay, Washington detonated. The blast sent a fireball a hundred feet into the air and shattered windows in Tacoma. The city was alight with rumors of a volcano, a massive earthquake, or a meteorite, as several such objects had been seen in the sky before the detonation. On the 22nd, unknown arsonists destroyed armored vehicles on Tacoma's Northern Pacific docks. German saboteur Emil Marksz committed suicide in his hotel room in Seattle on the 4th of July, and Walter L. Scholz, working under the name Herman Schultz, admitted to assembling the dynamite and detonator rig in a shack south of Harbor Island. This had seemed like a simple case, but then investigators connected the meteorites to the destruction of a major DuPont facility in Tacoma, associated with black airships in the sky. Similar airships had been seen over Tacoma in 1896 and in 1908 (along with Kent and Puget Sound). But it all seemed to be a red herring with the fall of Lothar Witzke's decisively earthbound network.

With these acts of sabotage satisfactorily explained, this skyship panic died down. However, there were still suspicions of some sort of aerial assault, perhaps a directed energy weapon likened to the Heat Ray of Wells' Martians, or low-visibility flamethrowers, but no explanation could be found for the diving action of the vessel; the most plausible theory was that the attacking airships simply killed its lights and dropped something into the water, such as an empty fuel tank, ballast, or an overheated weapon battery, to hasten its getaway.

Building on the "mysterious inventor" craze of the late 19th century scareships, American intelligence strongly suspected academia and alternative religions after the case of Erich Muenter, a German-American with strong sympathy for the Fatherland. In 1908, while a linguistics professor at Harvard, he poisoned his wife with arsenic. He fled to Mexico after probing questions by A.E. Long, an undertaker whose suspicions were aroused when Muenter was oddly persistent that his wife be quickly cremated. Her brother came forward, claiming that Muenter had previously tried to murder her and their daughter via natural gas asphyxiation, and several of the professor's colleges noted that his body became "wraithlike" in proportions in his pursuit of "ancient lore" and transcendental notions steeped in German romantic literature and alchemy[11]. He also sought to create a universal Germanic language blending High German, Nordic, and Scots, and what might have been a pan-Celtic language or an attempt to recreate proto-Celtic. Due to his obsession with linguistic, spiritual, and biological revival, Meunter became known as the Necromancer.

In Mexico, Meunter worked as a stenographer and bookkeeper for the Samuel Brothers mining operation in El Oro. One of the company's executives, a James Dean, thought he was a good worker, but noted that Muenter had a habit of gazing into the middle distance and going into a trance, muttering something strange to an unseen presence.

Soon recruited by Germany's spy networks, he re-emerged as Frank Holt, a metaphysics professor at Cornell, and developed a terrorist persona, "R. Pearce." The Necromancer used this pseudonym to write letters filled with threats and post-action gloating, and a 'C. Hendricks' to mask his shipment of materiel, including several hundred pounds of dynamite and acid-timed bombs. In rapid succession, he bombed the Capitol Building, shot the son of J.P. Morgan in a strong-arm home invasion, planted a dynamite bomb on the England-bound steamship *SS Minnehaha*, and committed suicide in captivity after examination by an alienist. After unsuccessfully cutting his wrist and stabbing his throat, he climbed to the top of his cell and let himself fall to his death. Unbeknownst to Meunter, a Bureau of Combustibles taskforce lead by Inspector "Owney" Egan discovered Holt's trunk-bomb in a warehouse before it was loaded onto the *Minnehaha*, foiling the bomb plot.

The alienist was baffled by Meunter's statements; the terrorist claimed that he never wanted to hurt anyone, and that he somehow thought his actions would end American involvement in the European war. He was quickly labeled "a paranoiac of the reformatory type" by Dr. Carlos MacDonald. Despite this unstable personality, he insinuated himself so rapidly and successfully at Cornell and the University of Kansas that a massive German infiltration of America's universities seemed terrifyingly real. A further scandal emerged when an investigation revealed that Meunter's suicide was possible because he was barely guarded, to the point that an anonymous county official

[11] *Seattle Daily Times.* 10 May 1906.

stated that "Nassau County [was] lucky Holt killed himself. If he hadn't, he might have walked away from us."

The most chilling detail of Meunter's case was that he keenly observed the death of his wife, hoping to measure the changes that occurred upon her passing, both biological and 'etheric.' Though the papers described it as a search for a 'vapour,' he was likely looking for measurable evidence for ectoplasm or animating ether[12][13], and he had previously alluded to the famous pseudoscientific 1907 experiment by Duncan MacDougall, which determined that the soul weighed "21.3 grams." According to his theories, the recent birth of a child left Mrs. Meunter in a vulnerable, or perhaps exalted, biological and spiritual state, at a climactic point in her life cycle that would make her departure far more tangible, by Meunter's strange metric – *the Annals of Psychical Science*, paraphrasing the *American*, furthers a romantic narrative that "he thought he had perfected a means of proving the existence of a soul which he could only test at the death of one whom he loved. Then he thought a vaporous substance would cling to him."[14]

Theosophists muttered about the case, because Meunter's cremation of his wife had been tied to their philosophy, but Theosophist spokespeople pointed towards something far more ancient, perhaps alchemical palingenesis or Zoroastrian rituals (though Zoroastrians historically expose their dead). Later, residents of Schaumberg, four miles north of Elgin, Illinois came forward after locals uncovered evidence that Meunter hid in their remote, German-speaking village. He appeared to belong to some local pagan cult worshiping an unknown serpentine deity (or a primordial sea serpent), blending ancient trappings with modern "German metaphysics," whatever that means, the belief in the transmigration of the soul, and the use of mind-altering drugs such as peyote. The cult appeared to be led by a Jopp family of Mecklenburg, whose patriarch could perform faith healings[15]. The cult appeared to

---

[12] *Daily Express.* 30 April 1906.
[13] Blackmore, Suan J. (1992) *Beyond the body: An investigation of out-of-the-body experiences.* Academy Chicago Publishers
[14] "Echos and News." T*he Annals of Psychical Science* Vol. III, January-June 1906. pp. 351.
[15] *The Sunday Herald of Boston.* 13 May 1906.

Christianized with the death of the patriarch, and merged with the newfound snake-handling movement sometime in the 1920s.

Not long into his enterprise, Edison was confounded by the submission of a plan by Dr. Orville Wilson Owen of Detroit, an enigmatic engineer and anti-Stratfordian. Owen claimed that he was in communication with Colonel J.E.B. Seely, former British Secretary of State for War, and sought funding to develop a machine to "neutralize gravity through ionic vibrations." When Britain declined the offer, he submitted it to the Naval Consulting Board. Owen's proposal relied on an electromagnetic principle that all things vibrate at certain frequencies, and that what we perceive as magnetic poles are, in fact, self-sustaining vibrations either joining with or repulsing their counterparts. This variability in vibrations was Owen's root cause for all aeronautical issues, including "zones of silence" lacking all vibrations that forced aircraft to lose all momentum and plummet to the earth. Artificial zones of silence were his explanation for the capability of phantom airships to seemingly drop straight into the water and function as a submersible without losing their rigid airframe.

Edison, at this point, must have been rolling his eyes, but Owen's final claim struck a nerve – Dr. Owen was a fervent admirer of Sir Francis Bacon, believing him to be the true author of Shakespeare's plays (a common assertion in the early 20th century) and a genius inventor. During an 1912 excavation of the River Wye, Owen claimed that he came across plans for the construction of a strikingly modern airship. This got Edison thinking – there was very little evidence that the Germans were behind these strange airship attacks, for if their engineering was so advanced, to the point of being invincible and untraceable, why were they still deploying the vulnerable, flimsy models seen in the European theater of war?

There must be some other force at work, a secret society of airship builders. The public had, as mentioned before, tried to pin the prior scareship waves on Edison, and he in turn had looked to the stars for an answer while on Ford's peace mission. He had been warned of the issue all the way back on 17 September 1908, when a strange airship buzzed the General Electric plant in Pittsfield, Massachusetts, accompanied by a "fiery mass," moving far too fast for a Zeppelin, far too advanced for a heavier-than-air craft in the same year as the Wright Brothers' historic flight.

Edison had recently heard of a man named Shivkar Bāpuji Talpade, an Indian scholar and engineer who passed away the previous year. Talpade received a blend of Western-style and classical Vedic education in Bombay, and was inspired by his mentor's tales of ancient aeronautics and books such as the descriptions of Vimāna by Maharishi Bharadwaja and the *Rigvedādic Bhāshya Bhumikā*. Talpade had also cited Edison and Hiram Maxim as inspirations to explore a way to mechanize these legendary flying vehicles, and claimed to have built a unmanned, steam-powered, electrical airplane called the *Marutsakhā* (Air-Friend) in 1895, which flew to a height of 460 meters in a poorly-attended exhibition. Edison had heard little corroborating evidence from contacts in India, and Talpade's working principle, that mercury could sublimate into hydrogen in sunlight, was patently untrue, based on superseded alchemical theory. The best lead he found was a barely-literate *pandit* named Subbaraya Shastry, who claimed to have channeled an ancient sage named Bharadvaja, and Bhagavan Das's *Utterances of Pranava*, published by the Theosophical Society in 1910-1913, who claimed to be drawing from the work of a sage named Gargyavana. Both men held to the notion an ancient aeronautical program more advanced than our own existed in the shadows, its secrets known only to the initiated.

Persistent rumors held that the British Raj had the bodies of several vimana passengers. An archival search of the *Houston Post* (2 May 1897) carried a tale of a Danish sailor named Oleson, who, in September 1862, witnessed the crash of an aerial vehicle during a storm in the Indian Ocean. He and six of his companions on the brig *Christine* had been swept overboard, forcing them to take refuge on a lifeless islet, where one man died of his injuries. Their despair soon turned to horror as a massive craft fell from the crowds, heading towards them, only to be blown off course by a ferocious gale.

The sailors swam to the wreckage of the machine, described as "the size of a battleship[16]" and with four large wings. Some scavenged what appeared to be food from floating storage boxes. Those who pressed

[16] Based on the ironclad frigates and similar battleships of the 1850s and 60s, the vessel was somewhere between 100 and 130 meters in length.

deeper into the vessel discovered the body of a dozen men with dark bronze skin, long silky hair and beards, each standing over twelve feet. One man, in a Lovecraftian twist, allegedly went mad and threw himself into the sea. The survivors stocked up on the food and built a raft from the floating elements of wreckage, and sailed to sea, to be intercepted by an Australia-bound Russian vessel some sixty hours later.

Oleson used an oversized thumb ring set with two unidentifiable red jewels as proof of his discovery. The Dane's report led to a brief search for the remains, and possible recovery, by British forces near Diego Garcia. Interest in this old tale was briefly revived by intelligence indicating that the German light cruiser *SMS Emden* had a secondary mission to search for signs of "Indian Ocean giants" during its 1914 commerce-route patrolling near Diego Garcia, a fanciful element that was cheekily supported when *Emden* captured the Russian steamer *Ryazan* and renamed it *Cormoran*, after the giant of Cornish legend.

His search for answers in India was ultimately fruitless, but the seemingly political nature of the scareship attacks led Edison to believe that there was something both earthly and occult behind these mysterious saboteurs.

And so, dangerous research and development moved to hidden bases and mobile positions such as Edison's yacht.

At Washington (or, rather, at a nearby city on the Potomac known as Scotland), Edison's crew gained a replacement navigator, a Captain Claude Stoughton, who seemed to slip in effortlessly despite his good looks and noble bearing. After his initial entry on the crew manifest, Stoughton is next mentioned during a striking sighting; passing near the island known as Tangier, two crewmen claimed to have spotted a large hippopotamus wading by the shore. Edison did not have a chance to see the beast. Aging and nearly deaf, runners had to alert him of such occurrences, and he could be slow moving despite his energetic temperament. When Edison finally arrived at the bow, Stoughton joked that the hippo must have booked a ship to the wrong Tangier. Edison at first dismissed it as a manatee, which the crew had previously spotted off Florida, but Stoughton insisted he had worked closely with the creatures, and there was no mistaking the teeth in those yawning jaws. Edison reportedly scowled, and asked where he'd worked. Soughton simply said he'd worked in Africa, before noting that he had never seen one that large before – it must have been a giant, "some freak of doubled proportions, likely incapable of supporting its bulk on land."

Edison said that he wanted to be clear of the island, as he didn't want to injure the beast with their experiments for the night, pertaining to "the absorption of light by seawater" and "underwater searchlights." Stoughton, rather cockily, stated that Edison must have had a change of heart since all those electrocuted critters and the Coney Island elephant. Edison balked – he said that execution was fifteen years ago, that Topsy had killed three people, and electrocution was more humane than the original plan to strangle the poor thing. He hadn't even shot the footage - that was Edwin Porter's work. His name was simply on every film made by his company, and there had been thousands of them. The topic appeared to have been an often-prodded sore spot – and, indeed, the idea that he executed Topsy as part of the War of the Currents is a modern fabrication, as the AC/DC conflict had ended well over a decade beforehand.

The main witness to the event, and our primary source, Dr. Henry Newlin Stokes (1859-1942), noted the crew immediately went tense and looked for other work elsewhere on the ship. Edison pulled away from the new captain – his hearing impairment could make him seem deeply confrontational as he was forced to get right up in people's faces. The voyage saw him forgo his usual clean-shaven and dapper looks; "there was something of the ancient mariner to him now, grizzled and gray-eyed with thin, wind-blown hair." He looked to be chewing at something before he slunk back into his cabin to make preparations for the experiments. Stokes followed him, though kept his distance.

Dr. Stokes had an interesting career and philosophical trajectory. He was ostensibly aboard the vessel in his capacity as a chemist. In his early career, he studied plastics and inorganic rubber, discovering Hexachlorophosphazene and its polymerization[17]. Once a strict materialist and agnostic, he gradually dabbled in esoteric publishing, yoga, and psychic sciences, and eventually joined the Theosophical Society. In 1917, he established the *O.E. Library Critic*, an outgrowth of

---

[17] H. N. Stokes (1896), *On Trimetaphosphimic acid and its decomposition products*. American Chemical Journal, vol. 18 issue 8, p. 629.

his O.E. Library League, which he would continue to own and edit until his death. He was something of a gadfly in the world of Theosophy, Spiritualism, and Rosicrucianism, criticizing their practices as straying from the First Object, the common brotherhood of man. Despised by elite esoteric circles for exposing their hypocrisy and fraudulent practices, he was a champion of the "Back to Blavatsky" contingent. He likewise was a proponent of religious freedom, which saw a downward turn in May of 1916, when Chief Michael Long's "wizard police" arrested the Rev. Mrs. Sarah Darling of Newark's Spiritualist Church, on charges of witchcraft[18]. Stokes was on Edison's mission under an alias, as he did not want his muckraking reputation to tarnish the important work of a fellow Theosophist – and journalism was a secondary concern to the chemistry, though he would record any interesting events for posterity, to be disclosed a century after the War.

The third notable Theosophist on the vessel had yet to make a name for himself: Edward Arthur Wilson. Wilson was not a scientist, but a mariner, who had arrived aboard the vessel after a sojourn from Prince Edward Isle. Stokes said that he resembled a young Mephistopheles, a sharp-faced man with a small, goatish beard. He was not a navy man, and was nearly turned away for this reason, but Edison saw something in him, charisma, intellect, and talent - and when Edison said someone had potential, people listened. Also, Edison noted, the name "Wilson" kept popping up, serendipitously.

Stokes waited two hours, until Edison finished his nap. Edison snapped out of his slumber suddenly, and looked rather distant and sad, prompting Stokes to ask if he was feeling well. Edison looked at Stokes and simply said "it was that damn elephant. He saw its death in a dream, but not as in *Electrocution of an Elephant.* The beast was enormous, larger than it was in life, electricity shocking its body and the whole thing smelled like brass and burnt-out light bulbs. There was the trumpet of an elephant, and something like a train whistle; this is what propelled him to consciousness."

Edison rose up, wiped his face with a towel, and got to work. The acoustic tests were successful, but they were unable to produce a

---

[18] *The Sunday Telegram..* 1 May 1916.

searchlight powerful and precise enough to reliably detect the buoys. After the retrieval of their test supplies, the crew plotted a northbound course.

Their experimental cycle continued for a week with little interesting activity, performing smudging experiments (that is, smokescreens, on the hull and against periscopes), further searchlight tests, development of mirror reflection systems, and something vaguely described as "night glass." It was during this latter test that Edison nodded off in his seat above deck, as he was prone to working for serial eight hour shifts, interrupted only by two hours of sleep.

From Stokes' report, Edison seemed unsure if he was awake or asleep. He felt the sudden crash of falling trees, which startled him into wakefulness, or so he at first believed, fearful that the ship was breaking apart. The pungent scent of sulfur and an intense heat wafted over him, yet a chill ran up his back. He then saw a man that resembled a timberjack, in blood red flannel and carrying an ax, suddenly walk across his field of view from the direction of the falling trees. The bearded, dark-haired man briefly glanced at Edison, eyes deep and sunken, and disappeared into the cabin. He closed his eyes in shock and bolted up from his chair. Nothing had changed, and he could not find the strange man, but it had seemed so real, with none of a dream's fogginess. He stumbled towards the lights, and flipped on the switch – the light, he would recount, flared up like the sun before burning out. He reached up with a gloved hand to unscrew the light, and found that the tungsten had been consumed somehow, or perhaps removed and replaced with a paper filament as some practical joke. Yes, he noted, there was paper ash in the bulb. The whole intrusive affair spooked him, and he mused on the lightbulb's label – Mazda, named after Ahura Mazda, the ancient Persian God of Wisdom and Creation, who warded off the evils of the world.

One experiment emphasized a paranormal bent to detection, based on the theories of Sir William Fletcher Barrett, discoverer of Stalloy, which would be purified into Permalloy by Gustav Elmen of Bell Laboratories. This silicon-iron alloy was known for its magnetic permeability and shielding, and used in transatlantic cables. Barrett was also a paranormalist, theorizing that the use of permalloy loading coils and quartz crystals could detect objects in water retroactively. Edison thought this experiment went beyond quackery and hokum, nothing more than "dressed-up divination," but it would sate the more spiritually-inclined engineers. Edison was more interested in the harder science of George Washington Pierce's study of quartz crystals, and other submarine applications of loading coils, known at the time as Pupin coils. At New York City, the crew corresponded with Mihajlo Pupin himself, who worked at a separate submarine detection program at Columbia University and advised the National Advisory Committee for Aeronautics, the precursor of NASA. From the docks, Dr. Stokes noted Pupin's secret communication with fellow Freemasons aboard the vessel.

As Edison's subordinates carried out the crystal experiments, Stoughton and Wilson watched with curiosity. Edison explained that understanding piezoelectricity was something of the Holy Grail of this research, as crystal structures could produce and detect sounds, generate high voltages and refract light, *and* regulate frequencies. A merger of sonic, ultrasonic, electrical, and optical technologies would be the culmination of his life's work.

Wilson suddenly asked if he put much stock in the concept of sacred geometry. Edison, always the pragmatist, said no, he never thought much of it, and said that when you get down to it, mountains and rivers decide human settlement more than any mystical lines of force. Wilson countered with the nature of these quartz crystals — what would otherwise be dead carbon, no more fascinating than ash, could take on far more advanced capabilities simply by reorganizing its structure; just as ductile wire could carry complex telegraphic signals even though it is nothing more than spun metal.

Stoughton laughed and slapped Wilson on the back, saying that he counted Wilson as a simple pile of sea-salt, not a philosopher. Wilson said he had traveled far and wide, and knew more about the shape of the world than most. Some places had an emerging spirit to them, and he'd seen it in action.

Edison asked how so, and Wilson mentioned Canberra, the capital of Australia. "It means the meeting place," he said, "Or the hollow between a woman's fine breasts, because of the mountains, or because there was a heart beneath that city."

Wilson laughed, and said that he had ferried its architects out from Chicago. They were a couple, Walter Burley Griffin and Marion Mahoney Griffin. The Australians held an international contest to design their new capital city. "They took a canoe trip just north of Chicago, when Mrs. Griffin started hearing voices. When they got home, she forced Mr. Griffin to complete his entry in the contest, locking him in his workstation. And suddenly, Mr. Griffin went into a fit, a trance, like he was channeling something. For weeks he did nothing but design that city, and they both said there was someone or something telling them what to do."

Wilson said that they won the contest, and became Anthroposophists not long after, "whispering to the gnomes in the land." He brought them down to Australia on a steamer, through the Panama Canal, a detail that caused Stoughton's ears to perk up. Griffin ran into problems there, because the government was lying to him, "feeding him falsehoods for some damned reason... Australia is dangerous," he said, because "the myths are animals and people and gods and places all in one. It's all geography." When he dropped them off at that river dock, he swore that he "saw something in the sky, the Kurra Kurra, the storm bird, or some kind of creature with wings and paws. I don't trust that place. There were queer lights over the Blue Mountains. And why is it called New South Wales? Why just the south of Wales?"

Edison stepped back and covered his mouth, to keep from laughing. He asked if Wilson was influenced by his departed companions' surname in his day-dream of a griffin.

Wilson said it was no day-dream, but dreamtime. Creation myths are not just an ancient point of origin, but always happening to the Aboriginals. There was something terrible in that snaking lake by Canberra, something locked up in the river and the stone, yearning to break out into the sky.

"They're building pyramids and lines of power with quartz. The Blacks there call it *maban*, the source of their magic power." He gestured at the piezoelectric experiment. He said he didn't trust that whole building project, because "it's a wet center of a dry plane, a powderkeg of fire and water, bird and snake. That's what it is. In the Hebrew, *Chol*, means both *sand* and *phoenix*, and how all the wicked lands of the Bible became people, both ancestral and personified. Edom and Magog. Or the Greek god-realm Hades. And something like de Camões' Adamaster, the drowned giant off the Cape of Good Hope, or Jasconius, the whale that was an island and a demon all in one. The Australian Blacks worship a rainbow snake as their high god, that snaked up the rivers, water and earth, and is still writhing over the land. Bad joo-joo, the stuff of evil alchemy. The Griffins're going to conjure up a phoenix. The Ziz."

At this point, Dr. Stokes remarks that Edison looks at Wilson, "as if attempting to ascertain whether Wilson is some undiscovered magus or the grandest idiot in Creation. He walked off, to speak with the experimenting physicists."

Dr. Stokes said that Wilson turned to him and said, 'He's too much of a scientist, that one. But we're on the cusp of an Aquarian Age. That means not just the stars, but the seas. The Depths of consciousness, the infinity of knowledge, the flow of life and death. You'll see, that's the important bit."

Dr. Stokes asked for clarification.

"The ancient dead were exposed to the air, to be eaten by birds. Then the dead were buried. Theosophists and Hindoos know to burn the dead with fire. But soon, all the souls will flow, the dead are in the water, changing and reincarnating freely. Think of Osiris on the Bark of the Dead, the Foremost of the Westerners. Serapis Bey on the islands. Think of the abyss. Think of Atlantis rising."

Dr. Stokes said Wilson was awfully interested in the esoteric for a sailor. Wilson retorted that seamen had always had their mythology. You need such things to survive on the sea, to give the chaos order. He said it was the same with America, when the white men had to give the frontier of the New World a mythology, from Columbus' Prophecies to the Latter Day Saints. It had always been this way – the Vikings had seen monstrous whales the size of islands in the Greenland Sea and off Newfoundland, the *Lyngbakr* or *Hafgufa*, and the coils of *Jörmungandr* off the coast of Nova Scotia. Or perhaps it was *Níðhöggur*. Wilson wasn't too keen on the difference. "One of them is dead, but will shed its skin and rise again in the twilight of the gods."

Dr. Stokes privately noted that there was, long ago, a sect of gnostics known as the Ophites or Ophidians, so named by Origen for their worship of the Serpent of Eden. They believed that Leviathan wrapped around the globe, just like the World-Serpent of Norse legend or the Ouroboros. Stokes knew that most Gnostics believed that a false god, a Demiurge, had trapped the human spirit in the Material World, but these Ophites alone seemed to believe that the actual separation between God and Man was itself a creature. Leviathan was the wall, eating up the spirits of the dead and spitting them back out into the cycle of reincarnation if they failed to pass through the seven spheres of the Archons. "It is very Hindu," he noted, to the point that such reincarnations could occur in non-human animals, a seemingly unique belief in even the weirdest corners of Abrahamism. Leviathan was slain by a pair of the Rephaim, according to Manicheans, a belief that may have been reincorporated into the Ophites. Mandaeism, from what he could recall, claimed that Leviathan was also Ur, a demon and a city in Babylon. Leviathan was their purgatory, swallowing up souls into prison-stomachs called *Mattarathas*.

Edison sat down to watch the final phase of the experiment, observing the faces of Wilson and Stoughton, trying to read their lips. He scowled when his junior engineers reported inconclusive results, and said that they would return to more scientifically grounded counter-signaling broadcasts.

That night, Edison dreamt -it was clearly a dream this time- of a lumberjack in red plaid and a great ox in the sky, bright blue and full of stars. Behind him was the Elephantine Colossus, a 122-feet-tall hotel and brothel on Coney Island in the shape of an Indian pachyderm, even more resplendent than it was in life. But it was burning, just as it had in 1896, and as it collapsed the great ox charged it and tore it to flaming bits. Edison jolted awake to the sound of women screaming and running, and the laughter of a scarlet harlot echoing through the rouge-painted sky. When he confided in Wilson as to its occult significance, Wilson laughed and said that was just "Paul Bunyan and Babe the Blue Ox. A tall tale from the French-speakers up in Quebec. Pretty new, not an old story. I don't know if it's based off a real man or anyone. People have giants on the mind these days. Maybe you saw him in one of those logging company ads."

Stokes asked if he had been around these loggers, and if they attributed any meaning to it.

Wilson said that it was just a bunch of stories strung together, silly japes like skating on a skillet to butter it. Bunyan didn't even keep a consistent size, sometimes just a large man, other times big enough to carve out rivers and canyons by dragging his ax. America's Dreamtime creatures, he noted. He said there were "weirder things up there to worry about."

Stokes, ever the journalist pressing mystics and obscurantists, asked for clarification. Wilson said that there were stories of men with heads like goats up around Cherryfield. They wore flannel and carried axes, menacing the bridges and train trestles over the Narraguagus.

Edison asked for the point of the flannel - was it just lumberjack fashion, or a larger symbol?

"Are you dreaming of the working man?" said Stoughton. "A simple life? Frontier labor?"

Wilson suggested a "Dr. Flannel," a nickname derived from "doctor's flannel," a heavy, felt-textured wool flannel often used to make shearers' shirts. "Do they call it that up here? They used that in Australia."

"I've never heard of it," said Stoughton.

"Was it double-headed?" offered Stokes. "The ax, the labrys, was sacred to Minoans, as was the bull."

"I think I would have recognized the minotaur," Edison said.

"Right, but it was also used by the Zeus of Labrandos, the Ba'al Shamin, and the storm-god Teshub," said Stokes. "Gods with an ax in one hand, lightning in the other. Or, electricity. Perhaps they're looking for modern company."

Edison wondered if it had something to do with the symbol of industry, conquering the forests. Railmen wore flannel and felled wood as well. Stokes suggested that the lumberjack is the woodsman archetype, but aligned to civilization rather than the wilds. A red man rather than green. "Red flannel and dark blue jeans, American colors...maybe that civilizing form explained the goat head, like Pan." He clarified that the buffalo plaid pattern was inspired by the MacGregor Red and Black tartan of Rob Roy – there might be something of the fey there, and, perhaps, a link between that blue ox and Rob Roy's cattle-thievery. Privately, he mused if these fey railway-men had something to do with Henry Ford's friend, Arthur Edward Stillwell.. Edison suggested that the checkered panels would indicate a kind of intelligence, the order of chessboard.

"A game for two players," Wilson noted.

"Buffalo flannel," Edison suggested. Stokes noted that Edison traced an hourglass figure through the tattoo on his arm, five dots arranged like the face of a die, and alchemical quincunx. "The beast of the American plains. We slaughtered them in the millions while crossing this fair nation. You could see the pile of skulls along the rails, like some...what are those mass sacrifices called? Hecatombs? Left in pyramids like the victims of the Khans, charred or sun-bleached bones, all black and white."

"The North Atlantic has taken many such sacrifices lately," said Wilson. "Think of the *Titanic*, and the *Bremen*[19]."

Edison then let out a grumpy grunt and said it was just word association at this point.

Stokes asked if he could turn off the radio. Edison said yes, he hadn't noticed that he left the radio on. Stokes noted that the detuned radio sounded sinister, like someone whispering in a crackling voice. Just as he turned the radio off, he heard something that sounded like a whale-song coming through. Edison said that he heard something, and Wilson yelped for them to turn it back on. Stoughton simply stood in silence, watching Edison struggle to understand the noise, ducking towards the speaker. Edison met his gaze, and asked what was interesting to him.

"Maybe it's a sanatorium patient," Stoughton suggested. "That doctor flannel – they also call it medicated flannel. Doctors prescribe it to people in sick wards, for patients with the chills. Turns out that the dyes were made of poison-sumac, and through that chemical treatment, soothed the skin and calmed the chest. Maybe you saw the ghost of a

---

[19] A U-151-class U-boat, which vanished in September 1916.

dying man. Or a madman."

"He had an ax," countered Edison.

"Then hope it wasn't a madman," said Stoughton.

"Perhaps it was a bit of suggestion, same as the Griffin," forwarded Stokes. "There is a fire ax in an emergency case on the bow-wall of the cabin. You must have seen it every day, and simply never thought much of it. But still, a weapon, even in the capacity of a tool, could cause some anxiety to the dreaming mind."

"Psychology is rubbish," said Wilson. "It's a ghost."

Edison appeared to have taken this as a joke, laughed, sharply snorted, and said he had to oversee the night's visibility experiments, involving exploration of the ionosphere via radio, a method to draw nitrogen out of the atmosphere, and the fitting of Elmer Ambrose Sperry, Sr.'s new arc lamp technology. He looked at the ax on the wall, acknowledged it with a 'huh,' and said he still had a bad feeling about that thing.

Pouring over the recent dispatches from Ernest Rutherford and speaking with a physicist with an interest in esoteric Christianity, Stokes records the parallels between the hydrogen atom and the City of New Jerusalem in Revelation 21:15-21: The velocity of the electron in the ground state orbit of hydrogen is 2,200 kilometers per second. 2,200 kilometers is the length, width, and breadth of the cubic city, rendered from the original 12,000 stadia. The walls were 144 cubits, or 65 meters, thick. The measured magnetic moment of hydrogen in its first excited state is $\mu H2=(0.88291\pm0.0007)\mu N$ [here, the nuclear magneton], the latter value which is equal to the ratio between the center point and the outer wall's dimensions; also an analogue with the reduced radius discovered by Niels Bohr in 1913, the distance of the electron of a hydrogen atom to its nucleus. Spuriously, and this is where Stokes starts to waffle in his interest, Rutherford predicted that a third, unstable isotope of hydrogen exists, with a half-life of twelve years. An elemental interpretation would be a far-fetched notion if the bulk of the passage was not focused on a precise description of twelve precious stones, an alchemical symbol of a gold so purified that it resembled glass, and the famous notion of the "pearly gates." That is, the gates of New Jerusalem are of a 'single' pearl, a shelled grain resembling the atomic model.

Stokes wondered what compelled the modern rise in attempts to build this Zion, from true Zionism, to the Mormons in Utah, to the Walla Walla Christ, to the Bedwardism of Kingston, Jamaica, the Taiping Heavenly Kingdom, and British Israelism. Wilson's statement on the nature of places had struck a chord, Stokes said. He also noticed, for the first time, how strange it was that Edison abbreviated his first name as "Thos." rather than "Tom."

Two days later, the *Sachem* reached Canadian waters, docking at either Dartmouth or Halifax, Nova Scotia, which Edison fondly noted as his ancestral land. He then idly wondered if something was rotting – others had noted a foul smell, while some claimed to have heard odd groaning and chimes, as if from melting ice – but some swore it was a bovine noise. Stokes spoke of an auditory phenomenon noted off the coast of Nova Scotia and Newfoundland. As reported in the April 29th, 1915 edition of the *Cincinnati Enquirer*, the Red Cross Liner *Forizel* encountered an iceberg two hundred miles off St. Johns, which emitted a choir of chimes and angelic singing. This sound, along with its twin spires, recalled a cathedral. Over the next two years, similar singing icebergs were encountered off Meat Cove, Little Harbour, Pleasant Point, Sober Island, McNabs Island in Nova Scotia, and St. Pierre (of St. Pierre and Miquelon), and Grates Cove in Newfoundland. The phenomenon was attributed to wind passing through tunnels forming in the melting ice as it drifted from the Arctic down the North American coastline. A second theory was that it was the crystalline structure of the ice itself creating the noise as they melted and cracked, supported by witnesses recalling percussive snapping and chiming sounds rather than the fluting, whistling, and howls produced by wind.

In Halifax, they received an update from the research team of Paul Langevin and Constantin Chilowsky, working on submarine detection via ultrasonic quartz transducers which would emit a high-frequency pulse – the echo would be measured, and used to calculate the distance of its target from the detector. Further research would be done to see if the piezoelectric effect, and specific interactions between electrical fields and salt water, could be used to generate optical and auditory mirages, and, knowing the mystical element of the yacht's research, stimulate paranormal influence[20].

There were suggestions of using the "spiritual telegram" of Dr. Richard Schleusner's Church of Modern Spiritualism, but no model or blueprint could be transferred in time, so the design instead pivoted towards that of British physicist Sir Oliver Lodge, who had drifted towards spiritualism after his son Raymond died under fire in Belgium in 1915. While he had used the traditional methods of automatic writing, table tilting, and talking boards, as chronicled in his 1916 memoir *Raymond, or Life and Death*, Sir Oliver soon moved on to using radio technology, with purported success. Others in the group believed that such electromagnetic stimulation would require testing on a vast receptive field, such as the sea or a salt flat.

Piezoelectrics generated by excited saltwater and salt-rich earth were suggested as a mundane explanation for various "spooklights," "Ghost lanterns," or "fata morgana" effects – Wilson floated the notion of "lights in Queensland," a then emerging phenomenon in Australia that would be dubbed "the Min Min Lights" in 1918. The coasts of Queensland were infamous for their fata morgana, with ships seen "flying" on the horizon. The spiritualist counterargument was that salt was not a mundane explanation, but a medium for spiritual contact – salt circles were long used as a way to create barriers against invasive supernatural powers, indicating that there was some inherent interaction between salt and the ethereal realm.

Stokes overheard a conversation between Wilson and Stoughton, telling him about the tale of a two-mast brigantine by the name of *Zebenia*, which sank off Port Grenville in the Bay of Fundy on the 13th of November, 1883. One of the survivors of the five-man crew, a Hatfield, said that he saw an angel, a terrible thing of wings and lights and eyes, dive out of the night sky towards him. He fled the deck, dove into the sea, and swam towards the beach despite the terrible and sudden storm. The vessel was overwhelmed and the three men in the cabin were crushed and swept up the Grenville River, and found by Fox

---

[20] As one historical footnote, engineer Maurice Jas Aykroyd, grandfather of actor Dan Aykroyd, was part of this Canadian research group from Bell Telephone, forwarding the notion that high-frequency crystal radios could be used as a medium to contact spirits.

Point. The wreck of the *Zebenia*, like the namesake imperial guard of Ethiopia, kept a still and silent watch on the harbor, eerily ignoring the winds that should have swept it up the coast. Hatfield wondered if there was some strange magic, as his captain miraculously avoided the disaster – that Captain Bill Parsons had something of the witch to him, and had made a strange sacrifice to something in the Nova Scotian waters, toasting the tides with a cup of oil and a cup of ale. "Never trust a Parsons," Wilson said. "Or a Barker or a Noun or a Cold or a Reeves or Reeve. Or anything with Hell or Hill in it, Helfins, Helfen, or Heller. Some names are just witchy."

Stokes was unclear on the details, but that night, they sent electrical and high-frequency sonic pulses into the waters off Halifax. Alerted by a sudden foul smell from the cabin well after midnight, he eavesdropped on a conversation between Wilson and Captain Stoughton, in which Wilson appeared to be reciting a poem and rocking.

"God is that deep, ethereal ocean, free,/whose billows kept their wide unbarriered place/Amid the stars that move before His face/In robes of hurricane and harmony..." Stokes moved away to adjust his position for better listening, noting that Wilson sounded almost ritualistic. He then began to struggle in his recitation, powering through it. "Now brightly in the sombre southern skies,/Between Aquarius and the Hunter's feet,/Above where earth and heaven in shadows meet,/Mira[21], the star of ancient mystery, lies."

This appears to be a melding of two poems by the spiritualist and physician Albert Durrant Watson, "God and Man" and "the Wonder-Star," rather than the supernatural invocation Stokes assumed it to be. Watson is perhaps most notable for conducting seances with medium Louis Benjamin to contact Samuel Taylor Coleridge, who allegedly pointed amateur astronomers to a mysterious light near Venus on 15 July 1919[22].

The horrible smell soon forced Stokes to cover his mouth as well, and he had to smother an audible retching. Stoughton raised the head of

---

[21] Corrected from the original, which Stokes misheard "Mirror the star."
[22] Watson, Albert Durrant and Louis Benjamin. (1920) *Birth Through Death, the Ethics of the Twentieth Plane: A Revelation Received Through the Psychic Consciousness of Louis Benjamin.* New York: The James A. McCann Company.

a frozen ox, blue from its storage in ice, and invoked the names of Angrboða and Antaboga. Even with the salting and freezing, "an odor of ancient rot poured forth when the Captain pierced its eye sockets with a line."

Stoughton offered up a prayer to Thor and an entity that Stokes later identified as Himinhrjóðr, after consulting with a Germanicist. Stoughton asked if this was all necessary. Wilson mentioned someone called "the Necromancer," who had wished to perform this rite, but Stoughton abruptly ordered him to shut up and keep watch. Wilson scoffed, said that Stoughton asked him first, and turned to the sea, standing near the depth charge racks. Stokes moved away from the two, and lost sight of them, but it was clear that they had thrown the oxhead into the water by the splash. Stoughton, alone, ran to the electronic broadcast station, and sent a pulse into the waters.

Their work done, Stoughton rejoined Wilson, and Wilson quietly asked if this "Necromancer" had shot J.P. Morgan's son over the alleged conspiracy to sink the *Titanic* with Isador Straus, Benjamin Guggenheim, and John Jacob Astor IV aboard. "The Napoleon of Wall Street," he said. "Another Antichrist."

Stoughton made a quizzical sound, and said, yes, "something of an Antichrist, but something even more like the prophets of Ba'al. Dead in Rome a year before the War," Stoughton noted that Morgan was not just a banker; he had helped form U.S. Steel, the International Mercantile Marine, the system of agri-business, and even Edison's General Electric. He tried to fund Tesla, until the latter swindled him. He had saved the banking system in 1907, and owned practically half the railroads. There were also hushed whispers that his son had Edwin James Houston, an engineer and writer who co-found General Electric, killed by heart failure, but Stoughton noted that such a thing seemed unlikely and rather fruitless for the younger Morgan.

Wilson laughed, and asked if Stoughton had done Houston in. Stoughton went quiet. Wilson prodded again, asking about the recent death of Johnson – who Stokes inferred was Edward Hibberd Johnson, the man who recruited naval officer Frank J. Sprague into Edison's organization and the Naval Consulting Board – by a freak electrocution. Stoughton remained quiet. Wilson made a strange face that Stokes could not read, and said it wasn't some cultic hecatomb, and noted that all of these modern witches speaking of workings and will were wrong- the most powerful magic wasn't world-shaping Will, but the subtle, unconscious evils the truly guide the world.

"When you get down to it, Cap, magic is just economics of the immaterial," Wilson said. "What do you want? And how do you get it? What do you invest in for the best pay off? Faith is a metaphysical war-bond. We don't give a damn about Ba'al, but we're slaves of Babylon's gold."

Stoughton said that Wilson should have a visit to Jekyll Island, off the coast of Georgia. Stokes vaguely knew of it from the first transatlantic phone call – in 1915, Theodore Newton Vail, president of AT&T, was on Jekyll when he received a five-way call featuring President Wilson in the Capital and Alexander Graham Bell in New York. Stoughton, though, noted that Senator Nelson Aldrich launched the Federal Reserve System there, in 1910, along with representatives of J.P. Morgan's empire, like Charles D. Norton and his catspaw Benjamin Strong, Rockefeller, Vanderbilt, Vanderlip, Warburg, and Treasury Secretary Abraham Ambrose. From all across the nation, the greatest financiers, investors, and industrialists traveled to an out-of-the-way Georgia island to "duck hunt" under false names.

Wilson asked why the place was so important. Stoughton said that in ancient days, the Timucua had dwelt there, seasonally, with their giant chieftains carried by a caste of hermaphrodite porters. George Jay Gould, the Railway Tycoon, had a fascination with archeology and mummies. His transcontinental railroads had uncovered the bones of giants across America, and Gould passed on his collection to the Jekyll Island Club, which also had artifacts bequeathed by its first president, Brigadier General Lloyd Aspinwall, from a family of art collectors and dealers.

The Club had other members as well – Joseph Pulitzer, Cornelius Bliss Jr., Marshall Field, and Henry Hyde. Wilson interrupted to laugh at Henry "Hyde" on "Jekyll" Island, but Stoughton shut him up with a nasty glare. It was at that Club, over the bones of giants and altars of ancient sacrifice, that the Mark of the Beast was worked and sealed. The National Monetary Commission, multiple reorganization bills and presidential acts, systems of national debt, massive consolidation deals ready for a great opportunity to bear fruit. And now, with Wilson's War, industry and finance and military are one crowned hydra, sunk into the ocean and bleeding out poison.

"That's the scary thing about sea monsters," Wilson said. "You see the dragon. You see the big charging brute on the land. But even if you know it's lurking out there, you don't see the sea monster until it's already dragging you under."

Wilson then quietly intoned an ancient prayer in what Stokes assumed was Icelandic, Old Norse, or some other ancient Germanic tongue – the only words he understood were Goð, Thor, and Miðgarðsormr. Once his incantation was complete, Stoughton and Wilson parted ways, with Stoughton moving to bow and Wilson moved somewhere that Stokes couldn't determine, as he had decided not to push his luck and ducked into his berth.

He briefly thought of the recent tale of Violet Jessop, an Irish nurse and British Red Cross stewardess from Argentina who survived the sinkings of *HMS Titanic* and *Britannic*, and the deadly collision of the *HMS Olympic*, all three Olympic-class sister ships. The papers had called her "Miss Unsinkable," but she seemed, perhaps, to be the most sinkable of women; it was her survival that was miraculous. Perhaps some people are walking disasters, the eye of a hurricane of ill-fortune. Or, "perhaps, at times, many unlikely happenings simply happen to happen at once."

Stokes nodded off for a short nap, waiting for the early shift.

It was not long after that the crew awoke to a phantom city in the misty sky. Murmurs rumbled through the crew, and some mystified awe. It was Edison who broke the spell, pointing out that it was the previously explained fata morgana, before he returned to unspooling wires and charging the test battery. Canada had seen many such phantom islands and sky cities, such as John Ross' ghost mountains in the Northwest Passage, the mirages of Lake Ontario, and the recent foolish expedition to "Crocker Land" by Donald Baxter MacMillan, a fatal wild goose chase for nothing more than a late Autumn Arctic illusion.

Then came a rumbling from the water, and several sailors on the port and starboard shouted that there was something moving in the harbour, something that looked like a partially-eaten whale or shark, spilling innards but still swimming. A groan echoed through the air, catching even Edison off guard as he felt the vibrations roll up through the deck. He pressed his hand to his ear and set his elbow against the back of the chair. The old engineer floated the idea that these sounds and movements were caused by an aquatic cryoseism, or ice quake, caused by the seismic movement of glaciers or breaking ice sheets. Uncertainty weakened his voice. As the crew scrambled for a better view of the aquatic monster, Edison continued to work, head down.

Stokes approached him, leaned in, and told him, briefly, about Stoughton and Wilson's strange ritual, and to beware of them. Edison looked at Stokes, almost eye to eye, and said that the man in buffalo flannel was in his dream again, and so was a blue ox, dead in the water. And he was sitting on the edge of his bed when Edison awoke. The timberjack said that his sisters were waking up, too – and then he vanished with a trumpeting noise, like an angel of the End Times and an elephant.

"There were cedars," Edison said. "Cedars in a train, ten thousand cars long. It was as if all of ancient Lebanon had been felled. I had a dream of a great whale skeleton fused into a giant ship, too, on Ford's damned Peace Boat...There's something diabolical, doctor."

"So sayeth Lucifer, the Lightbringer, who shall blot out a third of stars of heaven with his incandescent bulb," ranted Wilson.

There was a heavy splash from the stern. The yacht rocked, and Stokes grabbed Edison to keep him from falling out of his chair, as Edison had reacted by flinging the arm holding the wire wide and away from Stokes. The crew gasped as a high-pitched grinding sound, like the sound of an icebreaker plowing through glaciers, turned into a distinctly feminine shriek.

Stoughton approached Edison, ax in hand. Stokes froze. Wilson secured the vessel's pair of three-pounder 37mm guns, placed on the forecastle near the pilothouse on the far side of the yacht, by theatrically waving his pistol around. Two crewmen moved to the M1895 Colt-Browning machine guns behind the smokestack, but Wilson or Stoughton had the foresight to dismantle them. Edison looked at

Stoughton, scratched his stubble, and said, "yes, I forgot to shave this morning, but this is a bit extreme."

Stoughton raised the ax, signaling that he would swing if anyone moved.

"So, you're going to kill me for the Kaiser, Mr. Duquesne?" asked Edison.

The Captain paused, and he asked Edison who gave him that name. Edison said that the Captain did, when he mentioned a history of working with the hippopotamus. Edison had read of the "quite fascinating" proposal to introduce the hippopotamus into the rivers of America for food, by a man named Fritz Duquesne.

At this point, Wilson asked what was going on, but Duquesne ignored him as Edison said he was the same Duquesne that posed as a Russian duke on the *HMS Hampshire*. He signaled for a U-Boat to sink the cruiser, making his escape on a stolen life raft.

"That was how he killed Field Marshal Kitchener," said Edison. "Well, thank you for not torpedoing my research. The ax seems cleaner."

"I don't need a torpedo," said Dusquense. "I'm an inventor too. I've arranged for electromagnetic underwater mines, with your own signaling system. Lights, sounds, electrocution. Fitting end for the Wizard of Menlo."

"And I saw Satan fall like lightning from heaven!" said Wilson with a laugh.

"Oh, on that subject," said Edison, as he jabbed the live wire into Duquesne's thigh. Duquesne screamed and convulsed, and tried to bury the ax in Edison, but the head slipped off the handle and tumbled overboard, and Stokes wrestled the handle from the shocked – in both senses – assassin.

"I told you I had a bad feeling about that ax," said Edison. He mimed an unscrewing motion.

Duquesne shouted to Wilson for aid, to flip the signal. Wilson instead laughed and said that it wasn't a detonation signal, but a prayer that he sent out.

"Think of Morgan. Think of the Necromancer. The Titans, Olympia..." said Wilson. "The *Titanic* was more than blood money, but a grand sacrifice – to Leviathan, the arch-demoness of Pride."

"Shoot him, idiot!" Duquesne screamed, his voice mixing with the screeching wind.

Wilson stood up on the edge of the boat, balancing on the rail with "more grace than a cat."

A terrible rumble rose from the deep, "like thunder that shakes the bones," accompanied by "the wails of the damned."

"Behold!" he shouted, before a rogue wave swept him out to sea. The crew never saw him again.

Fritz Joubert Duquesne was bound in rope and arrested. Edison dispatched two sailors to return him to the US, where he was officially apprehended in New York City on 17 November 1917 on charges of fraud for insurance claims and illegally printing U.S. War Bonds. He was found with his files of newspaper clippings related to the sabotage of ships and dockyards, and a letter from the German Assistant Vice Consul to Nicaragua. However, this was just the public story, and secret arrangements between the British and Americans established that he would be extradited to the UK for his assassinations and high-sea sabotage. In prison, he would feign post-electrocution paralysis for two years, slowly cutting through the bars of his cell at Bellevue Hospital. "The Duke" escaped before he could be shipped to the United Kingdom, and would only be recaptured in 1932; he was released not long after. He continued big-game hunting, adventuring, and spying, and led an espionage ring during World War II. His final arrest would occur in 1941, and he would die in a New York City hospital on 24 May 1956.

Edward Arthur Wilson would reappear in the late 1920s under the alias "Brother XII," after a revelation in Tarascon, the city in which St. Martha tamed the legendary child of Leviathan, the Tarasque. He established a post-Theosophical cult known as the Aquarian Foundation in Vancouver, naming his settlement Cedar-by-the-Sea, recalling Leviathan and Behemoth. He declared to his small band of socialite followers that he was a reincarnation of the Egyptian god Osiris, and he accumulated a massive fortune in gold "from the sea itself." He rapidly grew paranoid and abusive towards his followers, and his mistress, a Mabel Skottowe – declared "Isis," "Madame Ziz," or "Madame Z"- forced his underlings into a harsh life of virtual slavery. When they eventually rebelled, Brother XII destroyed the colony himself, tearing apart the buildings and equipment, and scuttled his sailboat *Lady Royal*, before fleeing to France with Madame Z aboard the Tugboat *Kheunaten*. While reported to have died in Switzerland in November of 1934, eyewitnesses place him at a meeting with his lawyer in San Francisco several years later.

By the end of that Fall, Edison moved his research to Admiral Dewey's offices at the navy annex in Washington, D.C., before shifting to the naval station at Key West. He would return to the *Sachem* in early 1918, but the navy recalled the vessel for anti-submarine patrol service in New York Harbor at the end of May; He continued some maritime research on the SP-249 *USS Hauoli*, even past the Armistice. Edison's activity would only decline slightly in the years before his death in 1931, expanding his business ventures and taking automobile trips with his neighbor, Henry Ford. In 1920, Edison sent shockwaves through the press when he told B.C. Forbes, interviewing on behalf of *American Magazine*, that he was developing a piezoelectric "spirit phone" that would allow communication with the dearly departed. Six years later, he would brush it off as a joke in the *New York Times*, with a wry twinkle in his eye.

Red October.

During the October Revolution, the Bolsheviks formed an alliance with the Left Socialist Revolutionaries and various anarchic factions, breaking from the coalition of liberals and conservatives that made up the Provisional Government of the February Revolution. These opponents would soon become known as the White Movement.

With the November 7th armed uprising of the Bolsheviks, the Kerensky government crumbled rapidly, with its leaders fleeing Petrograd after a group of Red Guards broke into the Winter Palace, got lost inside of it, and accidentally wandered into the breakfast room that housed the provisional government.

The collapse of this transitory regime accelerated the Bolshevik's rise, with Lenin promoting a Soviet-based system. Soon after, the Bolsheviks denounced this position as anarchistic, mostly because it would interfere with their planned power-grab. The Bolsheviks wanted to control the October Revolution, and it was for this reason that they largely opposed the coalitions behind the February Revolution and the 1905 Revolution.

The Bolsheviks quickly established the All-Russian Congress of Soviets, which elected the Council of People's Commissars and several committees to seize control of and oversee the national economy, creating a bureaucratic tangle of a legislature that cemented their power, possibly because nobody else could figure out how the system worked. They also created the secret police force known as the Cheka and reinstated the old Imperial prison system.

When the Constitutional Assembly held elections in December, the Socialist Revolutionaries won most of the seats due to its support from the rural peasantry, leaving the largely urban Bolsheviks as a weaker, secondary power. The Bolsheviks betrayed the Socialist Revolutionaries by sending the Red Guards to shut down the assembly when it convened in 1918.

The Bolsheviks found that the Socialist Revolutionaries were popular throughout the Russian Soviet system, even among the Urban proletariat, and they reacted by overturning elections and shutting down Socialist Revolutionary meeting halls and papers and threw everyone who looked at them funny in jail. The last straw was with the Treaty of Brest-Litovsk, which took Russia out of the war and briefly ceded Estonia, Lithuania, Latvia, and Ukraine to the Central Powers.

The White movement quickly became an armed force, lead by generals Yudenich, Wrangel, and Denikin, and Admiral Kolchak, and revolted in June 1918, releasing a manifesto that denounced the Bolsheviks as agents of Germany. It must be remembered that the White movement was not purely monarchist in character by this point– it was instead a ragtag coalition of conservatives, democrats, socialists of several, non-Bolshevik stripes, some anarchists, and ethnic nationalists and separatists (seeing the writing on the wall, Finland and Poland beat feet at the first opportunity). It was more of an anti-Bolshevik movement than a cohesive ideology, and that was their greatest weakness. While the Whites are remembered as a conservative movement, this is because its leaders often formed military dictatorships to consolidate their gains, with democratic elections a secondary concern – and it did not help matters that the most powerful leaders of the movement *were* conservative military men.

It came to pass that by the middle of 1918, the Whites of western Russia were on the whole more liberal than the Bolsheviks, who had essentially become an openly despotic party banning all rival political assemblies and media organs, becoming the Imperial regime with the serial numbers filed off. Trotsky, for instance, reinstated the pre-revolutionary military structure and the death penalty, a major motivation for the initial soldiers' rebellion.

"The Bolsheviks have brought back the knout," Mihajlo claimed on December 17th, alluding to the brutality of the old regime in a debate with a man he called Dima or Dimitri Sergeyevich. He did little to describe Dima, beyond noting that the man carried a signature sawn-off Mosin-Nagant sniper rifle, "technically refashioning it into an inaccurate carbine or spring gun with a dremel. I would have asked him why he would do such a mad thing, but I have learned my lesson – 'Russians' are their own justification."

"Dima, his chest puffed and his *bogatyrka* stressing his image as an agitator, said that such actions may be necessary, citing the need for a strong military in the face of foreign intervention. He stressed the word *foreign*, so I would have no doubt that he was not happy with my return.

Such power, I said, was not something to be used lightly, and these hostile foreigners were less of a threat than an undemocratic, single party government. The Black Czar is dead, long live the Red Czar.

The problem with revolutions, Anna said softly but darkly from her perch in the corner, is that you end up in the same place a year later.

Dima wanted to give them more time to restructure the new government, and Timofey and Viktor agreed. This revolution is led from Moscow and St. Petersburg, and those of us in Arkhangelsk can only wait for news and react.

The phonograph, and the only record that we had looted, Nadezhda Plevitskaya's *Chayka*[23], warbled through the silence. We had,

---

[23] *Chayka*, "the Seagull," is an arrangement by Jurakovsky of Chevkov's play of the same name.

at least, taken a supply of delousing agents, hopefully enough to fight the threat of Typhus, which has killed millions.

I said that I was tired of this dawdling. I needed to take action. I held up the group's Avtomat Fedorov, one of the new and advanced rifles pushed out by Kovrov. There are no more than four hundred in the world, and quite a few of them are here. I told them of hundreds of Type 38 Arisaka rifles purchased from Japan, and endless stores of munitions housed in this port's magazines. I told them I was sick of looking at their boring Mosin-Nagants and Dima's ugly, boxy Mauser C96. And I told them that we were going to break into the munitions stores.

I asked them who was with me. Dima informed me that he believed that such an action could be construed as supporting the growing dissident forces, because the Bolsheviks officially controlled the port's munitions, while the right-wing Whites controlled them *de facto*.

I told him that I was sick and tired of the Bolsheviks and their broken promises, and if they wanted their guns they could come up here, fight me, and pull them out of their asses when I was through with them.

He finally got fed up with my insolence and told me that I was a foreign agitator and an idiotic anarchistic bully. I told him that I was not idiotic.

If you are so worried about foreigners, I said, worry about those British in the ports seizing their weapon stores and heading home. Because they have a word for when the British are already docked at your port but I would not use it in mixed company. If anyone in Moscow or Petrograd says we're undermining them, we can say that we seized the stores to keep them from falling into British hands. And then we can shoot them if they press us.

He told me to leave, and to take Anna with me, as I was obviously going to turn against him and join up with General Miller. I began shaking my head around slightly, to keep the twitching at bay and to work off some of my anger.

I don't side with powerful men, only ideals, I said, pointing at Dima with my pinky. I don't like tyrants or bullies. I am a Serb and a Bosnian, from the Land of Martyrs. I fight for the wretched and the weak, those in constant struggle against tyrants and authorities. I told him that I came here to fight against tyrants, and the Bolsheviks were turning into tyrants.

Dima said that the Bolshevik's had taken control of the revolution, and that Russian Communism must rally behind them to keep the Central Powers and the Czarists from winning.

I turned around and scraped my middle finger's nail over the gauze on my wrist. The gauze caught fire as it tore off. I turned my bandaged and flaming arm over and slid it through a ball of heated air and over my other arm. I balled them into fists and punched the ball of fire at him. I made sure it sailed past his right shoulder.

Everyone else had seen me turn into a pillar of darkness and fire for a second before Dima shouted in surprise.

I held my injured wrist as I waited for it to heal, and for Dima to stop hopping around trying to snuff out a flame that wasn't there. That boy is a jackass.

He pointed his blocky gun at me. The Polish man, Adam, Karp Griboyedov, and Radomir all rose to their feet, trying to figure out a way to stop the fight from escalating without earning the ire of Brave Comrade Dima or the fidgety fire Serb.

'Don't provoke me,' I said. 'I've punched through angels.'

Igor, Adrian, and Kolya looked horrified, Lana raised an eyebrow, Yuri laughed nervously, and little Galya got up and quietly walked away. Miloslav, already sickly looking, began to tremble and look off into the distance. He laid down the piece of wood he was whittling into yet another whale, and dropped his knife into the snow.

'Our Lady of Kazan is missing,' he said. 'All that's left is the copies. Our protectoress is gone...the Bolsheviks say that they found it, or people say that they found it, in a pile of Romanov gold, but it's not true...no, something else is coming. An anti-idol, a barren mother, an unholy mother...'

We try to ignore Miloslav.

'Who's with me?' I asked. Nobody responded immediately, other than Anna. She rose to her feet and stood behind me.

'You are a bully, Zrnu,' Dima said. 'You are nothing more than a bully. Two meddlers, a foreign freak and a Siberian with a Jew's Trill[24]. You can't scare my people into following you.'

'Yes,' I said. 'Just because someone has power does not mean you follow them. Glad we are in agreement.'

'Revolutions always flush out the monsters,' he muttered as he glared at me.

'If we're all doomed to die, I want to deserve it,' I whispered after appearing right next to his ear. 'Keep looking, and I'll run a razor across your eyes.'

Dima glanced at his feet and said, 'We seize the ammunition, Zrnu, but I'm still the leader. We need a Russian to lead.'

'*Zrno*,' I corrected. 'In Serbian, the word for bullet can also mean a hard seed or kernel. It makes sense. Plant the right *zrno* in the right body and watch something bigger grow. Tyrants are the richest soil for a new world.'

'The Imperialist War ends, and a new war begins. If this will bring peace in this city, I will follow you,' Galya said. She slung her rifle over her shoulder as she rose up from the fireside logs. She shook her head and moved towards Anna and I. There was no inspiration to be seen in those perpetually tired eyes, but her apathy had been replaced by a desire to do something.

'The exploiters, the capitalists, the old masters and the petty czars...they will be torn from their homes like a child from its mother's womb. And they can run to the edge of the world and hide among the cooling stones, but those stones will shout that there is no hiding place among them,' said Miloslav, a godless preacher. He looked at me. 'Follow the man who runs on the ice.'

Timofey spoke up, and said that he trusted in the power of Anna and I. He had been our lifeline to St Petersburg, as he had once been a

---

[24] *The Jew's trill* - Slavic languages, with the exception of Sorbian and some parts of Poland, use what's called an alveolar trill, and disparage the use of the uvular rhotics as nonstandard. The reason Sorbians and several Polish groups are the exception is the influence of German. Jews of German origin – originally Yiddish speakers – in Russia and other Eastern European nations often used this Germanic uvular rhotic trill instead of the alveolar, and it was seen as a marker of Jewish background in those regions.

laboratory assistant there. He had seen the powers of the invisible world, in those final lost notes of Filippov."

On 12 June 1903, Mikhail Mikhailovich Filippov died in his St. Petersburg laboratory. Born in 1858, in Oknino, Cherkasy Oblast (in what is now central Ukraine), Filippov was a polymath – a philosopher, journalist, historical novelist, Marxist agitator, encyclopedist, mathematician, physicist, and chemist – and generally considered to be one of the last people who could fall into that broad category of "natural philosophers." He is best known today for his positivist works, the two volume *Philosophy of Reality* and the essays collected as *The Future of Russian Philosophy*. As a journal editor, he published the writings of both Vladimir Lenin and K.E. Tsiolkovkiy's 1903 article "The Exploration of Cosmic Space by Means of Reactive Devices," which paved the way for Russian space technologies. He likewise translated Dmitri Mendeleyev's works into French, popularizing his periodic table in the west.

Due to his populist political sympathies, many supporters of Filippov, such as this "Timofey," believed that he was assassinated by agents of the Okhrana, presumably on the orders of the Czar, especially as police investigators confiscated his scientific papers and the manuscript of what would have been his 301st publication. His laboratory was dismantled, and rumors that Nicholas II himself read the manuscript before it was destroyed trickled down through the intelligentsia of St. Petersburg. What is known is that the work was entitled "Revolution through Science, or the End of Wars." Filippov had written to his friends that he had made an astonishing discovery, a method of inducing explosions using a "directed beam of short radio waves," and claimed that, hypothetically, a dynamite charge detonated in Moscow could have its blast wave transmitted to Constantinople. He believed, like many inventors, that his weapon would render warfare impossible.

Later notes indicate an even stranger path of research, describing the detonation of carbon monoxide and oxygen via radiowaves. It appears that he began developing something like the Radionic quackery of Albert Abrams, but rather than medical fraud, it presaged the psionics movement of America's 1930s and the later Soviet field of psychotronics, an attempt to make parapsychology and physical science.

It seems that it somehow worked. He had heated a small sample of cyanoacetic acid and acetic anhydride with a light ray and bombarded it with microwaves. Rather than the typical cyanoacetylation, it inexplicably resulted in a high-yield and radioactive detonation, as though he had caused some matter of nuclear decay using radio-waves in his laboratory. As even physicists of the day found this impossible knowing Filippov's means, they posited something supernatural, with a psychic influence transmitted onto the microwaves, a bizarre blend of death ray and psionic sending. The mysterious "spiralling" golden fabric in his surviving notes was rumored to be the Golden Fleece of Greek myth, gifted to him by a member of the Ryabushinskys, a family of wealthy textile industrialists, bankers, and liberal politicians. One of their members, a Pavel, in a search for exotic fabrics, had purchased an alleged piece of the Golden Fleece from Georgia in the middle of the 19th century, and artist Nikolai Ryabushinsky edited and published a magazine of the same name. He had seemingly given the golden fiber to Filippov for chemical analysis, with disastrous results.

"Timofey was," as noted by Mihajlo, "confronted by the reality of alchemy and telepathy, as I have seen with Winepress and Venetianer, and he worried that such powers would soon be in the hands of the world's governments. Anna and I were his counter-agents against any such Filippovian remote detonation.

That is why they followed me. They had done nothing for two months in the Arctic darkness of an Archangel winter but eat horrible nettle bread and Garden Orache soup. We drink freeze-distilled industrial lubricant, the traces of castor oil helping us expel the grainy, pebbly breads. Even death is preferable after this winter.

'There's this old story in the north,' Miloslav said as he resumed his whittling. 'That some predators have the same spirit, and that the wolves of wintertime become blackfish under the summer sun...but they're wrong, they're wrong, it's the other way around. The season drives them to the shores, and then the wolves take to the sea, and all the wolves in Russia and all the wolves in Canada and Alaska switch nations...the grampus-wolves have no borders, no nations, just rule by strength. Great She-Wolf is coming, Great She-Orca is coming, to rule by strength.'

Whom Gods Would Destroy, Part III

Maxim, Radomir, Adrian and Lana began to clean up the camp site. Lana, shivering in the night, wrapped a kerchief around her shaved head. Anna finished off a bottle of vodka and dropped it on the ground, observing the Russian custom of never putting an empty bottle back on the table. Anna quietly stumbled into the darkness and leaned her head against Adrian's back. She had not stopped drinking since we got back from Siberia, the poor thing. Annushka has become notably quieter, and I can't stand it.

I picked up the samovar and took a shot of zavarka, a heavily concentrated tea. The Russians dilute it with boiled water, but I like it strong, like the tea counterpart of Turkish coffee. I like the grit and the sludge washing up against the sugar cube pressed beneath my teeth.

When I had my fill, I reached down and rubbed some snow on my wrist.

'What is that on your arm?' Galya asked.

I showed her my tattoo. РевеР кка.

'Aren't you with Anna?' Galya asked, being one of the few literate members of the band. 'Is Rebekka your mother?'

'No, Anna's,' I said. 'She saved my life. Saved yours. Got it done in a port parlor over the last two weeks.'

'Decent work,' she said. 'Better inking than what you'd see on a drunk sailor.'

Galya and Yekaterina worked in the factories in the spring and sold their bodies in the dock houses in the winter, when the heat is scarce and the icy sea cuts off most of the port and many men are trapped in the Arctic wasteland. She had learned to do filling color on tattoos, for some extra money.

Galya nodded and walked away as I wrapped up my arm and knuckles. I explained the plan."

The next entry recorded the sudden animation of Miloslav after a long period of sickness and inactivity. Zrno previously noted that Miloslav occasionally carved "Косатка," meaning Orca, and Косаткаград, "Orcatown," into walls. Yekaterina noted that Miloslav began muttering and wandering towards the waterfront, and had to be forced back to the encampment. He began screaming in the middle of the night, striping himself down to an undershirt.

"She is coming! Grand Orca is coming! There is a city underwater, and she is coming, she is coming to beach herself at Archangel," he shouted, "The Orca-City, the drowned are there, burning, and the burnt men are there, drowning!"

Zrno, Yekaterina, and Radomir helped retain him, tying him down with ropes and belts.

The next morning, the encampment awoke to the sound of Galya screaming and sobbing. She cried for help, unable to restrain the much larger Miloslav, who barely acknowledged her as he stripped naked and walked into the freezing water, disappearing with nary a bubble. The bed that he had been bound to was soaked and broken, the belts and ropes worn-down and faded by water, as though they had been submerged for centuries. The belts that restrained Miloslav's arms even showed signs of being chewed by fish.

Galya claimed that Miloslav refused to respond to her questions and pleas, simply whispering "great orca" over and over.

Anna wrote that, while flying the next day, she happened to look out over the sea and heard the soft sigh of the waves become something eerie and feminine. She described it as the sound of a woman with shallow lungs struggling to breathe.

She stumbled in the air and began to fall, dizzily struggling to maintain altitude, and choking. She gasped for air, and sensed the painful, heavy sloshing of water in the lungs. She began to spasm violently, pushing the entire world away in her panic. She crashed to the ground, and began vomiting up and snorting out gray water.

There was something "in the water or over the water or of the water," something sickening and huge and ghostly, and it was coming to Arkhangelsk.

The Haligonian.

The Stowaway.

HMS C27 was a British C class submarine, laid down on June 4, 1908 by Vickers, Barrow and commissioned on August 14, 1909. The 38 class C's were the last British petrol-engined submarines, coast-patrolling vessels with limited endurance and range, offset by high underwater performance. The vessels had a length of 43.64 meters, a beam of 4.11 meters, and a complement of 16.

Trawlers frequently towed Class C submarines as a countermeasure against U-boats, their captains corresponding by telephone. When the U-boat surfaced to gun the trawler, the C sub would torpedo the U-boat. The *HMS c27* engaged in these operations with the trawler *Princess Louise*, sinking U-23 in the Fair Isle Channel between the Orkney Islands and the Shetlands. The C227 was redeployed to Tallinn after this success. There, the vessel took part in the Baltic Operations, designed to blockade German imports of Swedish iron ore.

The c27 made its way to Tallinn by a dangerous route. A large and vulnerable ship towed them around the North Cape to Archangel, Russia, where a barge took them to Kronstadt through the White Sea Canal.

At 10:22 PM on December 12, 1917, First Officer Roger Mitchener awoke from the last in a series of dreams about flooding boats, which he took to be omens of a death at sea.

It wasn't the only thing troubling him. One of the crew members brought aboard a Jenny Haniver, a ghoulish monster, a dried up ray carcass carved into a varnished gargoyle. "It looked like the Devil's foetus," Mitchener wrote in his journal on December 13, 1917. "I knew it was cursed, and I refused to go near it."

In any case, he swallowed his fears and joined the six man night shift.

The other five men looked worried. Something had smashed in a section of the deck, and a loud yet distant sound echoed through the ship, "rhythmic and raspy like the slow breath of a woman."

The compass began to spin so rapidly that its arrow disappeared into a bronze blur.

Mitchener ordered the submarine to surface. He went alone onto the deck to inspect the damage, pulling out his service revolver just to be sure. He had served on other ships prior to c27, and even encountered stowaways, but never one on a submarine. As he wrote:

"The first thing I noticed was the lung-stinging cold, far colder than even Russian waters in the dead of night. The second was a woman on the mangled railing. She was somehow heavy enough to crinkle the steel hull with the tips of her toes.

'How did you get here?' I said through shivering lips, wondering if we had some kind of female Stoker Brown on our hands[25].

'Though a hurricane of tears,' she whispered, the R's long buzzing sounds on her blue lips, like Yorkshire R's. Her words were cold dead things that leaked out of her mouth, hollow thoughts, graveyard tones. She lacked breath. The air was freezing, but no mist accompanied her words. 'There's a hole in the sea, a crack in the sky.'

I tried to place her accent. It was not English, Scotch, or Irish, but some kind of North American, a flat and deliberate drone without the lilt and thickness of the Newfoundland. Perhaps she was from the States, or Canada.

She wore a knit cap over blonde hair brown and grey with dust and soot. She wore some kind of admiral's jacket, Empire but not RN [Royal Navy], over her powder dress. Burns and bituminous stains covered everything but the cap.

She was a willowy thing, a waifish mess with lifeless, grey eyes and sallow, plastery skin. She looked pained and frightened as the steam curled up around her.

'Canadian?' I asked.

She tried to nodd [sic], with a twitchy, jerky spasm. 'Halifax.'

'Is this a joke?' I asked. 'Did one of the men smuggle you aboard? Keep you in his bunk for weeks?'

'Steam rising from the sea, entire world going to blow.
Dead, broke at the bottom o'the North Atlantic. Sea'll boil over soon,' she said.

---

[25]   A mangled reference to Stoker Chief Petty Officer William Brown, a British sailor who escaped from the submarine HMS E41 ninety minutes after it sⁿnk to a depth of sixty-five feet, on August 15, 1916. He survived the sinking by a feat of preternatural resourcefulness and nerve. He returned to the engine's control room, which was pitch black, half-flooded with oil-clouded water, choking with chlorine gas, and sparking with exposed electrical wires, where he built up the engine room's air pressure and let in enough water through a scuttle so he could freely blow the hatch and rise to the surface. He managed to be saved by the *HMS Firedrake*.

'What are you on about?' I asked. I had never experienced anything madder in my life.

The air cracked with a truly thunderous report. It was then that I noticed my watch fob had been magnetised - it clung to my revolver.

'Why? Why? They whisper behind me. Pain burned into stone and steel. The fear. Why? Why do we suffer? They ask. Body heat and darkness.'

In my confusion, I believe I asked her how she managed to cling to my boat and survive three hours of underwater operation in freezing water. I stumbled, shivered, and huffed my way through the question. I do clearly remember flatly observing that 'you aren't wet.'

Her head rolled down. It took a great effort on her part to pull it back up, her quivering lips and hanging jaw producing a deep death rattle and an industrial clanking. The waters filled with whalesong.

I dashed to the hatch, in fear of this dreadful spectre.

'Thank - you – for – safe – passage,' she whispered, bile and oil rolling down her chin. She fell backwards over the rail. She did not make a splash like a falling woman would, instead displacing enough to drench the deck and nearly capsize us. I tumbled into the hatch, and hastily closed it."

The other crew members did not believe Mitchener's tale, but could not deny that something rocked the boat. The breathing sound and the minor magnetic disruptions stopped, along with the flooding nightmares and the sense of being watched by something lurking outside the portholes, which all the men admitted to experiencing after Mitchener told his tale.

The Royal Navy lost ten C class submarines during the war. The C16 fell to a "friendly fire" ramming by the *HMS Melampus*, and six were lost to accidents and German action. *HMS c27* and two other C class submarines were scuttled on April 5, 1918 outside of Helsinki to prevent seizure by the Germans. The Royal Navy scrapped the entire C class line in 1922. *HMS c27* was salvaged by Finns in 1953.

Haunted Halifax.

Founded in 1749 in the Mi'kmaq-controlled area called Chebucto ("the largest harbour"), Halifax is a major port city, the hub of Atlantic

Canada, and a town of ghosts.

In 1745, New England sent a fleet to capture the Fortress of Louisbourg, and succeeded. The following year, the King of France countered with a massive expedition commanded by Admiral Jean-Batiste, De Roye de la Rochefoucauld, Duc d'Anville, tasked with the disruption of British colonization in the New World, up to and including the subversion of the American colonies.

Two major storms stopped the Duc d'Anville Expedition dead on the water, stranding it at sea for more than three months, completely destroying the food stocks, water supplies, and morale of the sailors. The British detachment stationed at Halifax Harbour met the Expedition as they arrived at Chebucto. They found a floating graveyard. Over 2,500 men lay dead and rotting in the French ships, with wretched, diseased sailors shuffling between them, trying to man the understaffed ships. The broken fleet soon limped back to France, suffering more disasters along the way, because Mother Nature never misses an opportunity to kick a man when he's down.

The Duc d'Anville was among the dead. His ghost is said to haunt his resting place on George's Island, slouching in the darkness in shame and failure. On the Northumberland Strait, a lost ghost ship of three or four masts burns at night, lost forever between Prince Edward Island and the Nova Scotian peninsula.

The sound of a phantom rowboat approaching the shores of the Bedford Basin of Halifax Harbour lead to the story of a fogblind fishing crew hopelessly searching for the shore.

McNab's Island is dense with the apparitions of Acadians and Mi'kmaqs, generations of the McNab family (Peter McNab, in particular, left behind a headless spirit), soldiers from the Halifax Defence Complex, phantom carriages rolling down the roads, and the spooky burial grounds of the choleric dead from the *S.S. England*. Of special note is Maugher Beach, or "Hangman's Beach," where the Royal Navy executed mutineers and left the bodies dangling in the sea breeze as a warning to incoming sailors.

The Brewery Market on Salter Street is home to Alexander Keith's pub, where Keith himself is said to haunt the brewery. He's said to be rather pleasant. On the other hand, a rather disruptive and disturbing specter runs down the hallways at night. The running ghost is frequently associated with the apparition of a man, apparently stabbed to death with knives, dripping with blood in the bathroom mirrors.

They say that a young Englishman fell in love with the daughter of a Mi'kmaq chieftain who lived across the Narrows, on the far side of a British bridge. The Englishman walked across the bridge at night to meet her under the cover of night. As the story goes, the chief cursed the Narrows, promising that the bridge would collapse, as would the next two bridges that followed. Two of them so far have fallen, though the Angus L. MacDonald Bridge still stands, the curse broken by a modern Mi'kmaq chief. Still, there are occasional sightings of the ghostly lovers on the bridge, and the Mi'kmaq tend to leave behind ghosts along the Narrows. Further inland, the ghost of a Mi'kmaq runs along Citadel Hill just before nightfall.

A phantasmal janitor in a yellow uniform haunts "the Pit" of Kings College. On Tower Road, a ghost stands around the altar at the Cathedral Church of All Saints. St. Michael's Church, a disappointingly non-gothic edifice on Herring Cover Road, is home to gentle music rising from a self-playing organ and an elderly-looking ghost that kneels at the pews. The historic buildings on the Waterfront are home to shadow figures that roam around at night.

"Ghost lights," the spectral, will-o'-the-wisp-like phenomenon associated with the restless dead, appear on Devil's Island and Deadman's Island, home to a lost mass grave.

Halifax collects the souls of the anguished dead like a spinster collects cats. Maybe it's simply a nice town and the dead people don't want to leave. Very few of them are actively malevolent – maybe it's because malevolence isn't a trait one associates with Nova Scotians, or maybe it's because when evil Canadians die, they go to Edmonton.

However, there is an exception – the ghosts that appeared in the wake of the Halifax Explosion tended to be far more disturbing and hostile. It was, after all, the single most traumatizing event in the city's history.

Whom Gods Would Destroy, Part III

The Halifax Explosion.

Halifax Harbour is the world's second largest natural harbour that isn't covered with ice. The military build up proceeding the First World War transformed Halifax into a world class port, an industrial rail center, a bulwark against German submarines, and the British navy's main hub in the American Atlantic[26]. Indeed, the British Empire forced all North American-bound neutral ships to stop in Halifax for inspections. Halifax became the staging ground for the Canadian armed forces and the point of departure for all British-bound materiel produced in Canada.

At 8:40 AM, on Thursday, the Sixth of December, 1917, disaster struck the city. The French ammunitions freighter *SS Mont-Blanc* collided with the Norwegian vessel *SS Imo* in the Narrows of Halifax Harbour (ironically, because both ships engaged in evasive manoeuvres) and caught fire. The fire ate through the cargo of 2,300 tons of picric acid, two hundred tons of TNT, stacks of benzol drums, and ten tons of gun cotton. The blaze destroyed or cut off access to the fire-fighting equipment, and the crew abandoned ship for Dartmouth.

At 9:04, the ship erupted, producing the largest accidental artificial explosion in history[27].

The fireball rose over a mile into the air, producing the first recorded mushroom cloud. The hot ash and near-molten shrapnel caught up in the blast rained down not long after; the lightest material, the carbon carried by the *Mont-Blanc*, fell for ten minutes across the city as a charcoal-black rain. The residents found themselves blackened by the soot, causing smoky tattoos on those with open wounds.

The shock wave produced a sixty-foot tsunami in the harbour, trampled buildings in much of the North End flat, shredded trees, ran vessels aground (including the *Imo*), destroyed the *SS Picton* with a one ton boulder pulled from the harbour bottom, scorched the landscape up to two kilometers in-land, killed two thousand people, blinded thirty-eight[28], and injured nine thousand others in Halifax, Darthmouth, and

---

26   It was a wartime boomtown, but using that term is tasteless.
27   Estimated to be the equivalent of 3 kilotons of TNT, or 12.6 terajoules. The atomic bomb dropped on Hiroshima released 63 terajoules.

Richmond. The damaged rendered tens of thousands of people homeless in the harshest winter recorded.

The pressure wave damaged the various sources of heat and stockpiles of fuel covering the city, coating the streets in a mix of petroleum, kerosene, and coal and igniting it. The various naval artillery magazines also suffered damage, releasing volatile chemicals. With the streets ablaze, the North End became a labyrinthine conflagration darkened by dust and burning, oily rain.

Soon after the dust settled, rumors spread through the rescue workers of a second fire at the smoking Wellington Barracks. The smoke was the result of military personnel putting out controlled coal fires, but the fear of a second explosion caused a mass evacuation to the high grounds, delaying rescue efforts.

The sound and force of the Explosion reached as far as Prince Edward's Island and the northernmost reaches of Cape Breton, 130 and 220 miles away, respectively. Windows cracked within a ten mile radius of Halifax, and substantial damage occurred as far away as sixteen miles. Part of the *Mont-Blanc*'s anchor crashed down two-and-a-third miles from the blast site.

The Royal Naval College was destroyed.

The next day's edition of the *Halifax Herald* carried a simple headline: "Halifax Wrecked."

Relief.

Despite all the horror, stories of heroism and human kindness emerged from the disaster.

As *Mont-Blanc* caught fire, the crew of the *Stella Maris*, a tug boat,

---

28   Most of these blindings, along with some six hundred less severe cases of damaged eyes, were caused by the hot glass and the white hot chemical flash of the Explosion. Physicians took note of the massive amount of eye damage inflicted, and a great deal of research took place in the city, advancing the field of ophthalmology considerably. Halifax is still noted for the treatment of blindness. In addition, the six hundred children injured in the event led physician William Ladd to establish the field of pediatric surgery in North America.

anchored alongside the flaming wreck and tried to douse it with its fire hose. The *Mont-Blanc* exploded just as they were preparing to tow it away from the pier, killing nineteen of the crew. Five survived, washed on the shore.

One of the fleeing sailors from the *Mont-Blanc* alerted an Intercolonial Railway dispatcher named Vince Coleman, who realized the implications of the munitions fire. Running to his post, he sent out a telegraph that read "Stop trains. Munitions ship on fire. Approaching Pier 6. Goodbye." He successfully stopped the incoming St. John's inbound train and any others that would have come later, saving the lives of the passengers and allowing those trains to be quickly re-purposed for relief efforts. Coleman died at his post.

Nine members of the Halifax Fire Department died fighting the fire, including the Fire Chief Edward Condon and his Deputy Chief William Brunt.

Help poured in from the rest of Atlantic Canada, Newfoundland, and the United States, but just to rub salt in the wound, one of the worst blizzards in Canadian history hit the city the next day, dumping sixteen inches of grey snow and hindering rescue efforts, brutalizing the unsheltered residents. Many of the unaccounted-for injured perished in the cold. Even most of those with homes didn't have windows after the blast, forcing them to cover the wind-swept holes with carpets. See my previous comments on Mother Nature.

Despite that setback, Canada, Newfoundland, the US and many other countries poured money and manpower into the city over the following week, and the city was restored to order peacefully and quickly, all things considered. Massachusetts in particular gave so much aid that Nova Scotia donates the annual Christmas tree to the Common, Boston's main park.

Fallout.

Johan Johansen stumbled into an American relief hospital in Halifax, begging for help in thickly accented English. The doctors, instead of helping him, locked him in a room and called the police. They found and confiscated a letter in his pocket, confirming their suspicions of a German spy ring.

This came as a great surprise to Helmsman Johansen, as he was a Norwegian from Norway who spoke Norwegian, and his letters had the weird slashed-through O's to prove it. He was one of the few survivors of the *Imo*, thrown clear by the blast that hurled his ship and his friends onto the shore.

Despite his insistence that Norway was a completely different country from Germany, and not just in that half-hearted, still-German way like Austria or Lichtenstein, Johansen was blamed by many for the blast[29]. Other rumors spread of German culpability in the explosion, and the *Halifax Herald*'s articles added fuel to the fire, fabricating reports that the German High Command had mocked the city's dead. Authorities rounded up the German population of Halifax[30], but released them not long after.

The Ghosts of December.

St. Paul's Anglican Church on Argyle Street is the city's oldest Protestant church. One of its parishioners had his head blown off by the shockwave with such force that it smashed through one of the windows. Even though the pane has been replaced several times, the silhouette of the severed head keeps reappearing.

The sea-food restaurant *The Five Fisherman* stood near St. Paul's, and was used as an *ad hoc* infirmary in the aftermath of the Explosion. Employees reported several ghosts, including an unusually violent poltergeist on the second floor. This ghost, that of a man, allegedly trapped an employee in a room and attacked another employee trying to open the door with thrown objects.

The ghost of a soldier dressed in a Canadian First World War uniform haunts the Halifax Armoury, simply staring at people in a disturbing manner.

The Narrows Spectre, known by the outside world as the

---

[29] Macdonald, Laura (2005). *Curse of the Narrows*. London: HarperCollins. p. 284, 342–341.

[30] "Elements Still Scourge Desolated City of Halifax, 1,050 Bodies at Morgues; All Germans Being Arrested". *The Halifax Gazette* **CXLVL** (295). December 10, 1917

Haligonian, is perhaps the most unsettling of the lot. She would appear in random households, military installations, or vessels, screaming or vomiting black oil, and occasionally with damaged or absent eyes, weeping shards of glass. She would frequently reach out for children before dissolving into in a puddle of fetid water.

This association with water is key to the phenomenon. Not only was she something of a storm-herald, like the famous Gray Man of Pawleys Island, she did not have the ethereal, spiritual quality of other ghosts, and appeared to be not only solid (and liquid, as the case may be) but incredibly heavy, to the point of damaging floorboards and decks.

Despite the Narrows Spectre's seemingly material nature, she had the inexplicable ability to appear and disappear through bodies of water, some no deeper and no wider than a puddle in the corner of a room. The Haligonian revenant's geography bending manifestations have sometimes been compared to the strange death of British Vice-Admiral Sir George Tryon, KCB. Vice-Admiral Tryon ended an otherwise highly competent career in disaster when he sent out an utterly insane order to turn his flagship, the *HMS Victoria*, directly into a collision course with the *HMS Camperdown* off the shore of Tripoli, on June 22, 1893. His last recorded words before he sank beneath the waves were a forlorn and distant "it is all my fault..."

At the same moment, a doppelgänger of Tryon was seen walking through his drawing room at 45 Eaton Square in London. His family, hosting a party with several guests, could only look on in confusion as this spectre gazed silently into the distance, not looking at anyone. It departed soon after, with the spiritual duplicate, or something similar appearing near bodies of water around Tripoli and London for several years.

The earliest known encounter with the Spectre appears in a document written by a Halifax resident, Michael Ferguson (1891-1968), in response to an investigation launched by provincial detective, R.O. Carroll:

"It was Thursday, the Sixth of December. You know what day I speak of. I wandered through a dirty haze, trudging carefully through a city of shattered glass and ash-blackened snow. Not a pane in the city survived the blast.

I found a pocketwatch in the ashes. The face, covered by the only piece of unbroken glass left, froze at the exact moment of the explosion. It would be 9:04 forever.

I searched for survivors along the coast. Some had been passing by, while many others turned out as spectators to the conflagration aboard the *Monte Blanc* [sic]. I found twelve bodies, complete, a torso, and an arm severed at the shoulder.

I found two survivors that day; one a shaken young boy who limped home after I removed the pile of rubble which pinned him to the ground, and the other was something remarkable: a girl in a grey dress, stained and faded like an old oil-cloth sat on charred rocks in the Narrows. Her eyes opened slowly, groggily, like someone waking up from a nap, but with the strain of a newborn opening her eyes for the first time and wincing in the needling shower of the world's new light. It was a fresh agony.

I asked her if she was hurt. She shook her head. I asked her who she was. She shook her head. Just to clarify, I asked her if she could remember who she was. She shook her head. There was something otherworldly about her. She was conspicuous, giving the impression of a mermaid blown out the water despite her obvious toes: her hair was short and had wet waves like a roaring ocean. It was golden but singed and packed with grey ash and spotted with black oil and dried blood, and held down by a curved iron supports rivetted [sic] like the belly of a steamship. Black water washed away the ash around her, replacing it with sludge and the liquidated viscera of dead fish. The gore did not seem to phase [sic] her.

I asked her if she felt anything. She nodded her head. A head that, as I soon noted while trying to move her, always faced magnetic north. Her body was magnetized, the stopped watch's fob clinging to her shoulder.

I took her cold, wet hand, trying to get her back onto her feet – and I saw the world through her eyes. She found herself in the middle of an invisible burning spiral, expanding outward to consume the earth, exploded and imploded. She looked around her, trying to find her bearings. She felt so big. Miles wide, even though she was a scant meter and a half tall waif.

At that moment, overawed by this bizarre experience, I lost my grip on her. Perhaps she pulled away, perhaps I slipped and let her go, and found myself waist-deep in the freezing water.

She tried to stand. She touched herself like she couldn't feel her body and she wanted to make sure she was all there, like people whose limbs have been blown off. She acted weightless, lighter than the air she fought through. She stumbled forward, barefoot and shaking, as if her body was about to fall apart, with every fibre of her being trying to go its own way, each wailing like a spectre, each wanting to go home and never return to her body.

As spooked as I, she crossed her arms across her breast, tried to hold herself together like a puff of demon smoke trying to find a bottle for itself. She ran an ash-caked hand up her arm. As she reached the shoulder, she stopped, horrified. Even though it seemed as if she just fell from the heavens, knowing nothing of this world, she knew that people shouldn't have cold, hard, angular creases in their skin. I gasped when I saw it. Running her finger down the crease, she felt a slight curvature to the side. She moved her finger over, tracing its circular outline. It was a rivet.

My heart skipped a beat. The girl pulled open the torn grey fabric of her dress hanging from her stomach. Her skin was branded with the stencilled word "IMO." And right above it, she saw the circular lead rim of a steam pipe, passing through where her heart should have been.

It was then that I realized that there was no stony barricade between her and me – she was simply sitting on the surface of the water without support of the rocks. She tried to scream, but only a gush of bubbling black oil came out, followed by the ghostly shock of a foghorn. I fled the stony path in panic. When I glanced back from high up the shore, she stood on the still grey water like a shipwrecked Christ, watching me with great and terrible fury in her eyes."

The Haligonian's next major appearance occurred mere hours later and drew comparisons to the case of "Ashpan Annie" (Anne M. Welsh née Liggins), a twenty-three month old girl who had been thrown under the kitchen stove during the Explosion, kept alive by a blanket of warm ashes for over a day. She was rescued by her neighbor, a soldier, and a search-and-rescue dog. Her mother and brother died in the blast, and her father was serving overseas at the time. She was placed under the care of her grandmother and aunt, and died in 2010.

While sifting through the wreckage of their house, a family on Gladstone Ridge came across a skinny female figure caked with gray ash hiding in the remains of their kitchen, clinging to a busted pipe. She had apparently been washing herself in the plumbing, perhaps cleaning out an eye socket that had been lacerated by glass – the wash basin was stained with blood and petroleum. The father of the house, who had removed the beams pinning the girl to the floor, ran out of the house upon seeing her damaged face.

The Haligonian, a girl no more than twenty, rose to her feet when the mother and her youngest child entered the room. She wore a pea coat over her tattered dress, her wet hair matted down by a black tuque.

She stumbled towards the child, her oil-caked mouth producing a strange gargling, wheezing moan. The girl reached out for the boy, only to have her freezing-cold hand swatted away by his mother.

The girl contorted her face and made a series of agitated croaking sounds. The kitchen flooded in her wake.

The mother grabbed her boy and fled from the freezing room, where she met her husband and the man he had left to retrieve, one of the wandering physicians treating the injured.

"It's not fair..." croaked the woman.

"I know," said the doctor. "But we can treat you. Your eye is in danger of infection."

"Your name, what is your name?" asked the father. "You're not from the neighbourhood."

"The dying screams... they blew a hole in the world, and I swam through..."

The Haligonian stepped backwards into the filthy puddle flowing in from the kitchen. The family and the doctor were shocked when the puddle exploded with a high-pressure whistle and the girl dissapeared into ash-heavy stack smoke and boiler steam that stained the warped ceiling black.

The doctor left behind the most striking description of the event, saying that she was accompanied by "a bitter cold, bitter with resentment and indignation. The sound of heavy feminine breathing and the sense of being watched did not leave us until the expiration of the hour."

On December 8th, a woman walked out of a waterlogged wood pile, grey smoke and grey fire on Waterfront. She was described by the crowd of witnesses as a girl in a tattered, oil-smeared grey dress. She had faded, dishwater blonde (or brown) hair and ashen skin with dead grey eyes. She march directly into the sea, without even acknowledging those around her. When one man dove into the freezing water to pull her out, he found nothing at all, as though she had dissolved in the sea. When interviewed by the papers, the crowd reported severe sea sickness and recurring dreams about drowning and flash floods.

The Haligonian, or something like her, appeared in other provinces not long after. Indeed, there are isolated reports of a strange woman washing up or appearing in several other harbors between December 9 and 12, 1917, including Sydney Harbour, on the Thames, and Snug Harbor, Staten Island, New York. In all such cases, the woman soon dove back into the water and vanished beneath the waves. It is difficult to put these seemingly random appearances in context; the more widely accepted appearances of the Haligonian in December 1917 are Canadian. The first of these is on a beach near Vancouver, but the rest are confined to Maritime Canada, Ontario, and Quebec.

While the people of Halifax called her the Narrows Spectre or the Lady-of-the-Harbour, English speakers throughout Canada dubbed her the Haligonian Waif after she identified herself as coming from that city in one rather dramatic sighting on December 11th, in which she climbed aboard a small boat on the Black River, shivering and gibbering about the city and its recent disaster. Later that day, she appeared in Eel River Crossing, New Brunswick, where she demonstrated, for the first time, the ability to speak French.

French-Canadians in Quebec and New Brunswick gave her several titles in addition to *l'Haligonienne*, including *l'Ondine* (the Undine), *l'Amirale* (the female admiral), or *l'Amiralette* (The Admiral's Wife, or the Little Admiral). She gained the last two names by appearing in the uniform jacket and cap of a Canadian admiral, worn over either the grey dress or nothing but a pair of black trousers. I imagine something similar to the woman depicted on Howard Chandler Christy's "I want you for the Navy" recruiting poster, except Canadian and disturbing; as with the Sopwith Aviatrix of 1918, there is a running theme of transgressive female transvestism in late wartime imagery, paranormal manifestations, and perhaps the androgynous fashions of the early 1920s.

During the December 12th encounter at Dalhousie, New Brunswick, One of the witnesses along the Restigouche River claimed that she had "no light in her eyes." She was accompanied by the sound of ghostly soldiers. Similar phantom marching was reported during her brief appearance in Saint-Omer, Quebec.

It is possible that the stress of the war had something to do with these alleged phantom soldiers. It is notable that they seem to pop up most frequently in places with mixed Francophone and Anglophone populations, where political tensions were highest. Canada entered the War on August 4, 1914, when Britain declared war on Germany. Canadian Minister of Militia Colonel Sam Hughs created a militia of 31,200 men, dubbed "Canada's Answer." The Answer arrived on British soil on October 14. Hughs quickly raised other battalions.

Francophone Catholics, discriminated against by the largely Anglophone Protestant officer corps and irritated by contemporary anti-French language statues like Regulation 17[31], rarely volunteered after the first contingent. Those who did preferred to join units such as Les Fusiliers Mont-Royal, which allowed French to be spoken among the troops. The English-speaking officers proved simultaneously reluctant to mobilize Francophone units while at the same time believing that French Canada was not pulling its weight, especially since Ottawa expected a 150,000 strong army by 1915. The demographics backed up this assertion – while 28% of Canadians identified as native French-speakers, Francophones composed only 5% of the Army in 1917[32]. Most Quebequois, however, saw the war as just and necessary, and simply wanted French-speaking units led by French-speaking officers, with some government and media personalities in Montreal advocating for

---

[31] Regulation 17, passed in 1912, prohibited instruction in French past the first two years of schooling in Ontario.

[32] Auger, Martin F. "On the Brink of Civil War: The Canadian Government and the Suppression of the 1918 Quebec Easter Riots", *Canadian Historical Review*. Vol. 89, issue 4 (2008).

Quebeqois units to join the French Army. The Dominion government soon allowed the formation of the 22nd French Canadian Battalion, CEF.

However, just as one recruitment problem was solved, another one began, as volunteers dwindled as the distant and ghastly war dragged on. The Battle of the Somme, especially, was a blow to morale throughout the UK and the dominions. Canada, with its population of only eight million, could not hope to provide the 500,000 recruits promised by Prime Minister Robert Borden.

To end the Conscription Crisis of 1917, Canada turned to its final option – a draft. Quebec opposed such a measure out of hand. While the English Canadians felt a stronger loyalty to the Empire, many weren't happy about the prospect. This nuance, however, was lost in the debate, as the political battle lines were hastily drawn up along the language barrier.

On 29 August 1917, the Military Service Act passed, allowing Prime Minister Borden to recruit from across the nation. He also used the Military Voters Act to draw support from Canadians serving overseas (soldiers and female nurses alike) and the wives, mothers, and sisters of such soldiers, who generally favored conscription. He also used a particular loophole to his advantage – such overseas votes could be distributed in any riding. Also, the act denied voting rights to conscientious objects and immigrants from enemy nations, basically giving Borden's Unionists effective control of the government. Wilfred Laurier, as leader of the Liberals, opposed both conscription and the formation of a coalition government. This lost Laurier a lot of Liberal support, but he wished to prevent his Quebecois-nationalist opponent Bourassa from having an excuse to agitate for secession.

Still, the Military Service Act came under heavy protest from French Canadians when it came into force on New Year's Day, 1918, culminating in a riot that lasted between Thursday, March 28 and April 1st, the so-called Easter Riot. It began when a mob demonstrated against the arrest of a man who failed to produce draft exemption papers to Dominion Police outside of the St. Roche District police station. Quebec City soon erupted into riots and vandalism, including the ransacking of pro-conscription newspaper offices, and rumors spread of a Quebec-wide uprising. It was during these events that L'Amirale was seen in Quebec City's port on several occasions, performing some sort of odd ritual by rearranging rocks. She disappeared in front of witnesses during the May 29th, 6:50 AM sighting, as a large wave crashed down over her. She would later be seen quietly watching the soldiers and rioters clash either somewhere in the St-Roch area or on Rue Saint Roch.

Ottawa deployed nearly eight hundred reinforcements in response to the rumors of a Quebecois revolution, with another four thousand incoming from other provinces. On the Monday after Easter, the rioters rallied against the nearly twelve hundred troops in the city, resulting in gunfire that lead to at least five civilian deaths, nearly a hundred civilian injuries, at least 32 military injuries, and $300,000 worth of damage, and the threat of an impending Canadian civil war. Ottawa's effective crackdown both suppressed (in the short term) and increased (in the long term) French-Canadian nationalism. The Crisis shaped Canadian politics to this day, crafting Quebec into a Liberal bastion for the rest of the century.

One peculiar area of contention was Kitchener, Ontario, where the cultural-linguistic divide was between German-Canadians and the Anglophone majority. The area was settled by Germans and Pennsylvania Dutch throughout the 19th century, and had been known as Berlin until its patriotic renaming in 1916. Kitchener garrisoned the 118th North Waterloo Battalion, known for its horrifically poor discipline. The 118th tore down a bronze bust of Kaiser Wilhelm I, erected in 1897 and previously tossed into the local lake just two years before. The statue was allegedly melted down to make napkin rings. The Battalion incited multiple local riots, including attacks on police, the mayor, a choral group, the Acadian Club, and local shops with German names and cultural-ties. On 5 March, 196, the Reverend C. Reinhold Tappert was dragged out of his home and beaten for his pro-German sympathies and willingness to conduct Lutheran services in German. On New Year's Day of 1917, a Sergeant Major Blood attacked the city council, due to rumors that the newly elected government would revert the city's name to Berlin. A simultaneous raid was conducted against the newspaper offices.

The Battalion saw 92 desertions on Canadian soil, largely during the August harvest furloughs, and twelve officers resigned from the unit. They were shipped to Europe in January 1917, where the unit was dissolved and largely attached to the 25th Reserve. However, many of their deserters remained in the area, and were even rumored to control local politics for some time, perhaps well into the twenties[33]. On March 7th, 1918, a deserter bandit gang attacked Mayor John Hett. A willowy woman in an oil-drenched dress was seen on King Street, in the midst of the attack. Rows upon rows of strange, ghostly hands pressed against the darkened café window behind her. These apparitions disappeared once she quietly entered the locked café by breaking open the door. The spooked bandits fled. This was the Haligonian's final appearance in Canadian territory.

A similar watery wartime waif comes to us from the flight bases in Norfolk, England. In September of 1916, Flight-Lieutenant Ronald Jacoby witnessed "the face of a beautiful girl mirrored as it were in the water beneath" as he flew over Barton Broad. He compare her beauty to the Lady of Shalott, and sought out local lore. As it were, local pilots had witnessed a similar face in the final moments before sundown, within an elevation window of 450 to 600 feet. The locals avoided the place, as a girl had been shot dead in the Broad several hundred years ago, while trying to escape from her father by boat with her lover. The girl not only appeared as a reflection, but occasionally left the water to circle the edge of the lake at sunrise, her eyes filled with sorrow[34].

Dagger Creed.

After the encounter aboard the c27, the next person to encounter the Haligonian was Halifax-native Edwin "Dagger" Creed.

Dagger Creed was a Black Nova Scotian, born in the community of Africville, an impoverished Black settlement south of Bedford Basin in Halifax. The poorly constructed houses were devastated by the force of

---

[33] Burpee, Lawrence Johnstone (1926). *The Oxford Encyclopædia of Canadian History (The Makers of Canada Series – Anniversary Edition)*. New York: Oxford University Press, pg. 477.

[34] Sampson, Charles. (1993). *Ghosts of the Broads*. Jarrold Publishing (Originally published 1931; Yachtsman Publishing Company).

the Explosion, though only five residents died. The neighborhood received almost no funds for relief and reconstruction.

 Africville had originally been settled by fifty Black Loyalists that had been promised free land and equal rights in Nova Scotia in the aftermath of the War of 1812, later reinforced by an influx of Jamaican Maroons. While it had never been officially incorporated, its inhabitants legally owned the land around the southern Bedford Basin after purchasing it in 1848. It transformed into a crowded industrial neighbourhood during the Great War build-up, and its population reached nearly four hundred before the community was destroyed and its inhabitants evicted in the 1960s to make way for the A. Murray MacKay bridge to Dartmouth. Many men in the community worked low-paying maritime jobs such as sailors, dockworkers, and shipbuilders, and the many trains dividing the neighbourhood employed many black Pullman porters. Sixty-five percent of the population worked as domestic servants[35]. It was largely centered, religiously and culturally, around a single Baptist church built in 1849. While Africville is the most famous of the traditionally black neighborhoods of Nova Scotia, there were other such communities scattered around Halifax and other cities in Nova Scotia, producing such figures as Summerville-native William Nelson Hall V.C. (1827-1904), a Crimean War and Indian Mutiny veteran who became the first Nova Scotian, the first black person, and the third Canadian to earn the Victoria Cross, and Haligonian lawyer James Robinson Johnston (1876-1915), the first black Nova Scotian to graduate from a university.

 The city government cared little for Africville, forcing them to use wells for their water, candles for night lights, dirt roads for transportation, and volunteers for teachers in an unfunded school. Halifax used the area as a kind of dumping ground for its prison, infectious disease hospital, rendering plants, slaughterhouses, garbage dump, and finally an inexplicable fecal waste depository, just to literally shit all over the area. Creed attended the Baptist church before his mother converted to the Seventh-Day Adventist movement, received a seventh grade education in the schoolhouse, and got the hell out of there as soon as a decent opportunity on a boat arrived.

---

[35] Africville Genealogy Society, ed. *The Spirit of Africville*. (1992). Halifax: Formac Publishing Company Limited. pp. 17.

Creed served a noncombat role during the war, and while a skilled arctic hunter, he preferred not to shoot or gut his targets. He was something of a trapper, honing his skills exploring the wild north of Canada and Newfoundland. However, his wilderness survival skills were just a plus; his true importance lay in his expertise in the field of winter navigation.

The Canadian military did not actively recruit people of color, turning away fifty Black Nova Scotians with a particularly condescending policy statement: "this is not for you fellows, this is a white man's war." Still, men of the First Nations were allowed to join a segregated 114th battalion in 1915, and roughly 3,500 Aboriginal Canadians served in the war, the Canadian Japanese Association mustered a reserve corps of 227 men in British Columbia, and over a thousand Black Canadians would serve in segregated units in the course of the war. Creed found something of a loophole, serving as a hireling, something of a consultant, to the Dominion Navy in its Arctic operations.

This is how he found himself aboard the Canadian steam-powered icebreaker *CGC Sir Peregrine Maitland*. The *Maitland w*as one of many icebreakers serving in the port of Arkhangelsk during the War, keeping the necessary trade routes open. Icebreakers are difficult to work on, prone to rocking and rolling due to their round, heavily armored keels, noisy, and expensive to construct and maintain due to the constant damage the icebreaking causing to the appendages. They shake as they break, keeping your teeth chattering when mixed with the freezing cold. The presence of German U-boats and Baltic naval mines did nothing to improve conditions.

Canada supplied a respectable amount of icebreakers to Arkhangelsk, the most notable being the long-serving ice-cutter steamship *Fyodor Litke*, original the *CGC Earl Grey* and renamed the *Canada* after 1914. Along with the Canadian-Russian icebreaker the *Lintrose* (or *Sadko*), the *Canada* escorted nearly a hundred and fifty British munitions ships around Murmansk between 1914-1915. *The Maitland*, laid down in 1911 by the Halifax Graving Dock Company and the Dominion Steel Corporation[36], also functioned as an escort ship in

---

[36] Possibly with the help of a third company with an even cooler name.

Russian waters. By December 1917, the Revolution trapped her in the Port of Arkhangelsk.

On December 17, 1917, Dagger Creed wrote:

"Still stuck in Archangel. White Sea still a block of ice, though some activity to the south on the Northern Dvina, strange fire to the large island to the north across from ML [Mainland?] Archangel. Colder than usual today, somehow. Wind strong from E. This sad wooden town must be creaking like crazy. The captain is worried about control of the railroad to Moscow. We have heard bad rumours.

* * *

Olson spotted a dark form wash ashore. I took out the spyglass and examined the mass. I handed Olson my glass and told him that I believed it to be a girl, who looked to be resting on a dark cloth through my goggles. I unfurled and descended on the ropes, letting myself fall at the midpoint. I buried the knife into the ice as I struck the ground, and used it as a toehold as I pulled the girl onto the ice.

She was unbelievably heavy for such a small person, so heavy it was a miracle that I brought her ashore. I did not find the shroud - she left behind a massive slick of glistening oil that turned the frosty water silver and gold, and a kind of dimness clung to her - queer thing. I shouted up at Olson and Wilkins to throw down a dry cloth and material for a fire. Merely setting her upright felt like hoisting a beam, and I searched her jacket for irons or a lead pipe, like someone tried to drown her by sinking. I could not carry her up on the rope, so I would tend to her there on the stones.

I pulled up her tuque and brushed aside her hair, blonde hair blacked by water and oil. She had yet to move in any significant way. Her skin was oddly hard, too hard, almost petrified or frozen. I placed my ear to her breast, and could hear the sea roar, her heartbeat the crash of a thousand madding storms upon a lonely, windswept shore. I could hear a hurricane howl inside of her, and it frightened me.

I pulled open her pea coat and recoiled at her bare breasts. I buttoned it up again and looked up, hoping that none of the men had seen me expose her. We made eye contact as I buttoned the top button. There was something oddly taught [sic] about it, like the coat was sewn to her. It had a weight to it, and clanked with metal; I though there surely must be plates bound into its lining, like the experimental armour of some tank crews. She looked fetching, like a distressed Hebe[37]. She had those large sad Dorothy Kelly eyes, dark grey. She made me sad and cold just looking at them. Extremely cold and with a faint light, like a winter's dawn. Glistening black oil trickled from the edge of her dark, purplish lips. I held out my handkerchief, and let her spit the blackness from her mouth.

She smiled at me and said in a husky, salty voice: 'Ahoy, my countryman.' Then she added, with chilling seriousness, 'There is a hole in heaven, right over Halifax.'

She closed her eyes again and appeared to pass out while against the rock, a single glass tear falling from her eye. I called to the men again. I started the fire and tried to dry her off as best I could, though she and her clothing always seemed to be wet. I placed her next to the fire as the men gathered around.

My hands trembled when I touched her, trembling with the cold of the dead and an overpowering fear. It sounds silly, being afraid of such a thing. She was a mass of exposed nerves in an open wound, all the

---

37   Hebe (born Constance Irene Vessellier) was an English model known for her large, sad, puppy dog eyes and innocent, waifish features. She was also known for deceptively youthful looks, to the point that her professional name derives from that of the Greek goddess of youth. She modeled for the fashion designers Edward Molyneux and Lucy Christiana, Lady Duff-Gordon, better known by her pseudonym "Lucile." Despite her current obscurity, Hebe was one of the first modern professional models, participating in the original catwalk fashion shows, Lucile's "mannequin parades" - mannequin being the Edwardian term for fashion model. She later married American millionaire Arthur Kingsland.

Lady Duff-Gordon (1863-1935) is a fascinating figure in her own right, a female entrepreneur who revolutionized fashion design and took on royalty, movie stars, and theatrical productions such as the Ziegfeld Follies as clients. She was also one of the first fashion designers to become a brand name, selling a line of clothes through Sears and Roebuck catalogs, and helped push corsets out of fashion and introduced lower necklines, slit skirts, and erotic lingerie, winning the favor of both working women and all the men. Not content with being a *Titanic* survivor, she later missed her berth on the final voyage of the *RMS Lusitania* due to a freak illness.

world's pain and hatred and fear of death and failure wrapped in a nameless loneliness, this little orphan.

    I looked at her again through the snow goggles, and saw again that dark shroud. I asked Spooky Marsters (one of the midshipmen) about what he thought it was. He was big on ghost happenings, like the Amherst Mystery and the Bell Witch, haints and Spiritism, and told spook stories at night. He asked me what I used to darken the lenses on my goggles. I said I painted it with a cobalt gloss. He smiled queerly, flashing yellow fangs, and said that there was an English doc named Walter Kilner who discovered that one could see the 'human atmosphere' (the etheric double of a person that became the ghost upon death) through his goggles. These used a cobalt blue coal-tar dye, dye cyanine[38] [sic]" to see the electrified radiation of a person, 'the N-rays,' something I had never heard of. He said to look up what the chemical make up of my lens dye was – maybe she was putting off a heavy 'aural radiance.' I can't remember where I purchased it, though."

When You See Millions of the Mouthless Dead.
    Canadian historian Tim Cook performed in-depth archival research on the subject of supernatural experiences during the First World War, finding that soldiers' journals and letters are overflowing with encounters with ghosts, phantasmal appearances of still living but dearly missed relatives, premonitions of doom from front line soldiers, and strange, calming silences during battles, even during the chaos of the Somme. The Haligonian was simply an extremely prolific haunter.

    Rather than ethereal "visions," these Great War-era entities typically had an uncanny solidity or hyperrealism to them unlike our typical understanding of ghosts. "The unnatural, supernatural, uncanny and ghostly offered succour to some soliders, who embraced these 'grave beliefs' to make sense of their war experience," Tim Cook noted, explaining the 'threshold borderland' of the Western Front. "It was a common response for some soldiers who lived in a space of destruction and death." No less a figure than Robert Graves reported multiple encounters with ghosts, including an alleged visitation by the ghost of

---

[38] Dicyanin.

his recently slain friend Private Challoner, smoking outside of his dinning hall in Béthune.

Other visitations, while tinged with the uncanny, still carry a sense of camaraderie. The Tuesday, 21 November 1916 edition of the *Liverpool Echo* carries a story of ghostly bilocation, starring the beloved colonel of an unspecified regiment stationed in Flanders, deprived of his arm by a hand grenade. The colonel, fitted with an artificial arm, "moved heaven and earth to get back there with his men, but that, he was informed, was impossible." He was instead attached to a garrison battalion leaving for the Dardanelles. Unfortunately, upon landing in Turkey, he fell ill with dysentery, and he died in transit to England aboard a hospital ship.

"Now the extraordinary part of this story is that at the exact moment that the Colonel died on the hospital train a company of his old regiment saw him in their trench in Flanders," read the *Echo*. "There was nothing out of the ordinary happening at the time, and beyond the number of exploding shells, the 'tick-tack' of a machine-gun, and the occasional bursting of a hand grenade, the morning was just as many others had been. The company were at their post when the company sergeant-major turned to the company commander: 'Beg pardon, sir, here's the Colonel coming round; I didn't know he was back again.' The officer looked up. There, standing with his cap just a little to one side, as he always wore it, stood the colonel. His field-boots were caked with mud, and an old pair of binoculars were slung around his neck. The company commander was surprised, and started to walk towards him, when he dropped his stick, stooped to pick it up, and when straightened up again the colonel had gone. The officer dived down a communication trench and rushed for company headquarters. 'Did you see him?' he queried, breathless. The three subalterns looked up at his question, 'See whom? Do you mean the colonel? Yes, we saw him, standing still, looking down the trench just here; we looked at him for fully a minute, and suddenly he WAS NOT THERE. Can't make it out at all' said the spokesman: 'thought he was in the Dardanelles; besides, all the men saw him too, and I don't know whether you noticed it or not— he had BOTH his arms.'"

Cook cited a similar case of solidity and liveliness in Canadian veteran Will R. Bird's 1968 memoir, *Ghosts Have Warm Hands,* in which

Bird's brother Stephen woke him in the middle of the night at Vimy Ridge, two years after his death in battle. Will began to rejoice, but "Steve" placed his notably warm hands over his brother's mouth to silence him. The apparition commanded his brother to get his gear and follow him out of the shelter, before vanishing into thin air. Bird's otherworldly bafflement collided with the mundane horrors of war as a stray shell demolished the shelter.[39]

Dr. Hereward Carrington collected multiple reports of war ghosts, including the case of a "Private Rex," who suddenly began to lag behind his unit. The commander, Lieutenant Smith, believed him to be ill, and watched as the private slowly fell out of line until he was standing behind the officer. Smith asked if he was feeling ill or cold, but Rex said no. Smith asked if he was hungry, and offered a package of malted milk tablets. Rex reached out, and it was then that Smith noticed the private's hand was icy cold. The color drained from Rex's face. Smith turned away for a moment, to command his men; Rex had vanished by the time he turned back, and could not be found. He halted his unit and gave search. A junior officer told him to call off the search, as the private had been killed three days before – and Smith had attended the burial. Smith's memory suddenly sharpened, and he remembered. Curiously, Carrington records Smith saying that such visitations by dead comrades were a "common occurrence," and that it "takes away all fear of death, for I know that Private Rex lives, though dead.[40]"

Michael Harrison gathered multiple reports from British sailors in the North Atlantic, where a spectral "Captain Jesselton" or a ghostly submarine would guide marines around unseen mines or away from U-Boats[41].

One Private Tom Easton, of the 2nd Battalion Tyneside Scottish (32st Northumberland Fusiliers), wrote in a letter dated to 1 July 1916,

---

[39] A prolific writer with multiple odd experiences, Will R. Bird would also recover a gladius churned up from the soil following a bombardment near his position at Amiens. Upon returning to Nova Scotia, scholars would date the sword to the Gallic Wars of Caesar.
[40] Carrington, Hereward. (1918). *Psychical Phenomena and the War,* New York: Dodd, Mead & Co.
[41] Harrison, Michael. (1981) *Vanishings.* Trafalgar Square Publishing

that he watched a dying friend undergo a religious revelation in the wake of the attack up Mash Valley, by the French commune of Ovillers-la-Boisselle:

"He called me over and when I got to him he asked me to sit down. I protested, telling him we had other things to do. He said it wouldn't take long and asked me if I could hear music. I could hear absolutely nothing.

He described to me what he could see: 'The whole sky was opening up. Orchestras were playing, choirs were singing, and all the ancestors were telling him to come and join them.' He held out his arms. 'There's my old father' he says, 'They're waiting for me.' He fell forward and I saw he had no back. A piece of shrapnel had gone through his chest.

These things shake you. But it was a momentous experience for me, and in spite of the shock, it gave me the courage to do my duty as a soldier."

During the grueling Battle of Verdun, French soldiers shared tales of a common visitation by a joyous warrior dressed in the kit of the Franco-Prussian War of 1870, consistently describing him with a long white beard and flowing hair and laughing eyes, usually preceding a period of recovery or victory. He was even seen leading a push, and at times tended to the wounded with enough efficacy that men said the the entity saved their lives.

1975 saw the publication of the famous photograph of an R.A.F. Squadron who served at the *HMS Daedalus* training facility, gathered in 1919 to attend the funeral of air mechanic Freddy Jackson, killed in a propeller accident two days prior. A phantasmal face appeared behind an airmen in the back row, whom the squadron identified as their recently deceased friend.

Premonitions of one's own death seemed to be commonplace enough that Anglophone soldiers came to call such dreams and visions "the call," and German soldiers developed a culture of aversion towards anyone that expressed a foretelling of death, hopefully to avoid going with the poor prophet. Dreams of family members, especially a departed one greeting or embracing the recipient, were commonly said to be the usual form of "the call," hence the name; in the realm of war folklore, there are countless tales found in letters that tell of a soldier receiving a premonition and separating from the unit to meet his fate alone. One repeated anecdote has the soldier receiving the call and moving into a barn loft, attic, or a side trench, only to be struck by stray shrapnel, a grenade, or a shell.

And likewise, such premonitions occurred in reverse, with those on the homefront receiving visions of their fallen sons and fathers. Our old friend Elliott O'Donnell, in his 1934 book *Family Ghosts and Ghostly Phenomena*, recorded a tale from Edinburgh, Scotland, involving a family by the name of MacKenzie. Their youngest daughter, Sylvia, was alerted to a tapping on the drawing room window. Her eyes met a malevolent gaze. The description, rather jarringly, resembles both the entity witnessed on Spike Isle and the classic grey alien – a long, narrow face without a nose, its slanted eyes set far apart. MacKenzie froze in terror as the grimacing entity slowly faded away. She hid in the center of the house until her parent returned home. When the related what had happened, her parents believed her, telling her that it was something of a banshee, appearing to herald deaths and disasters for the family. On the following day, Sylvia's brother, Robert MacKenzie, was killed fighting in Belgium.

Finally, there is "the crisis apparition," a ghostly figure of a departed comrade or family member that leads a soldier to safety rather than death. As before, the most common form of this legend is the dead friend or mother who beckons the soldier away from the very spot of a landing artillery shell. In the summer of 1918, multiple British soldiers at Verdun saw a spectral soldier beckoning themselves away from danger, usually a trench mortar. The soldier occasionally had a skeletal face[42]. The most famous crisis apparition of the Great War is that of a 28-year-old Adolph Hitler, who claimed to have dreamed of burial beneath a flood of mud and molten iron that rained from the sky. He woke up, feeling the pain of a mortal wound, and left the trench for a dug out, escaping a shell burst by moments. Of course, Hitler would have been well aware of this common wartime motif, and could have easily made up the anecdote to further his cult of personality. So many memoirists of the Great War share a similar story, to the point that one begins to

[42] H. Drummond Gault. (1929). *Ghost Tales and Legends*. London: W. & R. Chambers. p. 10.

wonder if every writer to come out of the trenches was a lucky sensitive or a plagiarist.

As with Carrington's tale of Private Rex, these crisis apparitions frequently overlap with the "Third Man phenomenon," in which a phantasmal figure appears alongside the moving troops, to the point that T.S. Elliot's famous *The Waste Land* mentions it:

"Who is the third who walks always beside you?
When I count, there are only you and I together.
But when I look ahead up the white road
There is always another one walking beside you."

Commentators on the Haligonian legend often wonder why she washed up on the shores of Archangel. The entity had an affinity for ports, but many major cities are ports, and most important cities are on either the sea or a navigable river. What made Archangel a likely choice is how closely it mirrored Halifax during the war – in an eerie parallel, on February 20, 1917, a munitions ship exploded in Archangelsk Harbor, killing roughly 1,500 people. Lev Vasilyev speculated that Halifax and Archangel became psychic sister cities via these explosions, two northern ports forged together in 1917 by trauma and fire and ice. It is as good an explanation as any why the Ghost that Breathes resumed her strange work on the icy shores of Archangel.

The Unexpected Ms. Halifax.

Dagger Creed had himself and the Haligonian hoisted aboard. He described the debriefing that followed.

"I asked her whether she felt symptoms of anything. She sounded like she had a cold, a bit stuffy. I had something of a headache, my eyes flashing like migraine phosphenes as she sniffled and snorted up oil and water.

'Don't worry, I'm not going to come down with the pneumonia,' she said, slowly and stiltedly as she dried her hair with a towel. Her accent was Nova Scotian, but the words seemed new to her. I merrily asked her how the Windsor Swastikas were doing, which puzzled her.

I asked her for her name. She avoided the question, asking me why they call me Dagger.

I pulled out the dagger.

'Ivory-handled, walrus-bone knife,' I said. 'The wounds don't heal.'
'Why?' she asked. 'Eskimo magic?'
'No,' I said. 'That's just what it does. It's Eskimo design, but I carved it myself just north of Frobisher Bay in '09.'
'That's far north,' she noted.
'I've explored the Arctic a bit. That's why I'm here. You're a canuck, eh?'
'Yes,' she said with a half-smile. 'And there ain't a more Canadian way you coulda said that. You their leader, these men? Captain?'
'I'm no Talented Tenth, I'm just the guy who carves up ice. So what ship were you on before you washed ashore?' I asked.
'There weren't none. I rode a submarine.'
'They have women working on submarines now? What are you, women's auxiliary?'
'No,' she said. 'I'm not part of this war effort. Just a product. The distant wars of distant shores – what do these mean to me?'
'They why did you come? You're a civilian, you weren't assigned,' I asked.
'I was drawn here,' she said. 'Not sure why. Pushed by the waves, pulled by the cry of gooneys, gulls, and turns.'
'It wasn't for the sight-seeing,' I said.
'I've seen the war...no man's land and no woman's sea...I'm just drawn to crashes of iron and chemical fire,' she said. 'No, not drawn, they call to me, like I'm the moth to a dulling flame, and it's rolling out to burn up all the Earth. This city... This bitch...everyone seems to be pissin' petrol.'
'I beg your pardon,' I said. 'What do you mean by that? A fire burning up the world and this city being --?'
'I don't like this city. Her cold isn't a crisp, cozy Canadian winter. It's harsh, brutalizing. This harbour isn't quaintly maritime; it's icy and cluttered. Her people are miserable. Nobody smiles.'
She looked out the porthole and added, "Things are gonna change around here.'
'What do you mean?' I asked.
'This port...it's gotta go.'

I asked for some clarification.

'I can do better,' she said. 'This place is sh--. This place is sh--, and it's still standing. It's not fair.'

'What isn't fair?' I said.

'Halifax fell,' she said.

'What?' I said. 'You mentioned Halifax earlier. You said there was a hole...'

'I came to during the death of a city. On a Thursday, in the Narrows, in a mushroom of industrial smoke, in the greatest harbour in the world, where all the neutral ships in the maelstrom had to come, past the forts and batteries,' she said, her voice a mix of haunted languor and port-pub saltiness.

I felt like someone walked over my grave. No, I felt like I was watching someone dig my grave in the darkest hour of the coldest night of the year.

'My father was Norwegian, my mother French, flying no flag and pregnant with explosives and acids. They danced with each other, trying to avoid each other, a death spiral that ended in a hull-cracking rupture and a fuse-lighting rapture. He was thrown to the carbon-blackened shore by a wave of boiling water, and she fell to the bottom in a halo of debris. I am the detonation.'

'You? You are the detonation?' I said. 'What detonation?'

'There was an explosion in the Harbour. Two thousand dead. And I felt the city's torment,' she said, rising to her feet. I did nothing as the news of my home's destruction settled in. 'The shock and the fear and the blue fire and the black rain that fell for ten minutes. I don't know if I was made then or I just woke up, but I pulled myself together from flotsam and jetsom on the ocean of tears that flows between the worlds. Bandages and amputated limbs from the hospital ships, the chill of U-boat terror...And oh Lord, the drowned... My bones are the city's concrete, my blood the salty crush of the Atlantic. My hair is the wind, my eyes lighthouse lenses, my teeth watchtower stones, and my tongue a chocolate wharf on a soda water sea, tasting the oily flavour of failure and the spice of calamity. My heart is an explosion, fire on water. Help me put the fire out.'

She was crying, the hot tears of a furious woman.

'Fire out?' I said. 'You want to die?'

'I want to rest,' she said. 'I want to sleep again. I want quiet. I want to stop suffering for something that isn't my fault.'

Her thin arms shook as she pushed down on the edge of the table. It began to creak. I got up. I touched her elbow. She looked down at my hand. We both looked away as someone knocked at the door, and recoiled from her when Connors came into the room with a tray of food – two water glasses and mashed turnips.

Connors set down the tray between us, saw our grim expressions, and silently left.

The men were not happy. Strange, nameless women who wash-up from Davy Jones' locker are bad luck. I'm not well-versed or place much faith in sailor lore, but even I sense she's a Jonah, or something else out of a whale. Yes, it's all a mash of odd ends: Sami can tame the sea – bring them on. Carribean [sic] cats may be mermaids under a spell. When you're in Bathurst or on the Northumberland Strait before a storm, look for the ghostly fireships. Knotted ropes are a sign of the malicious sea-goblin; never set eyes on its benevolent Baltic "cousin," the Klabautermann. Tattoos bring luck. Don't kill an albatross. Don't whistle, for it challenges the wind and it will win. Don't sail on Thursday, don't sail on Friday, or on a ship of walnut or a second name. Don't miss Sunday Mass if you're ashore or you'll bewitch the ship like *La Chasse-galerie*. Black cats are lucky and the bane of hold-mice. Don't carry bananas, murderers, debtors, or a man of the cloth. And especially not a woman.

But perhaps that's the point. The sea is an endless, terrifying, a chaos of life and death, riches and loss. It must be respected. And what tames it can only be guessed at; it is a wrathful deity without priests or precepts that still demands obedience from all who enter its domain. It's closest prophets are drunken, smokey men with salt in their beards and ropes around their shoulders. And this is why this young woman filled me with fear of the frozen seas ever since I heard the crash of waves in place of her heartbeat — this was Neptune's angel, as dangerous as the mid-Atlantic depths, and confusing as the coastless blue.

She pushed away the turnip mash, and I couldn't blame her. That's the normal reaction to rehydrated turnips. But then she ran her finger around the rim of the glass, contaminating it with some kind of dark grey cloud. It scared us both.

She smashed the glass against the wall.

'Fuck piss bugger and shite!' she shouted. Even though bluenoses[43] have the most obscene mouths in the entire anglophonic world, being the product of the union of sailors and Scots, hearing such words out of a pretty white girl caught me unawares. It threw a bucket of cold water over my dark and mournful mood.

'I am sick,' she said. 'I wish to see the captain of this vessel.'

I summoned MacCallum. He came quickly when I told him there was a woman involved.

'Parlez-vous Français?' I asked, adding, 'Many Russians of the upper-class speak it, some better than they speak Russian. And It's more likely for a Canadian-'

'Oui,' she answered as Captain MacCallum entered. 'I think I know Russia too...there's a lot of languages in here...'

She took off her tuque, soaking wet again, and pulled out a partially collapsed but immaculately dry naval officer's cap.

'Hello, sir. I'm commandeering this vessel.'

'You have no right,' MacCallum said, 'You can't just come aboard a vessel and say that you're in command.'

'I outrank you,' she said.

'I am a captain operating under the auspices of the Canadian Dominion, and His Majesty George V of the British Empire. And I'm licensed to work for the Russian government...whatever that happens to be at the moment.'

'I might be a shade or the capital of Nova Scotia,' she said. 'Or maybe something in the harbour. Or all three.'

'I don't get what you're saying, ma'am,' MacCallum said.

'I think I might be an echo of the city,' she said. 'I don't know what I am, but I don't think I'm a ghost of a person. I might be weeks old, might be ten thousand. Not sure. But not quite a ghost.'

'A ghost? Who said anything about a ghost?' MacCallum asked, with a hint of fright creeping into his voice.

---

[43] Confusingly, here a slang term for Nova Scotians, and not the other meaning of an overbearing moralist.

'Nobody,' she said. 'But...that's what I thought I was. I thought I was dead. But I'm too solid. A ghost is the slough people leave behind when they die. It's all a bit airy, like dusty shed skin and last breaths. I'm made of...Stuff.'

'Ghosts are slough?' I said.

'Yeah, not the body or the soul, you know, but the masks we wear. In society, I mean. That's why you never see any really ancient ghosts. They all seem to come from about fifty to two hundred years ago, maybe three or four hundred for really extraordinary cases in castles and keeps. You never here [sic] of cavemen ghosts, eh? Urban culture forced us all to put on polite little masks, you know, out in the street. Women haunt houses, men haunt businesses and barracks.'

'But you're not a ghost, you said,' I said. 'So what does that have to do with anything?'

'Well, I mean, imagine if an entire city died at once. What ghost would form from all those fallen façades? Think about it. And all of Europe's masquerades are ending. The ball's over, brother. The façades are fallin' like dominoes, and it hit us hard.'

'Us?' the Captain asked.

'Yeah, the wages of European arrogance struck the White Dominion's shore. And now the whole world's about to boil over, and old ghosts are risin' up like steam. A new city's gonna come up here, comin' up like a submarine. Let me get up on it,' she said, with a hot glint of madness in her cold grey eyes as she slowly raised her hands in the air. 'I washed up in the Thames once, and I said, I asked, Mother London, why did I have to burn for your ambitions? But...no, no...No need for self-pity. I'm no sooky baby. If brutish, backwards Russia can rise from the ashes, then so can I.'

I felt something stir inside of me, something inspiring and sickening. She turned, and walked out of the chamber to look out over the railing at the sea.

'What did you mean by things will change here?' I asked her.

'Things will change. They must change,' she said. 'The might of the river is in her motion. Change or die. The might of the mountain is in his permanence. Change, and die.'

'What would you have this city do?' I asked.

'Change and die,' she said.

There was a long, cold silence as she stared out over the white ice.

'There's a British munitions stockpile in this city,' she said softly. 'The Reds want it. I want it more. Do you have a Russian-speaker? I don't think I can run a translation for you.'

'There's a White Russian kid from Alberta on board, a Ruthenian, you know,' I said. 'Simon. He doesn't speak much proper Russian, but he gets us by.'"

The Haligonian uses the phrase the White Dominion, an imperialistic term used in the 1910s for Canada. Canada was one of the six trusted, largely self-governed, white-settled colonies of the British Empire, along with Newfoundland, the Irish Free State, Australia, and New Zealand, as opposed to the exploitable, non-white commercial colonies such as India[44][45]. While Australia and New Zealand were also considered white dominion countries of the British Nation, Canada's snowy climate cemented its status as *the* white dominion. India's potential dominionhood was up in the air at this time precisely because of its ethnic make-up. As A. Campbell, in his 1924 work *the Lost Dominion* put it, "You can have the white dominion, or you can have the Dominion of India, but you cannot have both."

The White Dominion policy proved to be highly important in Edwardian politics, as the British began to 're-Britonize' the colonies. British emigration to the colonies, and specifically Australia, peaked between 1909 and 1913, and almost one in five Australians were born in the UK by the beginning of the War[46].

The War, however, changed this dynamic. Before World War One, the Colonies were fervently British and traditional – the Australian response to the colonial wars of the 1880s to the 1910s was shockingly jingoistic, especially after General Gordon's death in Khartoum during the Sudan War of 1885. London was the center of the world back then,

---

[44] Walder, Dennis. *Post-Colonial Literatures in English: History, Language, and Theories* (Wiley-Blackwell, 1998)

[45] Louis, W.M. Roger. Judith M. Brown, ed. The Oxford History of the British Empire: The Twentieth Century. (Oxford University Press, 1999). (p. 77)

[46] Andrews, Eric Montgomery. *The Anzac Illusion: Anglo-Australian Relations During World War I.* (p. 10-12)

and a voyage to the imperial capital was a Colonial's *hajj*.

A series of military disasters signalled the rise of white dissent in the Empire. With the Australians and New Zealanders, it was the loss of ANZAC forces at Gallipoli and the Third Battle of Ypres, between July and November 1917. The public of those nations saw the British commanders as callous jackasses throwing Colonials into the meat grinder. English Canadians proved to be more content with the British, but Canada's disproportionate amount of victories in the war, such as at Passchendaele and Vimy Ridge, helped Canada form a patriotic identity. Before the Great War, Canada was the part of North America still held by the British Empire after the American Revolution. After the War, Canada was a true and modestly proud nation. Indeed, a lot of the characteristic cultural differences between Canada and the United States can be traced back to the effects of the war, such as Canadian views on militarism and imperialism.

"MacCallum was having none of it. He said that she would be confined to quarters.

'No quarter,' she rasped. 'I will come and go as I please. Look around you. Your ship rots around me like a wounded apple.'

I did, even as MacCallum looked at her in disbelief. The metal of the bulkhead showed signs of rust, and the glass of the portholes had been slightly fractured in a strange pattern that revealed no sign of impact, only inexplicable structural failure.

'Before you came in...she contaminated the water,' I said to MacCallum. 'With her touch. It thickened into an oily sludge.'

'I feel a bit feverish,' said the Captain.

'Cure this sickness...' she said. 'Kill me.'"

'Creed, kick her off the ship,' MacCallum commanded.

'I will comply,' she said. She held her head high as she buttoned up the admiral's jacket.

'I will escort her off the ship,' I said. MacCallum opened the cabin door as I lead the girl out. I threw over the ladder down to the most stable section of ice. The air grew so cold that my teeth chattered. I reached out my shaking hand to guide her down. While icy to the touch, the little bag o' bones was unfazed by the biting cold. Her calm, unstricken hand darted towards the holster of my knife.

She pulled out the deadly blade, the safety strap snapping at her corrosive touch. I retreated, fearing its incurable cut. She quietly and rather matter-of-factly ran the blade across her own throat.

There came a distant clanking sound as the engines showed signs of distress. Five men ran past us, alarmed by the sudden catastrophe.

Our eyes met as blood and bitumen oozed from her white throat. She show no sign of pain or even discomfort. Disappointment. She was disappointed as her throat clotted up. She handed my knife back.

'Don't tell stories,' she hissed, her voice rattling harshly. She told me to wear a jumper under my coat, adding that 'It's the Apocalypse, so I'd dress in layers.'"

The War In Heaven As A Class Struggle.

"I will not lie," Mihajlo wrote, about the events of 18 December 1917. "I mostly brought the others along to give them something to do and to help us carry out the haul. Anna and I could do this drunk and with a bum leg, which is good because that's how things happened to be as we hit the magazine on the pier.

Anna and I struck down at the entrance to the loading platform. Anna's mere presence did something to the guards' inner ears, destroying their sense of balance. They tumbled to the ground as the vertigo took effect, an effect worsened by Anna's slow, deliberate walk along the wall. She kicked open the door, breaking the locks with a ten ton boot sole, and fell into the magazine.

I led the rest of the group in, leaving Lana and Galya behind to guard the door. I handed Galya my suppressed Nagant M1895 gas-seal revolver. I kept my old Browning M 1910 semi-automatic pistol as I entered.

Dima led Adam, Yuri, Igor, Yekaterina, and Karp deeper into the facility. The loss of that bear Radomir to typhus was a blow to their strength; the rest looked like eager children. They spread out. Gena, Maxim, and Pyotr remained near Annushka and I, looking queasy. Maxim stumbled about, and Gena's untrimmed hair fell flat on his head until Anna finally came to a complete landing. Pyotr loudly gasped at that moment, the phantasmal weight pressing down on his lungs vanished. He covered his mouth in fear and embarrassment. I gestured that it was fine. I whispered that there was no one around to hear us.

That is when I wondered why. There was more security here when Anna and I scouted out the location. Dock workers, too.

I lead my squad down the hall to an open space filled with stacks of munitions, including bombs and shells bound to pallets, crates of bullets, and barrels of chemicals. In one corner, a sea boat half-covered in a tarp collected dust – a Grigorovich M-5, I think. All of this was ripe for the taking, with not a single dog in the orchard.

We all jumped in fright as a clanking noise echoed through the chamber, followed by a whistle, the sounds of steam being released from an old engine. As we crept forward, the faint bubbling sound that followed became distinct, the sound of water flowing from a pipe. Anna and I darted towards the source of the noise, a shadowy figure behind a pyramid of fluid munitions.

The man, his body obscured by a parka, ran away before I could see his face, splashing through a fluid on the floor. I shot forward. I took in my surroundings, and realized what he did. At first, I thought that this was the water from the pipe that he had opened, but the pool of water in the corner of the storeroom demonstrated that this was something else entirely, possibly leakage from one of the rusting barrels of industrial lubricant that littered the area. It took some time for the smell to waft up to my nose.

It wasn't a lubricant. It was petroleum, a fact confirmed when the friction of my sixth foot step pulling up from the floor ignited the pyramid of fuels. I sped up in an attempt to outrun the rising wall of fire and fumes, but could not avoid the bone-shaking force of the explosion. I was propelled into the wall.

Unable to control the conflicting and colliding forces, all I could do is push against the whole of existence to stay alive, decelerating so rapidly that I had something that I could describe as a miniature seizure. I sprained my ankle sometime before I regained my center of gravity, somewhere in a grey tumult of wet rubble and smoke. I was numb and covered in whiteness. The blast had ripped through the wooden wall, allowing the snow to tumble in around us.

Anna cried out to me, calling my name as she pushed through the thick smoke. For the first time since Chingis and Rivka had died, there was life in that distance voice.

She let out a shocked scream followed by a rapid series of nasal gasps as she retreated through the smoke. The gunshot echoed through the pipes and barrels, obscuring the source of the noise. Her smokey silhouette struggled in the air, her legs bound by a mariner's slungshot binding her legs like bollos.

I rose to my feet in pain as the shadowy figure ran past me, a recently unbound pyramid of barrels crashing to the ground in his wake. The cut band flapped in the breeze, a ribbon of metal cleanly and effortlessly slashed apart. I had to brace myself against the wall and stop a pair of bouncing barrels with my uninjured leg – which happened to be my bad leg, but searing, new pain is worse than chronic knee weakness and occasional paralyzing cramping in the morning.

I saw his face. He was, of all things, a Negro in winter garb. His eyes were hidden behind a pair of slotted bone goggles, disconcertingly similar to those possessed by Anna. The snow crunched beneath his feet as he fled the magazine. An enraged Anna saw his shadow through the smoke and the quickly forming fog and gave chase. I was grounded, but before I could pursue him, he discharged his rifle not at Anna or I but at the snowbank he was standing on, sending tons of snow crashing down into the magazine, cutting us off from the wilderness outside as he jumped clear.

'Who was that?' I asked.

'That was a normal human,' Anna said with a hint of disbelief. She kicked her feet until she was in the right position to saw through the slungshot with one of her utility knives. 'He beat us.'

'He cheated,' I said.

'Against two demigods,' she said. 'And he got away with it.'

'Yes, good for him,' I conceded. 'We'll find him. There can't be many black white Russians.'

'Still just a mundane human being,' Anna said.

A chill ran through the room. A short, thin, shadowy form coalesced in the fog and the smoke and the steam, rising from the filthy water. Out of the corner of my eye, it was simply an oil slick, but then it turned its head. I gasped and pivoted, and was met by a crouching and hunched over figure.

'I am not,' said a woman's voice. It was in English, actually, but I could understand those three words. The small woman continued to talk, but I could not make it out, nor could I see her face behind the black wall of fumes.

'She said *you were running around earlier, so fast*,' Anna said, translating. '*Why are you here?* She says. *These are British stores. They belong to the Empire, and we are seizing them in the name of King George for the Dominion of Canada.*'

I caught a brief glimpse of the young Englishwoman's face as she opened up her soaked coat. Litres of water poured from its shredded and oil-stained lining, extinguishing the flames. She continued to trudge forward, soaking up the acrid steam as she went, as if powered by it like some automaton.

The woman hissed something.

'She says...she says, *Kill me*,' Anna said. '*Storm warning*, I don't understand why, but she is whispering *storm warning*.'

I froze up, sick to my stomach with fear. I am glad she is a poor judge of facial expressions.

'Anna?' I said, my voice quaking. 'Fly us away from this woman.'

Anna complied. We embraced in the air as she pulled me up and away from the steamy ground and the glowering woman. As we rose towards the ceiling, Anna's down draft clearing the air, we saw that the woman had drawn a crude map on the ground in a circle of black stones. She had written words in English, in what a black patch on the woman's finger convinced me was ink until I saw that those words and the map had some depth to them. She had burnt and gouged and carved those scribblings into the ground with her soot-blackened fingers.

We landed on top of a block of crates, hoping to see the rest of our group so we could reorganize and leave this place. Everyone was gone. Anna ran around the side of the stack before rejoining me at the summit when we heard someone running in from the front section of the magazine.

It was Dima Sergeyevich, sprinting towards us, shouting warnings to run, leave. Anna and I flew towards him, hoping to lift him to some kind of safety. Right in front of our eyes, Dima vanished. He was gone, erased by a flicker of golden light.

We retreated. Flying backwards until the palm of Anna's right hand pressed against the southern brick wall. We slid down to the floor, so we could see through the corridor.

There were human shadows burnt into the walls and floors and across the ceiling, the elongated shades of flailing limbs scarring the walls, long after the bodies had flickered away.

We travelled down the hall to the entrance. I saw my silenced revolver on the ground, in the brown snow. I at first thought it stained with rust. My stomach turned as I realized my error.

Yuri stood in the center of a sunburst of boiled blood. The wind howled past him, carrying snow between us, each flake licking away a little bit of color from his already pale face.

'Yuri?' Anna asked as she picked up the discarded revolver.

'Uriel,' he corrected as his body erupted into a mass of light, his voice the crackling thunder of ice tumbling down a mountain. He seemed to crack open like molten stone, but burned with such a heat that it was brighter than an electric bulb. It had faces like the fish of the deep sea, jawless, abyssal things and eight swirling wings of scale and bone. A spiral of twisting, ringed bones rotated around him, like the shell of a nautilus, glowing with a living light. All around us, onto the bricks and tiles and remaining window panes, a letter that resembled a rounded honeycomb burnt itself into the walls – this was the Multiocular O, an obscure letter used only in a single-phrase, a famous bit of trivia: "серафими много⊛читїи.[47]" I think it was Aquinas who theorized that every angel was its own species – Uriel must have been some lost beast from the abyssal depths, glorified into the master of light in recompense.

We finally had our archangel of Arkhangelsk. Just the two of us, without the Rabbi and Céleste to leach away at its essence and energies, without Tom Noun and Winepress to break it open, without Siegfried to kill it. All we had was a small, fragile prison, and no way to capture him.

To my horror, I did not even have time to think. I accelerated myself upon seeing him, simply to buy myself some time. I gasped when I saw the angel move towards me, flowing like a torrent of liquid light.

---

[47] *Serafimi mnogoochitii*, Old Church Slavonic for "many-eyed seraphim."

Uriel is the Archangel of Light. Light is faster than me, much, much faster.

I decelerated, grabbed Anna, and sped up again. Uriel used that split second to engulf us in a burning star. Anna and I screamed in pain. We blew a hole in the world trying to repulse the creature of light, tearing open the the magazine's wall and breaking glass throughout the north shore of Arkhangelsk. The rubble did not hit the ground for several minutes in some places.

The angel held onto us tenaciously, even as we dragged it through the freezing clouds, hoping that the friction fires and the cooling effect of evaporating air would shake off the searing light.

Something inside of the angel coalesced into something sharp and solid, a core of knives ready to cut us if we slowed down.

Anna and I held onto this core and sent it shooting into an icy cliff in what would be known as Franz Josef Land – yes. The irony of the name is noted. A steamy avalanche came rolling down the snowy mountain. The impact of Uriel permanently changed the geography of the archipelago, not that anybody noticed. Even Uriel did not notice. It simply refracted out of the ice crystals right in front of us, cooling into its four headed form.

Our eyes could not focus, with spots dancing across our overwhelmed vision. Our skin still burned, raw and red and healing painfully. Our bodies shivered, both from the primordial cold and the shock to our nerves. The concussion of our rapid, reality breaking flight rattled our bones. I fell to my knees, and Anna heaved and vomited up a thin, pus-yellow gruel.

Here in this Arctic wasteland, Uriel was the midnight sun, and we were nothing than fuzzy grey shadows waiting to be obliterated at his rising."

Anna continued the tale.

"Uriel killed our friends, and he was about to kill us, a dozen murders carried out in so many seconds.

His eye were wrong. He must not have understood blinking, and sometimes his eye slid up under the lid instead of the lid sliding down, exposing a pool of light that seemed heavy like a jelly.

The archangel elevated his hand, and Misha rose with it. Misha twitched in the air, tracing a burning black smear above the ground, an impotent act of defiance. The archangel left him hanging there as it approached me with an adamantine blade of white fire. I did my best to hold it off, but he was too fast, too strong.

'Ahoy, angel,' said a voice from the bottom of the world.

The water below Uriel's feet, melted by his radiance, began to pool and blacken. A hand reached out, and grabbed the angel's ankle. The angel flapped its wings, dragging the Englishwoman from the magazine out of the disgusting puddle.

She screamed for the angel to kill her as as she attacked. She did not stab or strike it with a weapon. She simply charged at the archangel of light and weakly pushed it backwards. 'KILL ME! KILL ME! DO IT!'

'I can not kill you,' said the angel.

'You're a goddamn angel! Kill me, you arse!' she said.

'An angel cannot assist in a suicide,' said the angel, melting the ice binding its feet. 'I can not kill you.'

'I can't kill you either,' she hissed, stumbling back. Her voice was older than her face. 'But the dead...the dead are here, to claim you as one of their own.'

Uriel turned his head, as though he saw something that we could not.

'It's dark down there,' she said. 'They want your light. And would you deny the voice of that silent majority?'

And then hands, a teaming swarm of hands, emerged from the shadowy spaces around the archangel, restraining it, pulling it backwards. Imagine seeing someone dragged backwards through a doorway you couldn't see by a faceless, ashen mob...The silence...the silence made it worse.

Mihajlo and I tried to understand what she was. That was the problem. She's not alive, but she's not dead, and she's not even undead. She's not an angel, not a demon, not a woman or a god or a nephela.

'What are you?' I asked.

'Are you some kind of revenant?' Mihajlo asked.

'We are scars on the thin skin between worlds. We can only heal and die when the disturbance is gone. The injury salved....the grudge settled...But most of us forget this...we last forever, eating away at ourselves until forgotten and empty...until people stop believing in us and we stop believing in ourselves and we fade away... But the banks of the River Styx are overflowing, and the dead refuse to drink from the Lethe. They wont let you forget this war...'

'No,' I said to her, in English. 'You are no ghost. Not quite. Something is wrong.'

Her gaze filled us with her overflowing rage and grief...no, it wasn't just her anger and despair, but that of the restless, resentful dead.

'Then tell me what I am,' she said. She took deep, pained, rasping breaths, very solid and very much alive.

'I don't know,' I said, fighting this foreign sense of fury and loathing. 'Some new kind of abomination.'

'Can you kill me?' said the ghost that breathes.

'I'm not sure,' Mihajlo said, slowly moving away from the creature.

'Try,' she hissed.

'No...not...not until we know what you are,' Mihajlo said, his voice quaking in her cold.

'The rivers of the underworld can always sweep away another soul,' she warned.

We fled. The last thing we heard her say say was a loudly whispered 'Storm warning...'"

Urban Renewal.

"The girl had me track down a pair of freaks working for the Liberal Communists. She told me that they were powerful and truly astonishing, but I had no idea what I was getting into," Dagger Creed wrote. "They led a raiding party against the British munitions stores the girl was so interested in. I saw them from the roof. The man in the tarry black suit moved with such force and velocity that he melted the ice and tore up the ground. The female flew, somehow. My mind and my essence rebelled. While the girl had displayed a disturbing nature and troubling, inexplicable features up until that moment, I could not fathom this monstrous pair. I therefore chose to think of them, and hunt them, as a particularly fast and an enlarged bird of prey.

As they infiltrated the storehouse, I descended into the building through an emergency ventilation hatch situated over the chemical storage sector.

I covered the ground in a petrolium distillate [sic] as a counter measure to the fast-runner. I found a detonator wire and unravelled it into long strands and rigged them across two of the thin support columns of the warehouse, hoping to entangle the flyer. I waited on the far side of a pyramidal stack and waited for them with my rifle.

In hindsight, I should have searched for a nicer rifle to replace this rubbish Ross. Rosses cannot handle a little mud and cannot keep the bayonet fixed. Accurate though, and that is all I need for this task. I did not have to kill the pair, and the girl said that such a feet was unlikely. All I had to do was draw them out, bog them down, and flush them into her arms.

I did my job well. The racer set off the oil trap and crashed into the wall in the resulting explosion. The flyer snapped the tripwires as she approached, but I managed to force a landing with a few shots. Something happened to my eyes, I think, for there was something off about her size. She was a small thing, but there was a weight to her, a great shadowy grandeur to her; It's hard to understand, but you know how something can be deceptively heavy, like say, a pistol, and one had to give it a second before it feels right it your hand? This was the visual equivalent. There was something bigger there than a five foot woman should feel. I knew an old lady on my block that had a stroke and afterwards she swore her tiny little arm felt like was ten tons and she couldn't move the damn thing. Maybe it was some psychical projection of that variety of brain damage, sickening my optics- I don't know, ask a professor. I work with boats.

My eyes burned and my ears rang. I heard a buzzing, between bees and flies and a straining motor when the belt is about to snap[48]. I held myself together through the short ordeal, but by the time I blew the wall I was quaking and on the verge of vomiting. I could blame it on the

---

[48] These buzzing noses associated with the nephilim by outside witnesses seems to be related to a similar buzzing noted frequently in seances and paranormal experiences, particularly in the Journal of the Society for Psychical Research (See Volume XXXVI No. 662). May also be connected to the *Zamzummim*, that is, "the buzzing ones."

aviatress' emetic presence, but that would be dishonest. I ran into the winter storm, scared for my life.

This was apocalyptic, and demonic. When I was seven, my mom went over to the Adventists, because she was scared for her life and her soul and she put that terror into me. I pushed it down and away and kept it down in a hole in the ground for nearly three decades until I saw a woman flying around and it all came rushing out. She had been afraid the End was coming, reading the doomsday prophecies of that White woman[49] and the Child Guidance and the Great Controversy and Napoleon capturing the Pope and Satan and his angels and Earthquakes in Portugal and the Great Darkness and the comets in the sky and the fall of the Turks[50]. It all came back to me in a flood.

She was always afraid of a great worldwide war that was coming, a dispute over which day the Sabbath was on. And when she heard that the Ottomans had entered the war, she lost her mind and said I couldn't go off to war, quoting 'Thou shalt not kill,' because she said that Turkey was going to move its capital from Constantinople to Jerusalem and trigger the battle of Armageddon. The Russians had rounded up all their Adventist pastors and shipped them to Siberia, and all the young men who didn't want to fight for the Czar, the Caesar, were jailed for disloyalty. She handed me a pamphlet on the Eastern Question and I pretended to read it for her sake. I always laughed it off because honestly, very few folks in Christendom are on Mom's side, and the Jews and Moslems don't care.

There was no Sunday Law and no mark of the Beast, but there was certainly a worldwide war. Maybe that was the Mark of the Beast; the number of Caesar (or Kaiser or Czar or all the Kings in the World) is

---

[49] Rather than a racial term, Creed seems to be talking about Ellen G. White (1827-1916), a leading figure in the early Seventh-Day Adventist movement, with an alleged gift of prophecy. She authored *Child Guidance*, a pedagogic work.

[50] Part of Seventh-Day Adventist eschatology involves stretching the events of the *Revelation* over a long-form calendar: Creed alludes here to the Lisbon earthquake of 1755, the Darkest Day of North America (19 May 1780), and the Leonid Meteor Shower of 13 November 1833. In 1838, the Millerite Josiah Litch predicted the fall of the Ottoman Empire.

just being in this War. We're all damned, and we're all in hell or going there fast.

And that small girl was a giant, somehow. I knew it in my bones, and I remembered what the Eskimos told me when I was with them after that ten-legged polar bear was sighted just before the war. They called their giants the Tuniit, the first people who were there before they came across from Alaska. They were giants, tall and strong and with magical powers that let them fly and hide and string and move like the wind, but they were terrified of interacting with the Eskimos themselves even though a single Tunik could devastate an entire village. It seemed like nothing but a haint-tale, but the Europeans have also started grumbling about psychical giants living in the Far North, in Hyperborea.

And maybe my strange Haligonian was a living projection, like that Esther Williams case, and the Yukon Messiah."

Creed is likely referring to a popular ghost story that spread in 1916, appearing in *the Seattle Times*, 1 May 1916 Daily Evening Edition of *the East Oregonian, the Cook Inlet Pioneer* of 15 May 1916, and the 24 June 1916 edition *Nome Daily Nugget*, and . Donald Mack, a mining engineer from Juneau, Alaska, claims he was warned to avoid crossing the frozen Lake Taglish by a woman named *Ethel* Williams in his dream. She wore light summer clothing amid the deep snow, and told him to avoid the lake, or he would drown. Mack pressed her for further details, and she said she was from Syracuse, New York, and even gave him an address to write to. After awaking from what might have been the most helpful and straightforward of paranormal encounters, Mack reported back to his companions, "three Indians and a Frenchman" met on the trail. He could not convince them, and he took the long way around. When he arrived at his destination, he discovered that his companions had indeed perished in the freezing waters of Lake Taglish. The traumatized Mack tried to make sense of the events, and sent a letter to the address. After a few months, Mack was shocked to receive a reply from a real Ethel Williams, who also had no idea she had seemingly projected into the dreams of a distant stranger.

The Yukon Messiah refers to a mysterious individual reported by Anglican missionaries to Bishop Stringer. The Native of Dalton Post allegedly revived forty-eight hours after his death and claimed to be the

Messiah. The uneducated man demonstrated the newfound ability to suddenly speak English, Latin, French, and all other languages the missionaries could muster. He attempted to get local native Christians to convert to new and strict Sabbath rites, including renaming Sunday to "Special Day." His most striking ability was some form of astral projection into dreams and waking bilocation, appearing to Tlingit, Tagish, and Tahltan communities many kilometers apart[51].

"I ran at first until I sunk thigh deep in the snow and had to trudge back to the ship," Creed continued. "As I waded through the timeless white, my limbs had become numb and light, warmed only by a dying fire in the core of my body. The exhaustion of stomping through heavy stow began to dampen that fire even as it forced blood into my tingling extremeties [sic].

I was about to give up after the deathly chill of melting ice penetrated the tight canvas-and-leather footwear that I slipped into my felt boots. I needed shelter, any port in a storm.

I started started quaking and almost cried, asking my mom for forgiveness, and telling her from across the Atlantic that I went to war but never, ever killed anyone.

A rock flew in my direction, sinking into the snow several yards from me. It was then that I saw a man in the snow, piled up to his chest, but he seemed to be nearly naked, maybe wearing pyjamas. He seemed to be floating in the whiteness, passing through it easily, like a spectre. He was a white man with thinning hair – perhaps in his fourth decade – and striking pale eyes. There was an eerie grey coldness to him, and he seemed almost transparent against the white and black world. I had never seen him before or since. But he pointed off into the distance and silently mouthed something. Another rock shot out of the snow in a blast of white powder, and I decided it was a sign from God or the next best thing, and followed his direction. I nodded in thanks at the figure, who nodded and vanished on the winds.

Eventually I came to a hillock of snow as high as myself. I forced my weight against it, pushing it down into some ditch.

Halifax was on the other side.

---

[51] 15 May 1916. *The Nome Daily Nugget*. p. 3.

It was right there, the starburst fortress of Fort George, right up on Citadel Hill, the stone sun from which all of Halifax radiated. I could see the mouth of the Harbour, and McNabs [Island], the dockyards, and a thin strip of Dartmouth through the mist. I was back in the Warden of the North.

I was home. I was home. I probably would have cried if my tear ducts weren't frozen stiff. I took off a glove. I reached down and touched the snow. This was real snow, Canadian snow, cosy, home for Christmas with a cup of chocolate in hand snow. I began to slowly hum 'the Maple Leaf Forever' to myself, feeling patriotic for the first time in my life.

And then I heard a great rumbling. I was sent tumbling back by a great shock in the Harbour. The entire city began contracting into itself, the streets shrinking and the earth drinking up the Harbour.

Sackville rolled up beneath me, dragging bits of the nearby cemetery with it. Pier 21 snapped like a twig and folded back onto the city, scooping up Fenwick as this overpowering force dragged the piers towards the Fortress. From the southwest, a chunk of a diminished Dalhousie campus collapsed into the Public Gardens and soaked itself in the deliciously named Chocolate Lake. The northwest portion of the peninsula took longer to roll in, rising like a great crashing wave of urban material. It shrunk and shrunk around me as a great black cloud of ash and smoke covered the Harbour, bleeding out of a pair of broken ships.

I ran to the top of the hill as the city swirled around me in a maelstrom of pulverized streets. The cloud got thinner and thinner as the swirling cloud of debris swallowed itself like a snake eating itself. There was a statue of a wingless angel or a Greek goddess from the cemetery, its widening stone mouth ravenously swallowing up the cement storm.

As the black cloud settled over the city, I found myself on a naked Citadel Hill, alone with this angel. I walked around the statue. It turned its head to face me, the neck grinding away until it made eye contact with me. It was her. Its face warmed up until the mossy stone burned away or softened into pale, feminine flesh.

'Ahoy sailor! You'll lose your toes to the frostbite if you keep out in this cold, you know,' said the girl, working out a painful-sounding crick in her neck as her thin white Arctic tern wings drip-dried slowly in the crisp air, before becoming one with her thin white arms. 'We gotta get you back to the ship.'

'What are you, really?' I asked her.

'I think I'm the city,' she said. 'I don't know how, or even what that means. But I feel it. I'm the spirit of the city. Or the ghost of the spirit of the city. Or just a piece of its pain. A genius loci. *Full fathom five my city lies. Of its stones are coral made. These are its pearls, become my eyes. Nothing of it has faded, but suffered a sea-change into something rich and strange.*'

'In light of whatever this was, I think I have to agree.'

'I don't know. Maybe if the war goes on, another city will die, another city-spirit will be born. Maybe us urban spooks will be our own race, you know, replacing a dead planet. Just a few hundred of us, you know, but that's all we need. Lady London, in a fine dress, Mr Moscow in a regal coat, Madame Paris in a beret, having a smoke, there.'

'How can a place be a person?' I asked.

'It's possible. It's a nutty idea, she is, but it's true: God is heaven. He is a place, the shining city after the end of the world. Ah hell, everything is a place if you're small enough. You're a place to your lice.'

'Heaven is the city after the end of the world,' I repeated, letting the idea sink in. 'Well, I suppose that's true.'

'Heaven is real, by the way,' she said. 'I thought you'd like to know. I captured one of its councilmen.'

'You captured a councilman? What?'

'You know, one of the civic administrators, er, an archangel,' she said. She muttered something I couldn't make out.

I got quiet, this fresh news taking a while to sort through.

'I'm going to rebuild myself here. I've got the raw materials and the fuel,' she said, her hands in her pockets. She looked up at the black sky as the vast white expanse reverted to the blizzard-bleached Archangel. 'A pair of Archangels. One from Heaven, one from Earth.'

There was a twinge of creeping fear when I remembered *Two Babylons*, that book mom read that made her fear the Catholic Church and even our native Baptists. She said that the Roman Church was founded by a queen called Semiramis, from old Assyria. But what really chilled me is that she came from the sea, too. Her mother was a fish goddess from Ascalon, Ashteroth [sic], who gave birth to Semiramis with the seed of a mortal man. The fish goddess then drowned herself. When my mom read that story, I thought it was silly. A fish can't drown. A goddess, even a false one, couldn't die, right? But here was a drowned woman. And she's more than a woman – I don't want to call her a god, but there's something bad here, something great and terrible. A beast out of the sea."

The Two Babylons was an 1853 pamphlet by Alexander Hislop, which rose to popularity in the English speaking Protestant world before the turn of the century. It claimed that Catholicism, both its structure, iconography, and holy days, are pagan practices created by Semiramis; Hislop goes so far to credit all polytheism and goddess worship to this mythologized queen, along with King Nimrod, and claim that Semiramis gave birth to Tammuz, who would be deified by the Akkadians.

The goddess that Diodorus actually credited as Semiramis' mother was Derketo, though she is considered to be the Hellenized version of Atagatis, a fertility goddess tied to the cities of Ascalon and Hierapolis. She is conflated with Anat, Astarte, and other near eastern fertility, war, and sea goddesses.

None of Hislop's claims are considered credible by archeologists, Assyriologists, or historians of Christianity.

"'What did that horrible pair of people have to do with it?' I asked. 'Are they...also from the sea?'

'I will either die at their hands or be reborn,' she said. I only somewhat understood her grand and suicidal plan, but I no longer feared her. I actually found myself rather concerned. I didn't want to see her go. I think she could feel that too. She smiled at me, a little, until the wind blew a wave of golden hair between her lips. She forced it out of her mouth with a puff of dead air, and we both let out a chuckle.

She nodded towards the coast and turned away from me, sinking up to her chest in the snow. I slipped in behind her. We both laughed hysterically, but realized that we were stuck in.

She fell back into the snow. A fluid blackness leaked out of her spine, melting the frost into a grey sludge. We wound up in a pool of water.

She embraced me and set her head against my chest.

'Come with me, brother. It's all one water,' she said. She closed her eyes, and told me to do the same. I gasped as the earth gave way and I tumbled through the water and into a deep, cold space below, as something vast rose up to meet us. I forgot everything else about that murky place, for it wasn't meant for me. Not yet, at least.

We washed up in a tank of water aboard the *Maitland*, soaked to the bone and cold as hell. I don't know if I'd ever be dry, even after I changed by clothes and warmed myself by the boilers.

She took me up to the deck, where we looked to the north, across the delta, where the Northern Dvina meets the White Sea. I told her that it reminded me of my time on the Mississippi Delta, but the large, solid, relatively dry islands that almost closed off the harbour reminded me of New York's, especially the seven-or-eight-mile-long one across from Archangel that I dubbed 'Rusky Manhattan.' She said that she had been to New York, briefly. Very briefly. And a bit of time in Portland, Maine.

She smiled at the wide white world.

'*Dominium Canadae, Resurgam*,' she said. 'A phoenix of ice and steam...The Maitland's men...you've seen it, the fire in those eyes.'

'Yeah,' I said. 'They're starving, on the edge of a riot. Been having bad dreams even, thinking they're going to freeze to death in alien water. Not sure if I want to be here when they blow.'

'I am now their captain,' she said. 'I should do something.'

'I'm not sure that's official,' I said. 'You can't just browbeat the captain.'

But, I thought, she could, couldn't she? She was the Sea, or its Queen, or both. She was a place. And so was that Semiramis, wasn't she? The Scarlet Woman, both the Whore of Babylon, and Babylon itself, with practically all the great monuments of Syria attributed to her. Maybe those two strangers were also creatures, half-gods, of the land and the air.

'Still...I should do something. Stranded out here, and the Empire not coming to help them... That's the thing about the British – they only say we're British when they need something from us. Any other time and we can f--- right off,' she said, as the men gathered around us. 'And these Russians don't respect us either. We are the Dominion of Canada.

And we have done more than our share in the name of the King. At Second Ypres, our men were baptized in fire and chlorine. We were the first poisoned by gas. We fought through the green froth, our sons drowning on foot with yellow skin, stricken with the cruelest thirst, one that kills you when you try to sate it with water. But we beat the Hun back. We struck a blow at Vimy Ridge and at Thiepval. We held the line at Artois. We just broke the Germans at Paeschendaele. Britain was bogged down. The other Dominions were tossed into the meat-grinder. Currie will go down as one of the great general of the War. And where were the bloody Yankees during all this? Trying and failing to hunt down a pot-bellied Mexican. Can't even find Ambrose Bierce. And we have, man for man, the most effective fighting force in the fray. I think that the White Dominion has earned some f------ respect. What we're going to show Europe that it can't ignore the colonies...they are all affected by this War. A build up by the United Kingdom to fight a war against the Central Powers...led to two ships filled with munitions colliding in my harbour and two thousand Haligonians dying. And it led to millions of innocent people dying...dying everywhere. Just everywhere. And why? Why? The dead just want to know why. Why were we torn away from our families and our homes? Why do we have to scream in this darkness? I can't help them...I can't even ignore them.'

She began weeping black oil dotted with islands of hot glass.

'But I can give them a home,' she said. 'Then I can die.'

I clenched my teeth behind my quivering lips. The men gathered around the deck, to see what was the matter. But they soon found themselves drawn to her, as though they had heard her. They gathered around her, eerily silent as she whispered to them, before leaving the deck.

'What did you say to them?' I asked.

'*Avis de tempête*. Storm warning,' she whispered in my ear.

'What storm?' I asked.

'This one,' she said as snow began tumbling from the heavens and the colder hells.

A strange scraping sound issued from a patch of ice and snow, followed by a crushing clicking din. We both turned towards it, and I used my boot to scrape off the top layer of snow as she held my arm to brace me. I yelped as I uncovered a white being, an androgynous, beautiful human-thing frozen next to what must have been lampreys. It was armless, and its bottom half seemed to be wrapped in or composed of clanking, ill-defined machinery.

Its face burned through the ice, and it spoke to the woman.

'I heard you speak of yourself as the city - as a place. You are a place. And a time. And a state. And nowhere, and eternity. And a chaos.'

'What do you mean?' snapped the Haligonian.

The white thing said that it knew who she was."

Cocytus.

While the proceeding winter had been horrible, the Winter of 1917-1918 was the worst winter of the last two centuries and possibly throughout the entirety of the Holocene period, with a cold wave washing across much of the northern hemisphere[52]. The trenches of the Western and Eastern fronts became ice-glazed ditches, and the winter conditions set the stage for the 1919 flu pandemic[53]; Fifteen states in the US experienced their worst recorded winters, January 1918 was the coldest January registered in New York City's Central Park, Canada experienced severe blizzards, including the one that kicked post-Explosion Halifax while it was down, and Russia became exactly what you think of when you hear the words "Russian Winter," the bleak weather a fitting backdrop for the nihilistic violence that followed the October Revolution. Burning the country to the ground would at least warm the place up a bit.

Indeed, the climate was shifting – late summer and Fall of 1918 saw strangely weak Atlantic hurricane season, including a weak El Niño and one of the largest shifts in the ocean's surface temperature[54]; a crippling

---

[52] Day, Preston C. "The cold winter of 1917-1918." *Monthly Weather Review*, December 1918. pp. 570-580.

53 "Severe Winter of 1917-1918: Factor in 1918 Flu Pandemic." Suburban Emergency Management Project. Biot Report #637. July 23, 2009.

[54] Donnel, C.A., 1918: Notes on hurricanes of 1918. Mon. Weather Review. Issue 46, pp. 568. ; *and* Giese, Benjamin S., Compo,Gilbert P., Slowey, Niall C., et al. *The 1918/19 El Niño*. American Meteorological Society (February 2010).

drought in India was followed by a failure of the monsoon season, and late Autumn of 1918 in North America was freakishly warm.

Oddly enough, the winter of 1918-1919 was refreshingly mild, as though the spirit of winter decided to make the war more dramatic[55].

Any Port in a Storm.

Wounds caused by knives shall heal, wounds caused by words shall not. - Mongolian proverb

After returning to Arkhangelsk, Mihajlo and Anna found themselves lost and drifting apart. The archangel they had been seeking was gone, captured by a strange being outside of their context. They simply described the Haligonian as *Burevestnik* (Буревестник), the Russian name for several seabird species. It is frequently translated as "stormy petrel," largely due to Maxim Gorky's famous 1901 revolutionary poem, "Pesnya o Burevestnike," or "the Song of the Stormy Petrel." While this is a technically inaccurate translation, it fits poetically, as burevestnik literally translates as "storm-announcer," and the stormy petrel is both regarded as a herald of storms by Western Europeans and as a symbol of anarchist revolution.

Anna and Mihajlo initially decided that this strange creature was not part of their mission, and should be avoided, though that may be a far too strategic way of putting it. Mihajlo wrote that "The Burevestnik aparation's sudden, unannounced arrival and casual dismissal of our hereunto overwhelming opponent lead Anna and I to avoid it at all costs, and I attempted to depart from Arkhangelsk as soon as possible," which is an oblique, Edwardian admission of absolute panic.

Mihajlo's phrasing hints at Anna's apathy and listlessness. On the day of December 19th, she woke up at about 2 in the afternoon, and had

177-184.
[55] Ward, Robert. "Meteorological observations while traveling." Monthly Weather Review, March 1919, Volume 47, Issue 3, pp. 170-171.

to be badgered into eating. She refused to say a word that day, and had withdrawn completely into herself by the 20th, not even acknowledging Mihajlo's presence as she scratched her sunburnt skin raw. Anna's rapid weight loss especially worried Mihajlo. Since the death of her parents, Anna had lost roughly three kilograms (7 pounds) on an already rail-thin frame. At dinner time on the 29th, Mihajlo apparently gave Anna a light shove (from his account, he may have been more violent) in an attempt to get her to acknowledge the stew he had set before her. She quietly tumbled to the snowy ground and made no effort to get up, and apparently increased her weight significantly. Mihajlo had to drag her closer to the camp fire to keep her from dying of exposure in the blizzard. Mihajlo force-fed the nigh-catatonic Anna the stew, with one hand prying her jaw open, with the skilled patience of a boy who had carved out a familial niche as his brother's nurse.

By midnight, the lantern oil ran low and their makeshift shelter, a burnt out shack on the south-east coast of mainland Arkhangelsk, began to collapse under the weight of the endless snow and the high winds.

Mihajlo decided to leave the building, packing up and dragging Anna out. He pulled her bony snow-blindness goggles over her eyes and stole her aviator goggles as he carried her through the whiteout.

He soon found himself struggling, with Anna unwilling to move or even lighten his burden. He eventually dropped her into the snow and pulled her to her feet. He transcribed his frustrated outburst:

"'You can fly!' I shouted. 'Goddamn you, Annushka, you invalid! Fly!'

She did not move. She stood mute. She would not even look at me. Her insolence opened the floodgates.

'You're why we can't move to America, Anna,' I said. 'They wouldn't let us marry, or have children – they would sterilize you. You've already got the Oriental mark against you, we don't need amentia to show up on the exam[56].'

---

[56] In primitive psychology, amentia was used to describe a cognitive impairment that began at an early age, in contrast with the later-onset of various forms of dementia. By the 1890s, it was used to describe inborn mental impairment, and by the 1910s, it had expanded to encompass all forms of mental retardation or "feeble-mindedness," and was used as a pejorative.

She did not answer my insults. Her eyes fell, but almost imperceptibly behind narrow lids and the even narrower slit in the bone goggles.

I pushed her a few times on the shoulders, more forcefully each time. I had to restrain myself from throttling her. I walked away from her in disgusted. I lit a cigarette, hoping the hot smoke would act as an antidote to the venomous cold spreading through my blood and bones.

'Fine! If you want to die, just die! Just lay down and die!' I shouted as I trudged and waded away.

Anna responded by falling face first into a meter of snow. The cigarette slipped out of my mouth as I ran back to her. I dug her out, scrapped the powder from her hair and face, and put her hat back on. She looked around her, checking if she had lost anything from her kit.

'Do not touch me,' she said as I grabbed her arm. She winced.

'You finally decided to talk,' I said as I picked her up and carried her on my back. She stopped resisting, at least, negating most of her weight.

'Why are you doing all this? Carrying me around...' she hissed. 'I'm not a baby.'

'Because you won't fly, Anna! Because you're little and weird and you won't even fly us to shelter in the middle of a blizzard! A baby, babies would at least fly. If they could, I mean.'

'Why do you even care about me, then?'

'Because I love you, you idiot,' I said.

'You are being patronizing,' she said.

'You are being suicidally stupid. I win.'

'I'm never going to see my parents again,' she said.

'I know,' I said. 'I'm sorry. But I don't want you follow them. Please. I know that you're sad, but don't let it win. I need you. The world needs you.'

'You said cruel things about me,' she said.

I said that fear makes men violent, and frustration can make caretakers cruel. Maybe not that well. She went quiet, and looked off into the distance.

'Would they really not let me into America?' she asked.

Unlike its contemporary terms for mental retardation, like idiot, moron, or imbecile, amentia fell completely by the wayside.

'Possibly. That is what I fear,' I said.

'I could say that I am a Jew,' she said. 'America is good for Jews.'

'But you look Oriental,' I said. 'And they don't want you there.'

'Why?' she asked.

'The Yellow Peril,' I said. 'They fear the Heathen Chinese and the rising Nipponese.'

'I'm Tuvan,' she said. 'I don't think there are many of us in America. I don't even know if Americans know we exist. Papers will say Russia, Russia is white. I can go.'

'They don't care,' I said. 'If you look Chinese, you will be Chinese to them. Invading California and spreading opium. And I doubt people will stop thinking of you as a dangerous conqueror when you explain that you're more closely related to the Mongols.'

'California?' she asked. 'What is this California?'

'The word for the west coast of America,' I said. 'But we would go to the east coast. New York City.'

'The American west coast faces the Far East, and the east coast faces the Western World,' she noted. 'The world can't be just east and west any more, after the Americas. Columbus cut it up and also made it too big for you. Europe likes to think itself great, but it is a pair of peninsulas jutting out of Russia. That is why this great chemical war started. You saw the world was so much bigger than Europe, and it must be reduced and controlled. And your circles of control crashed into each other. Reactions. And Russia, Russia is so big it does not know what to do with itself.'

'Spheres of influence,' I corrected.

'Circles are flat. Europe does not control the sky or the deep sea yet. It only thinks it does. And influence sounds weak. Petitioners influence, empires control. I win.'

'You're right,' I said as I pushed down a particularly tall pile of snow. Anna let herself slide off my back. She touched down a few dozen seconds later.

'Are your parents still alive?' Anna asked. 'You never talk about your family.'

'My parents are still alive. Petar and Marija. She bore nine children. Three survivors. We grew up poor. I moved to Zagreb, my brother

Whom Gods Would Destroy, Part III

Gavrilo joined me. In '08, the Austrians annexed Bosnia. We decided to fight back. When the war began, the 1912 war, I mean, we joined the *komite*, the guerrillas of the Black Hand.'

'Black Hand?' she asked as she walked over to an unusually shaped mound of snow.

'The *Unification or Death* movement. For Greater Serbia. He had the spirit, but he was small and frail. We were often sick as children. I joined the Sokol movement[57] and I suggested it to him, but Gavrilo's body had been ravaged...and he knew it. Nobody would let him forget. Serbian life...it raises hard men. He needed to prove that he was a real man, willing to die for a Greater Serbian. He showed the world. And he sent a message.'

'Serbs are hard on the outside, brittle inside,' Anna said, rather distantly.

'And what does that mean?' I asked.

'You are easily offended,' she said, brushing the snow off the wooden object underneath. 'Easily angered, easily saddened and shamed. You don't like to show it.'

'We've been bullied by Turks, Germans, and Bulgarians, manipulated by Russians, and betrayed by Croats. Any race would be brittle...And now, everyone is dead. We've lost more than anyone. And part of that is on me.'

'Is that why you bring up America?' she whispered. 'You cannot see this Serbia, this Serbia that you have built in your dreams. So you run to the other side of the world.'

'I don't know why I wanted you to talk,' I said.

Anna did not visibly take offense. She simply went quiet and continued sweeping the snow from the wooden board, snapping off

---

57 The Sokol movement was a pan-Slavic athletic and cultural association founded in Prague in 1862. It spread throughout Czech-speaking regions of the Austro-Hungarian Empire and quickly proliferated across most Slavic regions in Europe. It also published a journal and held lectures on various, often nationalistic, topics, and sponsored mass meetings and gymnastic events called slety, from a Czech term for a gathering of birds. The 1912 All-Slavic Slet was a paramilitary gathering of over thirty thousand Sokols; the Sokol movement was disbanded in 1915 after encouraging a Czech defection to the Allies.

icicles and fighting the blizzard's attempt to reconquer its claim.

'Annushka, please, I apologize for that...but please, I want you fly us out of here,' I said. 'Please, just take us to the heart of the city. We need shelter. And heat, and food. We need to get to the city.'

'I don't know where we are,' she said.

'Due south of the city. It's a port, we just have to follow the waterline until it gets urban and dock-ish,' I said. 'Hey, earlier, you turned and stopped like you saw something. What...was it a gull or something?'

'Syih-tee-yof Hah-lyi-faksh,' she said. She read those words from the sign.

'What does that mean?' I said as I walked towards her. And then I saw the words over her shoulder. Latin letters framed in silver ice.

CITY OF HALIFAX.

'Where the hell is that?' I asked.

'It is a city in England,' Anna said. 'Rowan gave me toffee from there. I remember that. I remember all things candy related.'

'Why the hell is that here? And what is that sound? Is that you?' I said, noting a rasping, gargling, painfully heavy breathing noise underlying the howl of the storm. It sounded like someone, a woman or a child, trying to breath through a slit throat.

''The Englishwoman from the munitions...' Anna said. 'This is what I heard in smoke and steam...And I saw a ghost earlier.'

'Why didn't you mention it?' I asked.

'It wasn't her. Nor anyone I knew. Seemed unimportant. Woman pulled waterfalls out of her pockets, Lone Wolf fired at me, friends murdered, angel attacked,' she said. 'I'm taking you back to the munitions magazine. Woman might have returned. Possibly we interrupted something. If not, there are still many opportunities to start a fire.'

We embraced, and warmed ourselves in the burning sky."

Anna described how "the force of our landing uncovered not the stony roads of the factory district, but a fully paved road. We quickly made another sky hop over to and through the hole in the side of the magazine. It was deathly cold, and the walls seemed to seethe to the sound of distant, labored breathing."

Zrno wrote that it reminded him of birth pangs and Rivka's bedridden breathing.

"We found her there, in a circular clearing in the magazine that had not been there before. The munitions had been turned to face her as she scrawled strange, gridlike signs in oil upon the ground, the liquid running into the long grooves that she had burnt into the concrete floor. The long grooves resembled the shorelines of Arkhengelsk and the surrounding isles, the oil-lines some kind of map overlaid upon the city.

'What are you doing?' I asked her in English. 'Writing map?'

'I'm healing,' she said. 'Repairing myself.'

I did not know the word 'repairing' [written as "раперин"], but I knew that she was up to no good. There was some fundamental derangement in her existence, something that must be corrected.

Misha asked me what she said. I translated.

'What do you want?' I asked her, at Misha's prompting.

'I have to bring the city back,' she said.

'What do you mean?' I asked. 'I do not understand.'

'I come from...I'm part of a port that was devastated. Like Archangel. A massive munitions explosion in the harbor, just like what happened here in February. It wounded my head. It drew me here. So I drew it here.'

She pointed at the ground. It was until later that I realized she was punning in English.

'What is this doing?' I asked. 'The sign outside. It was English.'

'This city will be my city when the snow is gone,' she said. 'Not through conquest, but revision.'

'Will this kill people?' I asked.

'Possibly,' she said. 'Probably. I don't know. I don't know if living and dying even matters in a city for the dead.'

'Get out,' I said. 'Leave Russia. Leave now.'

'I know it's wrong, but what else am I supposed to do? I have a duty to the dead. They need a foothold, leverage, a bargaining chip, a seat at the negotiating table when the War in Heaven ends. Do you understand, Chadanite[58]? This is a chancery. Archangel...New

---

[58] Chadan is a city in Tuva, though it does not have an established demonym in English. Though Anna never mentions it, we can assume — or at least, the

Halifax...whatever you wish to call it. It will be an embassy for the underworld.'

'We can not let you destroy a city,' I said.

'I can't help it. This is a burden...I feed on misery and fear and death,' she whispered. 'I just want to starve. So unless you or the Sarajevan can end this torture, keep away, please.'

'I don't know if we can't kill you,' I said. 'But we can stop you.'

She let out a short, wheezy laugh interrupted by a popping sound, like a bubble rising from muck.

'The ocean...the ocean belongs to me, and the earth reshapes itself at my touch,' she said.

'The sky is mine,' I said.

'Ah, do you really believe that, miss?' said the *Burevestnik*. 'Do you feel that wind? That's a Nor'easter!'

'But the land is still Russian,' I said. 'As long as I'm here.'

'OK,' said the *Burevestnik*. 'Sorry about all this, then, but we've gotta do this.'

She pulled off her wool cap, and slicked her wet, yellow hair back to reveal her forehead. Black oil trickled down from a nick in her hairline.

She closed the narrow gap between me and her in two steps. There was a black blur and an explosive burst to my right that suddenly died out. Misha fell back against the wall gasping loudly. The Burevestnik was not affected by whatever attack he had made. It was like kicking an anchor.

She reeled back as she grabbed me by the shoulders. I managed to predict what someone was going to do, which is exceedingly difficult for me. I pulled my head back and repelled the force of her head-butt. It coursed through me, breaking up the floor and blowing out the back wall of the magazine.

Mihajlo and I both looked at each other, finally comprehending the full magnitude of our situation. We had seen her not only defeat but dismiss an archangel. She was indestructible, forceful, commanded the seas, and was full of screaming dead people. I initiated a fistfight with the *Titanic*.

Haligonian did- that Chadan was the city closest to her place of birth in the Tuvan wilderness.

I pressed my thumbs against her eyes and pushed her head back, stealing her weight. We rose up, grappling until our collision with the ceiling broke our holds. She crashed to the ground, pulverizing the concrete floor. I hung in the air, setting foot against the wall and running down to meet Misha. He leapt up to me, and I grabbed him by the elbow and pinned him to the wall until he could rise to his feet. He dashed forward and yanked a heavy door open. He pulled me down to the surface of the wall, using the door to shield us from the lung-mutilating blast of dust.

We pushed the door open as the dust settled. The Burevestnik looked rattled, her confused grey eyes wide like those of a fish and her purple lips open and quivering. The piping burst open around her, and she dissolved into the pillars of hissing steam. Several stacks of armaments cracked and warped in her wake. Misha and I embraced as we fell against the roof. I pushed against it with all my might, and a quick stomp from Misha broke open the ceiling as fire engulfed the the room.

We tumbled into the sky until I regained my bearings. The wind was all wrong, all directions reversed, and strange grey marks covered the city like oil stains and bruises. The winds revolted against me, and we rolled across the tortured sky, and the grey everything melted together as the horizon broke like a wave upon a rolling slate-blue mass that may have been the sea or the storm-clouds or both. The swirling chaos throttled my skull. The pressure made me want to scream and hold my head but I had to find this woman and I had to kill her even though she was probably part of, or the entire, afterlife.

'Maybe...' Misha started, gasping for air. 'Maybe we should let her have it. I never liked this city.'

'What?' I said.

'I would fight to the death for Petrograd or Moscow, but what does Arkhangel'sk have? The name? Sacrificing this city may put an end to the War. Maybe even to the War in Heaven.'

'No,' I said. 'Do not side with that evil creature.'

'If a city of ghosts suddenly appeared - right out in the open - the whole world would stop and listen. No war, no battle of Armageddon. One city dies so the world can live.'

'We have no right to make that choice,' I said.

'Who does?' he asked. 'Generals and kings?'

'Nobody,' I said.

'We have a choice to make right now,' he shouted over the wind. 'Nobody else can! Today, *we* are the gods!'

The wind whispered. It told us that 'he is right.' Misha and I spun around, scanning the clouds for her. 'You think this dying city matters? This nation is cracking like rotten ice. And Europe is a dead star, the better part of its light exhausted. It still has mass, yes, but just enough to drag us all down into the dark. Even us youngbloods in the Americas. Let it go. A bloody cancer has conquered Russia. It will survive the West, yeah, but its death will be slow.'

'I will not let one yard of my country fall to you,' I said.

'Listen, kids, I must win. I have seen broken futures, ones we can't let come to pass...neither the victory of the angels...All the world will be white, the skies unbroken grey...and all men will walk the rigid waters like a race of freezing Christs...nor the triumph of the demons...the rendering of all flesh for materiel, the world an engine for an endless war. The children will be processed in batches.'

'What did you do with the archangel?' I demanded.

'He is gone. Devoured. Melted into mortar to bind this city of souls,' she said, and the mists and the clouds parted, and the city hung down from the sky, alive and pregnant with the souls of the sleeping dead. 'Perhaps you can help me...I felt them following you...do you summon them, or do they find you?'

'We were hunting one, but it found us,' I said. 'We do not call them.'

'Oh, now that there's a pity,' said the sky and the clouds. 'But I'm sure you can still find a way to serve my greater purpose.'

'We do not kneel,' Misha said. I repeated him.

'Damn shame,' she said. 'Sorry about this. I guess if any angels were knockin' about right now, they'd be disturbed by this here male strum [*sic*]. Come try to heal the would, surgin' like blood to a clot.'

'Show yourself,' Misha commanded, and I echoed in bad English, 'we want to see the face.'

'The ocean does not flow into the stream,' she said.

'Show yourself!' I demanded.

'Look above you,' she said. 'And look below, at the sea. You're bound to meet me.'

My stomach swirled. Misha and I hugged each other tighter, my fingers digging into his back as we yelped in panic. I was falling. We were falling upwards.

I never fall like that, uncontrolled and terrible. I wanted to fly, but I could not find purchase in an alien sky, a foreign gravity, an enemy's wind. There was a city in the sky, and a vast creature in the water, a swimming, steaming beast that would dwarf a blue whale.

Misha decelerated mere hand-spans from the tiled roof of building. This was something I forgot he could do, but in retrospect, of course he could. Otherwise, he would have left nothing but a morbid red spray reaching to the horizon the first time he decided to come to a rest after moving that fast. He's the demigod of speed, any speed, even none at all. I nearly passed out, and Misha's long blinks indicated the same; the fall shook up my blood, and it needed time to regroup before it could marshal back to my heart.

We touched down on the roof of the dock house, holding on tight as the wind picked up. The wharf peeled up, rising up and curling towards us like a cobra to a Fakir's flute. It struck, and my attempt to push it back cracked the roof below me. Splinters stuck into our skin, and clothing and skin slashed by tiles, Misha and I tumbled into the building, smacking against the rafters. My vision nothing but a pained white mess, the violent opening of a door sent me reeling through the air.

It was only then that I felt the hellish heat against my back and the choking clouds of smoke gathering below me. The furnace had warped and the chimney collapsed at an impossible angle, engulfing the back wall in fire and releasing plums inside the building.

Mihajlo grabbed my hand and helped me to the ground. We clung to the floorboards, widening the cracks with our knives. We crawled like that, as though scaling a mountain, until we reached the door. Mihajlo swung around, kicking off the dock house's front desk and striking the door off its hinges before it could smack us again.

We exited the building with great difficulty, and we lost our grip on the packed snow and skin-stinging ice. Fortunately, we fell against the wall of the building instead of sliding back inside the smoking ruins. We made a run for the neighboring customhouse, easily clearing the gap between the facades but nearly being pushed back by the sudden outward -upward?- explosion of the building's glass windows. We braced ourselves against the snowy ground, and felt a sudden rush of steamy air as the building behind us collapsed into a pile of burning beams.

'No!' Misha gasped as he pulled me to the side, slamming my face into the snow. A bullet whizzed past my ear. He pushed me forward, and we ran across the front of the customhouse and flew to what appeared to be an ale house of some sort.

We looked up at the wall of ice and snow. 'There,' I said, pointing out an unnatural blob of white. The texture was wrong, a hooded, camel-and-white duffel coat, with a long metallic patch, the barrel of a rifle."

"Once I became certain that the creatures had spotted me, I stood up, rising to a better firing position," wrote Dagger Creed. "The woman crouched down against the wall, and slipped her hand into a falconry glove, its fingers steal-tipped and tapering into talons. The boy steadied his pistol and aimed high. But I was able to move, and his unnatural bent had him scrambling to orient himself. He became a blur. I tried to slip behind a snowbank I erected earlier before he figured out how to shoot at someone jutting out from, what was to him, a wall, but even that took too long. I would have been shot down if not for the timely collapse of the building on the opposite side of the street from his perch. He and his female companion dove out of the way of the bricks which rained down upon him. I watched in horrified amazement as the bricks defied all logic and sailed across the narrow road, smashing to red powder against the pub.

The pair hung on for dear life on the edge of the pub's roof, the woman sinking her claws into a twisting eavestrough. I felt a painful bubbling inside my ears, and let the rifle slip from my hands. I stumbled and recovered as the woman regained her strength, pulling herself up and steadying herself on the roof with an unnatural grace. She moved like someone dancing through water.

I noticed for the first time several shadowy figures walking through the darkness, leaving no footprints in the snow. One neared me, and I pulled back, walking like a crab with thin-soled boots and one hand, a hand that I got soaking wet in melting snow like a damn fool. I heard a great crash roaring in from the ocean, the waters thick and heavy, the wine-dark sea out of *Ulysses* [sic]. It crashed in all the wrong way, the sea foam, sticking to the beach like a jelly that rolled up the steap [sic] and oil-washed stones. There were bones in there, I thought. A soft red tinted the next wave, a wave of red wine, sticking flesh to those phantom bones. A third and final wave washed over it, pearly white with foam and black with oil. She sat up as the wave waned, and pulled her tuque out of the water. I placed my arm against my stomach as a cramp shot through me, like my guts were a rope being knotted.

The flying girl and the running man felt the effects of her presence, their breath frozen and clouded into a reedy rasping.

One of the shadowy people came to a complete stop on the prospect. The shadow pulled back, and the woman beneath it realized that she stepped into somewhere strange and wrong, a place where two strange people hung from a building in an impossible wrong way, and a girl who cried oil waded out of a foreign ocean, and other things from the dark part of the map. She screamed. She took two steps back, listening to the murmurs that surrounded her and attempting to avoid the intense and stony gaze of the girl from the sea.

Something like a malformed hand slipped from under the woman's hair, and pulled her back into the shadows, and her distant silhouette fell to the ground."

Erich Loesser[59] postulates that a major gas leak was responsible for the hallucinations of shadowy figures – not just humanoid but buildings, including an oddly-based structure that matches the Halifax Citadel. The gas-leak theory was essentially confirmed by Loesser's work, as he found that one British munitions ship moored in the harbor experienced a catastrophic containment failure on December 21st, 1917, at about 2 a.m. Half an hour later, a massive diethyl ether and ammonia leak occurred in a refrigeration facility near a mooring yard, because apparently they need icehouses in subarctic Russia. It appears that the facility, barely staffed in

---

[59] Loesser, Erich. *Not Only Rasputin: Miracles, Myths, and Monsters of the Russian Revolutions (*1986) Köln: Vogt-Horn Verlag GmbH.

the coldest winter on record, had been poorly maintained.

Citizens of Arkhangelsk began closing up, obscuring, or even barring their windows to avoid the sensation of being watched through them by some invisible, gigantic entity. Several porters walking along Lomonosova Prospekt witnessed a man without a head standing in a snowy field. The December 22nd minutes of the Archangel Committee for Port Affairs reported that workers at a grain elevator fled at the sight of long, white limbs seemingly "unfolding" from the shadows. Other animated yet disembodied arms and hands terrorized workers across Bakaritsy, the military cargo center of Arkhangelsk. Dockworkers and shipyard engineers reported the frightening noise of twisting metal near half a dozen of the port's thirty-six cranes and a nearly-human "howling from the pipes, as though the damned were screaming up at us." Black oil inexplicably pooled on the decks of the *Lebedin*, Arkhangelsk's first icebreaker, and the steam-powered cargo ship *Chichagov*. Smoke poured from the cracks of creaking wooden docks and from a pair of mooring berths, though no source of fire could be found. Indeed, whatever produced the smoke appeared to be sucking in heat rather than producing it.

Similar hauntings were reported in the downriver port of Ekonomiya, constructed a mere two years before, along with medical conditions such as blistered skin and shortness of breath.

Aleskander Barchenko was the chief chronicler of these events, dispatched north by his friend Bokii and operating as a spy in the guise of a biologist from Yuryev University researching the condition of northern wildlife in the wake of the Arkhangelsk explosion and chemical contamination. He tracked the movement of the two "aerial anomalies," his term for Anna and Mihajlo, believing them to be remnants of the psychically evolved giants of the Hyperborean race, which he believed to reside either in the Russian Far East or in the Arctic Circle above Scandinavia and Arkhangelsk's Northern Oblast, with ties to Shambala and other Eastern concepts. In particular, he drew upon the polar origin of the Aryan peoples proposed by Indian mathematician and nationalist Bal Gangadhar Tilak, whose 1903 work *The Arctic Home in the Vedas* approached the concept from a point of view steeped in then cutting-edge glaciation theory and Hindu literalism. He likewise attempted to date the Vedas, and this gigantic, polar past, in his 1893 book *The Orion: Researches into the Antiquity of the Vedas*, with the passage of the vernal equinox into and then out of Orion coinciding with the rise and fall of these ancient heroes. Despite his extremely conservative social views, Tilak had expressed his admiration for Lenin and the revolution, and Barchenko hoped, in a way, that validating his theories would lead to a Russian-Indian socialist alliance. The 1908 discovery of Paleolithic mammoth bone tools carved with svastika patterns in the Mezine site in Dnieper valley lead many anthropologists of the time to conclude that such arctic beasts played a key role in primordial Aryan culture.

Barchenko favored the latter identification with Archangel, as arctic explorers had recent found inexplicable stone spheres on what would be known as Champ Island, in Fridtjof Nansen Land (Franz Josef Land), though the theory was damaged by Polish aviator Jan Nagórski's 1914 polar flight, which disproved the existence of several proposed Arctic landmasses which would have constituted this hypothetical homeland.

The reports of two flying humanoid figures in the region proved his theory beyond doubt, in his mind. Such a pair of "spirits" had inspired the works of the 18th century monk and prophet Abel of Valaam. Brother Adam (the name which he assumed with his tonsure) spent much of his later life imprisoned or under government observation due to his public prophecies of the death of Catherine the Great, the Capture of Moscow by the French (which occurred ten years later, with Napoleon), and the downfall of the Romanovs in 1918, followed soon by the rise of the Antichrist. This later prophecy was sealed away, but became a source of dread among the Imperial intelligence service, and a proof of cause among the occultists and psychics which followed the revolution. Abel's case was popularized among the Russian intelligentsia after his appearance in the 1890-1907 *Brockhaus and Efron Encyclopedic Dictionary*.

He wisely, though undramatically, chose to watch the incident in Archangeslk unfold from a distance. However, he and Bokii "employed" captive industrialist, chemical engineer, and psychic Stefan Ossowiecki to track the pair from their arrival in Poland via his alleged talent at astral projection and divination of location.

Ossowiecki, a Moscow-born ethnic Pole, had some familiarity with his ancestral homeland, and knew of the radio-telepathic projection work of Mikhail Mikhailovich Filippov via his father. The elder Ossowiechi owned a chemical factory, and had been a long-term assistant to Dmitri Mendeleyev, through which he had contacts with Filippov, despite their political differences; His father had died not long before the war, allowing Stefan to inherit the chemical business, allowing him a few years of sybaritic joy in the court of Nicholas II before the Bolsheviks arrested him and confiscated the family fortune. The spectral form of a man repported multiple times by Sokoll and Creed may have been the astral projection of Ossowiecki. Due to his cooperation with Bokii and Barchenko's project, he was allowed a release from prison in 1919 rather than his scheduled execution, and he managed as escape from Russia. His isolation in prison gave him a great many things to think about, a spiritual rebirth, and a claimed increase in the psychic talents of his youth.

"I took my chance, hoping that the phantasm had been startled by the sudden appearance of the woman from across that uncanny veil of shadows," wrote Anna Sokoll. "I flew towards her, tackling her, and reducing her weight to nothing. The abomination shouted something at *Biriuk*[60] as he ran to her aid. He shouted 'NO' as she pulled something from his hip, snapping the leather thong of its sheath. I pinned her airy arms to her sides with a bear hug as the workshops rose up below us and we tumbled and twisted towards the glass of a lighthouse. The gold lantern light cut through the smoke and fog, the certainty of its surfaces drawing us close. The forces involved in our sparring match caused a pair of leading beacons to illuminate and shatter. The white light's milky cast on the polluted, drained harbour lingered beyond the destruction of the beacons.

We crashed against the glass caging the lighthouse's great torch. I shattered the glass with the back of her skull. She remained still for some time, her hair and scalp slashed up. She closed her eyes, and a great hissing noise arose from the tower below us. The strange smell followed seconds later.

'It's mighty queer how people think fire and water are opposites,'

---

[60] Russian for "lone wolf," Anna's nickname for Creed.

she said, immobile and unmovable, eye closed and leaking black oil. 'Just because water smothers fire. That's like saying pillows are the opposite of babies. Fire and water are the pillars of civilization, and their destroyers, boon when controlled, bane when let loose. A city is nothing more than a way for people to control fire and water.'

'I do not understand,' I said to her in English as she held me there, both locked together, unable to let go without forfeiting. 'I do not even know who you really are.'

'Take it!' she ordered. That's when I felt the bullet enter my back. She pushed me back, and I fell against the railings with the thunderous bellowing of a fog horn tearing through my ears. I underestimated the Biriuk again. The Stormbird left me, fading into fog the same grey as her eyes.

The hiss I heard, I remember, was the hiss of gas escaping from a bursting copper pipe. I did not realize then what it meant, far too stupid and far too distracted by the gunshot wound. I have been told that I do not feel pain like other people, and I have seen evidence of this in their reactions. A stubbed toe, a twisted ankle, a broken arm...I walk away happy, as though blind-drunk. But a loud noise, a sudden start, or a thunderclap causes me to double over in agony. I do not understand why, but the fog horn was more painful than the bullet in my back. But it did harm me, and I could barely muster up the strength to raise my head from one of the grey puddles pooling on the warped and freezing metal.

He came for me, limping up the stairs. He could not run, for a single spark or flash of heat would light up the tower. He crashed through the door, kicking it open and slashing down in one of the puddles. And that is when the abomination struck, reaching up to grab his ankle. He kicked at her as she rose, strong as a mule and a thousand times faster, but the strike that would have liquefied a man merely knocked her under the surface of the bewitched puddle. His leg disappeared with it.

Mihajlo screamed in enraged agony, but soon managed to break free and pull his leg back to the metal surface. He collapsed against the railing, wheezing and hissing as blood rushed from his Achilles' tendon. His boot had been ripped off, the sock soaked in blood and the long, thin cut polluted by that horror's touch.

The Haligonian rose up from an other puddle behind me, wielding a bone knife tainted with blood and oil.

'Leave,' she whispered. 'I gave you so many chances to just leave, but you wouldn't listen. You can't win now. Take him back to wherever you come from. That wound will not close, and that leg's corrupted beyond use. Hopefully, someone like you can break the magic of the knife.'

I crawled towards Misha, pulling out the vial of ether. I soaked the already wet tip of Zrno's scarf in it, and placed it under his nose. He held it there with his trembling fingers.

The ghostly woman used this lull to her advantage, tearing the prismatic camera from the strap around my neck. When I struck back at her, stabbing her in arm pit, she lunged forward at Misha and sent him falling over the railing.

I raged at her, grabbing her by the head and trying to burden her body with such colossal weight that I would rip off her head when I launched into the air. She responded by sending the wind down with the crushing force of a waterfall. I found myself on my back again when my head stopped throbbing and my sight sharpened.

She drank the light of the angel, her skin aglow with brief sparks of vitality, shifting from the color of waterlogged bone to a soft pink, as though blood finally began flowing under her skin. The false port around us become more and more real, if that makes any sense. It felt more and right, as though a foreign city had always been right here, commissioned by some George instead of Ivan the Terrible.

'How many times do I have to tell you?' said the ghastly woman, her eyes closed and her breath heavy with life. 'The sky is mine now.'

The lighthouse blazed, bleaching the sky with its solar fury. The fog thinned, the clouds parted, and the sky cut itself open. The bifurcated night dilated, and the universe was a gold and silver clockwork. The starry lantern rose to the sky, becoming the pupil of an alien eye.

'But you have no claim to heaven,' said Remiel, called haBarachiel of the Chorus of the Ophanim.

'Oh, and now there's this jackass,' the spectre said with a sigh. 'Please tell me you're here to kill me.'

'I cannot destroy a creature like you,' said Remiel. 'Only God Himself could do so.'

'Then call down the Almighty! I've got time!' she said. 'I'll trade you for a pair of whatever these people are! Your buddy in the Arctic seemed to want them dead.'

'I will not,' said the Archangel, its voice that of a sonorous wise-man calling down to children trapped at the bottom of a well.

'Oh, come on! Just admit that you can't!'

'He fell silent when the guns roared like lions,' said the Archangel. 'We no longer hear His voice.'

'You should probably look into that before you try to destroy the world,' said the ghostly woman.

'Our mission is known,' said Remiel. 'What if the silence is simply a test?'

'What if something is wrong?' said the ghost of the city.

'God does as God wills,' said the archangel. 'Nothing can be wrong.'

'And I've been to the bottom of the Atlantic, and saw a ship that couldn't sink,' she said. 'Words are words.'

The Archangel's iris cooled from solar gold to a stellar silver, its textures rapidly taking on the details of recently forged chains. The adamantine chains, clinking against each other in the gale like wind chimes as long as roads, snaked through the sky, roots digging down to drink the deep dark sea inside of the Canadian abomination. The glimmering chains wrapped around the girl's thin limbs, binding her from shoulder to ankle. She did not resist, nor protest. Her facial expression was hard to read; perhaps she was simply dismayed, or stoically confused, or witheringly contemptuous of the angel's foolishness, as befits the Anglo-Saxon.

'Fine, drag me down to hell,' she droned. 'Convince yourselves that the game hasn't changed.'

'I have no idea what you mean,' said the angel, its eye scanning the ground in confusion.

'I'm the afterlife now. The dead once slept, awaiting the day of judgement, when they'd be cast into the fires or allowed into the first city. But the city walls came tumbling down in that storm of tears, and that tragic rain quenched the fires. It's all washed away. I'm the city now, not gold but all in grey and bone.'

'That's not possible,' said the Angel.

'Then why do the dead come to me? Think. I came here because its my mirror. A great northern port, wounded by a munitions blast. But now I've got a bit of that holy light in me, from eaten [*sic*] up that angel!" she let out a cold, mirthless chuckle. 'If I can't have Archangel, I will take the shinin' city on the hill. Imagine that! Heaven'll be Halifax! Wouldn't that just rough up your plans? Next year, in Jerusalem!'

The fury that filled the Archangel terrified me. The white hot rage surged through the chains, and the alien metal shined like links forged in the heart of the Sun. The eye of the angel began hoisting her up, and none of the winds conjured up by the abomination could slow her rising or break the chains.

'You will find no home but the void below Creation,' said the Angel.

'I've been there,' she said. 'You don't...know what I am, do you? I barely did, 'til I started eatin' up all your friends.'

The great scanning eye shifted, as one contemplating.

'You...' said the Heavens. It whispered with the voice of the Northern winds. 'Rahab.'

She chuckled, as the chains tightened.

'Back in the before-all, the Lord sent His spirit out over the primordial waters, and with the Word sought to give it form. And then, in those uncreated waters called Tehom, something whispered, "No, thank you,"' she said. 'That was me. Rahab. Lotan. Leviathan. Tiamat. Ur. So God and I wrastled a bit. He won after an age, and tucked me away under the ice in the far corner of the Earth...now, Nova Scotia's pretty far from ol' Canaan, but people came, and then more people came, and they built a city on me, and I became that city, like how clay becomes a jar and forgets it was ever clay in the first place. Being a city ain't so bad, even if a city is the exact opposite of what primal form is supposed to be. Too many ghosts and too loud a blast woke me up. So I'm back, kid.'

'One does not threaten the Heavenly Host, Leviathan!' shouted the angel, in fear and surprise. 'You will have a chance to beg for forgiveness when the Final Battle is done, but not today! You will return to your tomb and your abyss!'

'And send everyone inside me down there?' she asked. 'How is that fair?'

'Their sacrifice is necessary,' said Ramiel.

The spectre cursed at him.

I took to the sky. She looked at me, her anger turning into obvious confusion. It was so cold. Simply hovering in her presence sucked the heat from my flesh and the breath from my lungs. My clothing and hair grew heavy with foetid water.

I decided to do her one better. I placed my hands on her shoulders, and pressed down. I pressed down on her, pulled up the world, and kicked against the sky, until she weighed as much as ten thousand cities. Doubling, tripling, quintupling and so on until the unbreakable chains buckled and the all-seeing eye bulged out of the clockwork socket.

I yanked the prism-lensed camera from the ghostly girl's damp pocket as I pulled my knife, one fluid motion that detached me from her and let the coiled tension in the chains escape. The air grew still and quiet for one painful moment, before everything snapped. The great white eye came out of the socket, its blood vessels breaking and spraying us with a glowing white mist. The spectre gasped as my release sent her plummeting to the bottom of the sea. The Archangel fell onto my knife. I sliced through the thick flesh of the eye, soaking myself in the vitreous humour. Disgusting, but warm. I increased the weight of the prism lens, and it became the bottom of an inescapable pit. The essence of Ramiel tumbled into the crystalline trap as I ruptured the eyeball and depressed the trigger on the flash-mechanism.

Just as I thought myself free, the ruins of its clockwork body slammed into me. I screamed. I saw my forearm dangle at an inappropriate angle. I'm so stupid it took me minutes to realize that the impact broke my arm.

Leviathan and the shards of Ramiel's body crashed into the grey waters of Arkhangelsk, and the bottom fell out of the world. A great grey wave roared out of the harbour, obliterating the phantom city, and a whale the size of the world faded into the depths. When the waters subsided, the stone Canadian city was gone, replaced by the dank wood of Arkhangelsk.

Exhausted, I let myself drift down to the earth, and settled on the snow. The once-pure snow bloodied at my touch. I was leaking from somewhere, and wet all over. I was so cold that my blood fled from me into the far more inviting snow.

I told myself that I was going to freeze to death. And I was fine with that. Three Archangels were dead or captured. Three for two, a perfectly favourable score. No, I thought, mother and father are dead too...but so was Apollyon and its infernal angels. Yes, the scales tipped in our favour. We damaged them enough.

No, not enough, I whispered to the white world below me. I crawled on my knees, my one good arm groping at stones as I pulled myself towards the direction of two black figures."

"I huddled in the ruins of the lighthouse, nothing but a short wall of brick after it had crumbled to dust beneath the wave," wrote Creed. "I had no idea how we survived, but this water was not of this earth, a phantasmal substance that swept away stone but left me and my captive unharmed. I stood guard over the monstrosity, this impossibly fast man who wore pitch and left fire in his wake. He was bleeding to death, but slowly, the droplets falling from him like autumn leaves. It took nine seconds for one ruby drop to fall from his elevated ankle to the ground, from the height of a pair of stacked bricks.

His female accomplice moved towards me, half-crawling, half-floating, shivering and painfully gasping for breath. She came to a rest at my feet.

It took her a long time to say anything, as the fight left her struggling for each breath, but she eventually found the strength to speak a single question, one delivered in a cold, harsh whisper - 'Why should I not kill you?'

'It would be kind of rude,' I said. 'It's not right to kill a man who doesn't know why he has to die.'

'Why you work with that?' she asked.

'You mean, why did I work with that girl?' I said. I had to think about it. 'She promised me a way home. I've been stuck her for months. I want to see my hometown again. I want to see another town, any town. I want to taste a good beer. I want to see my momma again. Something bad happened to Halifax...I don't even know if my family's still alive.'

'You do not want to hurt me?' she said, correcting herself to 'You did not?'

'No,' he said. 'I was scared of you. You do things that I don't understand. It's not a trick, but some strange power. Why do fly like that?'

'I push everything away, and then I forget to fall,' she said. 'And I don't let the world pull me back down.'

I asked how.

She asked me what I saw. I told her I saw nothing but the Narrows Spectre rising into the sky, and her flying into a raging storm after her.

She told me to go away and let her die. She closed her eyes and let her head rest against the snow. Pink feathers blew away from her wounded arm, rising and drying in her pooling blood.

A crunch in the snow alerted me to the arrival of a strange man.

'Go,' said the man, curtly. His features were neither those of a Russian nor a Britisher. He reminded me of the Greeks I met at shipyards. 'I will take them.'

'Where? How? This man will bleed out before you reach a hospital,' I said.

'I take them where that girl came from,' he said. 'I follow her through the storm. There is a meeting coming up, on an Island in the Aegean. So I must step into the future.'

'She said she was some kind of afterlife,' I said. 'I saw them, I saw the dead, sir. I saw them grab people, carry away angels, tear them apart. Do not follow her.'

'The dead will bow in the presence of the Master,' he said. He cradled the Oriental girl in one hand and effortlessly pulled the charcoal suited man up with the other. He walked off down the hill. I tried to follow him, but he disappeared beyond the horizon.

I slung my gun back over my shoulder, saw that I had nothing left to do, and trudged back to the ship. I can't stop thinking about those two strange Russians and that poor little terror of a girl. Never did find out what they were on to."

Phantoms on the Wing

The Inquiry of Lt Arthur.
   In 27 May 1913, Lieutenant Desmond Arthur of the Royal Flying Corps' No. 2 Squadron suffered a fatal fall when his BE2 biplane experienced two simultaneous unrelated failures, with his right wing folding and snapping apart and his seatbelt breaking at the beginning of the dive, tossing him out of the cockpit. The accident was pinned on a poorly repaired spar. However, the improbability of both systems failing conjured up suspicions of sabotage, internal or foreign, or signs of rank incompetence in British aviation. Arthur's Irish heritage added another political tinge to the arguments, which rose all the way to the House of Commons.
   In a June 1956 issue of *The Scotsman*, Thomas Fletcher lays out a history of strange events. September of 1916 saw the first appearance of a ghostly aviator at Scotland's Montrose airbase, with a man in pre-war flying kit walking to the mess, only to disappear into thin air before he could open the door. Major Cyril Foggins witnessed the ghost on five distinct occasions. A flight instructor was roused from his sleep by a presence in his quarters, warming himself by the fire. The phantom vanished when the flight instructor "challenged the intruder," which is a nice way to say that an officer screamed in stark terror for five minutes. The phantom would also appear in the barracks several times. The long cold case was reignited, and pressure to resolve the disaster that killed Lieutenant Arthur intensified.
   On Christmas Eve, Sir Charles Bright, chairmen of the investigation taskforce, released a rather lackluster finding – the machine had been damaged, and poorly repaired, likely by the negligent party to avoid punishment. However, the ghost of Lieutenant Arthur seemed content that he, at least, had been cleared of personal failure. Arthur's spectre appeared to multiple men in the first days of January, with a happy look on his face. He did not appear again.

The Long-Delayed Comic.
   In 1942, an alarm rang out on a cold November night at the Fairhop Royal Air Force Base in Essex. As all British assets were accounted for, and they did not respond to hails, all signs pointed to a

German bombing squadron. Spotters noticed shadows on the clouds, and the defensive batteries opened fired. The commanding officer ordered an abrupt stop. The base held its breath as biplanes emerged from the clouds, unharmed by the fire. In front of dozens of witnesses, a heavily-modified Sopwith Camel – known as a Sopwith Comic– passed out of the clouds, only to vanish in the middle of the air[61]. Research of First World War records quickly established that there had been a Camel squadron stationed at the base, then known Hainault Farm. Oddly enough, the Comic's idiosyncratic modifications matched those employed by a Lieutenant Craig[62].

The Aviatrix.
    The last of the mysterious aerial vehicle flaps of the First World War occurred in the first months of 1918, and featured a roguish, daredevil of a pilot that fought both the Allies and the Central Powers. We still don't know who she is.
    In the early hours of January 9, 1918, experienced pilot Lieutenant Frederick Ardsley of 49 Squadron patrolled a strip of northern France between Amiens and Villers-Bocage in a Royal Aircraft Factory S.E.5, searching for enemy balloons at an altitude of three kilometers. Feeling a presence to his left, Ardsley saw a second S.E.5 biplane bearing three machine guns and bizarre markings – a bright red nose, no Royal Flying Corps roundels or squadron ID, and the sign of Venus, painted on the fuselage in gold.
    The engines did not roar. They barely hummed. They were so eerily quiet that Ardsley could hear the feminine laughter of the unknown pilot.
    Getting a good look at her, Ardsley described a bob of blonde hair under a leather aviation cap and icy blue eyes under goggles. A confused Ardsley could only shout surprised curses as the pilot blew him a kiss, stood up, and performed a little dance that exposed her knickers. And remember, she's doing all this in an open-air cockpit.

[61] Haining, Peter (2008). *The Mammoth Book of True Hauntings*. Philadelphia, Pennsylvania: Running Press Book Publishers
[62] Dominguez, Luis. (1969) "The Winged Phantom." *Ripley's Believe It or Not! True Ghost Stories.*

Upon completing her mad mid-air cancan, she fell back into her seat, waved at Ardsley, and turned left. Ardsley pursued, observed and reported on from the ground. The woman's silent S.E.5 outpaced Ardsley at every turn, her erratic flight and ability to accelerate beyond the capabilities of her plane keeping her out of range. She eventually climbed to six kilometers. Ardsley's plane struggled to keep up, and mechanical failures and icing jammed both of his machine-guns and the Lewis gun. His engine whining and his body freezing in the thin air as he reached the biplane's flight ceiling, Ardsley brought his stalling plane down. The aviatrix's powerful plane disappeared into a mass of clouds.

Ardsley received a dressing down from his squadron leader, who did not like Ardsley's theory that someone's popsy nicked a kite for a lark (that's "someone's girlfriend stole a plane for a joy-ride," for those of you who aren't ridiculous Old Timey English pilots), and said that the report would state that Ardsley and another pilot engaged in a mock dogfight. Ardsley was confined to quarters.

Her legend spread on both sides – the British and French called her Lady Sopwith or Madame Sopwith, the Germans *Die Walküre*. A few weeks after Arsley's encounter, Albert Röhl's plane was shot down behind Allied lines and he was quickly captured and brought to the RFC field near Amiens, where Arsley had first encountered her.

Röhl politely asked if he could "meet her," the woman he described as the *Walküre*, a woman variously described as piloting either a red Sopwith triplane, Arsley's opponent's red-nosed S.E.5, or, one occasion, a Fairey Campania seaplane. He was not the last German pilot to make such a request. The Allies in Amiens adopted Dame Sopwith as a kind of roguish trickster hero, a beauty with "Irene Castle-styled bobbed hair" cutting down the Huns.

Civilians in the area around Amiens claimed to see her too – a family by the name of Tuchel saw the woman's plane fly low enough over their home to barely clear its chimney.

She would also switch teams depending on the witness – in particularly dire times, she became a blonde-braided *fraulein* in a Fokker.

Some theorized that she was a kind of living avenging angel, the tomboyish sister of the fallen ace Albert Ball or the Red Baron. She was identified with many of the women who had flown before and during the war, such as Hélène *"La Flèche Humaine"* Dutrieu, Marie Marvingt, Amelie Beese, Katherine Stinson, Harriet Quimby, Blanche Stuart Scott, and Bessica Medlar Raiche, but they all had alibis or didn't match the description. Some pegged her as a member of a secret squad of female pilots from America (not dissimilar to the Russian Night Witches of WWII), a Suffragette special agent dispatched by Woodrow Wilson, or a publicity stunt launched by George A. Creel, the American Director of War Information.

An American origin was inspired by her apparently singing a song inspired by their Atlantic voyage - "The trip was long, the boys arrived/They ripped off shirt and collars!/The pretty maids who welcomed them,/made thirty thousand dollars!"

Contributor to the 1928-1945 aviation fiction magazine *Flying Aces*, novelist, creator of the pulp pilot character Kerry Kenne, and former RAF pilot Arch Whitehouse had a theory about the legend of Lady Sopwith. He believed that this "flossy legend" originated in a field near Chipilly and the Somme. He recounted a story of an S.E.5 squadron that frequently engaged in pranks and theatrical skits. One of these young men just happened to be a fantastic female impersonator, and once flew as a pantomime woman during the Christmas of 1917, wearing a blonde wig[63].

However, that does not explain the power of "her" vehicle, the sightings on opposite sides of the war, and her ability to disappear into clouds and never come down to land. The fighter planes of WWI were not exactly long range vehicles, and Arch Whitehouse was never one to let a good story go unembellished.

The Female of the Species: The Women Snipers of Gallipoli.

Gallipoli, for whatever reason, became a spawning ground for absurd legends, including the previously mentioned "Vanished Battalion," the Sandrigham Palms of the 1/5th Norfolks.

The Germans told tales of trench-stalking, blood-drunk Turkish night-patrolling volunteers roaming the battlefield armed only with

---

[63] Whitehouse, Arthur George Joseph [Arch], *Heroes and Legends of World War I*, Doubleday, Garden City, NY, 1964, pp. 328-332

knives, paid in what they could pick from the pockets of their victims. The Turks told a tale that recalls the Angels of Mons, in which ancient Ottoman heroes returned from the dead to destroy the Norfolks.

Rumors circulated among the ANZAC troops of men being dragged under and eaten by sea monsters while bathing off-shore, bolstered by news that Georgian scientist Nikolai Marr had seen an aquatic monster called the Vishap, in Lake Van, near Mount Ararat; likewise, the Armenian writer Atrpet collected similar tales of such a lake monster.

However, one far more plausible tale, especially popular among Australian historians, is the alleged presence of Turkish women acting as snipers during the battle of Gallipoli.

Contrary to some objections to the rumors, the Ottoman Military did employ female agents, the most famous being Despina Davidovitch Storch, an Istanbul-born spy and socialite famed for her beauty and flawless French[64], known by many aliases: "Baroness de Bellville," "Madame Nezie," "Madame Hesketh," and "Turkish Delight." During the war, she operated in Paris, Madrid, Rome, London, New York, and Washington, often accompanied by Baron Henri de Bellville, from which she derived her most often used alias. The pair were arrested on March 18, 1918 by the US Justice Department with two other operatives while attempting to flee to Cuba. The quartet were detained on Ellis Island and became ill, with Despina Storch soon succumbing to either pneumonia or poison. She was only twenty-three at the time of her death, and buried at Mount Olivet Cemetary in Queens. However, the existence of female Turkish agents does not in and of itself prove that there were women sniping at Gallipoli.

One of the most commonly cited pieces of evidence was written by Ivor Lloyd Jones of the 7th Royal Welsh Fusiliers, who wrote home to his mother six days after the death of his elder brother Captain Edward Wynne Lloyd Jones on August 10, 1915, at Gallipoli. The letter contains the following passage - "Dolly" being the family nickname for Edward:

"There are plenty of wells, but each one was watched by a sniper, so you risked your life each time you went for water. The snipers there

---

[64] Barton, George. Celebrated Spies and Famous Mysteries of the Great War. NYC: The Page Company. (1919).

are dreadful, their name is legion. Every tree seems to hold one. They are in front of the lines and behind them. Fortunately they are rotten shots, or else it would be impossible to do anything there.

They paint themselves green and wear green clothes and then hide in the leafy trees. Some of them have been caught behind the lines and they had stocks of food, ammunition and cigarettes to last them a month or two. Some are young girls and some boys of sixteen. They get short shrift anyway if they are caught by the men. It is quite sport shooting into the trees in front of the lines in search of them. Some of them are tied to the branches and wont come down however much one hits them, but occasionally they come down like rooks, wallop. They always replace them by fresh ones though. It seems that poor Dolly was hit by one of them from behind the lines.

They are most cowardly brutes and take no notice of the Red Cross. A man was hit by one just near Doc. Davies's dressing station, and when a Red Cross man went to tend him, he was shot as well. Doc says that wherever he goes he is continually being popped at."

Ivor Lloyd Jones would himself be killed in action in March 1917, at Gaza.

Private John Frank Gray of the 5th Battalion Wiltshire Regiment, as collected in Walter Wood's "In the Line of Battle – Soldiers' Stories of the War," wrote that his unit encountered "woman snipers" at a well by a blockhouse at Chocolate Hill. "There was a big run on the well, and a lot of fellows were shot by snipers who could not be traced, till a fellow in a Welsh regiment swore he could see someone moving in some trees not very far away. A machine-gun was brought up, and fifty rounds or so were fired into the trees, which dropped some very rare fruit – four men Turks and one woman Turk, all snipers. When we went up we found that they were almost naked, and had their faces and hands and bodies and rifles painted green to match the trees. And there they roosted, like evil birds, potting at our chaps whenever they got the chance, which was pretty often. This was such a good haul that firing was directed on all the trees, and more snipers were brought down, including several women. Some of the women wore trousers, like the men, and some had a kind of full grey-coloured skirt. They were as thin as rats, and looked as if they had had nothing to eat for months. I think there were six or seven women snipers caught in the trees, and it is said that the Turks have women in the trenches; but I don't know if that is true. I saw one woman sniper who had been caught by the New Zealanders. I don't know what was done with her; but as the men came back they told us they had bagged her in a dug-out, where she had a machine-gun and a rifle, and that she seemed to have been doing a very good business in sniping." The detail of a single woman possessing a machine-gun reeks of confabulation – the Turks possessed relatively few machine-guns, with each infantry regiment issued only four machine guns placed in a single gun company allocated by regimental headquarters, and would not allow such a precious and resource-heavy weapon to be crewed by a single person, let alone a single woman in the terrible conditions of a sniper's dug-out. Especially considering that First World War-era machine-guns are possibly the worst weapon to issue to a sniper.

Professor Mete Tuncoku of the Atatürk ve Çanakkale Savaşlan Araştırma Merkezi claims an Australian named J.C. Davies wrote that he was personally ambushed by a "Turkish girl sharpshooter" who killed many of his fellow soldiers. He was, however, "still upset to see that she was shot dead before sunset by one of our soldiers." However, records indicate that no soldier by that name served at Gallipoli.

Similarly, the War Diary of the 1/4th Norfolks Battalions recorded that a rumor spread that "women snipers have been caught within out lines with their faces, arms, legs, and rides painted green" on August 15, 1915.

On August 22, 1915, Corporal Ronald A. Semmence of the 6th Battalion of the Royal Dublin Fusiliers wrote from a hospital bed of the British Red Cross Hospital in Cairo that he was "wounded on Sunday August 15th, when our lot along with the Munsters and 'Skins' took a Turkish trench and about 20 prisoners... I have heard that some female snipers were captures. How true it is I don't know."

"His [a concussion victim's] wife says that she has letters from him, in one of which he described how he killed a Turkish woman sniper. He does not remember writing this letter, but there is evidently some retrograde amnesia," wrote F.W. Mott, in his 1919 work, *War neuroses and shell shock*, (p. xvi).

The veracity of these rumors is often bolstered by the occurrence of similar phantom female snipers in the European theater, as attested to in a letter to the family of Griffith Piercy, a British soldier killed at Overs Ridge at the age of 21 on October 1, 1918. Piercy's squad mate, Alf Hughes, claimed Griffith was shot by a female sniper, and that Griff was avenged not long after.

There are other other reports of sniping Turkish women at Gallipoli, but these come from even more spurious third-hand accounts and gossip reported as truth, often written down decades later. The *Times* even reported as truth an obviously fictional tale of a little old lady in a white house (which did not, in fact, exist) sniping dozens of officers from her window. There are no flawless first-hand reports or photographs of these snipers, many of which end up dead at the end of the stories, despite the curiosity factor and propagandistic value of such an occurrence. Photographers would have jumped at the opportunity.

Seasoned Turkish soldiers were often highly skilled counterinsurgents and countersnipers, experienced with guerrilla tactics in the Balkans, and many excelled and preferred sniping and independent, mobile, squad-based operations over the larger-scale actions favored by their European counterparts. There was little in the way of officially sanctioning of snipers by the Turkish high command; individual mid-to-low level commanding officers instead trained their own *ad hoc* sniping squads, which could allow for the adoption of quickly-trained irregulars and civilian support as sniping units, though there is little documented evidence of this.

While the Sultan's Army frequently employed irregulars and was followed by blackguards of various types, the forces at Gallipoli were different, almost entirely composed of Anatolian Turks supported by Syrian Arab regiments, who made up roughly two-thirds of the first wave of resistance (Ottoman-loyal Arabs were often used as cannon fodder, and during the later years of the war were sometimes transported to training with bound hands). These were men fighting early in the war on home soil, not the infamously broken Ottomans of 1916 onward, wracked with internal strife, poor morale, and desertion rates up to 50% in certain units. There simply is no evidence of a civilian presence at the battlefield – there were more than twenty Turkish divisions defending the narrow front, no civilian support, and barely any space for any unaffiliated civilian (who, for some reason, ignored the evacuation order) to survive undiscovered for long. Furthermore, the army composition would have made the presence of a cross-dressing woman implausible - Turkish units were segregated by language group, prone to regular and German-inspired medical inspections, and lead by an imam who not only controlled the religious life of the men, but could even assume command if his battalion's nominal head was incapacitated or proved weak.

There is some grain of truth in the myth, however. During the Balkan Wars of the early 1910s, women served as snipers in the Greek Nationalist forces and as part of various Slavic partisan groups or the Armenian *fedayees*, and Turkish women took part in the conflicts that followed the socio-political upheaval of Atatürk's reforms. The Albanian *burrnesha*, Sworn Virgins, who swear off sex and live as men, occasionally took part in warfare.

In an incident that recalls the Christmas Truce, May 24th, 1915 saw the Pause at Gallipoli, a ceasefire in which both sides stopped all hostilities to bury their dead and retrieve any lost wounded. The men traded hellos, cigarettes, tokens, and even played football. Turkish civilians and the ANZAC's Arab retainers gathered to observe the initially rather eerie lull, but soon joined in on the 'festivities.' Under the orders of Capt. Audrey Herbert, the Diggers – what "Ozzies" and "Enzeds" started calling their soldiers around 1917 - lined up and shook hands with their Mehmetçik – "Little Mehmet"- and Ottoman Arab counterparts. Less than half an hour later, both sides returned to their trenches, and the fighting started up again.

During the Pause, an Arabic woman appeared among the Syrian Ottoman Troops, encouraging an uprising. The diary of the Syrian soldier Taysir Karm Al-Taba'i describes the event:

"We had settled down for a smoke after the retrieval, weary of meeting the British due to our captain's stern disapproval of such fraternization. Out of nowhere, my unit encountered a woman in a yellow dress, with a rifle strapped across a man's coat. She wore a cream scarf around her head, with a crude map stitched into it. She shouted at us, demanding that we take up arms against the Turkish conquerors –

her accent was not *shami* [Syrian], but she was easily understood by us. She referred to the Anatolians as *Juj*, and the European *Faranji* as *Majuj*, proclaiming they will soon be thrown down by God. Some of us jeered her, and many simply quietly turned away, but others listened to her, too fearful to voice our approval. Our *müfti* [referring here to the battalion imam] overheard her, and chased her off with his revolver and the toss of a shoe, calling her a harlot and a filthy looter, though to my knowledge she was lost soon after. Several cartons of cigarettes went missing during the uproar."

While it's easy to see the Wartime Ottoman Empire's internal politics as a simple Turkish vs. Arab conflict, especially in light of the Arab Revolt, three hundred thousand Arabs served the Sultanate at the beginning of the war, nearly a third of all Ottoman regular troops. As found in *Year of the Locust: A Soldier's Diary and the Erasure of Palestine's Ottoman Past*, the diary of Pvt. Ihsan Hasan al-Turjman of the Ottoman 4th Army expresses the resentment and self-loathing felt by many Syrian troops who fought for the Ottoman Empire, claiming that "the Palestinian and Syrians are a cowardly and submissive lot. For if they were not so servile, they would have revolted against these Turkish barbarians." Al-Taba'i would fall in battle at the Dardanelles in November 1916, while Al-Turjman would be executed by an Ottoman officer in 1917.

The Incomparable 29th and the River Clyde, a regimental history by George Davidson, M.A., M.D., Major, R.A.M.C. Mentions that, among a large number of Turks killed by an artillery blast near a redoubt nicknamed the Boomerang by Gully Ravine at Gallipoli, "one woman was found...but it was believed that many of them had their wives with them. Many of their underground dwellings were so elaborate that they had evidently made up their minds that they were to spend the coming winter here. (p. 115)" This event occurred on June 28, 1915. However, there is simply no evidence at all that Turkish troops garrisoned with their wives, and such a notion is incredibly implausible.

Davidson also mentions a "strange occurrence" that happened at W. Beach on June 23rd – "a figure appeared over the sky line in petticoats, as it was thought. Our men began yelling "A wuman, a wumman," and all tore out to see what they had not seen for months.

Lieut. Thomson and Corporal Morrice were the most excited. These two have not yet gotten over their disappointment on discovering this was an Egyptian – and a male one – in a long coat. (p.110)" However, a homebound June 25th letter written by Lt. Donald L. Pogue, one of the remaining members of the Dublin Fusiliers, reduced to nothing more than company strength by the attrition of the Gully, makes mention of chasing away a battlefield looter, an Arab woman with short cropped hair wearing a long coat and wielding a presumably stolen gas respirator and rifle of British issue. Her coat was somehow identifiable as originating in Cairo, though Blake did not clarify how he discerned this fact.

The second volume of the war diary of the 1/3rd The Scottish Horse contains an entry dated to 4 November 1915 mentions that a reconnoitering patrol was sent out "after Demonstration. They got within 15 yds of Turkish lines. They heard about 10 men working with picks & shovels at some kind of dug-out behind fire trench. They saw no wire of any sort. They say they distinctly heard a woman's voice in the trenches." That very day, the Turks experienced their own attack at the hands of a female sniper, in which two nightwatchmen were gunned down in their trenches, which a third man seeing a woman vanish into the darkness, carrying rations. A female sniper, presumed to be an Arab, was spotted taking potshots at the Turks during the disastrous, three-day-long, soldier-drowning rainstorm that concluded November of 1915, and during the harsh blizzard that struck Sulva at the beginning of December. A similar figure helped cover the Allied retreat of 27 December 1915, by lighting supply fires and sniping at officers until being spotted through binoculars. She was fired upon and was assumed to be killed or wounded, but no body was ever found. Later that day, after the ANZACS feigned retreats in utter silence, ANZAC supplies were set ablaze, looted, or booby-trapped by an unknown hand.

The nature of these phantom female attackers may seem baffling, but the Turks wrote it off as particularly aggressive Arab saboteurs and looters, possibly splinters of the English's Egyptian auxiliary forces, which largely consisted of people serving logistical roles. Bedouin women – and to a lesser extent, the women of poor, settled Arab communities - were absolutely notorious among both the forces of the

British Empire and the Turks for the practice of body-looting after the dust had settled. The shocking aggression, however, did raise some eyebrows among the Special Organization, and some of the attacks took place from within the Turkish lines.

The answer to this riddle may lie with an elusive woman born in the town of Baalbek in the Damascus Vilayet, Ottoman Empire, under the name Manon Chedid. This woman was known to the Bedouins as *Batoul Bint Boulos bin Luca bin Ishac bin Marcus bin Yacoub bin Gassan abou-Shedid*, known to her allies as *Batina*, Arabic for "hidden or esoteric one," and to her Turkish foes as *Fenike*, the Phoenician.

Batoul Chedid was seemingly fascinated by a Moroccan religious and resistance leader known as Sidi 'Ali Amhaouch. Born in 1844, Amhaouch traced his descent from a line of powerful, apocalyptic, and seemingly magical marabouts of the Darqawa faction of Islam, a dynasty stretching back at least ten generations, including a warrior that captured Sultan Mulay Slimane in 1818. Amhaouch claimed that his ancestor Bou Beqr foretold this victory in the 12th century of Islam (the 18th century of the Common Era). He supported several Moroccan tribes' struggles against the sultan's government before attempting to unify all Moroccan Muslims against their French colonizers under the banner of a defensive jihad.

The 1912 Treaty of Fez had officially rendered Morocco a French protectorate, and Amhaouch and other Berber leaders saw the outbreak of World War One as an opportunity for rebellion, as a significant percentage of French occupational forces had to be rerouted to the European theater. This insurrection came to be known as the Zaian War, after the Zaian Berber tribal confederation. Despite support from the Central Powers, the Zaian Coalition suffered heavy losses and the French lost little territory. Amhaouch died of natural causes in 1918, and his principle allies Mouha ou Hammou Zayani and Moha ou Said l'Irraoui lost the war three years later. Sidi Lemekki Amhaouch, his eldest son, continued to fight until 1932, with the help of his father's allegedly magical rifle cartridge[65].

Batoul visited the Jebel Toujjit mountain of Morocco, which

65 Peyron, Michael. "Tazizaout: une bataille oubliée." Al-Akhawayn University Press.

Amhaouch claimed to be sacred, but found no clue for the source of Amhaouch's claimed power. She did, however, record a prophecy attributed to Amhaouch, in Arabic and French:

"*Ai ushshan ni'wanargi, a wi ni'muriq, aggat/ gir tfeza, a'tannayim aferran ai-digz-ilan*"

"*Ô chacal d'Anergui, et toi, compère du Mourik, transportez-Vous vers Tafza ; contemplez l'incendie qui y fait rage!*"

This cryptic, apocalyptic declaration translates to, "Oh Jackal of Anergui, and you, companion of Mourik, take yourself to Taza, and contemplate the fire that rages there!"

Anerqui is a small, historically unimportant town in Morocco, while Taza is a city in a mountain pass in the north, domain to the recent and brutal tyrant Bou Hmara. It is the gateway though the Rif mountains to the Atlantic coasts, and saw successive waves of invasions – Almoravids, Almohands, Marinids, Turks, and most recently, the French in 1914. The fire, she supposed, was a coming conflict, symbolic of repulsion of the Turks and French throughout North Africa and the Middle East.

Her knowledge of such artifacts stemmed from tutelage by Salim al-Kari (or *al-Khouri*, meaning "the Reader"), an Arab Christian artist, translator, and *dragoman* who aided Moses Wilhelm Shapira in the forgery of Moabite and Israelite artifacts in the 1870s, often buried by Salim's Bedouin henchmen to be uncovered in public displays. Shapira's cottage industry of "moabitica" culminated in a leather inscription which enumerated eleven commandments, with the final translating from sloppy Hebrew "Thou shalt not hate thy brother in thy heart. I am God, thy God." It was sold to the British Museum for a million pounds. Christian David Ginsburg, a fellow Polish-born, Jewish-to-Christian convert, uncovered the forgery, and Shapira committed suicide in a Rotterdam hotel[66]. Salim kept his head down, putting his talents to work in support of Holy Land archaeology, largely around Dhibon and Jerusalem.

---

[66] Oddly enough, time may vindicate Shapira; many points of evidence towards the forgery theory, such as its state, discovery site, and wording were countered by the excavation and study of the Dead Sea Scrolls, found not far from the "Shapira Scroll." Indeed, the oddities in the Shapira Decalogue were duplicated in the Dead Sea Scrolls' prophetic books.

Chedid, as a teenager, participated in another artifact smuggling incident, the failed expedition of Captain Montague Brownslow Parker. The Finnish scholar, writer, and surveyor Dr. Valter Henrik Juvelius (widely known under the pen name Valter Juva) accompanied the thiry-year-old English archeologist on the journey to the Holy Land, which began in August of 1909 before its abrupt end in May of 1911[67]. In addition to their English and Scottish staff, they employed the services of a Danish psychic and local Jewish and Arab porters. Operating in secret, they began by entering Warren's shaft, dug in 1867 by the Palestine Exploration Fund, descending into the Virgin's Well. Beneath the Temple Mount, the Parker expedition allegedly discovered a labyrinth of narrow tunnels containing traps, lamps, and pots decorated with the Seal of Solomon[68]. At one point, Juvelius took the measurements of a catacomb which contained the sarcophagus of King Solomon, which he claimed was booby-trapped by two masses that generated 'radioactive rays.' This dangerous and poorly-described object may have lead to the belief that the Parker expedition uncovered the Ark of the Covenant. British and Ottoman papers claims that the expedition had to escape Jaffa by yacht during a riot engendered by the rumor that the crew dug under the Mosque of Omar.

Parker was arrested on charges of stealing King Solomon's crown and ring, and the sword of Mohammed, and the complicit governor Azmey Bey was beaten by a mob. However, as they were stopped in port, Ottoman officials and the Jewish authorities of Jerusalem could find no evidence that any such smuggling took place, and the so-called 'Desecration of Omar Mosque" was found to be largely a trumped-up yarn spread by the press (with the *London Illustrated News* implying that Parker's team had stolen the Ark of the Covenant) and a particular Rabbi Jonathan ben Jochai who became suspicious of the expedition's motives and Juvelius' claims of uncovering an ancient Biblical code.

Juvelius wrote, in 1916's *Valoinen Kameeli* (*The White Camel*), that his

---

[67] Kingsley, Sean. (2007). God's Gold: A Quest for the Lost Temple Treasures of Jerusalem. New York: HarperCollins.
[68] Silberman, Neil Asher. (1982). *Digging for God and Country: Exploration, Archeology and the Secret Struggle for the Holy Land - 1799 to 1917*. New York: Alfred A. Knopf.

main mission was a search for a cavern-tomb to prove the historicity of Moses and the true nature of the Tetragrammaton, which *the Book of the Creation* claimed was drawn on the prophet's shield; the Solomonic treasures were nothing but an ancient chair and frustratingly vague allusions to "ancient manuscripts," and the estimated millions of pounds worth of gold promised to the party's patrons was nowhere to be found. Juvelius was forced to return to Russia after falling ill in the first months of 1911, missing out on the dramatic final days of the expedition, and the remaining party was hindered by heavy rains and Baron Edmond de Rothschild's purchase of the surrounding lands to protect the tombs of David and Solomon. He wished to return to the site, but funds and the Great War prevented him, and he succumbed to throat cancer in 1922. Chedid's employer and contact with the largely English group was adviser Père Louis Hughes Vincent of Jerusalem's Dominican order, who Juvelius disguised as "Father Justinus" in his description of the expedition. Chedid slipped away into the Arab crowds before the English were inspected. Père Vincent would go on to write *Underground Jerusalem*, an exploration of the subterranean Holy Land.

Bones Without Number.

"They came in the night," wrote Tom Noun. "I spotted them, but not soon enough. I was so fagged out that I was on the verge of ending my watch. We had finished our last tins of bully-beef yesterday, and were running on foraged plants and stomach pangs. They made no noise despite being wrapped in underbrush, and crawled on all fours with monstrous alacrity, their arms swinging forward in semicircles as their legs pushed on. I yelped and woke the others, just in time for the ground beneath us to give way. They launched a simultaneous gas attack, glass bottles stuffed into dried frogs breaking all around us. Smoke, toxic vapour, and the strange cries of noisemakers filled the air. From below they attacked, and then from above – arrows came raining down upon us. Not many, and none struck true, but they spread fear and confusion.

Our attackers screamed. One of their painted gas masks chilled so rapidly that it stuck to its wearer's face before cracking. The other two, blinded by a darkness that bubbled over their eyes, were overcome by a terror of our making.

The assault was too much. We could kill them easily, but only Céleste could do much between the darkness and choking clouds, freezing the gas inert and burning our shadowy foes. But one of them had the grand idea of tossing an unlit petrol bomb at us. The Salamander ignited it unknowingly, blasting her to the ground where she was seized, like the rest of us, by the troglodytes, and an ether rag over her face took her out of the fight. She did manage to boil out the eyes of her attacker, killing him.

We were hacking, gas-choked, as the cold earth surrounded us.

"I am Thomas Noun, Scion of the Nameless House!" I shouted, until dirt filled my mouth and the gas stung my tongue and lips useless. My whole body tingled with pins-and-needles, and then I felt and perceived nothing.

I awoke in a black cavern. Or, even more terrible to contemplate, I was blind. I could not move. I can not feel my surroundings. I thought through a fog, my body weightless, timeless, defenseless, powerless.

"Is anybody here?" I said. I tried to move my fingers and stretch my neck, but I couldn't even sense my body. I could have been a brain in a jar for all that I knew.

I panicked as a rat would under the knife of the worst vivisectionist. I felt the hag, the hypnogogic phantasm that assaults you when your mind awakes before your body, the presence of some invisible malevolence pressing down on my chest.

But there was another presence in the dark, stalking around me, watching me as a Bengal tiger watches an Indian encampment. I felt its gaze in that inexplicable way one can sense someone staring at you from across the room. Those were maneater's eyes.

After what seemed like hours, the presence quit the room. After another eternity, I heard a weak gasp from across the chamber. It turned into a choking sob.

A wave of tremendous heat rolled through the room, while the walls chilled me.

'Me!' I choked out. 'It's Tom.'

'Tom?' Céleste whimpered.

'Yes,' I said.

'Your heat,' she said, in French. Not only could I barely hear her, I had lost the giant's understanding which preceded the Confusion of Babel, anaesthetised like everything else. 'It is like theirs.'

'I know,' I said.

'I am feeble.' she said. 'I can barely feel the heat. Barely move it...'

I nodded out.

I awoke to her hoarsely repeating my name, the closest thing to a scream she could manage.

'I passed out,' I said. 'The drugs.'

'What?' she asked.

'The drugs made me sleep,' I said.

'I did that,' she said. 'Before I knew you were there. Before I could feel even a little heat again. I lost consciousness trying to build a fire.'

'There is no one else here, right?' I asked.

'No,' she said. Then, there was a long silence, before she loudly whispered 'Yes, Tom. Now.'

The foot steps sounded like dabbled brushstrokes against a canvas. There was light, soon enough. Its bearer moved through the cavern with elfin grave, his wide, mad eyes glistening with a sickly green film. His fingers were long, and caked with mud, and his long beard was a black wasteland of stone and muck and dust. He wore a tunic of leather, dark grey trousers, and a helmet upon his head that held a shockingly sophisticated, cyclopean electric torch. It was the master of these Dark Elves, a Dwarf King. Around him scuttled small, twisted midgets, rendered hideous and imbecilic by deformations borne from disease, chemical draughts, and foolhardy breeding. They were of diminutive servant stock, hobgoblins or kobolds in contrast to the tall, thin, aristocratic dark elf, and would live no more than a quarter of the lifespan of their master.

Céleste proceeded to breath fire at them. One of the little goblins, a hydrocephalic creature whose swarthy skin was blotched with great patches of white, tumorous wrinkles, yelped. His rags lit up and he screamed. His eyes popped out of his head as his skin froze solid and his brain boiled. The King snapped into action, moving unbelievably fast to inject Céleste with a sedative. She howled through the gag of his sleeve, but her eyes closed and she was asleep within second.

The king moved over and crushed the twitching kobold's skull with a swift kick. The others of their kind began to laugh.

My skin spasmed and an impotent froth bubbled down my filthy chin. My bones and nails sharpened. Hot blood ran from my muscles to the needle-tips of my arm hairs, spoiling into poisons so strengthful that I would kill the first mud-caked abomination of a dwarf to touch me.

The King pointed at me. His servants approached, and I prepared to strike. But they took hold of two bars to my side, and wheeled me forward. It was then that I saw my predicament; I was on a frame, suspended by hook and chain, pierced with wire and tubes. I was caked with my own dried blood. My scream died in my throat.

I panicked, and the world panicked with me. One of the living dwarfs began to rapidly rot as the microbes in his body multiplied spontaneously. His veins twisted into newborn worms that turned against their former owner, burrowing deeper into muscle and bone. Sprouts and fungal hyphae twisted through the earth around me, and long dead seeds bloomed to life in the lightness chamber. The Dwarf King's skin turned a drowned-man blue, and irregular spurs of bone broke the skin of his knuckles. He hissed with indignant rage, the wroth of a king who could not believe that his prisoner would be insolent enough to rebel. He covered my face with a medicinal rag damp with laudanum or ether, and I was out.

I came to in a chamber lit by a suspended candelabra mounted on a crude chandelier of broken mirrors. I was pierced and impaled to an operating table, with drugs dripping through metal needles shoved into my wrists. There was someone, it seemed a man, on the table next to me. A surgeon hovered above me, all but his eyes masked by a veil of gauss and a miner's helmet.

My intestines coiled around a set of hooks chained to the wooden ceiling. My clouded and dazed mind took seconds to process the fact that I was being vivisected. I could not even squirm for want of the spikes driven through me.

'I am Thomas Noun, Scion of the Nameless House!' I pleaded. 'The Nameless Men of the Name! Anshe ha-Shem! The Witch Lords! My eyes! Look at my eyes! You must know us, Lilim! If I die, you all die! Every one of your kind for miles and miles! The Hungry Night will fall upon you, and you will die screaming! My father will twist your bones into knots! My sisters will melt your eyes and freeze your hearts! We live in secret places, and the dens of wolves! A hunted hart would sooner give itself up to the mercy of hungry hounds than trespass against us!'

The surgeon shook his head. Disappointment filled his eyes, and he dabbed the spit and foam from the corners of my mouth. He made an unusually, jerky pointing motion towards the slab next to me.

'For each word that you say, I remove a finger from your friends,' he said in badly accented English. 'Only nod yes or no to my questions unless otherwise prompted....do you know of any anatomical differences between the Descendants and true men?'

I shook my head, and he continued probing around my chest cavity. I could feel cool air hitting nerves. He reached in with bare hands, coating them with my blood like a hunter would when preparing game for the table.

I tried to turn away from reality, to drive my consciousness to some other, painless realm.

They had gone mad at the end of the last century, when eight hundred of their long hidden kind were discovered on that hill in Krapina. It was their Apocalypse, their Croatian Megiddo, the sign that their discovery and destruction were nigh.

'You do not appear to be lying. Unless it lies in the skull -- some have attributed uncanny powers to the pineal gland, for instance,' said the surgeon, before glibly adding, 'May I eat part of your liver?'

I panicked again, and strained at my bonds. He cut away part of my liver, and placed it on a brass saucer.

The Dwarfen King arrived, and the Surgeon told him that 'the client' would be disappointed by the lack of gross anatomical differentiation between nephilim and mundane men. The Dwarfen King said something in their tongue, before gagging, hissing, and letting out a great, gargling, throaty sigh. The apish thing that followed the King, a guard of sorts, lashed out at thin air, his head destroyed by a point-blank gunshot. The Surgeon screamed in terror before being silenced. His body collapsed in front of me, blood pouring from his open neck.

Gottlieb and his red knife became visible.

'Sorry,' he said as he cut my bonds. 'This chamber was well-hidden.

The others are safe and free, for now.'

He refused to look at my torso as he pulled the medical tubing from my arms. He stood guard, facing away, as I pulled myself together. When the wet coiling sounds stopped, he moved to help me to my feet and gave me a shoulder to lean on. He turned towards the man lying next to me, and pronounced him dead. I called for the others to recover his body.

The dark elves defiantly drummed in the outer chambers, knocking against the walls and howling, the kobolds of haunted mines.

He told me to close my eyes, and lit the tunnels with a blinding radiance. The Other Kind fell silent.

Groggy, and seemingly drugged, Céleste, Venetianer, and Winepress joined us. Céleste had fashioned a torch from a stolen dwarfen tunic and alcohol.

'Are you OK?' and 'What did they do to you?' asked the Captain and the Salamander. The Rabbi half-whispered, 'the blood.'

'They eviscerated me,' I said, too tired to open my eyes. Rowan came to support me as well, and soon picked me up, almost cradling me.

'Please tell me that those are animal bones,' Céleste said, pointing down at yellowed splinters packed into the mucked up wall nearby, bored and drained of marrow.

'Sometimes they take children into their communities, when births are infrequent or unsuccessful...they take them *dancing* in the woods, putting them under enchantments with fairy food and drink, to make them...Other,' I explained delicately. 'Some react poorly to the drugs. Some simply want to go home. None do.'

The appalled silence that followed was a painful experience. Gottlieb returned to us, holding the body of the other man, a French soldier from the Macedonian Front.

'Which way is the exit?' asked Céleste. We realized that we had no idea, and wandered for some time before coming across a white light pouring from a chamber. We came to it, and the Captain gasped.

'What is that?' Céleste demanded.

'I've never seen a machine like it,' said Gottlieb. I opened my eyes.

The room was not a cavernous hell-pit like the rest of the complex, but a clean, sterile room lit by circular electric lanterns mounted on the ceiling, decorated with dissonantly primitive cave paintings, depicting men with large teardrop heads hunting animals unlike any I have ever seen. There were no straight lines, and everything was made of layers and layers of brass and green wiring and what appeared to be glass, giving the structure the appearance of a hazel eye as viewed close up. At the centre of the room stood a humming cylinder. An engine perhaps.

'What is this?' Céleste fearfully demanded. 'The heating is all wrong, lines of coolant running out of it...and there's nothing inside but something generating faint heat to be pumped out. It's not an engine, it's not a tube, it's not...I – what is it?!'

'No, it isn't,' said the Captain. 'I've never seen anything like it.'

'This is not the others' technology,' I said. 'They know some chemistry that mankind doesn't, but nothing this sophisticated.'

'So if it isn't fairy, and it certainly isn't human, and angels wouldn't need it...' Venetianer said.

The Captain approached it, trying and failing to find a seem or a screw or a panel.

'I'm considering carving it open with magnesium fire,' he said. 'Would you be willing to help, Céleste?'

'What if we end up, perhaps, detonating it?' she said, and I agreed with a high-pitched grunt.

'I admire your curiosity, Rowan, I really do, and if anyone could figure out what this thing is, you are that man, but we don't have the time or the tools and the boy needs to reach the surface...' Venetianer said, trailing off, before adding. 'And this frightens me. Any demon or monster or untempered angel – these are things I understand. But this is wrong. This should not be here.'

'Let's leave here, now,' Siegfried said, visibly shaken.

The Captain stormed out of the room, knocking his hand against the door in frustration. I soon learned that my fear of the grave was unique among our band. The rest found comfort in the chthonic, now that our enemies were dead or fled, and wished to rest here for the night. The giants in the earth, so they say, the ancient heroes sleeping under mountains. But I started to panic, both from the memory of the surgical table and that night I was buried with the corpse and headstones in Belgium, and those memories of Victorian live burials and those men sucked under the mud and drowned at Paschendale [sic]. It was Gottlieb's sensitivity that came to my rescue; he allowed me to save face by suggesting that we head to the surface to spot any reinforcements or stragglers. We found a ladder out of the complex not long after, illuminated by the silver glory of the moon.

Siegfried saw a figure outlined on the horizon, which he described as masculine, bald and nigh-hydrocephalic. He attempted to illuminate it, but it was gone before we could track it."

Mine recovery personnel discovered similar subterranean machinery in January of 1918, in the wake of the Minnie Pit disaster in Halmer End, Staffordshire, England. While official investigations never established a point of origin, it appears that a firedamp ignition of the gases lead to the death of 155 men and boys, from tunnel collapses, burns, toxic gas, and suffocation. The tunnels were dangerous, even by the metric of coal mines, as a similar explosion had killed nine miners three years earlier. Investigators searching for bodies – and a source of the disaster – glimpsed a chamber on the fringe of the mine complex that resembled a heap of storage trunks and vertical columns of whirring machinery, with beings resembling humans in strange, "shaggy hoods."

Researchers such as Ronald Calais, writing for *the Newsletter for the Committee for the Scientific Evaluation of Psi* (Vol.1, No.6), uncovered a similar report from the Staffordshire mines dating to 1770, where a tunneler discovered a smooth stone stairway behind a wall, leading to a humming or "roaring" room filled with chests of treasures and machinery, lit by some unknown source that to modern readers is clearly electrical. In this industrial complex, the man saw a hooded figure wielding a wand or baton – the tunneler fled before the figure could acknowledge him. The secret chamber as entered occult lore as "the Rosicrucian Sepulchre," but why they were attached to this even is unknown, possibly due to a connection with the Vril-ya mythos.

"The soldier we recovered was indeed dead, surgically destroyed," Winepress said. "Céleste and I re-opened his torso, which had recently been examined by those subterraneans. We smoked snouts to cover the stench. His internal organs, rather than extracted as I expected, were now accompanied by new ones. The man had several new glands grafted into his liver, spleen, and heart, akin to the transplantation processes of

Drs Voronov [sic], Sequard [sic], and Zervos."

Winepress is referring to the xenotransplantation techniques of Serge Abrahamovitch Voronoff, Skevophylax Georges Zervos, and Charles-Édouard Brown-Séquard, who had famously grafted monkey and ape testicle tissue onto human testes for hormonal therapy. While ridiculed after their 1920s hayday, these techniques pioneered surgical methods in endochrinology. The earliest of them, Brown-Séquard, had injected dog and guinea pig testicle extract into his skin in attempts to retard aging.

During the war, Voronoff worked in a surgical laboratory at the Parisian campus of the Collège de France, and by 1917, gained the funding and affections of an American socialite, Evelyn Bostwick. Voronoff, over the next decade, would perform at least five hundred gland transplants between livestock, particularly grafting young testicles to older animals for rejuvenation purposes.

"I informed Céleste of these procedures, and she brought up the related concept of blood transfusion, already in popular use; she wondered if this was a military project to create a more vigourous soldier, perhaps by doubling the masculine hormones and sanguine oxygen in a body by a ghoulish harvest of the fallen. There was, more than ever, a surplus of donor tissues and patients. I said that it did seem that if anyone was doing it, it would likely be the French, considering their advancement in surgical grafting, but we had heard of no such project.

We smoked feverishly, both in a fettle. She told me of her encounter with a nephel named Tarrare, dating from at least Napoleon's Wars, who seemed to be able to shed his body like an exoskeleton or cacoon; she wondered if France's military medical corps had known of him, and his organ's rejuvinatory properties. What, she asked me, with some genuine concern, if these are graphs of nephili tissue?"

Shrieks.

Togoland was virtually isolated during the war, as Germany's West African colony was surrounded by enemies, with French Dahomey to the east, French West Africa to the north, and the British Gold Coast colony to the west. And of course, Britain ruled the sea. The Germans did not even bother establishing a military garrison in the colony. The people of Togoland were in a vice, defended only by a constabulary of six hundred and sixty Togolese police officers and ten German sergeants.

Togoland's key strategic asset was the *Funkstation Kamina* outside Atakpamé, the linchpin of Germany's East African communications network and the only reliable support for their South Atlantic shipping lanes. The Funkstation Kamina was a two storied building with three peaked roofs, painted a sunlight reflecting white, surrounded by six soaring transmission towers networked with wires.

The Gold Coast Regiment invaded Togoland and met police resistance on 7 August 1914, with soldier Alhaji Grunshi firing the first British volley of the war at a manufacturing plant in Nuatja. The next day, Togoland's commander of the police, Captain Pfähler, was sniped out of a tree, and a quarter of German forces were causalities in the ensuing Battle of Agbeluvhoe. German technicians sabotaged the Kamina radio transmitter on the 24th, and Togoland officially surrendered two days later, allowing the French and British to consolidate in West Africa, with complete control over the region's railways.

British engineers at ruins of the Funkstation Kamina experienced strange interference as they attempted to establish control over the network, a metallic scream likened to the snapping of high-tension cables. The chief engineer at the station, James Ferguson, ruled out deliberate radio interference, and it appears to have abated for nearly four years before returning with a vengeance in January of 1918. This electrical screech blotted out communications from the Funkstation Kamina, forcing the station's operators to hire local boys and young men as runners. The station crew considered disbanding, as persistent signal jamming was a rather strong hint that the Germans may be coming to retake the station – intelligence had, after all, indicated that a massive surge was occurring in Europe, and it may be that the German Empire's African holdings undertook a similar gambit. And, frankly, the radio station could not be defended and was strategically useless due the jammed transmission. Nobody on staff was willing to die for this building.

It was then that one of the runners was found dead. The boy was an ethnic Ashanti, no more than 16 years of age. The initial theory was that he had climbed one of the wire towers and slipped, breaking his back and shattered his skull. The cut marks on his body were believed to be impact with the transmission wires on the way down. One of the linemen took a ladder to the wiring, and found the point of contact with the wires. What baffled the crew was that the boy had hit the wire ten meters from the closest transmitting tower.

At this point an older man named Kwaku, who the British staff called "Wednesday" due to the Ashanti's birthday based naming system, took Ferguson aside and whispered something. Kwaku was well respected by the staff, and was known to be calm, collected, and sober, and a talented property manager and interpreter. That Kwaku was on the verge of panic alarmed everyone, and several of the native boys ran inside of the barracks. Ferguson went dead quiet, gathered his British staff, and said that the boy was dropped.

The following night, a dancing luminescence akin to the will-o'-the-wisp danced over the wires after a storm, explained away as St. Elmo's Fire, though behaving more like ball lightning.

Between January 10th to January 15th, multiple men, both Ashanti and British, witnessed what was believed to be a giant bat fly around the wiring, at times hanging from the aerial masts with strange, hook-like feet.

On the morning of the 16th, an older woman in Kamina was found dead in her family's hut, with a massive "ulcer" found on her stomach.

By January 16th to the 20th, a trio of real characters came to the station. The first was district commissioner L.W. Wood, a haggard man trying to keep control of the Ashanti region with shoestring resources. It was a nightmare task: the fog of war grew thicker every day, the fallout of several tropical diseases piled up, and now there was a bat picking up and dropping Akon kids. He brought with him at least one medical officer who autopsied the first victim and identified that the boy had been partially eaten and drained of blood via the navel.

The second visitor was a native hunter named Agya Wuo. Very little is known about him, as he did not speak with the white men who recorded the incident, and barely spoke with the Akon people. He spent most of his time patrolling and camping in the jungle.

The last man to come in was Osaze Giwa-osagie, a Fon from Porto-Novo. Note the striking surname, which first drew my attention to the incident. He presented himself to the white staff as psychic medium in French and broken English, but the black staff knew him as a vodun priest. He made the white staff uneasy, and the Ashanti were terrified of him, because he sounds like a monster from the descriptions – he stood just under six and a half feet tall, a tower of wiry muscle covered in a maille shirt, dark skin covered in scars, and with a horn growing out of his head. The rational explanation is that his scarification caused the development of an aberrant skin lesion on his scalp, known as a cutaneous horn (*cornu cutaneum*). It was rumored, however, that Giwa-osagie was fathered by the Yehwe Zogbanu, a horned giant of the Beninese forests. He appeared to have been widely read in occult traditions, both West African and European, and had spent his childhood as a *vudusi*, a slave to a fetish temple. He called himself a "Ghagiel," which is a Qliphathic demon in Kabbalah, the "hindering ones," proud, mendacious, materialistic black giants embraced by coiling serpents.

Giwa-osagie rapidly insinuated himself in the barracks, taking up a private room. It took a week or so for Ferguson to even question who let him requisition a room. Nobody approved it, but here he was, with a hold over the base. Ferguson and two of his men confronted Giwa-osaige at twilight on the 29th. The priest was discovered in the forest, seated, swaying, with a snake around his neck and several banded-legged golden-orb web spiders building up a nest around him. He was praying to Aldo-Hwedo, the rainbow serpent, whose coiling movement shaped the world, and Fa, the Vodun god of divination. Ferguson nearly exploded in rage at this frightful outsider, but Giwa-osagie put his finger to his lips, and shushed him with a serpentine hiss.

"It is coming," he said in English, and jumped to his feet. Ferguson demanded to know what it was, and Giwa-osagie simply said that it was the Asiman, what the Akon called Obayifo. The tall man swiftly ran to the open field around the transmitter facility, pointing at a ball of light. When the light passed out of view in a northwesterly direction, a "batty shadow" passed over the aerials, moving at what Ferguson estimated as fifty or sixty miles per hour. Someone discharged a rifle, and the creature ceased flying over the complex. Two other men briefly witnessed a man in a shaggy suit of "moss," like some ritual garb worn by Igbo dancers, but the hunters were unable to stop or shoot him.

Giwa-osagie noted that this menace was a person, a witch, not some monster. Someone must have chosen to transform into this creature, using rituals to leave its body, draining the life from children, crops, and animals. Magical transformations required such a cost – for a spirit to become flesh, flesh must become spirit, and a life would be comsumed. He said that he would leave for the villages by morning, looking for a suspect.

Agya Wuo approached Ferguson and Wood the next day and, through Wednesday's interpretation, apologized for missing the Sasabonsam, and said it would not happen again. He then stalked into the wilderness to resume the hunt, over Ferguson's demands that he at least have some tea and bread.

Wood spoke with Ferguson about whether they should warn the neighboring villages and city about what had occurred. The Ashanti workmen were already spooked and suspicious, and Wood was concerned about the wisdom of arming them all in the face of a possible German advance. The white workers were also put on edge by the Ashanti drumming during twilight to ward off the evil specter.

On February 10th, a fight broke out among the workers, with the majority Ashanti beating and nearly killing an Ewe man before Wednesday pulled him away. The Ashanti had misinterpreted the Ewe's protective Voudun rite as black magic.

"There is no medicine for fear," Wednesday muttered to Wood, though Ferguson did suggest a round of sedatives. The next night, at around three, a brilliant light alerted several of the sleeping workers, and explosive burst shook the rest of the garrison awake. The five men illuminated by the light experienced acute ulceration on their body that developed within hours, large patches of stomach skin turning a "peach" likened to British skin. Two hours later, a loud crashing sound echoed through the forest. The two Ashanti workers who witnessed the source claimed that they saw a peach-purple skinned 'ogre' with iron claws running through the bush, chased by a massive serpent, big enough to swallow an elephant.

Wood recalled the tale of the Grootslang of South Africa, a cruel, colossal snake said to have eaten English explorer Peter Grayson just the year before. The Germans under Freiherr von Stein zu Lausnitz, as they pulled out of the Cameroons and Congo, reported a creature known to the locals as the *mokéle-mbêmbe*, an elephantine river monster with a long tail, a serpentine neck, and a horn. He sent a message out to the local photographer J.B. Danquah, the only man he knew with photographic equipment, and to the Coomassie (Kumasi) 4th Battalion for military aid. Seven of the men deserted the encampment by morning, including the entire contingent of Guang-speaking Akyode, likely frightened off just as much by the Ashanti attack on the Ewe as the vampire and snake.

On the 12th of February, Giwa-osagie reported back to Wood and Ferguson. He claimed that he had detected the witch behind the attack, and wanted permission to kill him. Wood and Ferguson hesitated. Ferguson was the first to break his silence, saying that this was outside of his domain – he was an engineer, here to rebuild and maintain control of a wireless station, and could not order the execution of a human being. Wood, who did have the legal right to execute people, still believed that this was a matter outside of his culture, and that the witch must be apprehended and brought to trial. Wood said that he was, however, afraid of setting Voodoo religious crimes into British common law. Giwa-osagie lowered his head, emphasizing the horn, and spat, "It will be in self-defense then," before leaving the room.

"There is no medicine for crazy," said Wednesday, before recommending barring the Fon warlock from the building. Wood decided that getting drunk would be the best plan.

On the 15th, one of the men with ulcers was found dead, apparently attacked and drained of viscera, sometime between midnight and six o'clock. His thumbs had been bitten off or otherwise removed, and an intense light had flash-burnt his corneas.

On the 19th, Wednesday awakened Wood, and rushed him outside, where the Ashanti and Giwa-osagie held an old man captive. The man was estimated to be around eighty, and clearly blind, almost deaf. Furthermore, he was a Dagomba, from the northern savannah of

Togoland. It seems that he had collaborated with the Germans. Wood ran to the old man, holding a rifle, and yelling at the Ashanti to back away. Wednesday and Wood ran through the languages they knew, and it seemed that the man, who answered to "Abdulai," knew decent, if heavily accented, German, in addition to his native Dagbani. Unfortunately, Wood's German was limited mostly to basic questions, greetings, demands to surrender or stop, and engineering terms, and could not learn much else from the man. The tattoos and ritual scars on the man seemed to be the result of enslavement in his childhood by Pramprams. Abdulai was the victim of a witch, rather than a witch himself, as Giwa-osagie had claimed. Giwa-osagie protested, pointing at the man's back, where there were marks that vaguely resembled the bones of a bat's wing.

Wednesday said that they could be a bat's wing. But they could be many things, including sails. Or lashes.

Ferguson said that they had one usable holding cell, originally a stable for the old chief engineer's prized horse. Wood locked the old man up, mostly for his own protection, until an actual trial procedure could be established. Giwa-osagie wanted a Dahomey-style Voudon court, while Wednesday rallied for an Ashanti style approach to the process, likely simply to buy time.

Abdulai could not sleep, and was kept calm with copious amounts of wine and beer.

On the 22nd of February, Agya Wuo emerged from the woods, dragging a corpse behind him. Wuo was clearly haggard, not having slept for several days, drenched in rain and sweat, covered in blood and scratches, and undergoing a harrowing ordeal. Wou dropped the body under the wires, and went off to the dugout's ground well, where he bathed himself in the prior night's rainwater.

Wood and Ferguson examined the body. The creature was 5'5", thin, and with a wing span of some twenty feet. It was covered in black fur with white spots, with leathery patches on its wings and legs, which ended in hooked feet[69]. Its face was more like that of an ape, with thick, leathery skin, and it had an oddly squared beard that Wood likened to

---

[69] Shuker, Karl (2014). *The Beasts that Hide from Man: Seeking the World's Last Undiscovered Animals.* Cosimo, Inc. pp. 103

"the statues of the Babylonians." There were scaly ridges over its eyes, and on its legs, along with unnatural metallic spines, which matched it nail-like teeth. Its left thigh and shoulder had deep stab marks, matching the bite of a massive snake – though Wou's rifle-shot, dead in the heart, had brought down the monster.

Ferguson said that it must have been some aberrant, mutated fruit bat, but admitted that this did not have the foxlike face, and such a grotesque mutation from the baseline would have likely killed the creature in utero. Wou had noted that the creature had whimpered like a bat, allowing the hunter to find him inside of a hollow tree. Wood shuttered and flatly admitted that this was a *sasabonsam* - a vampire.

Abdulai was found dead in his cell, a few hours later. Giwa-osagie claimed that he was vindicated, and that Wuo had killed the old man's spirit as it left to terrorize the enemies of Germany, the nation that had freed him from his slavery. Wood noted how cocky the Fon looked, but he could not openly fight his tale. But privately he believed that the old man had succumbed to a heart attack, aggravated by sleeplessness, fear, and drink. Wood and Wednesday privately mourned a man who had died, blind, half-deaf, and illiterate, surrounded by enemies. The other Ashanti celebrated, and Giwa-osagie danced off down the road, payment in hand and a stolen pith helmet over his horn.

"There's no medicine for evil," noted Wednesday.

Members of the newly arrived Ghana Regiment brought the corpse to L.W. Wood's bungalow, where he had J.B. Danquah photograph the corpse on the 22nd of February, often misdated to February 1928. Local Ashanti artists sculpted images of the body, which were featured in the September 1939 edition of *West African Review*. Unfortunately, the body rapidly rotted in the climate, and Wood was forced to preserved it using slap-dash, pickling solutions. The corpse was shipped to England for examination by Knud Christian Andersen, but, in another case of misfortune, or worse, the Danish chiroptologist vanished without a trace in June of 1918, taking the body with him. The photograph, too, was lost by the 1920s, when Montague Summers investigated the case.

Visitors from the Dark.

Outside of the phantom airship flaps of 1886, 1909-1910, and 1913, the 1910s saw the rise of the modern "alien visitation" phenomenon. While it was fairly common to see or interact with the inhabitants of the 'airships,' especially during the 1886 flap, they were invariably eccentric human inventors. At their most exotic, they were vaguely foreign and had oddly advanced technology on their persons. With the 1910s raid, we start see truly inhuman pilots. Their vessels also begin to blur the line; while many are still dirigible-like craft, if advanced and far too maneuvrable, these aliens begin to use the more rigid craft or seemingly ephemeral spheres of light typical of mid-20th century UFOs.

Indeed, several events immediately preceding the 1886 flap are rather otherworldly. Bright lights, the smell of phosphorous, and eerie sounds filled the night skies of New York, New Jersey, and Pennsylvania on April 29, 1885, with witnesses illuminated by strange fires that did not burn, perhaps something like St. Elmo's Fire. Interviews with citizens of Delaware Valley uncovered that various older people recall a similar phenomenon taking place in Pike County in 1836[70].

Director Bonilla of Mexico's Zacatecas Observatory witnessed more than 283 objects cross the face of the sun while monitored sun spot activity on August 12, 1886. The resulting images are claimed to be the earliest photographs of UFOs.

One summer after the "Wallace Tillinghast" airship reports across New England and Maritime Canada, a child in Vodotville, Maryland, a Lawrence J. Crone, saw an massive airship with colored glass windows[71]. He could see the passengers inside watching him, possibly the earliest description of the "Grey" alien: flat, pointed heads without noses or ears, two spots for eyes, and long, "pigeon necks." These beings were described as bearing soft, downy fur, however. Crone called for witnesses, who quickly fled.

---

[70] *The Bucks County Gazette*. Bristol, Pennsylvania. 30 April 1885. Evening Edition.
71 NICAP.

During the turn of the century, Lord Kelvin, Guglielmo Marconi, Nikola Tesla, and David Peck Todd believed that they had detected radio signals that were possibly Martian in origin, though it was possible that Tesla and Marconi were picking up each others signals, or electrical interference from Jovian plasma toruses. In the early 1910s, refining of Marconi's signalling apparatuses lead him to believe that something was sending radio waves from Tau Ceti.

1912 saw a greater frequency of such encounters. Outside Gallipolis, Ohio, a mother and son witnessed a dark object descending into the forest where they picked berries. A figure emerged from the cloud-obscured vehicle as they fled, following the pair. The entity was dark, with a large head or helmet directly resting on broad shoulders, and growled at the mother as she made eye contact with the figure and screamed[72].

J. Allen Hynek recorded the tale of Abram Penner, who was six in 1912. On his farm in Vancouver, British Columbia, Penner encountered a helicopter-like craft (this testimony was collected decades later) and its pilot, visible through its glass cabin. One of the beings seemed to communicate with Penner telepathically. He could understand the words the being thought, but it was otherwise incomprehensible. The creature was humanoid, but with different hands, round, stubby feet, and no elbow or knee joints in their limbs.

On December 24, 1912, outside of Proskuriv, Podolia (now Khmelnytskyi, Ukraine), a village mayor saw a dim machine in a field, attended by a pair of humanoids in usually but military-style uniforms. In an unusually thuggish case of alien abduction, the beings chased the man, and wrestled him to the ground, dragging him back to their vessel and interrogating him with telepathic questioning. Frustrated by his silent resistance, they deposited him by the Riv in Bar, some sixty kilometers from his abduction.

In July, 1913, a farmer in Nuritopia, Australia approached a metallic vehicle in his field. A bald humanoid briefly ducked outside of its window and shot the man with a paralytic ray that left him stunned for some time. The vehicle rapidly departed.

---

[72] Bord, Janet & Colin. *Flying Saucer Review*. Vol. 25, issue 3.

Several days later, according to Donald Keyhoe, a pair of prospectors in the sand fields of the Montana Badlands discovered a silver, domed disc nearly a hundred feet in diameter. It lacked wheels. There were small brown men picking flowers and collecting geological samples. One small man startled them, saying "Peace be with you, my friends," and telling them that they were from an otherworldly culture that monitored Earth for hundreds of years. Unlike many telepathic aliens of contemporary reports, these creatures claimed that they learned English from their spy network, including a circus. The craft departed, only to return the next day. The inhabitants gave one of the prospectors, J.L. Buick, a guided tour the vehicle, five concentric rings with varying air pressures, the outermost serving as a transitional 'airlock' like space. The aliens explained that chemical rockets were insufficient for their needs, and instead used principles of electromagnetism to manipulate and simulate gravity. After escorting Buick outside, the pilots left for the second and final time.

Chilean newspapers reported on a flaming, metallic "bolide" that left a trail of white smoke over Chanco before crashing into the Pacific on February 15, 1914. It appears to have been a massive spectacle, with hundreds of witnesses.

In June, 1914, in Lajoumard Haute Vienne, France, a farmer returning to his home encountered a large, luminous green craft hovering atop a hill some 200 meters away. Several small men entered the craft, and it spiralled into the sky before streaking away. Days after, as dawn broke in Hamburg, Germany, a man named Gustav Herwagen encountered a shining-cigar shaped craft with glowing windows in a field outside of his house. Four white clad "dwarfs," just over a meter tall, returned to the craft. They noticed his approach, and returned to their craft and took off vertically into the sky[73]. A nearly identical encounter occurred the same year in St.-Leonard-De-Noblat, France[74].

---

[73] Vallée, Jacques F. *Passport to Magonia: ON UFOs, Folklore, and Parallel Worlds.* McGraw-Hill. (1969. Reissued 1993).
[74] Hall, Richard H. *From Airships to Arnold: A Preliminary Catalogue of UFO Reports in the Early 20th Century, 1900-1945.* (2000) UFO Research Coalition, Fairfax.

On August 2nd, a pair of women in Strizhov, Russian Empire (now Strzyżów, Poland), witnessed two beings in red suits moving around a gray craft resting in a field. The women fled. Other locals would corroborate their stories, seeing a large object flying through the sky, creating a rustling sound.

The next night, a *pied-noir* in Blida, Algeria watched a glowing sphere land, gently and silently, in his irrigation field, mere meters from him. He dove into cover behind a hedge, watching short men in helmets and red-pink suits exit from the sphere. They rapidly collect soil samples, returned to their craft, and flew off. Several locals supported his story with sightings of a glowing sphere[75].

In the waning days of August, a ten-year-old boy by the name of Arvo Kuoppala and his Swedish grandmother Maria Fält sat in his farmhouse in Alastaro, Finland at noon, when a total eclipse of the sun caught his attention. A burst of wind swept down through the house, and a brilliant globular light shined through the eastern window, where it hovered. An oval aperture opened on the side of the globe, and two humanoid creatures with large, broad heads and friendly eyes became visible. One of them was much shorter and uglier than the other, strikingly gnomish.

Arvo reacted with fright as the taller creature smiled and began to move his mouth without saying anything, but his grandmother calmed him down. The aperture closed. The ship produced a loud thumping sound and rose into the sky, disappearing to the west.

The boy became sick and tired and passed out on his bed. When he awoke, his grandmother eerily began to explain the nature of the creatures. She said that the creatures were not from heaven, but from a distant world, and the ship was simply a shuttle from a "sky ship." She explained that they were more intelligent relatives of humanity who frequently visited us. The question of how she came by this knowledge went unanswered.

On the same day, William Kiehl and seven friends witnessed five small men in light brown coveralls and cubic helmets draw water from Georgian Bay, Ontario using a green cone and some kind of hose. A

---

[75] *Le Forum de L'Ufologie.*

lead gray, five-meter-tall vessel with a silver rim flew off, leaving behind a white trail of water vapor.

In early September, a scavenger at a Pawtucket, Rhode Island landfill witnessed a grey, domed vehicle humming melodically as it hovered in front of a church[76]. Eight short humanoids exited the craft. They appeared to have large heads, and sang harmoniously in an unknown language, recalling a religious choir. They then returned to their vessel and flew away over the church.

Before daybreak on the morning of September 23rd, masonry contractor Vasily Aleksandrovich Sokolov set out from a job-site in a remote Kalmyk village on the border of the Astrakhan Oblast[77]. Not long after bridling his horse, a bright "star" descended from the sky, rapidly decelerating. The vehicle, a fairly standard "cigar UFO," landed in front of him, its bright lights illuminating a brown hull and a kind of underslung, boat-like cabin containing six men. Sokolov retreated to the village, alerting the local Kalmyks. The vehicle swept the village with a blinding light, before shooting off into the sky over Astrakhan. B. Krishtafovich of the Kalmyk Provincial Government alerted St. Petersburg, launching an official investigation into the possibility of German invasion.

In the Summer of 1915, a bell of dark metal descended on a hill in Sulitjelma, Norway[78]. Two large-headed, grey skinned dwarfs in brown coveralls exited the craft, and walked towards the witnesses, smiling. They circled behind the hill and returned to their craft, which flew away. While the beings superficially resembled Greys, they had long, wavy, jet-black hair.

On 29 February 1916, around 4:30 AM, dock workers on Lake Superior observed a large craft, fifty feet wide and a hundred feet long, with a trailing cable soar through the Wisconsin sky. Illuminated by its three lights, a trio of strange men could be seen operating the vessel through its portholes[79].

---

[76] CUFOs Associate Newsletter, Vol. 3, Issue 6
[77] Gershtein, Mikhail (1999). "Mystery of the Astrakhanian Steppes." *Crossroads of Centaurs* Vol. 2.
[78] Braene, Ole Jonny. *Pre-1947 UFO Type incidents in Norway.*

Later in 1916, eight or so little men in blue uniforms and "sailor hats" grasped the brass handrails of a hovering toroid disc in the marshlands of Aldeburgh, England. For roughly five minutes, a Mrs. Whitehead watched the platform rise to a second-story level, and disappeared behind some nearby houses[80].

As 17-year-old John Boback walked along the railroad to Youngstown, Pennsylvania, a heavily-lit, saucer landed in a field some thirty meters away[81]. He stopped to observe the vehicle for roughly two minutes, with its humanoid inhabitants visible through the oblong windows of its dome. The vehicle soon rose vertically into the air, producing a high-pitched whine.

The first days of November 1917 saw the arrival of strange visitors to the sleepy Spanish town of Cambroncino. Nicolas "Colas" Sánchez Martin, a 39-year-old pig farmer, and Maria and Pepa Iglesias encountered strange flying lights above a river as they returned home from market. The sisters fled, but Colas drew his machete and rode his donkey into the shallow river.

The light intercepted Colas, darting forward and coming to a sudden, hovering stop on the opposite side of the river. Every time Colas corrected his course, the light darted in front of him. Colas raised his machete and shouted at the light. The light responded by lunging forward and shocking the donkey, bathing both of them in a strange, irritating glow. Colas struggled to regain control of his mount, and was forced to ride home.

The once healthy man's health rapidly deteriorated, dying nine days later. The attending physician, Victor Sánchez Hoyos, diagnosed him with a sudden pulmonary edema, but later observers believed that he had instead died of acute radiation poisoning.

Not long after, in Peñascosa, Albacete, a farming family, the Alguacils, witnessed a flying saucer with a prominent dome – the craft resembled a hat with an 'H' engraved on its side– extend quadropedal landing gear and settle in a field. Two extraordinarily tall men in silvery

---

[79] Clark, Jerome, *Unexplained! 347 Strange Sightings, Incredible Occurrences, and Puzzling Physical Phenomena*; Detroit, Visible Ink Press; 1993, ISBN 0810394367.
[80] Creighton, Gordon, *Flying Saucer Review*, Vol. 15, issue 1.
[81] Hartle, Orvil. *A Carbon Experiment*.

uniforms disembarked and walked around for a while before turning to the craft.

The sad fate of Colas Sánchez Martin recalls an incident in Maracaibo, Venezuela recorded in the December 18, 1886 issue of *Scientific American*. A bright, humming object appeared from the perpetual thunderstorm of Maracaibo, hovering over a hut. The inhabitants of the hut quickly sustained what we now recognize as severe radiation exposure, while the nearby tries withered and died. An alternate theory is that it was some form of ball lightning that released dangerous levels of ultraviolet radiation.

As a final note, there is an often repeated tale that a 105-year-old pilot named "Peter Waitzrik" made a deathbed confession, claiming that he and his fellow German ace Baron Manfred von Richtofen, the Red Baron, witnessed some manner of advanced, silvery aircraft with orange lights appear out of thin air in front of their triplanes while flying over western Belgium on 13 March 1917. The Baron shot the craft down without resistance. It dropped into the woods below, ejecting a pair of small bald men who fled from the craft. However, the earliest source of this tale is the August 31, 1999 issue of *the Weekly World News*, a tabloid known for joke articles. Likewise, there is no military or civilian record of anyone named Peter Waitzrik who served as a pilot in the First World War.

Mari Lwyd.

"Traditions die hard," wrote Tom Noun. "We awoke to a cold, wet day. I had found, weeks before, the skull of a horse. I was unsure if it belonged to a mare, but I kept it for the Midwinter.

We had a bitter Christmas Eve, without presents or wassail. We only had simple songs by Céleste and Winepress. Our tree was a small pine, uncut, and decorates only by Céleste and Captain Winepresses' baubles of ice and handcrafted tin.

My Mari Lwyd became the most interesting sight for the others; I wore the horse skull within a gas cape's hook, bringing luck while singing in Welsh and stumbling around the camp.

'Wear the horse skull and walk the crooked way.'

Rabbi Venetianer's confusion became its own source of joy.

At midnight, we spotted a strange light in the sky. Our Christmas Star sent us into a state of alarm, as it passed over head. The Geisterritter hid us from its sight. It was a cold white thing encircled by coronas of faint green and red, as if mocking the hues of Anglo-Saxon Yuletide, and sent out a beam of flashing red light at one point. But it was no angel, Loyal or Rebel, naked or haunting a dirigible. It seemed somewhat mechanical, as Céleste and the Captain could sense mechanical materials and heat, while the Crow-King sensed a vague and inhuman mind. It passed overhead without incident.

The Captain let out a dark chortle when Siegfried asked if it was from another world, and said that the Francis Younghusband had a theory of contact by cosmic rays. Winepress noted that the explorer had struggled with a lingering guilt over his *de facto* invasion of Tibet, for which he was belatedly awarded the Knight Commandership of the Order of the Star of India just this year. He wandered up a mountain, had a revelation of universal brotherhood and love, abandoning his Evangelical past and dabbling in Aryanism, spiritualism, a belief in the divinity of all people, and finally telepathic experimentation in the high hills of Kashmir. He had projected himself out into the universe, only to be detected and penetrated by a ray conjured up by the giants of Altair, an alien species with transluscent skin and vast mental powers. Altair was an awakened, enlightened world, with living creatures and the world itself in harmony, guided by a figure that can best be described as an Otherworldly Christ.

I quietly noted where I remembered the name – Younghusband was the man who put the bloody Blake poem to song in 'Jersualem.' Not even the true bit about the Giant Albion, but that insipid legend that Christ walked at Glastonbury."

A diary entry dated to December 26th noted that "we saw our 'Christmas star' once more. It is a flying machine, neither aeroplane nor rigid airship. Walking the crooked way will not bring us luck this season – there is not a thing of magic, but a thing of science."

The Serbian Prophet.

War on the Serbian front was perhaps the most vicious theatre of the war, not sparing civilians. While the powers of the West burned with hatred for each other, the Balkans are home to a special kind of ethnic strife that never really dies down, leading to some of the most appalling tragedies of this war.

Having fought two wars in the 1910s already, the battle hardened Serbian Army put up a decent fight against the combined forces of Austria-Hungary, Germany, and the Ottomans. An Austro-Hungarian monitor on the Danube shelled Belgrade on July 29th, the opening salvo of the war. The use of artillery favored the invaders, as the Serbs lacked effective units, and had only a single heavy ammunition factory, which could only churn out about a hundred shells a day.

Serbia won the first Allied victory of the War, the Battle of Cer, and its forces pushed back the Austro-Hungarians with such success at the Battle of Kolubara that Kaiser Wilhelm II actually congratulated Serbian Field Marshal Radomir Putnik on the victory.

However, in 1915 Serbian forces faltered and the Kingdom fell under occupation by the Austro-Hungarians and Bulgarians. The Serbian Army suffered huge losses before fleeing to the safety of several Greek isles, dropping from 420,000 to 100,000 men. The Austro-Hungarians, who blamed Serbia for the war, and the Bulgarians, who hated Serbs because it's the Balkans and everyone hates each other, carried out systematic atrocities against the occupied Serbs, often under official orders[82]. The Austro-Hungarians massacred Serbian prisoners of

---

[82] Particularly infamous is the following document: "K. u. K. [*kaiserlich und königlich* – Imperial and Royal, referring to the Habsburg's monarch's dual role as Emperor of Austria and King of Hungary] 9 Korps Kommando. Directions for conduct towards the population in Serbia. The war brings us into a country inhabited by a population animated by fanatical hate against us, into a country where murder, as the catastrophe of Sarajevo has proved, is recognised even by the upper classes who glorify it as heroism. Towards such a population all humanity and all kindness of heart are out of place; they are even harmful, for any consideration, such as it is sometimes possible to show in war, would in this case endanger our own troops. Consequently I order that during the whole course of the war the greatest severity, the greatest harshness and the greatest mistrust be observed towards everyone. In the first place I will not allow

war on principle, while the Bulgarians took out their rage against the civilians, raping women, burning down towns and orchards, and making a wall of skulls out of the people of Surdulica. Once the winter typhus epidemic of 1914 (which killed 150,000 people, making it the worst typhus outbreak in recorded history) and the later Spanish Flu are factored in, the Kingdom of Serbia lost 1,100,000 citizens during the War, out of a pre-War population of four and a half million. Of the survivors, over a hundred thousand disabled veterans and a half million orphans faced an uncertain future. Serbia lost over 27% of its population, and 57% of its male population, by far the greatest loss ratio incurred by any belligerent in the war. When the *New York Times* quoted Bulgarian Prime Minister Vasil Radoslavov's 1917 pronouncement that "Serbia ceased to exist," he was not contested.

In the wake of the war, Serbs looked for some meaning in this *tremendum*. One form of comfort was the discovery of a set of prophecies that at least evinced some structure to the arc of history, no matter how cruel it could be.

Illiterate Serbian peasant Mitar Tarabić, who lived between 1829 and 1899 in the village of Kremna, allegedly foretold the crises that lead

inhabitants of the enemy's country, armed but not in uniform, who are met either alone or in groups, to be taken prisoners. No consideration is to prevent their execution. ... In going through a village, they (i. e. the hostages) are to be conducted if possible until the queue (sic) has passed through, and they will be executed without any question if a single shot is fired on the troops in the neighbourhood. The officers and soldiers will keep a rigourous watch over every inhabitant and will not allow him to put his hand in his pocket, which probably conceals a weapon. In general they will observe the greatest severity and harshness. The ringing of bells is absolutely forbidden and the bells are to be unhung; in general every steeple is to be occupied by a patrol. Divine service is only to be permitted at the request of the inhabitants and only in the open air in front of the church. No sermon is to be permitted on any condition. A platoon ready to fire will be kept near the church during divine service. Every inhabitant who is found outside a village, especially in the woods, will be looked upon as a member of a band who has hidden his weapons, which we have no time to look for. Such people are to be executed if they appear in the slightest degree suspicious. Once more discipline, dignity, but the greatest severity and harshness."

to the First World War. His prophecies, recorded by a local priest, claimed that "After the assassination of the king and queen," here, Alexander I and Draga Obrenović - "the Karađorđevićs will come to power. Then we will again make war with the Turks. Four Christian nations will attack Turkey, and our border will become the Lim river. Then we shall finally conquer and avenge ourselves on Kosovo."

Indeed, Draga and Alexander I Obrenović were assassinated in the May Overthrow of 1903 by army officers under the command of Colonel Dragutin Dimitrijević. Dimitrijević, also known as "Apis" or "the Bee" due to his energy, eventually became the head of the Black Hand that backed the assassination of Franz Ferdinand.

House Obrenović was a staunch ally of Austria-Hungary, and their extinguishing shifted the tides of Yugoslavian politics. Dimitrijević was in the pay of Russia at the time, and the Russian-and-French-aligned Petar Karađorđević was installed as Peter I, the last king of Serbia, and war broke out between Turkey and a coalition of Serbia, Montenegro, Bulgaria, and Greece.

Tarabić also predicted that a time will come when evil would prevail and ravage the earth, with men dying in droves. Soon, Serbia would be forever changed after rule by a mysterious "him" - suggested to be either Tito or Peter I by those who buy into Tarabić's prophetic power- and ruled by a new, republican government. And then, though the wars of old would be forgotten and the people will again know wealth, Serbs will fall into factionalization, deny that they are Serbs, and brother will make war against brother. Some unholy force, described like the Devil, will bed with Serbian wives, sisters, and mothers, and sire children among the Serbs, evil creatures unseen since the world was young. Those women who are untouched by this evil will bear only weaklings, and Serbia will not give birth to a true hero for ages.

Those who believe that the "Him" is Tito believe this refers to the Balkan War of the 1990s, with the evil offspring and weak generation referring to the killers spawned by the conflict and those disenfranchised children who inherited the crumbling Balkans. Those who hold that Peter I is "him" believe that the infighting between "Serbian brothers" refers to the horrors of the Balkan front of the War, and the evil offspring of the devil unseen since the early earth refer to the nephilim.

Tarabić also predicted that the world would soon be plagued by a mysterious pandemic that would know no cure, men will soon build mechanical boxes that display images and write books using only numbers and think themselves geniuses, that man would soon travel to other worlds and find nothing but lifeless wastelands. He also optimistically predicted that one day mankind will rediscover the true power that lies within themselves, and will regret that they ever forgot this greatness, because such "knowledge is so simple."

Other prophets arose in the period, to less note. The Polish psychologist Julian Ochorowicz subjected his patient Stanisława Tomczyk to hypnotic experimentation in 1908-1909. Allegedly, this gave rise to an entity called "Little Stasia," who claimed to not be a spirit, and could probably be described as some sort of regressive personality. According to Ochorowicz, Little Stasia possessed psychokinetic power, rigging roulette games and dice rolls and stopping clocks remotely via invisible rays projected from her fingers. In one surreal incident, Little Stasia announced that she would produce a photograph of herself – Ochorowicz was instructed by Tomczyk's alter ego to enter an empty, completely dark room alone and take a picture. When developed, the image was that of a doppelganger of Tomczyk, with an empty, menacing facial expression. Tomczyk and Dr. Ochorowicz traveled to Paris to demonstrate her psychokinesis to one Professor Theodore Flournoy, and spent the next several years in labs attempting to recreate these psychic powers. One of the supervising doctors was the Nobel-prize winning physiologist Charles Richet, who had previously worked alongside Ochorowicz observing the then world-famous medium Eusapia Palladino, the host of the popular Warsaw seances of 1893 and 1894. Palladino claimed that her powers rapidly diminished and finally failed her just before her death in 1918, though skeptics believed it was simply the increasingly controlled conditions she was subjected to lessened her ability to engage in sleight-of-hand – she had previously demanded that her channeling sessions only occur in darkened rooms, and her ability to manifest forces and ectoplasmic objects seemed inversely proportionate to how well lit she was.

An American medium named Arthur Ford claimed to have heard phantom voices whispering the names of his company compatriots doomed to die in battle or, later, of the Spanish flu epidemic. He would grimly record them and match them to the casualty lists[83].

At the age of 16, Argentine artist Benjamín Solari Parravicini allegedly received visions from angels and fairies, who told him that a war would begin in 1914. These entities would soon be joined by his guardian angel, José Fray de Aragón, and his white-eyed Nordic aliens abductors. Between 1936 and 1972, Parravicini produced thousands of cryptic "psychographic" drawings that allegedly predicted the launch of Laika, the rise of Fidel Castro, satellites, television, artificial insemination, and the two terrorist attacks on the World Trade Center. Though he also claimed that evolution would be disproved and that humanity actually came from another world, and many of these prophecies require a liberal interpretation of the drawings. For example, the claimed 1939 prediction of attacks on the Twin Towers actually show the Statue of Liberty and read "The freedom of North America will lose its light. Its torch won't illuminate like yesterday, and the monument will be attacked two times"; applying this the World Trade Center rather than Lady Liberty requires some mental gymnastics.

Through the horrors of the Second World War and the Greek Civil War, Professor George Papahatzis poured over the notes of his late teacher "Paul Amadeus Dienach," translating them from the German. On Christmas Eve, 1944, the notes were confiscated and never returned, under suspicion that Papahatzis was secretly corresponding with German forces. But Papahatzis kept his nearly complete translation, and visited Zurich a dozen times during the Fifties and Sixties to confirm the details of Dienach's life, dodging the probing questions and intimidation of Freemasons, the Theosophical Society, the Teutonic Lodge, and other mystics, who did not want the diary spread.

Despite his Swiss-Austrian nationality, Paul Dienach had allegedly fought in the German Army during the Great War. Allegedly, of course, being the key word, as Papahatzis claims that this was an alias used by his teacher to distance himself from his past, a deeply suspicious claim that leads one to believe that he was fabricated by Papahatzis. But in any

---

[83] Ford, Arthur, with Margueritte Harmon Bro. (1958). *Nothing So Strange: The Autobiography of Arthur Ford.* New York: Harper & Row.

case, real or fictional, Dienach's spent the final months of the Great War comatose from the effects of Encephalitis Lethargica. His health never recovered, and he fell back into a year long coma in 1920. After his recovery in 1921, he traveled to Greece to teach French and German, hoping the climate might help him. In his free time, he "rewrote" the diary that he kept during his year long coma. He would die not long after its completion, bequeathing the volume to his favorite student, Papachatzis.

Slowly working his way through Dienach's Swiss German notes, Papachatzis soon realized that his teacher underwent a period of astral travel to the year 3906 AD, coming to inhabit the body of a man named Andreas Northam, who had lost consciousness after a vehicular accident.

Now, one issue in Dienach's tale is that its details are astounding if they are indeed from a man who died in 1923, but unremarkable if we assume it is a work of fiction developed up until the 1970s. Dienach's language was identified by his doctors as an archaic dialect of German, a language that was long abandoned. The world's primary language was English, as American culture had come to dominate the world after a second world war and the ever present threat of nuclear war. The world had grown overpopulated and globalized. Family structures fell apart as an ignoble, materialistic, technology-obsessed culture dominated. The late 20th century saw a rise in anti-globalist violence and terrorism, and young people became obsessed with idols – actors, the idol rich, and other ignoble celebrities. People lived without dignity, and the family structure fell apart into nihilistic, selfish cruelty, to the point that the world suffered from a neuropsychiatric pandemic. The world experienced race wars, a Latin American colonization of Africa, a Christianized Israel dominating the Middle East, the northern latitudes warming to the point that Scandinavians and Russians migrate towards the pole, and Australians, New Zealanders, and South Africans inhabit Antarctica. In 2204, a group of dissatisfied idealists colonize Mars, but the settlement failed after sixty years. Society rapidly decayed, and racial wars erupted across the globe, leading the extermination of multiple races. However, an age of enlightenment began in the death throws of that century, inspired by a sudden revelation of a simple man by the name of Alexis Falke, a new philosophy known as the *Nibelwerk*, at least in Dienach's German reckoning of the philosophy. By the time of Dienach's projection, the world had reorganized into an anarcho-socialist utopia, with a new form of humanity known as *Homo occidentalis novis*.

Shortly after the end of the Second World War, rough translations of the diaries circulated in the occult circles of Athens, and Papachatzis faced a great deal of pressure when he published the diaries in 1972 as "the Valley of the Roses," including threats from the Orthodox Church[84].

Time.
"Evvel zaman içinde kalbur saman içinde pire tellal deve berber iken, ben anamın beşiğini tıngır mıngır sallar iken…"

Ender Hoca was a professor, translator, literary editor, ethnologist and philologist specializing in Turkology, Iranology, and Arabic studies. In 1915, he was completing a manuscript on the humor and storytelling methods of the Hemshinli people of Turkey, incomplete sections of which were found in his papers. He had continued to edit this and other drafts of his ethnographic works in his spare time well into 1918, but never got around to publishing it. He lived among the Hemshinli for much of 1914, and carried with him a master-crafted pistol of Hemshinli design during the War.

Ender belonged to *Teşkilât-ı Mahsusa*, the Special Organization, a highly secretive branch of the Ottoman War Department most likely created by Enver Pasha at an unknown date during the pre-war build-up for the purpose of suppressing Arab nationalism and Western interventionism and imperialism. Süleyman Askeri Bey was placed in command of a reformed Special Organization by Enver Pasha in November of 1913, though its first head was likely Civinis Efendi, who once served Czarina Catherine II. The reformed organization's central command relocated to Erzurum, and quickly began carrying out the

---

[84] Sirigos, Achilleas (Editor). (2015). *Chronicles From The Future: The amazing story of Paul Amadeus Dienach*. This Way Out Productions.

relocation of Greek men to forced labor camps. Ali Bey Başhampa would replace Süleyman Askeri after the latter's death in April 1915 and held this position until war's end, while Eşref Sencer Kuşçubası may have been the Arabian and North African operational director, though he is not mentioned in the military archives. If he did serve, he would be replaced in the last two years of the war by Hüsamettin Ertürk. The Organization evolved into the Worldwide Islamic Revolt and the National Defense Society after the war.

The Special Organization drew its thirty-thousand-strong membership from the ranks of academia, physicians, engineers, and pardoned prisoners known as *başıbozuk*. These *başıbozuk*, traditionally rendered "bashibazouk" and meaning 'wounded head' or 'leaderless' were irregulars notorious for their expendable nature and undisciplined, brutish behavior. Indeed, they were often unpaid, expected to survive off what they could loot from their victims.

Ender was one such operative drawn from the Turkish university system, given a commission with the Organization on 15 December 1914 after volunteering to serve his country at the beginning of November. He wrote of his relatively quiet experiences during the early months of 1915, with the major source of drama the suspicion cast upon him due to his claimed abilities and mixed heritage. "They [his superiors in the Special Organization, who are addressed only by nicknames and titles in Ender's journal] called me many things – Operative Eleven, the Storyteller, the Liar, and, with disdain, the Circassian. My grandmother was a Circassian of the Ubykh Tribe, a refugee from the Russian empire's expansionism in the Caucasus, and that was enough to stain my reputation among the most extreme members of the Organization. I had done thesis work among the Western Circassians, and proudly wear a long, loose-sleeved bandoleered coat of Cherkess make, dyed a princely white, along with the traditional dagger and the *Shashka* [sabre]. They are a disciplined race of courageous warriors and fair women so famed in the west for their beauty that Blumenbach elevated them to the Platonic epitome of the Caucasian -and human – race. Said to be the very image of Allah's First Woman, Blumenbach counterfactually named the white race after their mountainous point of origin.

But I am a true Turk, born south of the village of Illuh[85] with the name Göker – named Ender by my wife – of the Qaji tribe of the Ghuzz, as was Osman the Great."

Ender became a specialist in social oddities and unusual resistance among the minorities of the Empire, rising to promise when he easily flushed out pockets of Cappadocian Greek resistance from the underground city of Derinkuyu, which he had mapped in his undergraduate years at Istanbul's Darülfünun-ı şahane. This troglodyte complex was said to have been built by giants aeons before its recording by Xenophon, and spared the locals from the deprivation of Tamerlane. His actual place in the command structure is hard to gauge, but he employed an Alawite aide-de-camp named Berker, and a Dönme researcher and diviner named Talut, an expert in mysticism with a private spy network in Russia, Greece, and the Polish regions. His two-dozen strong staff and anomalous research team set themselves up in the Bakırpaşa Mansion in Bakırköy, Istanbul, with another branch at the so-called Perili Kosk (Haunted Mansion) on Istanbul's Baltalimani Hisar Street. While Ender seemed to keep quiet about his activities, he felt it was important to record one incident in particular.

"I went on leave after the Austro-New Zealand attack on Gelibolu was repulsed. I went to see my wife and my daughter in Bâlâ. This was one of the great torments of my time in the army. I could not write to my wife because she was illiterate, so we had to make do with tri-yearly leave visits. My lovely wife made the perfect meal and kept the most wondrous household, a palace in five rooms. She really tried, but I couldn't muster up any romantic notions. Ever since Gelibolu, I've felt distant. It was that Australian boy's intestines spilled on my feet. The image that still haunts me is the boy looking up at me, gasping, with the cold, flat eyes of a land-bound fish. The machine gun fire had destroyed his genitals, shredding him from hip to navel. The boy lived for another minute and a half, just lying there, before I slew him.

That's behind me. That was in another place at another time in another lifetime. Like a snake shedding its skin, leaving behind its superficial scars in the process.

---

[85] Iluh was a minor village until oil was discovered nearby in the 1950s; the area was then renamed Batman, after the nearby river.

I returned to my command post with a great emptiness in me.

I was sent one hundred and twenty kilometers west of Aleppo, to a rocky inlet the shore of the Mediterranean Sea. There, I came across a village where there should not have been one, just as Talut had inferred and the outriders had confirmed.

I dismounted and watered my horse, pulled out my satchel, and walked into town. The streets were stone and the buildings wood and clay, long-standing and well-weathered, the simple residences of olive farmers and the owners of a cherry orchard. The only structures of note were the *hilwah*, the Prayer-House, and a grain silo.

Two dozen men walked the streets, most with mustaches, some wearing baggy *shirwals* and others in Western trousers, most with red and white checkered keffiyehs and a couple wearing fezes. A handful of children played and screamed until an old woman in a long black dress hushed them.

I closed my eyes and listened for the sound of war, and found myself drawn to the nicest house in town, on a rocky hill overlooking apple-covered slopes leading into the sea. Nobody in town reacted to me, even as I rapped on the door.

I was answered by a woman in an apron-covered blue dress with a white *naqab* wrapped over her hair. Her green eyes, far lighter than my own, shined like emeralds held up to the light. She was tall and full-faced, and unexpectedly young and beautiful, incredibly so.

'Good day, madam. Would you happen to be Sahar Halabi?' I asked. Halabi was Arabic for someone of Aleppine extraction – her family had presumably migrated from Aleppo a century or so prior, perhaps during the plague and the cholera outbreaks of the 1820s or the anti-Christian mob riots and Janissary coup of 1850[86].

She held the door open with one hand, and wiped flour from the other across her apron. She looked somewhat alarmed, but not yet frightened.

'I don't like being alone with men who aren't my kin,' she said. She reached up to slide a strand of hair back into place under the *naqab*, leaving a streak of powder across her forehead.

---

[86] These dates have been Westernized from the original Islamic calendar.

I smiled at that, and she laughed in embarrassment.

'I am here in my capacity as an agent of the Sublime Ottoman State, Sahar *Hanımefendi*,' I said. 'We are going to speak.'

She nodded, and her smile collapsed. She lead me into her home, a humble, spartan affair with a low wooden table in the center of the room, surrounded on all sides by cushions and rugs. A long, high table set in front of a well-stocked pantry held a coffee maker, wax-wrapped goat cheese, bags of burghal and rice, and old bottles filled with sesame and olive oil. Next to the table stood her most expensive possession, a treadle-powered rotary hook sewing machine.

'Is this a search?' she asked.

'No,' I said. 'I only wish to talk. You may sit. Return to work, if you wish.'

She knelt down, resting her shins on a cushion, and resumed kneading the dough left on the table. Without looking up, she told me there was already some coffee in the decanter if I wanted any. I declined her offer.

'How long have you been living here?' I asked.

She hesitated for a moment, her eyes flashing up to the ceiling, and said, 'All of my life.'

'You had to think about that,' I said.

'I've never been good at remembering things about myself, to be honest,' she said. 'I remember my marriage day, the day I was thrown from a horse, the birth of my kids, and their kids...the rest is a blur.'

'About those grandchildren,' I said, trying to phrase my question perfectly. 'This is not mere flattery, *Hanımefendim;* it is hard to believe that a woman such as yourself could have grandchildren.'

She stopped kneading, looked up at the ceiling again. She tapped her index finger against her pursed lips, shrugged, and returned to her work.

'I never really thought about it,' she said, distracted. 'It doesn't make much sense, but most things don't.'

'How can you not ask yourself these questions?' I said.

'I'm not the kind of person who has to question everything. I like things the way they are,' she said. 'You're always squinting, like the sun is in your eyes, or like you are sizing up a merchant to see if he will cut your throat.'

'When were you born?' I asked.

'Early in the year,' she said. 'It was rather windy, I remember them saying.'

'What year?' I asked.

'What a rude question to ask of a woman,' she said. 'I'm old enough, that's all you need to know.'

'I need to know, and I think you need to know,' I said, opening up my satchel and rummaging through it.

'Why is this so important to the State that they had to send you all the way out here?'

'Simple curiosity,' I said, pulling out the paperwork. 'You are an anomaly.'

I got on one knee and held the papers out right under her nose.

'Is this you?' I asked.

'Sahar Halabi, born to Mansur and Hawaa Halabi in this village, notified in the Aleppo Vilayet,' she said. 'I do not know who else it could be.'

'Read the date of birth,' I demanded.

'Oh, you're right, that is embarrassing,' she said.

'You were born on the first of Şaban in the year of the Hijra 1274 [17 April 1858],' I said. 'You don't look like a woman in who is nearly sixty.'

'Thank you,' She shrugged again. 'I must be blessed. God be praised.'

She began cutting and spinning the dough into circles.

'Are you going to fine me?' she asked. 'Are you a tax collector?'

I denied that.

'Good,' she said. 'Will you be returning to Aleppo soon, or do you need a place to stay for the evening? I will grill a few more aubergines for you. You look like a man who can eat. Big and strapping... I am sorry that we have no meat. There is no butcher in our village, and the goats are better used for milk.'

'Thank you for your kindness, but I will be leaving shortly,' I said, playing with the tassel of my fez. I shifted it to the left. 'So these holes in your life story don't concern you at all.'

She smashed up two cloves of garlic with a stone mortar and pestle.

'There's holes in every story if you look hard enough,' she said. 'Don't question them. You have to let yourself enjoy the telling.'

'This is your life, *Hanımefendim*,' I said. 'And you have no curiosity whatsoever.'

She made a short humming noise, looked up at me again, and shook her head.

'Is it true that *al-Muwahhidun* believe in "reason above all?" The Druze educate yourselves in the great Greeks,' I said. 'But it appears that you are as mad as your prophet.'

'Al-Hakim bi-Amrih Alla may have been mad,' she said, not losing her temper. 'But an incarnation of God would have to be mad. Imagine how stressful that would be, being God. It would ruin my head. But being crazy doesn't make one wrong. I like my place of madness. We look after each other here.'

'The Child of Maruf saw the light-' I started to say, until a sharp pain shot through my skull, and something pushed my head back. Sahar cringed, clutched her head, and closed her eyes so hard her eyelids wrinkled up.

'I don't know what that was, but never do that again,' she mumbled.

'Well, that confirms my theory,' I said.

'What theory?' she asked.

'That you're the reason that it's hard to tell my tales in this region,' I said. 'You are interfering with the truth.'

'What truth?' she snapped. There was fury in her eyes, and painful pressure and buzzing built up in my ears, with a sickness stirring in my stomach.

'Explain what happened in 1837, Sahar,' I said. 'Explain to me how this village still stands.'

'Nothing happened!' she said.

'This village was depeopled and the population relocated so that a naval base could be built along the shoreline.'

'Then where is it?' she said. 'I don't see soldiers or sailors! I don't see buildings or boats!'

'The project was canceled,' I said.

'Fine, fine, then tell me where the people are?' she said. 'If this is all a lie, someone would have told me before you!'

'The Kurdish soldiers and the janissaries assigned to handle the relocation had disciplinary issues,' I said, my voice softening.

'Disciplinary issues?' she asked. 'What disciplinary issues?'

'I tried to piece together what happened. The troops overreacted to some act of resistance...They never returned to base. We found them months later in the wilderness, starved to death after eating nothing but dirt and rubbish. They were a two day march out of base in fair spring weather, and looted food from this village was found in their rucksacks, uneaten. Inexplicable. Until now.'

'Are you saying that I killed them?' she whispered.

'I was implying that,' I said.

She stood up, slowly, painfully, her breath labored and weak. Her eyebrows rose like dead fish to the top of a tank.

'I killed them, didn't I?' she said. 'I lead them astray... I made them think that they could eat sand and stone...I avenged this village...None of this is real, is it? My sons and grandchildren, the town...'

Her voice choked up, and she fell silent.

The mask fell away. Her hair whitened in an instant, thinning and curling, weakening and breaking. Her skin sagged, and her once bright eyes dulled and clouded like water mixed with milk. Her left nostril peeled away, becoming an arch of scar tissue that cut deep across her nose all the way to the purple edge of her right eyelid.

She stumbled outside, and let out a soft croak of a sigh. The rising wind swallowed it up, and the town was nothing but rubble and dust.

'I wasn't looking for an answer,' she said in a cracking, time-ravaged voice. 'Simply a place to call home.'

'I'm sorry,' I said. 'But you needed to know the truth.'

'I doubt that,' she said. 'How is this better?'

'It isn't. I will not justify this selfishness. I, and I alone, needed you to know the truth,' I said. 'We are of the same kind. You lie to yourself, and the world comforts you. I lie to the world, and the world truly believes. Your lies were interfering with my lies. That is all.'

She sat down on a large stone, her face pained and joints audibly popping. She had been using sixty-year-old limbs as though she were still in her prime, and all that differed time had come to collect on its debts. Self-delusion is powerful, but time is the supreme law of life, and can only be denied for so long.

She pressed a balled-up fist against her chest, applying pressure. Her jaw flapped down, and her head quaked.

'Your lies and tales become truth,' she said, so flatly that I could not tell whether it was a statement or question.

'Yes,' I said, taking a seat next to her.

'Then damn the truth,' she said. 'Please, *effendim*, lie to me.'

I whispered in her ear, a long, sad tale with a short, happy ending. She looked into the setting sun and the shining purple waters of the Mediterranean. There was a final illusion; to the north, the great Mount Hermon arose, the Jabal al-Shaikh, the seat of Druze authority. She smiled. The mountain faded as her eyes closed.

Her head collapsed against my shoulder. I buried her under the rubble of her town, in an unmarked cairn."

Bulgaria.

It can't be said enough how unappreciated Bulgaria was, even by its Romanian neighbors. Germany was the young military powerhouse, Austro-Hungary was the aging, decaying, diverse empire, the Ottoman Sultinate was the exotic empire of the East, while the Kingdom of Bulgaria was simply wedged in the eastern power bloc, having joined the Central Powers in October 1915 in an effort against Serbia.

After the First Balkan War of 1912, the Balkan League that expelled the Ottoman Empire from Southeastern Europe signed the Treaty of London, breaking up the won territory between Greece, Serbia, Montenegro, and Bulgaria. The Second Balkan War began on June 16, 1913, after Bulgaria demanded to redraw the borders of Macedonia, which had been decided by Serbia and Greece alone, probably over a cup of weird, gritty coffee. In the resulting Treaty of Bucharest, Bulgaria lost more land than it had gained in the First Balkan War, especially to the Ottomans and the Romanians. Also, France and Russia hated Bulgaria for this destabilizing incident, closing the door to an alliance with the Entente.

The humiliated and devastated Kingdom of Bulgaria stayed neutral during 1914, wary of war against Russia. They were desirable allies for both sides – the Bulgarian army remained strong for the nation's size, and it was a geographic linchpin of the Eastern Front – but nobody wanted to acquiesce to their territorial claims against four other nations in the Balkan powder keg. The major powers really hoped that the Balkans would finally settle down after the War, and carving off pieces of four nations for the benefit of one sounded like a horrible idea to everyone.

By 1915, the Central Power's success seemed to open the door to Bulgarian territorial gains, so an alliance appeared profitable. On the other hand, Russia. But in the end, the Bulgarians hated the Serbs more than they loved not being killed by Russians, so they joined the Central Powers in 1915. This opened up a vital trade route between Germany and the Ottoman Empire, and put a fatal amount of pressure on both Romania and Serbia. The Bulgarian campaign met with a great deal of initial success before being bogged down in trench warfare like everyone else.

The Allies launched the Monastir Offensive against the Bulgarian First Army in August 1916 in an attempt to tie up the Bulgarians so the Romanians could mobilize. The Germans and eventually the Ottomans moved in the support the Bulgarians in the Macedonian Front.

By November 18th, the Germans began to fall back, forcing the Bulgarians to regroup near the Chervena Stena. The exhausted Entente forces could not break through their lines. The Front basically frozen in place by winter, and on 11 December 1916, General Joffre canceled the offensive. Allied casualties, mostly Serbian, numbered roughly 50,000, with 80,000 more dying or removed from the fray do to illness – all in all, a third of Entente forces in the Macedonian front became casualties of the Offensive. A massive failure, the Allies only seized fifty kilometers and failed to crush Bulgaria or defend Romania. The Bulgarian and German casualties numbered roughly 61,000, considered acceptable due to how outnumbered their soldiers were by the Entente.

Eventually, the Allies formed a coalition to break the Macedonian Front, causing the Bulgarian Army to launch an rebellion, declaring a Bulgarian Republic in Radomir. Bulgaria sought an armistice on September 29, 1918. Czar Ferdinand of Bulgaria abdicated on October 1918, narrowly avoiding the hot new Eastern European trend of Czar-killing.

Bell-Ringers.

"Just after New Year's Day, we crossed the border into Bulgaria at Tsaribrod[87] from occupied Pirot, moving some fifty-five kilometers Southeast to make camp at an ancient heap of stone. There was something about it that seemed comforting to us. We settled in. Céleste and Gottlieb had an idea about sterilizing some creek water with ultraviolet light, inspired by a project in Marseilles, from before the war.

Earlier, on the Danube, we encountered a community of Russian exiles who seemed to universally drive coaches. Most seemed to be from Bucharest, but they moved to the Rumanian-Bulgarian frontier for the war effort. They were a bizarre sect called the White Doves, who did not reproduce, for they believed coitus was the Mark of Cain and the source of Original Sin, with the forbidden fruits of Paradise grafted onto their body in the obvious rude positions. They were also known as the Skoptsy, the "castrated," as they underwent a truly horrible series of rites known as the Greater and Lesser Seals, applying hot irons and knives to all erotic organs. They spoke in high-pitched voices, and man and woman all looked like haggard boys. They did not seem too friendly, but had ties to some other Great Russians in the region, the red-haired Lipoveni [Lippovans] of Bulgaria, and gave us safe over-land directions. We purchased provisions and automobile parts from them, and tried not to scream.

As Céleste and the Captain prepared to fix the ambulance, only to be disturbed by the sudden appearance of bell-ringers, men Venetianer identified as *Kukeri* or *Kukari*. Gottlieb said that they reminded him of

[87] Now part of Serbia, ceded in the 1920 Treaty of Neuilly, renamed Dimitrovgrad.

the Alpine *Kausentreiben*. They were some pagan relic, dressed in sheepskins and belts covered in bells, their faces masked with the wooden skulls of snarling animals. Three of them were in shaggy wool costumes resembling those of the wildmen – I have seen those before, in more sophisticated forms, on the Lilim, ancestral recall of the other men. There was a single girl among their ranks, wearing a grass skirt that made her seem almost Polynesian.

One held goats on leashes, seemingly being lead to a slaughter. My heart went out to them – war goats were something of a Welsh military tradition, ever since wild goats wandered into camps during the American revolution. There was a Welsh Regimental Goat at Mons and Ypres that won the 94 Star, the War, and the Victory Medal, a billy named Taffy IV, descended from the herds gifted by the Shah of Persia. I read in *The Sphere* that he died in '15, at Givenchy, I think. Poor, poor thing.

The procession walked in twilight, so the holy sun would not find them upon the road, and threw stones at the cairn. A primal sense of oneness with humanity filled me; these men drew upon the same Aryan foundation as the Mari Lwyd, across millennia and Celtic-Slavic divisions in two far corners of Europe.

There are so many tribes in this part of the continent that it renders the histories of Celts, Germans, and Latins clean and clear. I understand the clash of Romans and Goths, Gael and Saxon. I know where these differences derive and the borders lie.

I really cannot even begin to understand the difference between a Serb and a Croat, a Slovak and a Czech, Roumanians and Moldaians and Wallachs and Bessarabians, Bulgars and Lipovans, Poles and Silesians, Kashubians, and Lemko, Great Russians, White Russians, and Little Russians. But perhaps those divisions strengthen the need to retain those old ancestral rites and particularities.

But there followed an unsettling revelation. This ritual is intended for the arrival of spring, though it could be invoked to drive away evil spirits. They predicted our coming. They were fearful, and mad enough to invoke the rites of spring in the heart of winter.

It was bad magic. Improper magic. Magic that calls down punishment. Unfated, unforgiven...unforgivable.

One of the Bell-Ringers leading the procession spotted us among the crowd, and turned to face us, but his expression was illegible behind the ram mask.

The Crow-King quietly ordered Gottlieb to follow the ram."

Siegfried wrote that, he "pursued the odd reveler down the dirt road to a modest house where the parading men disrobed and returned to their everyday attire. The man under the ram was a simple looking man of somewhat advanced age, likely in his late fifties. He was stout, balding, with dark black eyebrows and a wide nose. A crucifix and a pair of medallions hung from his neck, one of the Virgin and the other of a saint. The other men talked, walking off in pairs or small groups. The Ram, however, stayed behind, quiet and morose. I assumed this was his property.

He began muttering to himself, and went to his cabinet. He slipped chains around his neck, and began to mutter clearer – it appeared to be a chant. I audibly gasped as he pulled out a bottle of blood.

He heard me. He stared at a point not far from my head, and approached the spot. I moved, but the tight quarters and the fear of being caught caused me to stumble and drag a chair with my boot.

He called out a word like 'Kroi-ak' several times, and invoked what was clearly Mary and Christ and Saints Dimitri and George.

I moved around the corner, and decided that fleeing would only cause more problems for the villages. I became visible, went to my knees, and raised my hands.

He was horrified, both by my sudden appearance and my appearance; I could see that my albino skin only hurt the case for my humanity.

He used that word again, 'Krojak,' pointed the open bottle of blood at me. My eyes shifted from the bottle to his face. He looked perplexed. He drew closer, raising his medallions and chanting, until he gently prodded my lips with the lip of the wine bottle. I obviously refused to drink, and reeled back in disgust. He fell silent, his eyes narrowed, and the corner of his lips turned up.

I realized what he thought I was.

'Ya nyet vampir, ya...Mensch, albinus,' I said in some horrid and likely insulting kludge of every Slavic sound I know.

He snorted and waved his hands in front of his face. I didn't understand until he angrily closed his eyes while pointing at them. I had forgotten to explain the invisibility, and the, in hindsight horrifying and inexcusable, fact that I had tracked him into his own house.

He pointed at himself with a thumb and called himself 'Djad-ed-jie.'

I did the same, and said my name.

He nodded his head, but said 'no.' I later found out that this was a peculiarity of Bulgarian culture, the inversion of the negative head-shake and affirmative nod. He reached into his pantry without taking his eyes off of me.

He pointed at me and said "Krojak" again. I said no again. He thrust the bottle and a handful of drying blackberries at me. I snatched the bottle from his hand and placed it far away from me to signal that I was not interested in drinking it, pulling an exaggeratedly disgusted face.

A look of contemplation crossed his face, and he said a word that sounded like a suggestion: *Ispolin*. He waved the blackberry vine at me like a warding talisman.

He responded to my confusion by gesturing at me, then miming a circle around me, and piled stones – he knew the word *Steinen*- likely revering to the old stone pile my party encamped near when his parade passed us. He then raised his hands and stretched up towards the ceiling, and drew a mannish outline. Exasperated with my confusion, he simply said, *Gigantes*.

'*Da*,' I said. 'Giant.'

This man had a basic understanding of what was happening around him, even if ignorant of the finer details. That is why he was not overcome by the appearance of an invisible man, only suffering the shock of intrusion. I soon tried to tell him of the others, and waved my companions, hoping they could understand him better.

He indicated a short person, or a dwarf. 'Dzhudzheta,' he said a few times. Then he indicated a giant, and said 'Ispolini.' Then he indicated a normal person, and then himself, and said, 'Mensch.' I assumed he was referring to three ages of humanity. I recalled that the Greeks or Romans believed that there were similar ages of men, men of gold, bronze, and clay. Perhaps the Bulgars believe in ages of dwarfs, giants, and modern men.

He held up three fingers. He turned towards his cabinet and pulled out a sackcloth bundle. He unfolded it to reveal the skull, or perhaps skulls, of a three faced animal, either a goat or a ram. '*Triglav*,' he said. I assumed that the *Tri-* meant three, but I was unsure of *glav*. I repeated the word, and the man indicated his head.

'*Cheren Arap*,' he said, pointing at Céleste's skin. I knew those words, probably, and repeated 'Black Arab.'

Céleste blinked heavily and said, 'Sir, you are making me uncomfortable.'

He poured a handful of cornmeal onto the table and drew a mountain and a giant beside it, indicating '*Ispolin*.' He drew the giant again, this time with a sword and a fire or lightning emanating from his left hand, and gave him three giant friends, one flying, another raising the mountain over his head. He drew a shack, surrounded by three small people.

He looked at me hopefully, pointing to the giants and then me.

He added the opponent of the giant warriors. Its head resembled a long-necked bird, but the man added a snaking body with four clawed legs.

He said yes when I slowly asked him if he was seriously proposing that we slay a dragon."

Draconic.

Thomas Noun wrote, in an entry dated to 28 December 1918:

"Venetianer said that we have already encountered 'dragons,' which are seraphim, the fiery serpents. They are the closest to God and his highest ambassadors, which is why in Psalm 18:8, God oddly has smoke coming out his long nostrils, and devouring fire spews from his mouth; Deuteronomy 32 describes Him exhaling fire and burning the world in a form that is Lo-el (Not-God)l; further symbolized by the fiery serpents and the copper icon of the Nehushtan. There are strong associations with volcanic action, such as Isaiah 29-30:37, Exodus 19-20 and 24:17, Deuteronomy 4-5's smoking mountains, and His anger as the flame consuming the earth beneath the depths of Sheol, and Daniel 7:10 rivers of fire. There is even an oddity in God's declaration that his name is

Qin'ah, a word often translated as *Eiferer* [Ger. Zealot, Fanatical] , *Jaloux* [French. Jealous], or Jealous, [Sic, Eng.] but actually meaning, 'inflamed or reddened.'

The earliest work of post-Biblical Jewish mysticism, the *Sefer Yetzirah*, records an entity called Tali, Thele, or Theli, whom Shabbethai Donnolo [corrected from Sabbetai Donolo] described a draconic king of the cosmos who sits upon his throne while encircling all of creation. Though commentators speculated upon its nature for centuries, and attempted to merge it to Leviathan, it is hard not to see it as God Himself, with power over the motion of the stars and planets. And of course, there is the dichotomy of a dragon of flame and copper mountains destroying the dragon of the watery abyss, Leviathan. God, too, is associated with not only flooding such as the Deluge, but the storm-floods that plague the Levant, with the Song of Deborah in Judges 5 rejoicing as God goes out from Mount Seir, causing the heavens to flood the trembling earth.

A Cabbalist known as the Ramak – a Spanish Jew born Moses Cordovero- even portrayed Lilith's steed as a kind of evil anti-god called Tanin'iver, who brings about the unholy union of Lilith and Samael. This "Blind Dragon" is also contrasted with a Dragon in the Sea, perhaps Leviathan – the Rabbi went on something of a tangent, noting that the Talmud records an obscure myth that there were once a mated pair of Leviathans; God castrated and crippled the male and cooled the female, either literally freezing her, driving her into the sea, or perhaps rendering her infertile. Perhaps God's draconic aspect is to simply show His superiority to Leviathan and other serpentine beasts, just as God is often anthropomorphised as an ideal patriarch above the Patriarchs.

Shemiel was one such Fiery Serpent, as seen by her serpentine eyes. Those evil dragons slain by heroes and saints such as St. George were Rebel angels who had warped the flesh of beasts, perhaps crocodiles and eagles. Angels can do the same with any great beast, or force such a transformation upon men, hence stories of were-animals and chimerical creatures such as minotaurs and centaurs and griffins.

I disputed Venetianer's notion that all dragons are angelic, recalling old family lore about the great serpents, such as the famed Christchurch Dragon, the worm in St. Leonard's, Sussex in the early 17th Century, and our encounters with the draconic culti of England. The Captain interjected, briefly, on the Lambton Worm of County Durham, south of Newcastle. The once Danish regions of the Northeastern coast speak of Shoney (or Seonaidh), who demanded supplication in the form of human sacrifice. The Danes tossed their crewmen overboard, either the loser of lots or the infirm. In the Hebrides, particularly the Isle of Lewis, they toned down the sacrifices to cups of ale. Yet there were cases of consumed bodies washing ashore in Newcastle and Lindisfarne, but the maddest, most frequent cases occurred at a pub called Marsden Grotto, on the Bay, where the sea still belches out dragon sacrifices to this day. There was even the case of Captain George Drevar, whose 1881 sighting off of Cape Verde escalated the veracity of sea serpents to the Old Bailey. Winepress noted that the Sokolls had encountered clans in the Far East, in the wilderness outside of Khabarovka[88], who practiced similar rites to appease giant serpents. These creatures appeared to be animals, not celestial intelligences. Likewise, a dragon fell from the sky in Russia in the early 18th century, brought to the court of Peter the Great[89]. This man's dragon did, indeed, seem to be a mere beast, but it was hard to tell from his charades and drawn description.

This may be one of those little secrets nobody knows, like dragonflies are so called because they keep the fantastical world at bay, stitching any tears in the fabric between the shadow worlds and our own; that's why they hover in one place for seemingly no reason, darning back and forth. That's how the magical world works, foolish,

---

[88] Now better known as Khabarovsk, central city of Khabarovsk Krai. The change from Khabarovka occurred in 1893, but hadn't necessarily filtered to the West.

[89] This would appear to be the *Gad Arzamas* (Гад арзамасский), or *Zmeya Gorynycha* (Змея Горыныча) which was felled by a storm on the 4th of June 1719 (Old Calendar). As described by Vasily Shlykov, a zemstvo commissar, the scaled monster was "ten arshins and five inches" (7.24 meters) from mouth to tail tip, with a pair of leathery wings "nine arshins and ten inches long" (6.65 meters). It had four avian talons with four claws. The teeth were, on the average, nine centimeters long. It also had a dorsal sail, some seven meters tall at the center, resembling a dimetrodon, according to historian Liliya Heydarovna.

arbitrary rules; there is a family in Ibiza who, for thirty generations, lights a candle every Thursday night. Their neighbours have wondered if it is some garbled Jewish tradition, as practised by those of Marrano stock, but no, this is less tradition than instinct. If they ever fail in their duty, fifteen stars in the night sky will burn out.

For once, Gottlieb interjected with occult knowledge. He had heard many tales from the Americas of frontiersmen seeing giant lizards, dragons, 'thunderbirds,' and ancient mammals in the Wild West, or mammoths in the great frozen reaches of the Yukon or Alaska. There was a tale from the *American Scientist*[90] of explorers killing a three-headed dinosaur in Bolivia, with scales like armor, in the 1880s. Percy Foster saw a similar creature, and 'not long ago,' Franz Hermann Schmidt and Rudolf Fleng encountered a twelve-meter-long creature with flippers and a serpentine neck leading to a beer-keg-sized head in the waters of a Peruvian river[91]. It was on a rampage, and had to be scared away with rifle fire. It may be, he excitedly said, some kind of living dinosaur from some subterranean Lost World.

Djadedjie – I hope I am getting that name right - treated us graciously despite his means, offering us two spring chickens, bread, and two dozen eggs. Pukka! Céleste and Gottlieb were virtually in tears over the experience; young chicken flesh was something of a delicacy, well above the organ meat and the gamy muscle of hens past their egg-laying prime with which the poor had to content themselves. As we left his house, the Captain turned the eggshells and bones to gold and silver.

We asked around, quietly, brokenly. If only we had our Slavs with us the best we could do was Venetianer's half-forgotten academic Russian.

---

[90] The actual tale here comes from a report entitled "A Bolivian Saurian" by William E.A. Axon, published in *Scientific American* (Vol. 49, No. 1). The animal was reportedly 12m long, with short legs, and a trio of long necks terminating in oddly dog-like heads. It was allegedly shot thirty-six times just before July 1883, in the El Beni Department of Bolivia, with President Narciso Campero ordering it to be preserved and sent to La Paz.

[91] This incident appears to have occurred in 1907. Records indicate that "Rudolph Pfleng' is the proper spelling, and that he died of yellow fever in 1908. See "Prehistoric Monsters in Jungles of the Amazon," *New York Herald*, 11 January 1911.

We spent the better part of the evening tracking the local problem to a farm on the outskirts of the village. The house was empty, for our entire stay on the land. The slit in the window revealed nothing but a bare kitchen. It must have been recently abandoned, perhaps only a night or two before our arrival.

The reason why became apparent. The barley covered the ground, blackened with rot. Not the rot of long decay but a rapid necrosis, which reminded me of the acidic destruction of bog water. Some manner of poison pooled around it. Gottlieb and I thought we had seen such a thing before, the pooling of gas after a rain, but it was a thick black goop unlike the chlorine and mustard. Among the surviving barley stood thick green grass. Gottlieb and the Captain thought it might have been some exotic cultivar of barley, but its spines grew thicker and its seeds smaller and less appetizing than even the most unpalatable wild barley.

Venetianer let out an odd hoot as he rounded the bend and saw the backyard of the farmhouse, adding, 'I didn't realize how big they got.'

Gottlieb and I leaped to our feet and ran to him. He was right, they didn't get that big.

There were three dead domestic pigs in the pen, showing signs of poisoning, a telltale pus dried around their snouts. But behind them was a great wild boar, primeval and cruel-looking. It must have weighed well over a tonne, and nearly four meters long. It had died in combat at the hands of an even greater beast, it's right flank ripped away. Worms and grubs had their turn at the measly flesh, unlike the pork of the lesser pigs, seemingly sterilised by the poisons.

We turned to see blue flame rising from the field.

'Celeste, what have you done?!' the Captain shouted.

She stood there amid the smoke and roiling blue light as the entire farm went up.

'Why are you blaming me?' she said, with a look of genuine confusion on her face.

'You're a vicious pyromaniac who can conduct heat,' I said. 'And you were alone. And staring at the flame.'

'Oh, no, I started the flame,' she said, breathing heavily as she watched the flame. 'But I'm not to blame. There is fire and light trapped in everything...Why is it a sin to free the fire?'

'*Oida*, what happened?' Gottlieb said.

'Oh, don't you see? Those crops need to be purged,' she said. 'A strange, aggressive weed that produces inferior grain? Thriving in an unnatural field of poison? No no no, burn it all away.'

'Did you save a sample?' the Captain said, falling to a knee to search for a stalk of the barley.

'Why?' she asked. 'You have no laboratory. Are you planning on pressing it in a book?'

'She has a point,' said Gottlieb. 'Dragons like fire, don't they? Perhaps this so-called dragon will be lured here.'

'I don't like that we've accepted that this creature is an honest-to-God dragon,' the Captain said.

'Angels, fairies,' I said. 'Why not dragons?'

'I don't know,' he admitted. 'Perhaps it's just another leap too far. Especially after seeing that strange machine underground. What else is there? I don't like living in an absurd world.'

A chill passed through, as the flame subsided. Céleste turned around as the embers faded on the ground and suggested that we leave before people start investigating the flame. We swept the surroundings for tracks and other signs of this dragon's wake, but we found nothing. The boar must have sufficed.

The locals seemed fearful. Not just of dragons, but less fanciful evils. There were whispers in town of a manhunt for a Hungarian deserter named Kiss Béla, who was rumored to have been spotted in the area. He was a monster that pickled the bodies of twenty-three women and one man in seven metal petrol drums, discovered by his landlord while he was off to war, intending to distribute the fuel to marching troops.

The constabulary's search of his house found books on the occult and love letters from many women that he had defrauded and murdered. Kiss had openly worked as an astrologer, fortuneteller, and matchmaker, but the macabre revelation of his nature inspired a darker interpretation – there were some who wondered if he was a witch or necromancer. That some of the books were on poisons and other vile brews further supported the notion. The final detail of the murders was reported in hushed tones – the women bore puncture marks on their necks, and Kiss had drained their blood.

One rumor claimed that, rather than drinking blood, this boogeyman was using them for a magical rite, or perhaps a folk medical treatment. I was reminded of the Crime of Gador, when that jug-eared witch-doctor Francisco Leona harvested the fat of a young boy for a tuberculosis treatment. I saw him in the newspaper, I think, looking like some evil fairytale goblin.

The last known whereabouts of Kiss were a hospital in Serbia, which further spread fears that he was a vampire, especially when contradictory telegrams stated that he had been pronounced dead and had later left the hospital. When investigators attempted to clear up the issue, they found a dead soldier in his allotted bed, decidedly not Kiss. He had fled from manhunters in the night, and was spotted in several places – in Romania, arrested for burglary, one time on a ship to Turkey, and most frequently, in Bulgaria. It was assumed he had stolen a series of identification papers off the dead.

It was said that Romania's Special intelligence Service dispatched its Section Zero[92] to hunt for the criminal. Some wondered if Kiss was searching for an occult lecturer noted in his books, Peter Deunov – founder of an exotic Christian philosophy, mixing Orthodoxy with some revision of Theosophy. His followers called him 'the Master.'

I shivered at the thought, and said that this Kiss fellow sounded like an even worse version of the murderer George Joseph Smith –two time recipient of Old Blighty's Most Generic Name Award- a bigamist who drowned three women in the bath for insurance money. They executed him recently, finding him after great breakthroughs in forensic pathology. There was also this Italian Anarchist Simone Pianetti, who slew seven people in a spree of cold rage before disappearing into the Val Brembana mountains as the war began.

Even without this Kiss ghoul, the atmosphere chilled the blood. A sense of absence haunted the land, same we saw in Serbia. We dare not speak of Serbia. It was worse than the trenches. Not for what we saw, but what we didn't see.

England, France, and yes, Germany, we all knew these would still

---

[92] A remnant of its origins as Secţia a II-a (Second Section).

stand. That one day, we could return home. See our lands, listen to our songs, see our monuments and histories.

Serbia was a vast emptiness. There was mobilization, still, but only of the Bulgars and their Austrian allies. There were no men, at least below an advanced age. Even the women seem sparse, as though the Serbs as a people had been swept up in a vast whirlwind. They are scattered into the mountains of Albania or to Greece and the sea, a great retreat across Kosovo's Field of Blackbirds, army and civilian mixing as never before. They dragged their blind King Peter, ailing in his seventh decade, through the mountains in an ox cart, a debasement of national dignity.

It still came to me in my sleep, that cutting emptiness of the Great Retreat – what they called the Albanian Golgotha. There were bodies there, thousands of them, soldiers and men and children and elders, thawed and eaten by dogs and birds...oh, the sky was black with carrion birds. They died in groups of hundreds, to Austrians, to Albanian tribals, to Bulgars, to exhaustion, to typhus and flu and plague, to frost, to the wolves that haunt the East. We all but ran through the nation, afraid of the decay.

I wondered what had happened to those directly under the Austro-Hungarian heel in Bosnia, shuddering at the thought. I stopped counting the dead children after my thirtieth. I was glad Mihajlo was not there to see the devastation of his race.

Feldmaschall von Mackensen eulogised the Serbs, remarking that their resistance in Belgrade was an army only heard of in fairy tales. It was in the papers, as if the enemy was certain that the Serbs were a dead race.

The next day, Céleste, Gottlieb, and I headed into what passed for Tsarichina's town center. The War with Romania had sapped the town, but she was overjoyed to learn that rosewater and its oil was plentiful; Bulgaria contains a region aptly known as the Rose Valley, and its town of Kazanlak produces rose oil in copious amounts. She also managed to find a tin of lanolin – a wool wax- and some witch hazel.

'It's rather hard to care for my hair,' Céleste noted. 'But I can make a good treatment out of lanolin, carbonated ammonia, the witch hazel and rose oil. Maybe Sal Tartar, to get it to stick. Lard's a rather nasty substitute. I hope I can one day find bay rum again, but it's from the West Indies. The boche U-boats made it rather expensive. Oh, and I hope *eau colorante* comes back into fashion.'

I asked her what she meant. She explained that she used to rinse her hair with a blue-silver dye. It never looked a pastel blue like it would with the blondes and auburn-haired girls of Lille, but it gave her black hair a midnight blue quality under the light.

I asked her why she went through so much trouble, since she usually wore her hair under a hat or a Dahomey head-wrap. She smiled and said it was because of 1 Corinthians – a woman ought to cover her head with a symbol of authority, because of the angels. That's how we got into this mess, Na'amah's beautiful red hair.

She quietly grumbled about the lack of a 'cellucotton' in the east, a new product made of wood pulp with five-fold the absorbency of cotton. Nurses used it to stem the flow of blood in patients, and, as she fumbled for a euphemism, at other times.

She quickly changed the subject to local politics and racial strife: she spoke of the Cagots, an obscure people from southern France and the northern regions of Spain. Everyone hated them for some reason. Nobody, not even the Cagots, knew the source of the animus, and yet it lingered. Some claimed that they had tails or lacked ear lobes or had overly large ear lobes, but this was demonstrably untrue. They looked, behaved, and spoke like everyone else around them. Some said they were once lepers, or Conversos or heretics. Or perhaps they were the first Christians of the region, and the hatred remained even as their neighbours turned from paganism. But for whatever reason, the hatred lingered. Looking at the Balkans, she wondered, if the same thing would happen. Centuries and centuries from now, after the wake of the Turks is forgotten, perhaps the Balkans would forget their hatred. Céleste thought no. They might forget the source of the hatred, but never the hatred.

I wondered if they were similar to, or of, the Basque people. The Basque were an ancient people with a language isolate, and had long contact with nephilim and the others, who built great stone circles across the Country. They strangely referred to the giants with borrowed words for foreigners – jentillak (the gentiles), the mairuak (Moors), and the one-eyed Tartaro (Tatars) – and to the wildwose as the Lords of the Wood, the Basajaunak. Their version of Father Christmas, Olentzero, was the last of these Pyrenees giants, as all the rest fled the surface world or died of fright at the sight of the Christmas Star, though they were later said to throw boulders at the Frankish forces of Roland at Roncevaux. It was for their giant and neanderthal blood and strange traditions that they were put to the torture by the inquisitions.

We managed to procure some lamb sausage and bread. Gottlieb found some delousing powder for his officer. Captain Venetianer was fastidious in his grooming routine, oiling and powdering his hair to ward off the hateful torment of lice. Many men shave, but he was forbidden to shave his beard and locks by the law of the Covenant. He had run out of it a month ago, and had developed a neurotic, paranoid itching habit.

Nothing much happened that day, as we looked through the local fields. The main point of interest is that the Captain came to believe that the strange weed was in fact a primordial form of barley, though, oddly, one sample stalk appeared to have been hybridised with wheat. In the fields, we looked for an increased frequency and diversity among these crops. Diversity, he said, was usually the sign of an evolutionary point of origin before a rapid expansion; for example, there are many dialects of English in the British Isles, but fewer accents elsewhere, and while there are many Romance languages in Spain, only the Castillian form spread to their America colonies.

The effort proved – forgive me – fruitful. We came to a field with many oddities, with ancient grains blended together, strange chimerae sharing one stalk. This was a project, with deliberate alteration and culling. Some manner of venom pooled in the ground; Gottlieb alerted us with a yelp and a waving of fingers. He claimed that it stung something like pepper in the eyes and nose.

Winepress wondered aloud if this was some mad experiment to thwart the artificial famines forced by the blockade, that No Man's Sea. Rather shamefully, the Allies had planned on buying up a majority of Bulgarian produce in 1915, both to keep it out of the mouths of the Central Powers and to create a local grain crisis, hobbling the Bulgarian war effort. Sofia uncovered the plot, and arrested the agents. By September, they had joined the Powers.

One of the crueler tools of a maritime empire is the cutting of imports. Conquest, War, and Death ride with terrible, dark glory, yet the worst of all is Famine. Anyone would rather catch a bullet than die of a swollen, empty belly.

Would Germany face a similar destruction, with its people stoically facing their death by blockade? When the Teutons and Cimbri struck at Rome, Gaius Marius crushed them in retaliation, chaining their King, Teutobod, and dragging him home in a triumph. The Teutonic women slew their children and committed suicide by mutual strangulation rather than submitting to slavery, entering into Roman legend as a defiant last stand. What of the German women? Will they surrender? Will they enter our legends? Or shall they gnaw forever at the English conscience?

Something slowly dawned on all of us, a secret sense that something vast and ancient lie beneath the earth, a lost treasure of the ages. Venetianer called it a kind of Plutonic sensitivity to things long buried, the chthonic, the occult. The field was not truly open; to the east stood an old steeple or watchtower, of raised planks with a tiled canopy, rising from a small shack against a chest-high stonewall the length of two football fields. The field was stony, clear signs of geological flow from the nearby mountains. A root cellar lay embedded fully in the earth some 10 meters west, among the densest part of the stone deposits. Perhaps it covered some ancient quarry, we thought.

Venetianer joked about the local legend that Tsar Samuel buried treasures plundered from Basil II's Byzantium in these hills – he hoped the hiding place wasn't so obvious, for the sake of the locals' reputation.

We voted and entered the cellar, Céleste warping the lock with the cycling of heat. Gottlieb stalked in, unseen. A flash of light led us down not long after. We raised our pistols as we descended the stairs into the earth. We descended into a spiralling tunnel, leading several hundred meters down. It seemed less mined than carved deep into the earth for living purposes. It seemed like a great working of slabs and silvery floors, ancient beyond reasoning. It should have been foreboding, frightening to the senses, but it seemed like some gentle home.

In the dark, faintly illuminated by Gottlieb's foxfire glow, writhed our beast. Our hearts collectively skipped a beat, before quickening into a Flight of the Bumblebee.

It looked like no dragon I've seen illustrated. It was a disgusting, loathsome thing, a creature with four mud-and-gore-caked chicken legs and the body of a boar fleshed like a crocodile, dotted with nasty bristles and running sores. Its legs were turned inward, and it had a quivering, unstable gait. Its wings were small and skeletal, between bird and bat, its veiny skin feathered with rotten quills. Its neck was serpentine, but its face lacked any kind of nobility. It had a nose that vaguely resembled a man's, but flattened and flared as long as a forearm, ending with a boney angler's hook. Its mouth was a bird's beak coated in a thin layer of grey-green flesh filled with sharp and crooked teeth like arrowheads. Its piscene eyes were the worst part of it, the size of saucers, unblinking and wet, weeping yellow pus. It held its mouth open and its head to the side.

It was a fear born of unnatural abhorrence and that of an unpredictable and large animal, not the grand and noble villainy of the storybook dragons. It was pathetic, insipid and idiotic, and I hated it. I wanted to kill it, and Nature cheered me on.

We fired on the thing with a shocking enthusiasm, the deafening cracks echoing through the subterranean complex. It counterattacked with a noxious gas. There was some strange, oppressive force emanating through those carved stones, projected by some kind of golden statue of a bird of prey. Gottlieb fled up the stairs, but marked the beast with a halo of light that shone through the roiling haze. The rest of us fell back as the Captain attempted to convert it to harmless air, but the heat was oppressive. Less like that of flame, more like the unctuous heat of influenza's phlegm. The strange gout barely touched us, yet our noses, ears, and mouths were inflamed with a foul, acrid spice from Hell's cruelest plantation. Céleste gagged and asked if it was lye. The crack of a rifle interrupted the Captain's lost answer. Three more shots floored us.

We cursed and cried out, between a rock and a hard place, back in the trenches of gas and invisible gunfire. My heart stopped, time stopped, and I was back at the Somme. We went to ground, with the exception of Gottlieb, who passed by us, unseen, after pushing me into the stairwell for cover."

What followed was recounted by Gottlieb in his war journal.

"A creeper tank slid across the field. I had seen these things one before, a tool of the Entente. Something of a mobile shield, used to crawl forward behind three cm of metal, to snip wires and fire rifles. It was unpowered, yet there were no feet pushing it forward, only something thin and wet. Still, a pistol peeked from its firing port.

I moved to the abandoned watch tower, replacing my pistol with the rifle, splashing through the dragon's envenomed country. I stumbled on my way, in what I first thought was a muddy hole. There were several such holes in the ground around me, but in the moment I thought them simply some kind of obscure agricultural boring.

I slowly opened the door. I waited for seven seconds, anticipating the possibility of suppression fire. I slipped inside. I heard a man sobbing quietly.

The man asked who was down there in French, with a strange accent. The voice echoed down from his sniper's nest at the top of a wooden ladder. A ghoulish helix of barbed wire and intestines guarded the rungs. A black bile greased the barbs and the thin, flaky flesh, serpent's teeth on a serpent's skin. It was hard to tell if they were intertwined or if the barbed wire was generated by the organ.

There was a machine gun planted there, facing towards the door. A twitching red mass of fingers embedded in muscle tissue and nerves wrapped around its firing mechanism – with a naked eye gazing out. And again –'Who is there?'

The thin concrete floor had been broken, probably by a sledgehammer or similar, with several similar holes bored into the ground. Dust puffed up, wheezing from the ground. I moved back outside to look at the hole I had tripped in. A body-wide shiver followed the slow realization that these tunnels were winding, breathing channels lined mucous-slick skin, something between throats and intestine. There were organs under the old tower, leading in, feeding on the ground like roots.

The person behind this was clever, I realized – having noted someone enter the tower, but unseen by those detached eyes, he began to exhale from this tangle of throats. It was an acrid, slimy breath. I remembered when I had been gassed, when other men had been gassed, and heavy, liquid breathing, when bits of your lung start coming up. He was checking for some invisible presence, spraying it with droplets and hoping to sense some kind of deflection or run-off.

I thought better of returning through the front door, and used a brick jutting from the wall as a foothold. I scratched my hands up and left a cleft in a fingernail, but I made it to the second story window.

A strange creature landed on the chest of my cuirass. I, at first, thought it to be a beetle, but I shuttered when I noticed it was some kind of lobster with wings. It's body was maybe eighteen cm long. I had never heard of such a thing, and wanted to brush it off, but feared the noise it might cause.

The man was there, hunching near my window's opposite. He gazed through it with a detached eye worked by a small mass of glands and muscle.

I created a scoping lens to examine him closely. He was a lanky man, with wiry limbs. He was dark, with black hair, brittle from malnutrition, and perhaps in his fourth decade of life, or approaching. He looked like one of the Indochinese the French use as support, probably from their operations in Greece – unless he too made the long perilous trip across Germany and Austria from the West.

He huddled with one limb tucked under his dusty French army uniform. The limb was missing. So were his eyes. Their lids were closed and flat.

I sneaked up on him, invisibly, as his senses were trained on the ladder and the other window facing the cellar. I pressed my knife to his throat. Then, I brushed off the flying prawn.

He gasped, nicking himself, and the gun below fired, tearing off the door by the sound of it.

I covered his mouth, and told him, in French, that I did not want to kill him, to surrender. His face did not move, but the eye on the wall did. I pulled my hand away. We appeared to have a ceasefire.

Bile rose in my throat when the eye detached from its fleshy perch, skittering back to its owner. He opened his empty socket and let the eye crawl back into place, scaring off what looked to be a mating pair of the flying prawns[93].

[93] I have no idea what this creature could be; it matches with one creature I can find, spotted in Bacuit Bay, Palawan, the topic of a 1914 paper. See Worcester, Dean C., Alvin J. Cox (editor). "Note on the Occurrence of a Flying Crustacean in the Philippine Islands." *The Philippine Journal of Science*,

'Monsters,' he said. 'There are monsters out there.'

I said that I knew, that I saw the dragon. I asked if he worked for them, or had been hiding up here, defending himself from them. And I told him to speak freely.

'They found me,' he said in his native tongue, one bloodshot eye looking up at me. 'I had wandered from my work line. I was so afraid. The shells, the bombs, the machines. I can't sleep. I only see myself tangled up in the machines. I dream of it. Pain, men marching into the meat grinder. I am the raw red meat man. A flesh factory.'

He showed me his stump of a hand. He had severed his hand to the wrist to operate the machines. The flesh was already growing back, ready to be stripped off and used as more autonomous engine parts. That was why he so thin – his organs and muscles were lining this gunner tower, powered by thin blood vessels and feeding into this sweaty body-heat.

He must have been operating and foraging here for some time, as he was armed with the Mannlicher magazine rifle typical of Bulgarians rather than a French weapon. A small tin plate sat next to him, holding what appeared to be small hearts in rice paper.

'I dug out the bad dreams,' he said, pointing at what looked like a cluster of grapes hanging from the ceiling. They were parts of his brain, the size and shape of wrinkled peas or walnuts. 'They harvest them, put them into other men. I started wandering, left the war camp, left the war. The dragon and the bloody man found me. I knew I was a monster like them. I saw it in the water when I was a kid.'

I asked him what he saw, who he was.

'It was...thirty-four years ago now, in Hong Gai. I must have been a little child. The thing's head washed ashore by my house, an insect thing twice the size of a man's skull. The body came out not far away...it was a centipede of bone and fins, the Con Rit. Its plates rang like bells, like bells... it was thirty meters long, and smelled like death, and the war-gas. I kept the head, dried it....The monsters live around us, on the edges. The wild people of the forest, the monsters in the sea. The monsters lived on the edges, until they came for me.'

I asked him if he wanted to work with them. He said no, not really,

Volume IX, 1914.

but he had no choice.

He said that he grew up near Hong Gai, in the Bay Where the Dragon Descends to the Sea. There are dragons in this world, and the thrashing of one such monster formed the valleys and peaks of his home and the limestone pillars that jut from the Gulf of Tonkin. The Chinese pirates of the bay saw the dragon, and when the French came, they saw it too, and called it the Tarasque. The Tarasque killed the Con Rit, he thought. Water and Sky defeating Steel and Earth. The French doctors cut him open, and put organs inside of him, organs from the Tarasque, and took his organs and put them in other places, and so he became a machine, a factory of flesh.

There were people in the sky and the water telling him to run away from the war, and these monster people were the only ones who could stop the war for good. I asked him how they were going to end the war, and he said that it was a secret between the dragon and the man from Mars.

I had nothing to say to that, puzzling over the idea, wondering if he truly worked for a Martian. I simply sputtered out a suggestion that he couldn't possibly mean that.

The man said it was so, and he convulsed with fear. His long arms bristled with goose-flesh, skin literally crawling over a void of muscle. The Man from Mars had powerful machines and could stop his organs' distant workings with some electrical force. He did not understand the workings of the others, but they would stop the war and save the universe.

I said that I had to leave him. I told him my name. He said his name, Wong Wan Tei (*sic; likely* Vương Văn Tê, *a Vietnamese deserter from 2ème combat battalion of the French Colonial Division of the Armée d'Orient, Salonika/Macedonian Front*). I told him to piece himself back together and dismantle his traps, but I would come back to help him, if I could. He shook nervously.

When I returned down the ladder, I stripped the machine gun of its magazine, just to be sure, and left through the door. The creeper tank had been overturned, leaking a boiled mass of blood and gelatinous flesh.

My companions were still suppressed, on the ground by the cellar door. I told them that the sniper and machine gun in the tower wouldn't be a problem.

I paused when I saw that a great circle had been trampled down in the wheel field, like the Devil or the black fairies are said to do in old stories, the kind of thing you see in woodcuts.

They asked me who was up there, how many men. I said it was one man, a nephel, someone who tore himself apart to run the machines. I said I talked him down. Winepress asked me if I was sure he wouldn't betray that promise. He was interrupted by a loud, hissing voice from the dark of the cellar.

'Come through the flames,' said the voice. It had a scratchiness to it, like the voice of an old man, but with an inhuman hardness, the sound of wood scrapped across horn. 'Have you seen the Anastenaria? The villagers come to walk and dance through fire with icons of Constantine and St. Helen...When an old church burned, the icons cried to the people to rescue them...they say the saints protected those villagers who braved the flame. Will you brave the flames?'

A great blast of oily flame filled the darkness of the cellar. Céleste ran down, knife in hand.

Céleste continued:

"I charged into the vast cellar of stone as the rasping madman ranted.

'Serpent-footed Gigantes, Daityas, Asuras, Jötnar, Emmim, Anakim, Rephaim, Nephilim, heaven's bastards. There were giants in the earth in those days, and after then. We are the fallen, the dead of war, slain over and over across time, the Dead Rephaim rising from the earth, reincarnating in new flesh. We drowned in the flood, fell in gigantomachies, hunted by the Red Indians of the Americas. We were extinguished with Og of Bashan. And with Goliath, and Gogmagog, and with a hundred other generations of the living dead. We are trapped, as long as history continues, diminishing without dying, never escaping, over and over again, reborn in war. The wheel turns back, we have forgotten.'

The cellar was far deeper and longer than seemed possible for such a rural structure. It must have been excavated, and yet the walls were stone, and lined with machinery, piping filled with cables- perhaps bundled copper. There were slabs carved with what must have been some magical symbols, and an eagle statue blazing with electrical heat. It may have been some galvanic medical device, or a tool for torture. That oily venom burned all around me. There were snakes, there, some with toothy horns or leathery wings. I ripped out the heat, pulling it with me, smothering some of the flames and chilling the winged serpents.

'The sound of pounding hooves, chariot wheels, clashing blades and burning powder and horns and drums and endless calls to war.'

Siegfried called after me, and soon followed, braving the smoky heat. By the sound of it, the rest came with him. I did not stop for them – hungry curiosity compelled me to see how deep this passage truly was, with its exotic wire arcs and monoliths, and I found a strange joy in the earthy darkness. The scent of the wet loam was a perfume as familiar and comforting as mother's favorite. There seemed to be a vast expanse into the cold darkness, a crypt of giants in coffins of black stone and pitchblende. I knew them, somehow, as kindred souls, even across a gulf of ten thousand years. A great door was at the end of the chamber, pulled aside, and marked with the image of a primordial giant. He seemed like an old friend. I could have stayed in that tunnel all night, but fought the urge and ran until I saw moonlight and heard the sea.

I knew this place. I had seen its likes in travelogues and histories. We were in Greece, in the islands.

'Look down to that stone,' said the rasping voice. It was an old stone with vague letters carved into it, a bit of Greek.

'I can't read Greek,' I said, looking for the source of the voice.

'It reads *Desai*,' he said. "Take that.' A stone thrown from an ancient sling, with a sentiment we still hear today. We have never changed. Only the tools. So let us change that.'

I said that I have heard this. That he was not telling me anything new. I felt it. The pointlessness of war, the oppression of prophecy.

'What is rebellion when rebellion is pointless?'

I asked if he was the dragon. He was above me, on the mountainside, behind the rocky outcroppings. It was then that the men arrived. Siegfried, panting, touched my arm and asked if I was hurt, and Winepress seconded him. I hushed them and pointed at the stranger.

The dragon appeared from behind the weathered stones. Then

followed a hunched man, a brute of a man covered in coarse black hair. A snake circled his neck, flicking its tongue, and a bird perched on his shoulder, an exotic creature with scales covering its head and needle-like teeth in its mouth. The hairy man petted the dragon with affection.

'I am Typhon,' he said.

'Better question - what are you?' I asked.

'A giant,' he said, with a thick, striking manner of pronouncing the T-sound, 'Same as you. We strive against the gods.'

'When you say you are Typhon...do you mean the Typhon?' Noun asked. 'Of myth?'

The hirsute man chuckled, revealing two rows of teeth. 'Perhaps, in some way, in the cycle of rebirth. But no, it is an adopted name, the *Imago Typhonis*.'

Typhon was a Greek, though that name was recognizably a Latin term. I had heard that when Greece threw off the Ottoman yoke, the new government sent messengers to the villages to inform the populace that they were not the Sultan's slaves, but free citizens of a new Greece. The peasantry was often shocked, believing themselves to be Romans, heirs of Byzantium, most famously in the case of Lemnos in 1912. Though I was not even certain that this man even thought of himself as a mere mortal man.

'I was born Nikolas Evangelopoulos, on Chios. But I was in Thessaloniki, for the assassination of George, for your invasion, for the rebellion, for last year's hellish fire...it convinced me I had to come here, to the Cave. I recognize Thomas Noun. Who are the rest of you?'

I introduced myself. As did Winepress, and the Rabbi.

Noun demanded to know why this Typhon or Evangelopoulos knew him. Typhon explained that he had been active in the medical field, specifically organ transplantation, and had implanted one of the Tonkinese man's odd organs into his body. Through this, the living factory had been tracking him.

Noun twisted in discomfort, and felt at the place at his side where the surgery had occurred.

Typhon laughed, and said that the organ had already been removed, during the subterranean surgery, along with other 'hysterical oddities,' an addition that only he and I understood. He had learned much about

Noun's wild talents from its adaptations. Noun made a sound between a hiss and a grunt, pushing air through his teeth in a wolfish rage.

'I see,' he said. 'I knew there was another group out there. The Martian Man[94] encountered you with his allies, beneath the earth. Sorry for that savaging, but we needed to secure your blood and specialized tissue. That of the Phoenician provided our great tunnel. And I believe the English captain stabilized its walls.'

Winepress moved to hide his compact case of tin and lead, and spoke up: 'How so? How could our blood do that?'

Typhon moved closer, and now it was clear that there were many snakes on his person, writhing through his clothing. Some were not true snakes, but something with small limbs. Ancestral snakes, perhaps? He held a bundle in his arms, dearly like a swaddled child.

'Perhaps the best way to say it is that I can reverse-engineer,' he said. 'I can revise things to their ancient forms, extrapolate and exaggerate the primal natures of things. I can restore broken things, force things to revert, return animals to their ancient form like some fever dream of Darwin. And from your blood, I can isolate the processes, expand them to their purest properties, and keep them functioning away from their source – though I needed Voung's help for that.'

'That's how you made that...dragon...chimera...beast,' said Winepress. 'It's actually a chicken, isn't it?'

'Yes,' said Typhon. 'It's a chicken forced through aeons of atavism, and warped with possibilities that could have been, but weren't allowed

---

[94] Some speculation here: Céleste writes "L'homme martien" here, while Rowan records that he heard "Lamb" - Aleister Crowley describes a psychic encounter with a large-headed entity called *Lam*, a drawing that both resembles the "hydrocephalic," pinched-eyed description of this so-called Martian, and is a forerunner to the Grey aliens of the mid-to-late 20th century. To go further, the image of God's body – the *Shi'ur Komah*- found in early Jewish Merkavah mysticism also maps onto Grey-like dimensions, with an oversized head, small trunk, and long fingers, though measured on an enormous scale of *parasang* (a Persian unit equal to 5.6km) and with a fetching beard. This suggests that such an image may have something to do with humanity's sensory homunculus and transcendental experiences.

by our history's winding course.'

'Like the cockatrice of legend,' I said. 'A dragon out of a chicken.'

'Fascinating,' Winepress said. 'You're a step away from reviving the dinosaurs.'

'Yes,' Typhon said. 'You may have heard tales of great crocodiles rising from the sea, with flippers, or from torpedoes ships, or serpents out of Loch Ness spotted in the Dardanelles and dragging men into lake Van[95]. My work. My gifts of enlightenment.'

'This was our great sin,' said Venetianer, in haunted whispers. 'Our nephilim progenitors corrupted the world, its animals and grains, giving rise to horrible chimeras and hairy wild men. It all had to be destroyed in the Flood.'

'Yes, I dabble, unwholesomely, in the heredity of beasts...But it is the nephilim's right. We and our work are the Mark of the Beast.'

'The Mark of the Beast is...is it not the Kaisers, czars, and kings, their greed and trade? Their empire and coin?' Siegfried asked. 'Isn't 666, or 616, Nero Caesar?'

'What a petty mark,' said Typhon. 'This is eugenic. The other mark, the Mark of Cain was also a eugenic matter. And the Flood was an act of eugenic murder against our people. And it is somewhere in Luke[96], that 'as it was in the Days of Noah, so shall it be in the days of the Son of Man.' The very existence of Nephilim make humanity less human, less godly, and we make God less godly by our stolen domains. And so it shall be.'

'Is that the plan?' I asked. 'Make everyone nephilim? Bring back every antediluvian beast? Remake the world in your image?'

'Oh, yes. But I wonder if our crime was even greater than that,' said Typhon. 'Perhaps we corrupted time itself. There must be a reason why Genesis chapter one and chapter two don't match up...but we do only show up in Genesis Six...Perhaps we should rule, and make it so we always have ruled.'

He laughed, and continued: 'We were never supposed to know the

[95] This seems to be a reference to an incident recorded in the 29 April 1889 issue of the Ottoman paper *Saadet*, in which a scientific survey was sent to Lake Van after a dragon-like creature pulled a man underwater and ate him.
[96] He is specifically quoting Luke 17:26.

vastness of our world's history. They are slipping in their control of our scope. Professor Abel is finding giants[97]. The Other Men are undone – we've found their bodies for the first time, the Neanderthal Man of Germany, the Engis caves, the Gibraltar woman, the burial of Chapelle-aux-Saints and El Buxu. We have them now, we named the wild man, the fairy, the troll, the strange people of the burial mounds. We have found the dragons, the dinosaurs. We grind up the Cave Bears and the dragons of Styria for phosphates. And now we will find the alien and the angel. And we will have the cosmos under our dissection knives. Do you not understand that that's what the Apocalypse is? The Revelation?'

'That's what this is to you?' Noun asked. 'This is a war, a dying off, not some great discovery.'

'Physicists are discovering that existence is not limited to our galaxy,' said Typhon. 'That the continents are ever-moving. That the Earth is billions, not thousands of years old. That even time is not fixed.'

'The Euro-Nietzschean War. Read the Devil, in order to fight him the better,' said Noun.

Both Typhon and I let out a quiet 'what?'

'I saw it on a window display in England,' Noun explained. 'Europe is fighting Nietzsche. Or rather, modernity, the death of Christianity, a culture trying to suture up a break in history. "*It scares me stiff to think that, some day, I may be pronounced a saint.*" That's what this is, to you, what?'

'I see,' said Typhon. 'When sacrilege stands in the holy place, Judea must flee into the mountains. And sometimes vice-versa. When Pompey desecrated the Holiest of Holies, he did not exit the Temple as the same man. And here we are, on the mountain of the Revelation.'

---

[97] This is a reference to Professor Othenio Lothar Franz Anton Louis Abel (1875-1946) of the University of Vienna, known for founding paleobiology. He also speculated on the universality of giants, dragons, and solar myths, and the investigation of giant bones in Sicily, identifying European pygmy elephant fossils as the root of the Cyclops legend. This work came to the attention of the English-speaking world through *The Times Dispatch* of May 17, 1914. While an important trailblazer in his field, his latter day reputation was destroyed by his enthusiastic support of the Nazi Party and membership in the Bärenhöhle, a secret society at the University of Vienna meant to harass Jewish students and faculty and suppress their scholarship.

'Patmos?' Winepress muttered. He looked east. 'That must be Turkey, right... We're on Patmos. They knew. They knew this was the meeting place.'

'Did they? Or is it...is it Raduriel?' muttered Venetianer. 'I don't understand, where is the angel? Is it even real?'

I demanded to know what anyone was talking about.

'You are the Rabbi?' Typhon said with a twisted smile. 'How does it feel to see another faith's end time come? Strange, to see it all fade away without you.'

'This is a madness,' said Venetianer. 'A cosmic sickness. We will survive.'

'Will you?' said Typhon.

'Babylon. Rome. Tyre. The Pharaohs. These were Europe's forebearers; our contemporaries,' said Venetianer.

'We were here, too,' said Typhon. He then added, rather bitterly. 'Even if the Italians occupy Patmos. Rome again, always penetrating our holy places. But what are worldly politics at this point?'

'That's the problem, this is above politics, a cosmic politic. There is always Babylon. Babylon is a thought-plague, the great mystery, the temptation of the mind of man. Since Nimrod and Semiramis. Ur, Uruk, Chaldea and Kassite, Elam and Assyria, Hellenes and Persia and Rome. Empire is Babylon. The War is Babylon.'

'Then let civilization fall,' said Typhon. 'I know you are fascinated by dinosaurs, mammoths, ancient beasts and sea monsters. All nephilim are, in a way, drawn to such giant things. We all secretly want things back to the way things were, before the Flood. Help me turn back time.'

'Humanity is nearly a million years old, by Martian reckoning. Yet the current phase of civilization has only lasted about seven thousand years,' said a new man. 'Why is that?'

He appeared from around the mountain path, an uncanny figure. He was a hairless man – not simply bald, but lacking even eyebrows – his eyes black, and his sallow flesh marked with red earth like some kind of Zulu warpaint. His head seemed swollen, hydrocephalic, but I didn't believe he was inhuman, just twisted, mutated.

Winepress looked up at him, sharing my scepticism.

'You are no Martian,' said the Captain.

'I was a gondolier back home, in the flooded trenches of our final war,' said the man, flippantly, in perfect English and an indeterminable accent. 'A lovely place, even as it dries. But now I am an emissary of our Augoeides, and I may never see those red canals again.'

'No no, you had the good folk working with you,' said Noun. 'Why would they work with you?'

'A solidarity of Little Green Men, perhaps?' said the Martian. 'It's simple. I promised to cure them of some medical issue they have developed from their isolation and diets. Issues with heredity and brain degeneration. They don't see the full picture, but they were useful in gathering blood and performing surgeries. And better company than the ghoul...'

'Why do you look like us?' said the Captain. 'An alien race evolving in vastly different conditions would not resemble man.'

'Think of me as a homunculus,' said the Martian. 'I was conjured across to England, your Chatham, naked and half-mad in the January before your war[98]. My people were in contact with your English magicians for some time. The transit to Kent was easiest.'

'I don't understand,' said the Captain. 'What is this? What is your game?'

'We must stop your world's death spiral,' he said. 'We will return it to its primordial state, a hot, fresh world rich with promise. Will you join us?'

'I would like you to join us,' said the Rabbi. 'We have another plan to stop this war. A peaceful one, on the whole, to save lives.'

'We can't brook the destruction of humanity,' said the Captain. 'And we out number you. Joining our cause would be the best for everyone involved. Everyone. Rewinding the clock seems too much.'

'I don't think your race understands our perspective,' said the so-called Man from Mars. 'You giants are but the last remnants of the influence of Orion surrounded by half-mad apes. When you passed

---

[98] He seems to be referring to an incident recorded by the 10 January 1914 edition of *the Chatham News*, popularized by Charles Fort's *Lo!*, in which a naked man suddenly appeared in High Street, Chatham, Kent.

through the tail of Comet Halley, you entered into a decade of psychical intensity, dangerous beyond words. Why should all the peoples in the universe be snuffed out because of the politics of your world? I came here to disrupt your cosmos-ending ambitions.'

'This is some Nicolas Camille Flamel nonsense[99],' I said.

'Yes,' said the Martian. 'We have attempted communication. We have spoken to your scientists, and there was potential. Marconi has not acted. Esnault-Pelterie is designing atomic rockets powered by the decay of radium, but he is unknown to the world. Tesla could speak with the heavens with his radio science, but he has fallen to dabbling and destitution, dismissing our calls as mere fairy taps. Tsiolkovsky could have expanded the human mind and its place in the cosmos, but the Russians have collapsed to internal war. You do not listen to these men of science. You have turned to warlords and the heirs of warlords, and you are lost.'

'We are also trying to make the apocalypse impossible, Mr. Lamb,' the Captain said. 'We have a common cause. I know that an extreme solution seems like the only way at this point, but we want you to know that there is another way out.'

---

[99] Céleste appears to be conflating alchemist Nicolas Flamel, a popular subject of occult speculation, with Nicolas Camille Flammarion (1842-1925), a French astronomer, publisher, and author of over fifty popular science and science-fiction works. He was known for integrating his spiritualist beliefs into his fiction; "Lumen," in particular, involves an alien soul capable of faster-than-light travel and serial reincarnation across the evolutionary histories of alien worlds; this is likely what Céleste is referring to. He could be considered something of an early paranormalist as well, attempting to research reincarnation and other topics using the scientific method and, oddly, his own idiosyncratic take on skepticism. He also inspired a flap of panicked speculation when he claimed, in 1907, that Martians had contacted humanity, and that a seven-tailed comet was coming to earth. Three years later, with Comet Halley's passing, he stated that the comet's tail would potentially disrupt the atmosphere, killing all life on Earth. More soberly, he wished to see a love for astronomic wonder to unify mankind, "If they knew what profound inner pleasure await those who gaze at the heavens, then France, nay, the whole of Europe, would be covered with telescopes instead of bayonets, thereby promoting universal happiness and peace."

'Perhaps, but you would never ally with our cosmic council,' he said. 'Your race must be annihilated utterly, and the Earth destroyed. There are many races here, creatures who dance in the heart of stars and ghosts who fall backwards through time. Some are great minds, skinless buddhas bound to a single world but projecting their consciousness across the universe, and others are soulless machines who have made a conquest of a million stars. I am the spearhead of a Martian invading force that has monitored your world for centuries. We are not here to conquer or devour you. We have all come here to save ourselves by invalidating your parochial Armageddon. If we let Earth survive, such an event may occur again, a similar pattern of holy destruction...but without a hill in Megiddo, there can be no Armageddon.'

I muttered the word of Cambronne[100].

'You don't believe me?' he said. 'What you see as angels are merely exotic entities of exotic energies. You so called nephilim are nothing more than hybrids with other races, cosmic Koolakambas, with the expected hybrid vigour. You are the spawn of Annunaki descending from the stars, with stimulated pituitary and pineal glands. We have recreated your kind with surgical implantation. I have said that the history of this planet is far longer than the history of man, and nearly all of it has been forgotten. Typhon?'

'What became of the giants in the earth in those days?' said the Primordial Man. Or something to this effect; it was odd and difficult to recall in full. 'The true ones, the terrible lizards? I've been making them in the sea. Some got loose and swam to the Dardanelles. Our patron tried to ship one of Cuvier's Mosasaurs on the *Iberian*, but perhaps you heard what happened. Majestic creatures. What if they continued evolving, into birds and minds comparable and superior to those of men? This is a war across time, unbound by history's arrow. Why does the dragon haunt us? Why was Satan the snake? Why are seraphim winged serpents? The Star Wormwood hit the dinosaurs just as it struck us in Tunguska.'

'Haddaway, man...No, no, I'm done,' Winepress said.

---

[100] *Le mot de Cambronne*, that is, *merde*.

'Dinosaurs did not evolve into angels. I've seen how angels work, this is patently incorrect.'

'Yes, it's madness,' I said. 'I was trying to humour you, but this is absurd.'

'Yes, I thought it was impossible as well,' Typhon said. He turned, briefly revealing that the bundle was a stone with a face like a baby. 'But think of Plato's *theia mania*, the divine madness. Not insanity, but the ecstatic inspiration of the sublime, which leads to Apollonian prophecy, Dionysian mystery, the Music arts, and the Aphroditic appreciation of beauty and pleasure. This madness is the love of wisdom.'

The Rabbi chewed at his lip before noting. 'There may be something to it, I believe, with the ancient aeons of the earth giving rise to the choirs of angels. They at least seem to match the extinctions known by modern palaeontologists. Why else would He perform a wastefully long creation? Why else that use of 'aeons?"

'Why indeed?' Typhon chuckled, and added, 'I have seen this traveller's gifts, and the span of the cosmos. That is why this war is the last stand of the Host and the Rebellion. After this, comes a wild, untameable future. You know the end of the goddess Metis, whom Zeus swallowed to break the prophecy that her son would overthrow his father, as he had Cronos. We have the power to break providence. We are done here. Stand with us, leave, or die.'

'We don't want to fight you,' Siegfried said.

'Then don't fight us,' said Typhon. He and the Martian departed up the mountain road, towards the Cave of the Apocalypse. We could not stop him, realizing that we were powerless before them. I could not see the heat in things until they were far away, when the world flared up again in all its screaming, quaking glory. So that was what the world looked like to others.

Siegfried held his hands over his eyes, no longer able to alter the light to his poor eyes' needs.

I asked if everyone felt that sudden helplessness. Siegfried said yes, and noted that it felt like someone was sitting on his chest. Winepress said it felt like some enervating stroke.

Siegfried pulled a grenade out of his bag, giving the rest of us a fright.

'I can barely see straight without my optics. But you don't need fine detail with a potato masher,' he said. He followed our newfound enemies up the hill, ducking behind the trees and ridges.

'Well, we can't let Heinrich the Hypopygmented Hun go it alone,' said Noun, before charging after him, bayonet fixed.

The captains and I followed. Noun explained the stone baby between breaths as we found cover on the side of the road, waiting for an ambush: 'Nature and Divinity despise our race; very few nephela spawn more than one live child after years of stillborns, clots, and, more rarely, the boon and bane of a lithopædion, calcified in the abdomen.'

Such a 'stone-child' sterilises the mother, but if this lithopædion can be extracted, it is source of great power. Such a living stone can stabilise the effects of a nephilim's workings, allowing them to survive past death. This island was once an island at the bottom of the Aegean, dredged up, they say, by Artemis when Selene shined a moonbeam into the depths. Hence its ancient name of Letios, after Artemis' mother.

'Maybe it was a story,' he suggested. 'A cover for the working of that stone child. Or perhaps I'm spouting nonsense and they got it somewhere else...so, what was that name you mentioned earlier – Raguel?'

'Raduriel,' said the Rabbi. 'He is a supposed angel that eternally sings the praises of Adonai. The register and archivist of heaven that sits outside the hierarchy, superior to all others. He is the angel of the muses, inspiration, and creativity, who sings the other angels into existence. He is the enemy of Penemue, the watcher of literacy and internal thought, who taught men to read and write with ink and paper. He turned men away from the emotional praise of song to the way of reason.'

'He doesn't sound so bad,' I said.

'It's hard to condemn him, either,' said Venetianer. 'It's a strange part of Enoch's mysticism, antithetical to most Jewish thought, but writing was said to lead men astray, and let men carry on their words beyond death. Raduriel is, perhaps, *continuous* creation, the enemy of a dead man's legacy.'

'We didn't know for sure that it existed,' said Winepress. 'It seemed insurmountable. If he existed, then how could we win? How do you beat the infinite? But if the Rebellion was willing to mount their final assault at this time, perhaps we were wrong, and nothing like Raduriel truly existed. It was our only hope. He...he doesn't seem to be here in his alleged seat of Patmos.'

Winepress looked cold and drained. This seemed to be his greatest fear, the greatest complication in the plot, even more than the Battle of Armageddon itself. He pointed up to the summit of the mountain, to the cave. His finger quaked, yet he lead the charge with a keen ferocity, pistol and knobkierie in hand.

'We must continue our prospecting,' he said. 'That's what it was called at Messines. What the Australians have started calling Peaceful Penetration.'

Céleste interrupted with a loud snort and an apology.

'This whole mountain is a no man's land, up to their cave. We patrol around their front line, infiltrating from the flank and creeping in behind,' he said, as Céleste absolutely struggled to stifle her laughter. 'We need to destroy their morale, take them captive. They're more useful alive than dead.'

He looked out over the sea, to the sliver of Turkey on the horizon. He touched his head, as though aching, and added, 'Moseley died there...'

'Someone you knew?' Venetianer asked.

'Henry Moseley. Physicist, English lad, only twenty-seven...he proved Bohr's model, figured out how to derive atomic numbers from their X-Ray spectra...He taught us so much about the atom. Genius work. Could have done so much more. Boy deserved the Nobel. But, Gallipoli. Some sniper,' Winepress said. 'Twenty-seven. Same age as Alain-Fournier...Ever read him?'

He looked at Céleste, who shook her head in the negative.

'Nobody has. Schwarzschild was in his forties,' he added, distantly. 'He solved the Einstein field equations. Imagine if...what we could know about the universe...Sorry, it was the Mars mention, space is on my mind...'

Winepress seemed to drift a bit, his eye turning back to the mountain. He let out a yelp as eyes opened from the stones.

'*HaNephilim*,' said a voice echoing from the stones, an emotionless shout rumbling from the earth.

'Do not be afraid,' it said. Those burning, golden eyes rotated on the stone as if lining the rim of a wheel. The eyes routinely rotated into naked air at one open point in the rock. The second wheel revolved through the plane of the walking path, passing under our feet in some queer humiliation.

'I am Qafsiel Ha-Kaziel,' said the stones. 'The Watcher of the unfurling ages, the angel of Solitude, Tears, and the Death of Kings. I cannot interfere, merely shorten the way.'

'You won't fight us?' I asked.

'I cannot,' he said. 'I could lead you to wander, but I cannot kill. Only watch the cosmos unravel and bend the threads of fate. You spoke his name, the Archivist.'

Winepress breathed a sigh of ragged despair. The Rabbi covered his face.

'I can take you there, to the cave,' said the angel. '*Kefitzat Haderach.*'

'Why would you help us?' said Winepress.

'I am trapped here,' said Qafsiel. 'As is Raduriel. I am bound here, stretching from that miserable dragon pit to this sacred island. It is the doing of that woman's blood and the fell sorceries of that stone; she has the same mastery of space as I, stolen by her ancestors before the World's Rain.'

'Maybe the better question is why we would help you,' I said. 'Freeing some universal observer and the angel's factory for a shortcut is a fool's bargain.'

'I do not want Raduriel freed,' said the Angel.

'Are you a rebel angel?' Noun asked. 'Or a new treachery?'

'This is no rebellion. My sole duty is to watch,' said the angel. 'And I can see that Raduriel's continued existence will guarantee an eternity of war across the Inheritance of the Meek. And I would rather not watch that grinding horror. Bear witness to this: two armies clashing day after day in the mountains, dying in the mud and rising again with morning dew. That dew runs from their skin, wearing away at the mountains. Day after day, licking away at that solid stone until it's nothing but more dirt in the mud. That's nothing but a flicker of eternity. This war must have an end. I can't bear witness to this.'

The Rabbi nodded vigorously, almost teary-eyed. We all had this sense of crushing weight grinding down on us, a grim solidarity to do anything to stop this. Oblivion was preferable to eternal war. Forever reincarnating into this battle, perpetually banging my blood-blind head into Armageddon Hill like that six-fingered hand plinking against my skull - That heavy drop of the thumb, five fingers in quick succession, a miserable mantra.

Maybe we could live on, protecting humanity, but we would lose in the end, and fade away. We could have our own rebellion, our uprising, but in the end, these two collossi would beat each other flat with all mankind as casualties. We would be reduced to rats, scurrying in the trenches, nibbling on their waste. Thunder split the sky like the war in the other world, and we sealed our bargain."

The Jersey Devil, the Snallygaster, and the Maryland Testing Grounds: If the angels are unkind or the season is dark...

For reasons unknown, people continue to live in New Jersey, despite it's distressingly high devil population. The eerie, primordial New Jersey Pine Barrens are home to many legends, including the helpful White Stag and the traveling ghost of the "Black Doctor" James Still, an African-American who taught himself medicine in order to help sick Piners sometime in the 19th century. But the most famous legend of the Pine Barrens is the notorious Jersey Devil.

The legend goes that, centuries ago, the impoverished Mother Leeds (sometimes a Mrs. Shrouds of Leeds Point, sometimes an anonymous witch) expected a thirteenth child. As the winter winds howling through the Pine Barrens drowned out her evening prayers, she cried, "Lord, let this child not be a child, but a devil!" Because that's the kind of things expectant mothers prayed about in the late 18th Century, apparently. And indeed, when she gave birth to the child, it came out as a demon with golden eyes in the head of a horse, hoofed limbs, and batlike wings, because just go with it. The Devil, born down in a dead man's town, flew out of the chimney and out into the winter night.

Other, less popular, origin stories involve an American woman cursed for falling in love with a British soldier during the Revolutionary War, or a Piney woman who either seduced or mistreated a minister. There are many variations, most of them portraying God as a capricious and spitefully literal genie.

Sometimes the monster is said to visit its mother every day until it understood that it wasn't wanted, which brings to mind a series of rather awkward conversations at the Leeds residence[101]. Other times, it kills her, the family, and the midwives, and apparently takes the time to write down the events of the story because there's no other way it could have spread. It may all seem unbelievable, but show a little faith - there's magic in the night.

Atlantic County Historian Alfred Heston traced the names mentioned in the legend to several early New Jerseyians, including a Daniel Leeds who established Leeds Point in Great Egg Harbor in 1699, and a Samuel Shrouds who lived in Little Egg circa 1735, across from a "Mother Leeds."

It is often claimed that the Leeds Devil acts as a kind of ill omen, appearing before shipwrecks and the outbreaks of war, but I see no evidence of it, unlike the similar incidents surrounding the Mothman of West Virginia. 1909 is a bit premature for an omen of World War One, and as the next flap of sightings occurred in 1950, the Devil missed out on a rather important conflict. It may, in fact, be a publicity whore, appearing soon after Charles Skinner's 1903 book *American Myths and Legends* declared that the Leeds Devil legends were dying out, and after a period of obscurity in the 30s and 40s.

While reports of the Jersey Devil began in the 19th Century at the latest - Joseph Bonaparte allegedly encountered it on a hunting trip in the 1820s- the flap that concerns us is the January 16-23, 1909 sightings, in which thousands of people reported seeing a creature[102].

---

[101] "Sorry, J.D., but I've got twelve *non*-monster children to raise..."
[102] The following narrative was pieced together from the *Philadelphia Record*, January 16-23rd, the *Philadelphia Zoo*, and McCloy, James. F., & Ray Miller, *The Jersey Devil* (Middle Atlantic Press, June 1979); Beck, Henry Charlton, *Jersey*

Simply a creature – it had no definitive attributes other than being an animal. The most common description is a mammalian, hoofed animal with bat wings and a horse's head, but this is a more recent invention meant to smooth over the wild discrepancies in the description of the 1909-version of the Devil. Some reported the typical horse-headed bats and a similar yet wingless kangaroo horse, while others witnessed wingless demon-dogs and reptilian figures. The two universal traits are its piercing eyes and terrifying, otherworldly cry.

It must be noted that a kangaroo might be the explanation; In a similar incident in 1900, a kangaroo hopped around Mays Landing, New Jersey, terrifying families with its screams. And on June 12 of the previous year, a kangaroo baffled and terrorized the citizens of New Richmond, Wisconsin.

The flap began on the morning of January 16th, when a man named Zack Cozzens encountered a creature with glowing eyes flying down the street of Woodbury. Cozzens said, "I first heard a hissing sound. Then, something white flew across the street. I saw two spots of phosphorus-- the eyes of the beast.... It was as fast as an auto." Not long after in Bristol, Pennsylvania, John McCowen saw the creature shrieking near a canal. Bristol's postmaster, E.W. Minster, saw a gigantic bird with a horse's head, again screaming. Patrolman James Sackville fired upon it.

The next day, the citizens of Bristol found hoof prints in the snow. It should be noted that snow is an awful material for footprint identification, as snow prints are easily distorted by melting, variations in gait, and wind. Deer prints easily distort into diabolic hooves when exposed to the morning sun and terrified eyes.

The Lowdens of Burlington, New Jersey found their trash can knocked down and ransacked. Like their neighbors, hoof prints covered their yard, running up trees and across roofs, before disappearing in the middle of the road.

A party of hunters attempted to track the Devil, but the dogs refused to follow the tracks. The next day, a pair of professional hunters tracked the monster to Gloucester, following a trail that hopped

Genesis (New Brunswick,NJ: Rutgers Univ. Press, 1963), with some additional local flavor from McPhee, John. *The Pine Barrens* (Farrar, Straus and Giroux; 7th ptg. Edition - May 1, 1978)

five foot fences and squeezed under eight inch gaps. Soon, the diabolic hoof prints covered South Jersey, the tangled tracks of a beast on a rampage through the Delaware Valley[103].

At 2:30 am on the 19th, Nelson Evans and his wife awoke to the creature's characteristic shrieking. They watched the Devil from their bedroom window in Gloucester. The Devil wandered around their yard for about ten minutes, and Mr. Evans' detailed description of the creature became the definitive one:

"It was about three feet and half high, with a head like a collie dog and a face like a horse. It had a long neck, wings about two feet long, and its back legs were like those of a crane, and it had horse's hooves. It walked on its back legs and held up two short front legs with paws on them. It didn't use the front legs at all while we were watching. My wife and I were scared, I tell you, but I managed to open the window and say, 'Shoo', and it turned around, barked at me, and flew away."

The Devil was busy over the next few days. Both a policeman in Burlington and Reverend John Pursell in Pemberton saw the Leeds Devil almost simultaneously, while hunters in Haddonfield found more dead end tracks. It flew past a crowd in Collingswood, towards Moorestown, where John Smith and George Snyder saw the Devil at the Mount Carmel Cemetery. Soon after, hoof prints appeared on rooftops and around a dead puppy in Riverside. It appeared before a loaded trolley and by the Black Hawk Social Club in Clementon. Hoof prints appeared around the arsenal of Trenton. The West Collingswood Fire Department attempted to hose the devil down; it charged them before flying away, this time appearing as an ostrich-like creature with larger wings.

Mrs. J.H. White saw the creature curled up in the corner of her lawn while taking her laundry off the line. She fainted from shock. Her

---

[103] The occurrence of a tangle of inexplicable, hoofed footprints crossing the countryside is eerily similar to the Devil's Footprints phenomenon of Devon, England, which occurred between the 8th and 9th of February, 1855. Oddly enough, the tracks were also linked to escaped kangaroos. ("TOPSHAM. THE TWO-LEGGED WONDER". *Western Times*. 24 February 1855./ Household, Geoffrey (ed.) (1985). *The Devil's Footprints: The Great Devon Mystery as it was Reported in the Newspapers of 1855*. Exeter: Devon Books.)

husband rushed outside. The Devil responded by "spurting flames" at him and fleeing, an act both indisputably metal and paralleling events in the legend of Spring-Heeled Jack.

Schools, such as Mt. Ephraim's, and various workplaces shut down due to a lack of attendance. Trolley services in Trenton and New Brunswick armed their drivers. The pews in churches filled with the citizens brave enough to leave their houses. Chickens fell dead by the hundreds in the darkness on the edge of town.

As one would expect from a demonic entity, the Leeds Devil sought out the most hellish domain imaginable: Camden.

There, a Mrs. Sorbinski found the Demon of the Pines tormenting her dog, suddenly seizing her prized pet in its jaws. Sorbinski, fighting instincts honed by life in Camden, counterattacked with a broom. The Devil retreated, barked at the gathering crowd of over a hundred Camdenites, and soared away as the crowd charged the Devil on Kaigan Hill. The police fired at the creature.

The streets of Camden stayed clean that night.

The next day, police officer Louis Strehr saw the devil drinking out of a horse trough. There were a few other sightings in Salem and Blackwood, before a final sighting in February, the devil finding Camden inhospitable.

Even in its day, the Jersey Devil sightings were met with skepticism. The *Philadelphia Zoo* even offered a mocking $10,000 reward for its capture, and a pair of pranksters and dime museum operators named Norman Jefferies and Jacob Hope played along by purchasing and painting a kangaroo (because you could do that back then), gluing claws and wings on it, and claiming that the Jersey Devil was in fact an escaped specimen of Australian vampire bat. Others, from contemporaries to modern experts, proposed various birds, such as the now locally extinct four-foot-tall Sand Hill Crane, various herons, and an escaped central-African hammer-headed fruit bat (*Hypsignathus monstrosus*) as answers. Slightly less serious or credible experts blame a surviving population of pterodactyls.

The 22 January 1909 edition of the *Asbury Park Evening Press* carried a possibly related, but far more uncanny, sighting by Dan Possack of Millville, New Jersey. As he toiled outside of his home, a stranger called out his name. Turning to look, he saw a birdlike creature which he estimated to be eighteen feet tall, who asked him where his garbage can was. Possack, overcome with terror, fled, but was seized by the bird's massive red beak. Possack retaliated with a blow of his ax, which revealed that this bird was made of some rather solid, wood-like substance that could be split into distinct chunks and slivers. One such fragment was the beast's glassy eye. The creature dropped Possack, whispered something he could not recall, and retreated after another ax-blow to the face. At that point the bird flew away, but without using its wings – it instead inhaled air, became comically round, and floated away like a balloon.

This "awful struggle" recalls an 1892 incident in which Joseph Lassalle, a farmer from Sainte-Emelie-de-l'Energie, Quebec, shot and killed a tall, bird-like entity. The creature stood roughly 150 cm tall, with a nearly five meter wide wingspan. These wings were covered in black feathers, the legs resembled those of a wolf, the tail feathers covered a calf-like tail, and its head resembled something vaguely like a monkey or ape. However, this tale is almost certainly a bit of yellow journalism, as the body was allegedly taken to McGill University largely intact, yet nothing came of it.

A similar entity, the Snallygaster, haunted New Jersey and Maryland in February and March of the same year. The Snallygaster – an anglophone corruption of the German *Scheller Geist* ("fast ghost")- was a chimerical folk legend with reptilian and avian features, though it could also have octopus like tentacles or odd demonic features. In its 18th and 19th century tales, it grabbed people, flew off into the sky, and drank their blood, but its 1909 version was a massive, avian being with a single eye and a shriek likened to a train whistle. Alerted by the prior Jersey Devil case, the Smithsonian offered a reward for its hide, and Theodore Roosevelt considered hunting it. However, the bulk of the reports were found to be fabricated by editor George C. Rhoderick and journalist Ralph S. Wolfe of the *Middletown Valley Register*.

On Halloween of that same year, a pair of Baltimore boys had a Lovecraftian encounter with an entity in the so-called Baldwin House, a decrepit mansion on 28th street[104]. Charles and Clarence Legare, respectively seven and nine years of age, were drawn into their neighborhood's infamous haunted house by rumors of ghostly howls, phantom lights, and ghoulish entities, including a deformed figure frequently spotted through the windows. The boys rushed from the estate, faces twisted in terror, and could only communicate through guttural grunts and irrational violence. Their condition only grew worse, with Charles destroying household objects and Clarence frequently attempting to return to the Baldwin House. Their parents relocated to a house near Johns Hopkins University, where local doctors and government authorities erected a barbed wire fence around the estate. The boys simply burrowed beneath it. They were shackled, and eventually confined to cages in the backyard.

Maryland would also see the emergence of the Dwayyo, a folkloric creature associated with parts of Frederick County, particularly the forests that would become Gambrill State Park area. Local lore has positioned the Dwayyo, a bushy-tailed wolf that walks on its hind legs, as the arch enemy of the Snallygaster. The name itself was coined in 1944 in the papers of West Middletown and Wolfsville, with a major flap in November of 1965 and sightings in Fall of 1976, but the beast appears to be based on early tales of the Hexenwolf of Pennsylvania Dutch lore. It may also be tied to wider elements of American "dogmen," like the creatures spotted in Wexford County, Michigan in 1887, the Beast of Bray Road witnessed in Wisconsin in 1936, and related boogeymen such as the Bunny Man of Washington D.C. and the Goatman. Between 1893 and 1917, Crawford County, Michigan was haunted by similar dogmen, along with a menagerie of 'witches,' ghosts, lights in the sky, and prowling men. The town of Pere Cheney seemed to be the epicenter of the events, suffering multiple diphtheria and cholera outbreaks, resulting in its eventual abandonment.

Oddly, this wave of Delaware Valley monsters all seemed to spring from, of all things, 1898's Spanish-American War. The government had learned the power of yellow journalism, the capacity for media to inspire public terror and outrage. McKinley had fought against the call for war,

---

[104] *The San Francisco Examiner*, 4 November 1906.

but his successors would learn to embrace it. Which brings us to the origins of the US military's psychological operations: a Maryland facility known as Edgewood Arsenal, "the Place God Forgot."

Edgewood Arsenal

> "We began to hear about the terrors of this place. Everyone we talked to on the way out here said we were going to the place God forgot! They tell tales of men being gassed and burned."
> - Anonymous Private, 1918.

In 1917, Woodrow Wilson established a federally-owned chemical factory on the Aberdeen Proving Grounds of Gunpowder Neck, Maryland. During the First World War, privately-owned civilian contractors held much of America's vast industrial output; the 5,300 hectares of Edgewood Arsenal were needed for more controlled production and research. The Arsenal produced phosgene, chloropicrin, mustard and chlorine gas, and sealed them in shells produced on site. Between January and November 1918, Edgewood produced 10,817 tons of toxic gas (not including containers and shells).

The government's direct oversight was rooted in a need for secrecy; any whistleblower from the facility could be prosecuted for treason rather than simple industrial espionage. Between its establishment in 1917 to its dissolution in 1975, the American government used Edgewood as a site for human and animal experimentation. In the fifties through seventies, this heavily involved the use of PCP, LSD, and various psychotropics; it's much less well-publicized World War One era experiments involved simulated gas attacks and drugs such as cocaine and cannabis. These experiments were generally more academic than the *ad hoc*, trial-by-fire experimentation of the "Hellfire Boy" units of the U.S. Chemical Warfare Service fighting in Europe[105], and dabbling in the fringe elements of chemical and exotic warfare. Elements of these early

[105] Emery, Theo. (2017). *Hellfire Boys: The Birth of the U.S. Chemical Warfare Service and the Race for the World's Deadliest Weapons.* Little, Brown.

experiments proliferated, with descendants as wild as MKNAOMI's bioweapon programs and the Stargate Project of the late 1970s at Fort Meade, and as mundane as the domestic turkey breeding programs that gave rise to the Beltsville Small White. The most direct descendant, perhaps more of a resurrection, was 1953's MKOFTEN, an occult parallel project to the psychotropic and internal terrorism focus of MKULTRA[106], which recruited psychics, palm-readers, witches, and demonologists.

One logistical officer, a Corporal Carl (or Carlos) Fontana Garcia, began working at Edgewood Arsenal in February 1918, shipped in alongside many personnel from Sandy Hook, New Jersey. He had previously been a military liaison in Picher, Oklahoma, which produced half of the lead and zinc exported and used by America during the Great War; unfortunately, the mines leached cadmium and lead into the local aquifers, leading to Picher's dissolution a century later. In the meantime, they served as a useful test case for heavy metal poisoning. Fontana Garcia's writings would only be released in 1977, eight years after his death, largely for legal reasons, though he defended his actions, believing that any whistleblowing would have been treated as high treason under the Espionage Act of 1917.

A Mexican-American of partial German descent, Fontana Garcia at first believed his work at Edgewood dealt with the transport of marihuana from Mexico, general medical-agricultural logistics, and as a Spanish and German interpreter. Things quickly took a turn for the worst. Despite native fluency in English, Carlos Fontana wrote in curt Spanish, perhaps as a protective mechanism from prying eyes.

"Feb. 6 -New trains in from Mexico. Components for gas. 12 tons of Machinery. 1 ton 600 lbs. of crop. 400 lbs coca leaves. Remaining ten cars to be sent forward to Baltimore docks, donkeys, war horses. Oversaw the transfer of civilian labor from Maryland Dredging & Contracting. Lost one man on the train since prior station – presumably jumped off, no body found. The four barracks are simply tar paper over board- shoddy, tile brick shipments incoming. The soldiers came to one of the cars armed. It did not contain the crops, but men and women.

---

[106] Thomas, Gordon (2007) *Secrets and Lies*. p. 295-299

Some of them loaded in at Kansas City- many prisoners from both Fort Leavenworth and the Leavenworth Penitentiary. Mostly negro, a dozen white men, and, in a separate compartment, two white women, poisoners. Fourteen men were loaded in from Boston; these men were noted as Haitians. The remaining were Indians from Mexico, Apache it seemed, some Yaqui - pacificos. Unfortunately, few of them seemed capable of speaking Spanish. I was reassured that these were savage guerrillas, criminals, idiots, imbeciles, and the lowest grades of moron; they would have been executed or euthanized elsewhere. Some had already been sterilized off-site. Others were left normal so our doctors could see if germ-plasm could be altered with gas exposure. One of the weaker subjects died in transit, perhaps of tuberculosis, and was moved to the crematory, her bones to be sent to Dr Hrdlička for anthropological research. One of the Apache women panicked when she saw the corpse, and the soldiers held her down with the crooks used to shepherd the bleatless goats. One old gray goat stopped to watch, eyes swiveling in the socket."

Fontana Garcia soon realized that he was handling the installation of a gas chamber, refurbished from the air-tight compartment of a scuttled German naval vessel.

On the 8th of February, Fontana Garcia was forced to attend a lecture on the subject of the notorious Kallikak and Juke Families and "genetic hygiene." Later, perhaps on the 10th, he and others watched anti-German propaganda films. He mentions watching one member of the staff, a Viennese physician named Dr. Max Matschek, a cancer researcher. He noted that Matschek was an older man, an enemy alien trapped in the United States due to the declaration of war, and coerced into working with the staff. "Blackmailed with young prostitutes," was the rumor. Matschek's activities were not often recorded, beyond studying the carcinogenic effects of mustard gas, tobacco smoke and what were probably aflatoxins (caustic derivatives of chilies and cottonseed) on goats, birds, pigs, and humans.

It is hard to piece together due to Fontana Garcia's writing style, but there appeared to be some controversy with a Dr. Frank Crozer Knowles of Philadelphia, who, despite earlier partial experimentation on unwitting subjects, had refused to participate in full body iodide exposure tests on humans – seemingly using Hydrogen iodide gas and red phosphorous- and threatened to send information to higher authorities. His attempts were quickly stifled, and Edgewood's research proceeded. Fontana Garcia had to guide several subjects through the effects, including a man who had been briefly blinded by gas, and two people exposed to a chemical that caused massive red welts on the body. They knew Fontana Garcia as "Cabrera," a tongue-in-cheek alias derived from "the place of goats." They often saw him standing on the hill on the Aberdeen grounds, watching the goats suffer experimental gas attacks.

On the 10th, William Buehler Seabrook arrived at the base for medical examination. Seabrook, a native of nearby Westminster, Maryland, suffered a severe gas attack at Verdun in 1916, as part of the American Field Service. He was awarded the Croix de Guerre for his service, and published *the Diary of Section VI* a year after. For reasons unknown, there were some oddities in his medical record. It appears, though cannot be confirmed, that elements at Edgewood looked for such anomalies in German gas attack victims, hoping to spot signs of new chemical weapons in the enemy's arsenal.

On the 11th, the Master Sergeant began exposure tests on what Fontana Garcia called "a dozen Am.[107] negroes – three morons, seven of average intellect, two of above average intellect, tested with the Dix test[108]. Exposure to distilled cannabis in extreme concentration. Resin and liquid. Cocaine is proposed next." The marihuana tests would later be repeated, on the 16th, on a group of vaguely defined "neurotics" from a Baltimore institute. These groups were then separated into a control group and an experimental group subjected to "the lights."

As Fontana Garcia explained, "The youngest man was Sardara Bucha, finishing his doctorate here. He is interested in using power [sic]

---

[107] This "Am." seems to be his code for African-Americans, to distinguish them from the Haitian group.

[108] This would be the test created by Carl Brigham while serving as a first lieutenant in the US Sanitary Corps – he was a psychology graduate student at the time. The test was implemented at Camp Dix. It would be used to justify anti-immigration practices, though Brigham would later disavow his earlier eugenicist statements, and develop the SAT.

lights to disorient crowds. He studies photosensitivity, keeping test subjects in darkness for hours before subjecting them to rapid flashes and intense pulses. He has induced vertigo. He is willing to talk, though it took time to learn his given name, which he does not use as many find it feminine. He is an Asiatic- family comes from Lahore, but he's from Washington. His family was terrorized in the Bellingham riots – none were killed, but he became fascinated in nonviolent crowd control. Non-chemical, he always clarifies – he calls the gassing barbaric. He focuses on sonic and optic weaponry."

Another Bucha experiment involved an unmedicated control group of soldiers, a second test group overdosed on THC in the form of oil in their rations, followed by a subtle whining sound played by phonograph. Most men in the control reported headaches, unease, nausea, apprehension, and even chest pains, while the medicated group resulted in panic and extreme irritation, with one man cutting into the wall to find the source of the noise. Bucha was given a steady supply of hyoscine salts, a medicine used for motion sickness and nausea with side effects of blurred vision and sleepiness. Though not true, it was widely believed in the 1910s that powdered hyoscine- called "Devil's breath"- could be used to create a hypnotic state, destroying the ego and allowing a poisoner to verbally program their victims.

Fontana Garcia was most fascinated by Joseph Scheider, a psychologist who believed that the conduit between the physical body and the mind was fully electro-chemical, with a system that "Matschek deride[d] as an electrical reinvention of the humors, though Scheider insists that his work is building on the work of Silvanus P. Thompson." He had severely psychotic patients strapped into a Bergonic chair, a form of electroshock therapy also meant to stimulate and exercise the muscles.

Scheider's innovation lay in the use of Tesla coils and electromagnetic rigs to attempt "remote electro-chemical stimulation," using magnetized gas shells as a delivery mechanism. According to Fontana Garcia, "Sch. and others are proposing a terrible amount of money, an attempt to increase the conductivity of air with various methods: mixing other gases – Ar[gon] and He[lium], dusts of metal, graphite bursts, electrification of air using high power transformers, the latter of which, he must admit, would make a better weapon than the psychological stimulation. Planes, airships, and high-power wireless transmitters are considered, but too difficult to test on grounds at this time." One specific subfield here was the attempts to recreate ball lightning via electrical stimulation of the atmosphere.

The mission, it seems, was to replicate the Angel of Mons sightings: One of Scheider's hypothesis was that troops in Belgium and northern France experienced mind-altering electro-chemical effects, a mixture of combat stress, socio-religious suggestion, and the ionized air of thunderstorms magnified by the amount of soil and trace metals displaced into the atmosphere by artillery and entrenchment. He wished to weaponize these factors, projecting angelic and demonic imagery to bolster allies and terrify foes. One idea was using metallic droplets and signaling lights from airplanes and airships to frighten troops out of the trenches.

During an electricity allocation dispute between Bucha and Scheider's group, Fontana Garcia finally sought out the Master Sergeant, who led from a small office in a wing dedicated to "Lamarckian and hereditary chemical effects" – what we would now consider environmental epigenetics. The section is usually mentioned under the euphemism, "the hygiene wing." Fontana Garcia was rather, it seems, frightened of this department; chemical and drug effects were one thing, but this sector covered experiments including "chicken, turkey, rats, hog, and goat modification," "bird training and disruption," including attempts at killing birds with radio and a virtual graveyard dedicated to poison gas victims. Black goats roamed freely in the hall, to occasionally be fitted with a collar and a mask and lead to a gas chamber.

The event that terrified Fontana Garcia out of the wing was a grant from the Carnegie Institute funding "systemic public eugenics tactics." Fontana Garcia does not elaborate on this euphemism, but from his outrage, it appears to describe a germ weapon program. During this quick trip into the wing, the sound of muffled screaming was a constant, alarming presence.

"The two white female prisoners were there. The elder was treated with mescaline and locked in a dark room of caged rats. The younger was in another room. Her screams were muffled. I was not frightened until I signed the pay order for a civilian obstetrician, who had lost his practice for performing abortions. Everywhere, there were the goats. The old gray one sat with its ear to the door."

He knocked on the office of the Master Sergeant. He noted that "due to nerves," he opened the unlocked door and entered the room without being granted permission. However, nobody was there. "Box on the desk," he noted. "Linwood, NJ. There was a human hand inside, charred black. Instruments on table were set out, bores for coring bone. Dried marrow had been extracted into a vial. I placed my notes in a capsule and left."

The people on base used metal cylinders to deliver internal documents, to prevent their consumption by goats.

"I ducked into the next hallway to allow a team of porters to wheel in two heavy crates on carts. I had approved imports from Mexico, but was not given details apart from volume. They were from the ONI contact in Mexico, Guatemala, and Honduras, with notes from a Dr. Maximus Neumayer of Brazil."

After a period of examination in Matschek's wing, Seabrook spoke to a Haitian patient. "The man was barely coherent," wrote Seabrook. "There were now dozens of these Haitian captives (for there is no better word for it), but this man, Pentecouste Albinet, had awakened. It took some time to understand him, as he spoke a French Creole rather than the European tongue to which I was accustomed, and his recent string of miseries had rendered his speech slurred and disjointed. He and his wife (Osane) earned the scorn of a sorcerer or some kind of shape-shifter known as a Zobop, who disguised himself in the form of a goat. He repeatedly spoke of a "Hasco" – it took some probing, as he did not understand the English acronym, but it became obvious that he had, essentially, been blackbirded[109] and corralled on a Haitian American

---

[109] Blackbirding is a form of human trafficking that emerged just as European nations and their New World colonies were beginning to ban plantation slavery; vessels would abduct villages from one island and work them to death elsewhere. The practice usually ended in the death or stranding of the enslaved, as a stable, long-term plantation was illegal. While most common in the Pacific Islands, it occurred on the west coast of Mexico and in the Caribbean to a lesser extent. The people of the Gilbert Islands were trafficked up to at least

Sugar Company plantation, like the kidnapping of free negroes for sale in the Antebellum South.

Albinet referred to someone called the Green Sailor, but I am not sure if this is separate from this zobop ring. He spoke of strange coaches (perhaps motor cars), with blue and red lights that dazzled people so these zobops can abduct peasants to work on these sugar plantations[110]. I remember, not long ago, the distressing tale of a negro family discovered in Georgia that were completely unaware that slavery had ended, their white family keeping them in servitude through the Emancipation - I wonder if our nation's companies have continued to trade in Caribbean chattel slavery.

Albinet said that many zobop cars came during the anarchy following the downfall of President [Vilbrun Guillaume] Sam, torn limb from limb and paraded down the street by a rebel mob. He said it was the police chief Charles Oscar Etienne who sold them off; he purged the jails of Sam's opponents, gunning down the dangerous and selling off the most vulnerable – Albinet's friend, Vespasien Lamour, had disappeared into the police cars, only to be found in a ditch near the farms. It seems that Etienne had become something of a demon after death, Le Chaloska."

William Seabrook attempted to get the names of the other Haitians detained at the facility, but the men were completely inarticulate, moving as if in a hypnotic trance. He describes them as "automatons" with "ceaseless, clockwork laboring." Albinet appeared to play along with there actions, afraid of what the military men would do to him if they realized the spell had been broken.

In private, Seabrook asked what the zobops did to the men, and

1908, with 4 out of 5 Gilbert Islanders dying. [McCreery, David (1993). "The cargo of the Montserrat: Gilbertese labour in Guatemalan coffee". *The Americas*. Vol. 49 (3), pp. 271–295] It is related to the concept of Shanghaing, though this form of abduction specifically refers to kidnapping sailors or men in related professions to forcibly serve aboard vessels.

[110] This appears to be related to the Haitian urban legend of the *auto-tigre* or zobop cars. The major, best-known flap broke out in the Port-au-Prince area in the 1940s, with reports of cars with blue headlights abducting people from the countryside.

was told that the sorcerers used a powder to force obedience. Seabrook managed to write down the recipe phonetically, but had to consult a dictionary later, as the terms were obscure: a melange of bufotoxins, pufferfish organs, datura, and strange white "salts" distributed by Americans. When Seabrook asked for clarification on which Americans were providing what he assumed were psychoactive drugs, Albinet said that they were navy doctors who came during the 1915 invasion, which lasted into the 30s. Albinet said that these slaves could not eat meat or salt, which would break the spell. Seabrook was introduced to the word that he would go on to popularize in the English language – *zombi*. It must have been the greatest of all evils to the Haitian, he noted, slavery by chemistry and magic, toil unbroken even in death.

Seabrook tried to help these "zombies," but his ability to move about the base was highly restricted, and he quickly realized that his plan – to gather meat and salt from his meals – had been anticipated by the base. His rations were sweet, heavy in fruits, vegetables, and chocolates. That was one thing he enjoyed about his stay, "fantastic desserts," though the realization that the bananas and sugar likely came along with these slaves ruined the enjoyment. Seabrook's plotting was also hindered by the experimental treatments for "chemical penumonia," better known as pneumontitis. From what was disclosed to him, the treatment involved adrenal gland extracts injected by needle into pulmonary arteries. Now, this is clearly a precursor to the cortisone treatments pioneered by Philip S. Hench in 1929 and widely used in the 50s, but the medical staff had very little understanding of its efficacy. By the end of the first week of treatment, Seabrook's respiratory issues had improved, but his mind was foggy. He had problems telling time, slept twelve hours a day, and his muscles ached.

One night, Albinet took Seabrook to the window and said that there was a mystic who could save them, a wise man named Lucien-François Jean-Maine[111], who had learned voodoo and the ways of European magic from Crowley himself. Albinet, pointed at Sirius, and said that

---

[111] Lucien-François Jean-Maine was a member of the Ordo Templi Orientis, and founded its first lodge in Haiti, along with his own cult of the Black Snake (*La Couleuvre Noire*) in 1922, which synthesized Hermeticism with Vodun. Though the OTO was founded by Crowley, he was in fact taught by Papus.

Jean-Maine spoke to beings from that star, and that there was a *lwa* called Lam from Mars, who was coming to change the world. "L'Etoile Flamboyante," he said, quoting Albert Pike's description of Sirius' place in Scottish Rite Freemasonry.

The next thirteen days of Fontana Garcia's activities are written in plain lists of distribution actions, mostly notes to self such as "Refill flour stock. Requisition canned beans. Tell Annapolis no further small arms needed."

Shortly after this lull, he translated a report on the faith healer Bárbara Guerrero, known as Pachita. Born in Chihuahua, this woman participated in the Revolution as a strikingly successful *curandera,* so much that the Rio de Janeiro building in Colonia Roma, Mexico City bore the sobriquet "la Casa de las Brujas." Witnesses gave testimony of wounds closing beneath her passing hand, the rgeneration of missing organs, bullets rising from entrance wounds, and perfect transfusions performed by inserting surgical tubing into her mouth and exhaling blood. She claimed that she channeled her knowledge from Cuauhtémoc, the last emperor of Tenochtitlan, though Fontana Garcia thought it unlikely that a 16th century Aztec ruler would understand the recent science of blood transfusion.

Fontana Garcia was summoned to the Hygiene Wing on 26 February, to act as a translator. One of the workers, in gloves and a mask, led him to a storeroom that had been fully sterilized by a still working janitorial crew. Laid out on multiple surgical tables, Fontana Garcia watched the workers assembled a skeleton, while other men drilled into what looked like a petrified baby.

"The skeleton was today's shipment, from Middleboro, Massachusetts. On another table, several men unpacked a crate. Two other large crates sat beside other tables, ready for unpacking. These four were shipped from Mexico. The one on the table was from Mexico City. The skinny, long one came from Guanajuato. The smallest one was from the Yucatán. The final one, though bearing Mexican shipment, was from Guatemala. They were shipped with notes from our ONI contact, Sylvanus Morley. Photographs were attached, images from an Atzec tomb in old Tenochtitlán and a site labeled as 'Tula (Tollan Xicocotitlan).' Tula, it was noted, was 'built by Quinametzin (giant people) and the Feathered Serpent (Quetzalcoatl), in alignment with the Morning Star. Cholula's pyramids were built by Xelhua, a towering giant.' One of the workers, Professor Gunnison, explained that Hernán Cortés had learned of these giants from the indigenous kings. This mummified body was one, 'Tzilacatzin,' a mighty Otontin warrior who met the Spanish at the gate of Tenochtitlán - a goliath, 3m tall, who killed several Spaniards with thrown stones and dodged the bullets fired in retribution. Despite fighting naked and his terrific height, he was able to dive into a crowd and disguise himself as common men and women, harrying the conquistadores without fear...This was his body, a marvel; a shriveled, blackened mummy that still took nine feet of table-space to display. I glanced at the now half-assembled skeleton of Middleboro, and saw that it must have stood at least 2.2m in life. The crate from Guanajuato contained the skinny bodies of albino giants found in volcanic caverns - the Seven Luminaries of the Valle de Santiago, 2.5m long. The old grizzled goat watched me as I looked into the giant's face, his conical gas mask still hanging around his neck. I met its gaze, and it put its head down and walked out the door.

The doctor handled another set of documents, which had been lost in the mail for months, inadvertently shipped to a cousin of our Morley with the same name, down to the middle name, a setback that cost the team three weeks. There were other bones there, gigantic in size, transported by crate from Washington and New York. I stood silently for much too long, forced to take it all it.

It was then that I was asked to leave the room. When asked for a reason, I was simply told that the Master Sergeant wanted the bare minimum of necessary staff - security purposes. I was frustrated, but could not justify staying with my credentials as a logistician.

As I walked past the Master Sergeant's office, I saw an orange light on the wall, waving like a flame, and was called in. The phonograph was playing a record- Little Tich's 'One of the Deathless Army.' The Master Sergeant often played comical records, Tich and Maurel especially, to drown out the sounds of his wing. The room was dark. The Master sat in his chair, facing away. I greeted and saluted, even if he could not see me, and asked what he needed. On his desk was a skull made of crystal, and a mask of jade. He asked me if I knew what they were. I said that I believed they were Aztec artifacts. He said no, despite the legends, they've never found a crystal skull in Mexico, nor do any of its Indian races mention such crafts; all such artifacts seem to originate in Germany from Brazilian quartz crystals, dealt out by a French huckster named Eugène Boban. Same with the Jade Olmec masks. He asked me how much of history was artifice, how many artifacts in museums were a frauds to make money and promote comforting lies. History, he said, not the past but the recording, was a war of mystics against scholars. His strange, strained voice sounded almost feminine, like a croaking old woman. I had heard that before, to the point that some wondered if the commandant's reclusive nature was hiding 'his' sex, but he didn't sound too different from some small old men.

I asked him if those skeletons were indeed giants. He asked how large the skeletons appeared. I said about 3m. He then asked if that seemed unusually tall for a man. I said yes, and he said, 'then they would seem to be giants.' I clarified, asking if these were oddities, tall Mexican men, and not their own racial strain. He said he knew what I meant; it was still a mystery, he said, but they do seem to be freaks that arise from normal populations, as the heroes and folk legends of old. But, perhaps, as with the giants of Patagonia, they may exist in small clans or tribes in the remote parts of the world. On his desk was a somewhat elongated skull with large eyes resembling a child, but it was about the size of an adult woman. He abruptly noted, even though he couldn't have seen where I was looking, that the expanded occipital lobe explained the magic in the eyes of giants. The cyclopes, seven-cloaked Balor of Ireland, the Indian giants with freezing stares. It was really all glandular; an enlarged pituitary gland and an over-developed pineal gland. It had been known since ancient days – the Eye of Horus even resembled the pineal gland.

I asked if he needed anything from me, and he simply requested that I keep the giant's bodies off the records; he did not want knowledge of their existence to reach the Smithsonian Institution. I said of course."

It seems that the bones of giants collected at the Smithsonian dissappeared as part of a deliberate "coup," of sorts, that wrestled control of the collection during the power vacuum left by Samuel Pierpont Langley. Langly was a polymath - a solar physicist, inventor, astronomer, aviation pioneer, and skilled administrator of a massive, multi-discipline organization - whose career came to a tragic end when the Smithsonian's accountant, William Karr, was caught embezzling.

Despite no connection to the crime, Langley took the loss of funds as a personal failure, refused his salary, and, not long after, suffered a delibitating stroke that would soon kill him. He was succeeded as the Smithsonian Secretary by Charles Doolittle Walcott in 1907, a brilliant paleontologist who began an ambitious reorganization of the Institution and its resources. While simultaneously heading the United States Geological Survey, Walcott excavated and analyzed the Burgess shale fossil formation. Walcott's talents and imagination soon turned, unexpectedly, to founding the National Advisory Committee for Aeronautics in 1915, which sought to rapidly improve American air power. During Walcott's reshuffling, some force behind the scenes seized control of the collection of giant bones amid the administrative chaos.

The primary suspect is considered to be Aleš Hrdlička, a eugenicist known for distorting and destroying the remains of Native Americans to fit his theories of human development – which red-haired giants would obviously disrupt. Some point the finger at Walcott, working under the directions of Major John Wesley Powell and other military and government connections, in exchange for the approval of his NACA proposition. A more nebulous suspect is someone in the Department of Anthropology connected to Karr's embezzlement, a possible artifact theft ring that continued well into the Second World War.

Harrison Gray Dyar Jr., an etymologist with ties to the spiritualist movement, is speculated to be involved, mostly for his bizarre hobby of tunneling beneath the Smithsonian's property and his own home; a massive set of tunnels, some of which had even been electrified, were discovered in 1924. The rumor mill acted quickly, cooking up ties to bootlegers, artifact smugglers, secret Confederate storehouses, the Underground Railroad, and the lab of a German chemist and wartime saboteur named "Doctor Otto von Golph," who appears to have been invented by the Washington Post.[112]

112   Epstein, Marc E. (2016). Moths, Myths, and Mosquitoes: The Eccentric Life of Harrison G. Dyar, Jr. New York: Oxford University Press.

Others implicate head curator Otis T. Mason, based soley on his position at the time, though William Henry Holmes' fervent debates over the antiquity of human presence in America give him a (tenuous) motive in addition to his opportunities. Holmes had previously debunked the Calaveras Skull, a hoax by Josiah Whitney that placed humans alongside mastodons and mammoths in the Americas, attracting a media circus of Theosophists, Creationists, and crackpots. Alongside the Cardiff giant, Holmes may have simply wanted to toss all of this giant and anachronsitic skull nonsense into the crank pile to keep it from contaminating real anthropology. However, the Master Sergeant's statement seems to validate the smuggling theory:

"I asked the source of the enmity with the Smithsonian. He, in return, asked for my theory, and I considered that men of science might destroy giants to preserve their evolutionary theories. The Master Sergeant laughed: 'Darwinists at the Smithsonian? Please. In what world does anyone listen to scientists? No, it's a racket. Those bones are collected by weathly parties, for their own selfish aims. Some simply collect them, some grind them up like Chinese rhino horn. Some have even tried to graft giant-bone tissue onto their own. But there is no conspiracy – the Grand Architect of the Universe is enlightened self-interest. There are only wealthy individuals who want to make themselves and their spawn truly greater than you.'

The Master Sergeant then asked if I knew of Arjuna. I said no – he said that it was the secret name of Francisco Madero, the deposed president of Mexico. Madero was a Spiritist and a medium, who claimed to be in communion with his late baby brother. He had visited the grave of Allan Kardec while educated in Paris, spoke to Gabriel Delanne on psychic physics, learned of theosophy under Annie Besant, and, some say, was initiated in secret lore of Indian sorcery, dating back to the priests of the Aztec gods. He had met strange men in Europe, learned of secret doctrines, and had even been the first head of state to fly in a plane. He believed, drawing on Kardec's 'Genesis,' that 'the Time is at Hand,' a sort of Apocalypse of society but not the world itself, when man would be forced to abandon all previously held beliefs and create a new ethical paradigm of science and spirit, without regards to nation, faith, or race. Too bad, noted the Master, that Ambassador [Henry Lane]

Wilson and General Huerta had to engineer his downfall and murder. But Huerta had no regard for the work of giants – he was a pygmy, a moral midget. And so these mummies fell into American hands, and not those of the Kaiser's Necromancer."

In 2013, the CIA declassified "The Adam and Eve Story," a long-form essay on cataclysmic geology and paleoarchaeology written by Chan Thomas in 1965, in a .pdf. titled "Declassified in Part – Sanitized Copy Approved for Release." Thomas, drawing from his research at Baalbek, Tiahuanaco, and Easter Island, held that much of what we know of the Flood Myth is based on an 11,500 year old Ur-langauge of the East known as Naga (distinct from the language of the Naga of Northeastern India). The reason for the disparity between *Genesis 1* and *Genesis 2* lay in their later, Ezra-era combintation; the first chapter is recounting a true "Genesis" event that took place 4.5 billion years ago, and the second a cultural "Regenesis" which occurred some 11,500 years ago.

The essay is rather disjointed, at times, due to CIA deletions. After a map of the accepted Earth's interior, the photocopyist covered another four pages with random articles from the 11 March 1966 issue of *Time* Magazine. A requisition for tools and repair supplies takes up page 48 to 49, between the tale of Indra, King of the Gods, striking down the Titans with global destruction events (from *the Brahmavaivarta Purana* and *Krishnajanma Khanda*) and an except of Plato's *Timaeus* describing the world's destruction by "earth-fire and inudation." However, Freedom of Information Act requests indicate that the excluded sections are something of a brief inventory of giant bone finds from different parts of the Americas, connecting them to various lost centers of Native American civilization, particularly the Mississippian mound builders of the Angel phase. These shipments of bones are labeled as arriving at Washington D.C. sites associated with the Smithsonian's vast archives, and with a site in Gunpowder Neck, MD that is almost certainly Edgewood. Rather than nephilim, however, Thomas alludes to a theory that these giants with the Naga of Hinduism, a subterranean and aquatic race of snake-people or reptilian humanoids, but it is hard to clarify using the censored texts.

The end of the released document contains the following poem, without attribution:

> "A little bit of knowledge can be a dangerous thing;
> Or it can be a vibrant seed
> Giving rise to verdant forests
> And awakening sleeping giants."

During the next four days, Fontana Garcia oversaw a massive shipment of gas shells to Calais, a ramp-up in the construction timetable of a tertiary storage site, and made preparations for members of the the National Parks Service to come and inspect the Edgewood site's water table for chemical contamination. The site planners needed to find a relatively safe spot for a munitions dump. The issue, as he noted, is that "The Arsenal is a swamp leaching from streams and rivers. Bosses complain about price of cement basement site."

The base's authorities circulated a transcription of the 1910 lecture series of one Reverend W.A. Laughlin, M.A., Minister of the Methodist Episcopal Church, which covered Nephilim, Rephaim, Gibborim, "The Men Before Adam," and the intermarriage of giants with the Irish race. Fontana Garcia bribed Matschek with "an exceptionally youthful prostitute," to worm himself into the Hygiene Wing and find what was in the other boxes.

"It ate at me," he wrote. "What secret could be more shocking than a giant?"

Dr. Matschek managed to make his way in, faking approval to examine the skin of the mummy. Fontana Garcia tried to intercept him later in the day, but Matschek slipped past him, "Bloodlessly pale and in a daze[...] and locked himself in his office." The next day, Fontana Garcia confronted the oncologist as he arrived, helping pin him down with the help of Bucha.

"He then asked me if I had ever heard of something called a Huay Chivo. I said no. Matschek told me to ask Porfirio's Prisoners. I asked why the Indians would know, and this set off Bucha, who hated the term – he would tell you that he was a proper Indian of the Punjab, one of the purest remaining tribes of the Aryan race, and that Columbus' idiocy should not diminish his ancient people. Matschek told him to go flicker some lights, and that shut Bucha up. Matschek waited for Bucha to leave earshot before he said that it was some kind of Mayan sorcerer. Some kind of goat, I noted. He shook his head, more of a shiver than a no, and said those bodies had goat heads. And legs, he said, but it was the heads that made him jump out of his skin.

Maybe it was sewn on, I said, to break the silence. Like a carnival mermaid. Matschek said yes, it must have been some kind of Mayan ritual.

After the day's rounds, I went to the pens, asking around the prisoners if any were Maya, and telling them that I was not with Whitehead," he wrote. Whitehead was a figure alluded to several times by Fontana Garcia and others at the base, a cruel man who seemed to be a rank sadist. It was discovered that his D.O. was the product of a mail-order diploma mill created by a spiritualist group called the Philosophers of the Living Fire; rather than firing him and pressing charges, he was pressed into the role of the Master Sergeant's enforcer and the bases' boogieman, with those prisoners and volunteers who misbehaved or threatened to complain sent to his office. Nobody mentions what went on there. Only the screams, and the sudden silence.

These prisoners had previously been processed by a linguist, checking for populations of obscure languages and bilingualism. One proposition involved recruiting Native Americans from the American Southwest and Northern Mexico as field telephone messengers, based off of the innovative method of Col. Alfred Wainwright Bloor, who recruited Choctaw soldiers stationed in France to transmit messages in languages virtual unknown in Europe.

"One of the men came forward and said he was from the south, and had been a soldier and fought in Chan Santa Cruz, and knew some of them. Everyone else seemed to be a Northerner. The man said he might know some Maya, but he'd need to be let go if he helped me, his records destroyed. I said it wasn't up to me. He leaned against the bars and whispered to me in broken English, so the others could not hear – 'I am a traitor. To the government of Mexico. But not to God. I see God. The cross, she said to me, not to battle Maya. I see an angel. *Chakub*. No Jacob, *Chakub*. One of seven Chakub. He has...*alas de un ave*, he said in Spanish. Like the macaw. But his head, a jaguar. I thought a lion, but no, jaguar. He told me to battle my captains and the *Kasal-Ikub*, no the Maya. So I do that, and they take me. And I am here, instead of dead.'

I had the handlers take the soldier out of the cell. I asked him if her knew what the huay chivo was. The man answered that there were 'Kasal Ikub, evil spirits, they must be driven out. The devil makes them by blending man and beast, tricking people into deals that transform them, or if evil men willingly defile their own kindred and take up the skin of animals. 'The angel' showed him sleeping giants in the great watery cenotes under the Yucatán, where these ancients had kept 'elefantes peludos' - mammoths - and sea monsters as pets. I asked if the Maya ever sewed the heads of such animals to human corpses. He said no, and asked why I asked. I said it was nothing, and told the handlers to ship him back to Mexico, under cover of mental defect incompatible with pharmacological study."

Fontana Garcia then writes, almost as an aside, that the pharmacology and linguistic research was tied to a clairvoyance study under the Master Sergeant's direct control. There were organic attempts to induce psychic powers, hinging on alchemist Giuliano Kremmerz's contemporary work on synthesizing Latin American shamanism and Paracelsian philosophy into a "sacred materialism."

The Master Sergeant's chief subject, however, was the practice of remote viewing, under the less euphemistic term of clairvoyance. It was triggered by a case of a minister of the Congregational Church, Frank Hampton Fox, who claimed that he was, since his infancy, in a peculiar form of psychic contact with his youngest son, Clement. In childhood, such ESP was usually triggered by injuries, sometimes as minor as falling on his face during a high school footrace. However, in his twenty-third year, his son sailed for Europe as a corporal in the Signal Corps. Twelve days from port, a psychic disturbance effected his father, who stopped suddenly in his study back in Decatur, Illinois. "I leaned back in my chair and closed by eyes for a few moments in order to regain my composure," he would write. "Instantly a sea scene was before me; I saw clearly a large convoy of ships. In the midst of them I saw the dark form of a submarine come up out of the water and prepare to launch a torpedo. It was so close to the one transport that I saw most clearly that our gunners could not fire on it. From somewhere beyond the range of my vision came a shell sinking the submarine. The sinking was the only thing that was perfectly clear." The elder Fox quickly noted down the date, time, and all remembered details, and tried to get a message to his son. His son sent a letter weeks later, reporting the details of the event. What was fascinating to investigators was that the Rev.-Dr. Fox's letter was still in the mail, and thus a sealed and dated testimony of a premonition. The event sent the paranormalist community into a frenzy, and research into the military application was quickly initiated, a field inquiry would continue into the seventies, in the Stargate Program. The tale of Rev.-Dr. Fox would later be published in 1920, the *Journal of the American Society for Psychical Research*, Vol. XIV.

Three hours later, Fontana Garcia, encountered a man in a well-tailored suit who asked him what he had seen in the laboratory. The man, according to his description, was "tall, tanned, Asiatic[...] with overly-long fingers." Fontana Garcia wrote that he simply said the he saw some mummies from the Yucatán. The man nodded and abruptly mentioned Agustus and Alice Dixon Le Plongeon, two psychic archeologists who uncovered the Pyramid of the Magicians and the Mayan site at Chichen Itza. The couple believed that they had found elements of an ancient Atlantean civilization, and were reincarnations of the Mayan Prince Coh and Queen Moo. The strange man said, in a threatening manner, that they both died in the prior decade, from exposure to strange radiance. The folklorist Yda Hillis Addis had been driven mad, and disappeared from the asylum. The man then asked if he could speak to James Churchward, "and grew strangely frustrated when I said that I neither knew him or where he was located. He said that this Churchward was 'making magical steel, armor for ships. He was arming the ships. There were monsters inside the ships, sailing from Greece,' and he had to find the people behind these creatures." He oddly told Fontana Garcia that "He would have no skin in Tamoanchan." The man then stormed off, but with an almost comical, waddling walk.

Fontana Garcia immediately returned to his barracks and locked the door. Not long after, he left the room to ask his superiors about this strange man, but nobody in the complex matched the description. When he asked some of the chemists about Churchward, they referred him to an index, from which he learned that Churchward had patented NCV steel, named after
nickel, chrome, and vanadium. Chromium, he learned was derived from "Siberian red lead," while Vanadium was derived from red salts of

Mexican "brown lead," named after Freja, a Nordic goddess of war, death, fertility, associated with the Egyptian Isis. Baffled about the significance of all this, Fontana Garcia wrote to Churchward's Lakeville, Connecticut estate.

The next day, Fontana Garcia noted that "the mathematicians demanded difficult to find dies for their calculating engines's moving parts. They also wished to consult directly with Babbage, but he was found to be ailing." The Babbage here is Henry Prevost Babbage, the son of the more famous Charles Babbage, inventor of the Difference and Analytical Engines. Henry Babbage promoted his father's work throughout his life, and tried to update the engines' principles to the electronic era, with little success. Edgewood duplicated his successful 1910 model four-function calculating engine, using the prototype stored at Harvard as a guide, adding elements of Herman Hollerith's punch-card tabulating system[113]. Fontana Garcia found the calculation team's activities a mystery, puzzling over their use of William Walker Atkinson's works on divination through crystal gazing, and various recent works on numerology.

The team was comprised of an Ismaili Persian scholar who dabbled in the numerical alchemy of Geber, an expert on St. Augustine of Hippo and the early Church fathers who had been recruited from the violent debates against the American Catholic Church[114], a "Pythagorian" mathematician, several cryptologists, and a follower of L. Dow Bailliett, who blended classical numerology with tonal theory and Biblical exegesis. Fontana Garcia expressed bafflement at what they were doing, mentioning that they believed that the universe was "calculable," and

---

[113] Hollerith's tabulating system became the basis of the Computing-Tabulating-Recording Company, renamed International Business Machines in 1924 under the leadership of Thomas John Watson, Sr. These Hollerith punch-card systems were infamously used to manage the logistics of the Holocaust.

[114] The American Catholic Church was an odd schism/folk reformation of the Catholic Church, largely involving integration of elements of Orthodoxy and liturgy in various Eastern languages, such as Polish, Hungarian, and Lithuanian. There is some circumstantial evidence that this figure is Victor von Kubinyi, but this identification is very dubious, as he was moving between South Bend, Indiana and New York City during this time.

spiritual ideas could be communicated through mathematical, "Pythagorian" expression. They referenced the *Kybalion*, likely also written by W.W. Atkinson, and the idea that upper and lower planes of existence were simply vibrating on different 'scales.' Everything in the universe was fundamentally gendered, with male and female poles interacting to generate new entities, whatever they may be – both in easy analogies to sex, and something more in line with the thesis-antithesis-synthesis dialectic of Fichte. This group tied this into Leibniz's studies of the I Ching, and emerging developments in Boolean algebra and its application to machinery.

"The world was just the cypher resulting from self-calculating numbers," wrote Fontana Garcia. "Everything came from some system checking itself, formulas like ritual spells conjuring things into being. Strange people. They called it Caldean [sic] numerology. Everything is based on a 1 to 8 system. They say an 8-based number system is better, though 16 also worked. There's also something about the law of fives and atomic triads, and the Number of the Beast. When I asked about that last one, they mentioned an ancient priest named Irenaeus, who said 666 came from *Lateinos*, the Greek word for Latin. Not Rome, but the Latin tongue, and the spread and mutation of language. The lesser known number of the beast, 616, could be alluded to the base 16-system. The Persian said language should be abandoned. Numbers were the holy way of communicating and describing ideas, truth over the illusions of language. I demanded to know what the military application was; they said code-breaking. They could, with these calculating engines, decipher any code and create unbreakable codes. They even said that advanced number systems could one day model and create physical objects and allow for some sort of advanced telegraphy and 'non-physical space.'"

Four days later, Fontana Garcia was approached by an unknown communications officer, James Churchward's reply letter in hand. Fontana Garcia had to read this letter with this officer looking over his shoulder. Churchward was rather mystified that someone from the military wanted to hear his story, but he explained that he had learned advanced metallurgical secrets from the ancients. While he was a Sri Lankan tea planter, an Indian mystic told him about an ancient civilization that extended across Polynesia, the ancient site of the Garden of Eden. The inhabitants of this antediluvian civilization, the Naascal of Mu, established colonies that became all the great ancient civilizations – Babylon, Egypt, India, Persia, and the Maya. The mystic taught him the dead language of the Naascal, and he learned the applications of the brown leads of India and the red leads of the Himalaya. The vessels of the US Navy, he claimed, are now clad in the armaments of ancient Mu. Fontana Garcia read the letter slowly to remember its details. The man from communications snatched the letter out of his hand, tore it up, and told Fontana Garcia not to tell anyone of what was written there, before leaving the room.

The events of the next three days caused Fontana Garcia's narrative to break down. "Bucha started screaming in the hallway, along with several of his test subjects. He passed out not long after. When he recovered, six hours later, he did not know what happened. Several of the men were forcibly treated with derivatives of heroin, tinctures of laudanum, codeine variants, the authorities deciding not to let an opportunity go to waste."

Fontana Garcia soon recorded a splitting headache, and went to sleep. He awoke to the screams of rioting prisoners in the middle of the night. When he shouted for an answer, one of the prisoners turned and charged with a club made from a chair's leg. He quickly retreated into the room, the rioters beating at the locked door.

William Seabrook, spent a blurry, nightmarish week largely isolated, drugged, and bedridden, coughing up a dark fluid that his doctors would not explain. The riot shocked him into a state of lucidity, and he soon heard the 'zombies' screaming and pounding on the door of Matschek's wing, searching room to room. The way he describes it, the Haitians were active but still not fully lucid, filled with a feral energy – but where there had once been "sedated control, there was undirected anger and maniacal disquiet." Seabrook pushed his bed to the door, and covered his mouth so his raspy breathing would not alert the zombies.

The next day, Fontana Garcia reported nothing. The third day, he recorded what had transpired. The riot had been quelled, with three prisoners dead and two security officers wounded. It began when the prisoners learned that, to Fontana Garcia's surprise, his informant on the *huay chivo* had been isolated and executed with injections of an experimental stimulant, escalating the dosage until he died. Judging by the label of "Edeleanu's synthesis" and the description of "bruxism...and joyous laughter," the substance was MDMA or a similar substituted amphetamine, acquired when American government confiscated the Merck Group's American assets in 1917. It was likely that Whitehead had taunted the others with his death.

A strange haze filled the room at about eight o'clock, and someone rang an alarm. There was a fire in the Hygiene Wing, and Fontana Garcia donned a gas mask and run to the wing.

At the door to the Master Sergeant's room, he saw the old goat. "The thing stared at me through its gas mask as I passed. That is when it made a chortling noise, despite its debleting. I turned to look – the goat was standing on its hind legs, and leaning in the door frame. As silly as it may sound, the damn thing held itself like a man, a boss looking into an employee's office. He was supervising me, interested in my reaction. There were people stumbling around, naked to the waist, wearing only work pants. All negroes, with no reaction to what transpired but hoarse coughs. They moved without purpose, as if blinded by the haze but no will to call out to one another for guidance. When I turned my head, through the flame and the smoke and the gas, I saw a creature – the creature on the slab. It was the *huay chivo*, a goat-man, the classic devil, alive and walking. It pointed at me with its free hand. It held a fire-ax with the other. I screamed, and ran from the wing."

The following morning, Fontana Garcia was at work, dealing with the fallout of the fire. The officers explained the panic away with the leak of an experimental hallucinogenic gas. Indeed, Fontana Garcia saw with his own eyes that there was little in the way of fire damage in the wing, and he suspected that the smoke, heat, and light was a deliberate bit of stage-magic, a show put on for the Master Sergeant's research – or entertainment. Bucha believed this to be the case, as he had somehow lost control of his own experiments, though Matschek believed it was foreign sabotage, having seen "someone in a strange mask" leaping away into the darkness, or, as he nervously confided to Fontana Garcia, "a man with the head of a goat or ram." Fontana Garcia went to the Hygiene Wing once more, and made his report of the creature. "They laughed it off," he wrote. "They said the goat-man people had seen on base was in fact an escaped experimental kangaroo. When I said that I had the records of all experimental stock on site, with no records of imported kangaroos, I was sternly told that I was mistaken, and that I was not, in fact, at all responsible for the logistical input of the entire operation. I was told by Jameson that further questions would lead to official reprimands."

Within a week, Fontana Garcia would be allowed transfer out of the base to Fort Meade. He accepted.

Doctors had quietly dismissed William Seabrook three days earlier – he was blindfolded, driven to the closest train station, and unceremoniously removed from the car. He soon traveled to Haiti as a journalist, where he would meet with Constant Polynice, who would relate the story of the Ti Joseph, a "sorcerer" who drugged peasants into a zombified state and gave them mock burial and resurrection ceremonies. These "walking dead" were sent to work on the HASCO plantations, with Ti Joseph pocketing their wages. The scheme fell apart when Ti Joseph's wife fed several of the slaves pistachio nuts, sending the workers "back to their graves," which, reading between the lines, indicates that he may have murdered several of his victims after they rebelled. While HASCO feigned ignorance of the scheme and the zombie "resurrections," it's rather implausible that nobody at HASCO saw something wrong with these "vacant-eyed" slaves. Seabrook would expose these events to the world in his 1929 book, *The Magic Island*, best known for inspiring the Bela Legosi film *White Zombie* and kicking off a voodoo and zombie craze in American pop culture.

The experiments at Edgewood would continue for decades, shifting focus as the scientific understanding of psychotropic drugs increased.

A "goatman" would haunt Maryland sporadically, until an intense flap of sightings in 1950s and 1970s, associated with the Belsville Agricultural Research Center.

The mysterious Master Sergeant John Amy disappeared into classified military records, with vague ties to the "Stargate" psychic warfare program of the 1970s. Research into nephilim would decline significantly after his leadership, though in December 1952, medical researcher Andrija Puharich and mystic D.G. Vinod, working from information Puharich uncovered during his time at Edgewood, channeled a group of entities known as "the Nine," associated with the Egyptian Ennead, the Annunaki, the Nine Unknown Men, and the Nephilim.

The Phoenician and the Circassian.

This excerpt from Ender Hoca's diary deals with notions of race that have become obscured by time - the Ottoman Sultanate, in order to discourage nationalist unity among the Arabic-speaking peoples of the Empire, stressed their diverse origins as various preexisting nations. The Levantine peoples' Phoenician heritage was played up, and Arabic-speakers in the provinces roughly corresponding to modern day Syria and Iraq were considered to be members of the prominent Eastern Aramaic-speaking culture variously known as Assyrians, Syrians, Syriacs, Babylonians, Chaldeans, and Arameans. These non-Arabic origins were more often embraced by the Christians of these regions than their Muslim neighbors, but this is not a hard and fast rule -there were many Christian pan-Arabic nationalists- though Muslims have an obvious incentive in connecting themselves to the culture that produced Mohammed, and the politically powerful bloodline that he produced.

In previous centuries, the Ottoman Empire posited itself as the center of the Muslim world, and stressed its dual heritage as the inheritor of the caliphate and the successor to the Roman Empire, the latter through its conquest of Constantinople. In this way, it positioned itself in a similar manner as the Habsburgs, holding onto the monarchal model of a state, based on fealty to the sultan rather than ethno-nationalism.

However, the Young Turk coup brought about a highly racialized worldview that promoted Turanism or pan-Turanism, which originated among the Ottoman intelligentsia in the 1870s. It also found some purchase among the Magyars of the Austro-Hungarian Empire, who wanted Turkish allies against the German hegemony of Central Europe and the rising tide of Panslavism to the east and south, a notion propagated by the work of Hungarian Turkologist Vámbéry Ármin. In the long-discredited annals of scientific racism, the Turanid race was the alleged blend of the Uralic and Altaic peoples, the combination of the Europids/Caucasians and Mongolid races. The Turanids included the Turkic peoples, Hungarians, Tatars, and Finnic peoples, though some radical theorists included, even more spuriously, the Tibetans (who speak a Sino-Tibetan language), the Japanese and Koreans (who speak the Japonic language family and a language isolate, respectively, whose alleged ties with the Altaic languages are highly disputed), and the ancient Sumerians (who spoke another language isolate). In Turanism, the Turks in particular were considered to have brought civilization to Europe. The Ottoman Turks promoted this view under the form of *Türklük*, "Turkishness," and the integrity of this race became enshrined in national law, with insults against Turkishness became a prosecutable offense.

No longer viewing themselves as the center of Islam, the Young Turk's empire wished to become the ruling power of a union of the Turanids. This promised pan-Turanid Empire would be truly massive, spanning from Finland down to Hungary, across the Ottoman Empire at its greatest historical extent, and practically all of Central Asia: southern Turkic and Tatar-inhabited Russia, Mongolia, the Turcomen regions of Persia, Uighurstan, Tibet, and as far west as Manchuria. Since this was obviously a non-starter that would have enraged the Russians, Chinese, Persians, Germans, Arabs, and most of the people who would have been absorbed into the empire on a racial pretext very few had ever even heard of, the Ottoman establishment focused on consolidating Turanid power within the Sultanate. Its extreme interpretation meant the elimination or assimilation of all non-Turanid peoples within its borders.

The most prominent of these efforts include systematic genocide of the Armenians, Greek Christians, and the Assyrians during and immediately after the war, though these persecutions began as early as the the Hamidian Massacres of 1894 to 1897, which were motivated by the final gasps of pan-Islamism in the Empire and resentment against these relatively wealthy Christian minorities. Roughly one to one and a half million Armenians, half-to-three-quarters of a million Assyrians, and nearly a million Greek Christian and members of other Christian groups were murdered under this policy. While not at widespread, Turkish forces carried out massacres, expulsions, and suppression actions against other minorities such as Jews, Maronites, and Caucasians.

"I entered the drawing room, pulled my notes from under my arm and set them on the table, and took my place in a chair in front of my commanding officers, with my "morning couple"- a cup of salty ayran with a sprig of mint in it, and a hot cup of coffee," wrote Ender.

"'I finally have a suspect in my investigation into some of the queerer acts of sabotage carried out across the Sublime Ottoman State. These incidents, generally involving the twisting or welding of metal without the application of heat or explosions, and the displacement of heavy machinery, have occurred in Istanbul, Izmir, Trebizond, Basra, Bitilis, Damascus, Haifa, and at our facilities at Lake Van. I believe I have found our saboteur.'

The Commander said he understood, 'this group you are calling the Phoenicians.'

I said it was not a group, but an individual.

'An individual?' asked the Kadı, 'Your report lists an attack in the Beirut Vilayet and the Sancak of Zor on the same day, followed by the Basra Incident the following day, and a strike in the Archipelago that night. A strike in the lower Hejaz, followed by the Lake Van attacks less than forty hours later. No one man is that mobile.'

'The Eternal State is facing an omnipresent enemy. Let me tell you a story, a strange, long tale: It begins with my investigation into acts of Bedouin sabotage at Antioch. My unit had chosen to detach itself from the main body of troops in the region, as the Arabs' main advantage had been our inability to react to their light horse and mobility, and I had become concerned with the seemingly unchecked movement of their saboteurs in the region. So I took advantage of their greatest weakness – their propensity towards infighting. I sent off one of our loyalist Arab detachments to harry the rebel force near Antioch, asking them to only engage Arab forces speaking conspicuous dialects on the hope of pinpointing our Arabian Bedouins. They were also tasked with interrogating any Sedentary Arabs they met.

I settled into our command center and researched documents pertaining to the Antioch sabotage, and ordered one of the remaining depots restocked for use as bait in case the initial lure failed.

By the end of the month, my Syrian outriders retreated to base, our Bedouin enemies in hot pursuit. The commanding officer had the forethought to send a message ahead, and my task force and the local garrison prepared an ambush. Our outriders entered the encampment and turned to prepare a defensive position behind the high hill.

The enemy rode over the hill and into the blinding sun. The first one to shield his eyes let out a cry of alarm as he saw the vanguard of Turkish defenders hidden behind stone and steel. He fell to Berker's rifle. The next two Arabs were unhorsed, the the third and fourth killed outright, and the fifth unsaddled and dragged to his death by the panicking horse.

And then the sixth rider came over the hill, and the defenders lost their nerve. The light of the sun was now, through some sudden mirage, behind the golden rider.

I saw a thin figure on an unremarkable gray mare. The men would claim that they saw a glowing, golden colossus on the back of a brass destrier. A dread fell upon the troops as they quickly realized that even the machine gun was useless against this monster. Several of them fell dead, seemingly shot with
their own bullets. Another man tumbled to the ground and sobbed out the Throne verse[115], covering his face in horror; a second man recited the 113th sūrah[116].

'There will be no peace until the wolf no longer preys upon the lion; until the fig tree no longer strangles down the cedar!' it screamed as it rode. The voice echoed from all around the hill. 'Until the Turks have fallen, until Gog is cast down and buried in the Valley of the Hordes! Until the *Faranji* invader is drive back to the land of Magog and the tombs of Scythians, Romans, Goths, and Persians!'

Berker stayed at my side, paralyzed by a mixture of duty and fear. He soon found the strength to raise and aim his rifle, but I put my hand on the barrel.

---

[115] Ayat al-Kursi, the common name of Al-Baqara 255, is a verse of the Qur'an stating the sublime majesty and incomparable power of Allah, recited as a protection against djinn.

[116] Al-Falaq (Daybreak), a brief chapter recited to ward off the evils of Shaitan.

'Rise against Gog, Magog, Eshkenaz, Humnaye, and all the twenty-two kingdoms!' It shouted.

My German adviser shouted that it was a trick in his plain Turkish - *Lies! Do not listen!*

'This is no trick, but the blackest sorcery! I am the child of ghouls, fed on corpse-meat and blood! I hunger!" the figure screamed. I saw and heard nothing but a small, mounted youth in sand coloured scarves and a grey jacket screaming high-pitched and muffled words through what I believed was a British respirator, perhaps looted from the Australians. This melodrama terrified the men, however, the survivors reporting a booming voice and fire pouring from the diabolical creature's needle-toothed mouth, its eyes nothing but empty sockets behind veils of still dripping human skin.

And then, with the sun in our eyes and terror in our hearts, the Arabs came charging down the stony hills like a spring flood.

I pulled out my sword and my pistol as our line dissolved in panic. Only Berker remained with me, covering my charge with rifle-fire.

'The wire rose, and the horses fell,' I said, and there was a line across the rocks, hobbling a pair of horses about to run me down.

The strange, small rider dismounted on the far side of the saddle as I reached its horse. Its feet landed three dozen meters behind me, against the machine-gun. I made an about-face, shot an Arab out of the saddle, and ran in blind panic for cover.

'The thief looked upon his prize, and his smile faded. He felt heat in the engine, soot in the barrel, fire on the trigger,' I said, hoping to disable the gun as I approached it.

I found the youth fiddling with the tools in the gun nest. I grabbed him and pushed him against the hot barrel, and pressed my pistol against his throat. I pulled the scarf away and tore down the mask, and realized that it was no boy, but a girl no older than my eldest daughter, in her middle twenties at best. I wondered, briefly, if I had come across the famed Cossack adventuress Maria Yurlova, who indeed fought against our troops for the Armenian cause.

Beneath the Bedouin scarf and robes, she wore a sandy yellow dress a decade out of style, a liver-grey jacket over a pair of leather-protected bandoleers, and a silk neckerchief the color of dried bone, adorned with a sewn-on map too folded for me to read. She was well-above average height for a woman, fair-skinned as far as Arabs go, neither beautiful nor ugly, but striking. She had a recessed chin curving into a swan-like neck, large ears, a long, prominent nose, short-cropped black hair in the European mode, and large, dark eyes whose whites seemed to shine like pearls. Her left hand had a rather disturbing deformity, her right index finger swollen, as if the bone was doubled under the skin. Our eyes met, and hers burned with what I thought was defiance in the face of death.

I hesitated, for I have never killed a woman in my life.

'But it was just an Arab,' interjected the Commander.

I glowered at him until he looked away, and continued.

'The corner of her mouth rose, and I knew it was not defiance, but arrogance, pride, and the trickster's triumph.

The Arab started to laugh, and slipped through my fingers, taking the machine gun with her.'

'How?'

'The scarf fell, and she simply stopped being in front of me,' I said. 'I was being literal. I swore we would meet again, and we did. Because I said so. I fell ill not long after.'

We speculated that she may have been a foreign agent, such as the German's woman in Istanbul, this Hilda von Einem by way of Lawrence[117].

What followed, I dared not relate to my superiors. I took the famed mad honey, dyed red by rhododendrons. Utnapishtim appeared to me, in a dream. Green. In robes of green, in a turban of green, in a world of churning green water. He was the great wiseman of the sea, Hızır[118], the Babylonian companion of Ibrahim who drank of the river of life. He was mistaken for many scholars and mystics in history, including the

---

[117] Lewis Einstein's *Inside Constantinople: A Diplomatist's Diary During the Dardanelles Expedition, April to September, 1915* refers to an unknown female German agitator operating in Istanbul at this time; Hilda von Einem was a popular fictional character from John Buchan's *Greenmantle* (1916), an alluring mastermind who plotted to stir up a jihad against the Allies. Lawrence is, of course, T.E. Lawrence.

[118] More commonly seen in English as an Arabic transliteration, al-Khidr.

Canaanite craftsman god Kothar-wa-Khasis. He says that he had met the Two-Horned Alexander, who appointed him to oversee the gates of Gog and Magog – an event highly important to Syriac apocalypticism since *the Apocalypse of Pseudo-Methodius*.

The idea of Hızır has haunted me since the loss of Said Nursi to the Russians[119]. He was relatively young – he would have been forty this year, if I'm not mistaken – but recognized early for his vast wisdom, to the point that scholars dubbed him Bediüzzaman, 'the most superior and unique,' a truly irreplaceable man. He was a Kurd of Nurs, arrested for his participation in the countercoup against the Liberals (of the Committee of Union and Progress), but was released and became an education reformer, and was eventually recruited into the Special Organization.

The scholar had said that Hızır lead a twilight existence, still alive but in the second of the five degrees of life; he is truly free and transcendent, free of bodily needs and able to appear to many people in many places at the same time. He will return to proclaim the falsehood of the Dajjal, humiliate the Antichrist, and challenge the evils of the end of the world. He was there at the beginning, with Ibrahim, and will be there at the end. He instructs saints, initiating them into the secret truths of the cosmos, and the nature of the world before the Deluge. He was the man in the pyramids, the scholar of Alexandria, Serapis Bey - the old sage of the oasis.

He showed me, beneath the waters, the bones of ancient men who came before man and jinn. He showed me a vast cavern in the Selma Plateau of Oman, the Majlis al-Jinn, the Parliament of the Hidden Race. And he showed me the bones of giants, buried in silt and reaching out in their terrified final moments. It surely was some grand justice – but I saw one skeleton clutching a child against its chest, a babe the size of a man. What had it done?

In my drowsy haze, I awoke to hear two knocks at my door – there were two children there, fair and black-eyed, asking me to be let it. I denied them, for I knew in my fear-clenched heart they were Munkar

---

119 Though Ender speaks of him as though he had died, Said Nursi had in fact escaped Russian captivity after two years and was making his way back to Istanbul as he wrote this, dying at the age of 83 in 1960.

and Nakir, the Denied and the Denier, the angels who question the dead in their graves. I said my Lord was Allah and that Muhammed was his prophet, and closed the door. I collapsed into a deep sleep.

I dreamt of the Peri race, descended from those fallen angels of Persian myth, denied paradise until they repent for some unknown crime, eternally ambivalent between angelic and diabolical natures. They live among the mortals, hidden like the djinn, but only their beautiful wings are invisible. They must instead hide themselves with guile and sorcery, forever hunted by angels and the divas of Ahriman, or in their keeps in Paristan, hidden in the Caucasian valleys of Koh-e-Qaf. There was some secret to their redemption, in the the ruined temples of Baalbek, or beneath them, when the region was called Ubelseyael, where the Watchers gathered. I flew there, in my sickened and sickening dream, spinning into the darkness of the earth like a drill. And there, beneath the world and among the bones, I knew peace.

I continued with my tale to my masters:

Two months later, I heard news that someone had come to collect on the bounty that the Attache had placed on the woman's head. One of the Bedouin saboteurs had turned her in for amnesty and a hefty sum, claiming that he had grown tired of working with a vile, half-mad sorceress. The bedouins kept her in a separate area apart from the men in the main camp, and he had sneaked up upon her as she slept, painted "Allah" in the middle of her brow, bracketed by a crude *damga* or Seal of Suleiman on each side of her forehead, gagged her, and bound her arms with rope. He placed her on his horse and spirited her away in the night towards a prison camp. His one condition was that she be granted a swift death by hanging, beheading, or firing squad so she could not let out a final curse upon his tribe.

I doubted his story, and attended the execution with Berker.

The bailiff mounted a raised platform on the already raised platform of the gallows and began shouting out crimes and sentences, exposing himself as a untrained fool. The executioner, however, acted with all the dignity and skill one would expect from an Ottoman executioner. He examined the condemned, writing down notes in a copybook as a shopkeeper would compose a supply order, a habit we share. He was a gypsy, as all executioners once were, with the eyes of an owl and the grim countenance of a man considered damned by the Empire he served, condemned to be buried in an unmarked grave in the Eyüp. He passed behind the prisoners, performing a final inspection. There were seventeen Arab rebels and the witch, who he took particular interest in.

The woman named Batul bınt Bülos bın Luka bın Işac bın Markus bın Yakob bın Gassan abu-Şedid stood accused of treason against the Sublime Ottoman State, terrorism, multiple counts of murder, sabotage and subversion against the Imperial war effort, collusion with the state's enemies, agitation, provocation, arms smuggling, horse-theft, sorcery, apostasy, prostitution, slander, and theft of government private property.

He gave her a chance to speak, noting that if she took this opportunity to perform an act of witchcraft, her sentence would be changed from the mercy of hanging to the brutality of flaying.

Besides me, Berker cringed at the mental image. I whispered to him, telling him to shoot the woman through the head or center of mass seconds before she was dropped, hoping to counter what I assumed was her plan.

The woman smirked, as though the world were a joke that only she got. She said that she wished for her sentence to be accurate, and that the false accusation of prostitution should be replaced by an accurate charge of planning and carrying out a breach of the Ottoman penal system. She looked out over the crowd, and her eyes lit up when she saw me. She smiled.

'My Arab brothers, do not fight to support that which deserves nothing but your scorn,' she said swiftly. 'Reclaim your pride. And to the Christians, the iron wall has tumbled down, and Gog and Magog are coming for you. This is the Apocalypse.'

The fool began translating her words into Arabic when the woman stomped down on the platform, breaking through the trap door. Berker fired off a meaningless shot that scattered the crowd around us. The trick of the reversed sun was repeated, and when the blinding flash faded and the sun returned to setting behind us, the Bedouin raiders were gone.

The woman, however, remained, popping out from behind one of the scaffold's beams and firing directly on my position using a pair of fresh revolvers and a bandoleer. The bailiff lay across the platform wheezing and choking on his own blood, a primitive dagger made from beaten down scrap fused through his thin neck.

Berker pushed me back, retreated several meters, and took a defensive firing position behind a boulder. Instead of following him, I walked forward through the dispersing crowd, slipping behind a guard tower.

I noticed that one of the men in the crowd, a thin Arab who had been standing near a pair of penal officers, no longer wore a bag over his shoulder. He had taken cover against the earth and thrown it forward under the gallows. As expected, the betrayer had been colluding with the woman all along. I dashed towards him, hoping for a useful hostage.

I waited for her to reload the revolver, but she never did; every time her weapon would have been depleted, the leather cover of her bandoleers simply sagged, and another six bullets appeared in the gun without a pause.

'The gunner's hand ached, her eyes grew sore, the chambers filled with dust, the grip burned like desert sand,' I said as bullets whizzed past me. She shouted a curse, and the barrage stopped dead, punctuated by the soft crash of metal against sand.

She scurried to the Betrayer, took him by the hand, and pulled him out of the world with her. The sands beneath them twisted up towards the sky, and they were gone.

She reappeared behind me, alone, and wrapped her arms around my neck. The world folded around us, and we tumbled backwards, closer to Qasr el Azraq, among the ruins of a Roman fortress cooled by the shadows of palms. I got one good look at her reflection in one of the beautiful, clear blue pools that supported that old Roman garrison. She now wore a small, domed hat the same hue as her dress with a black brim upturned so dramatically it was nothing more than a useless liner, but her outfit was the same as our last meeting.

She soon loosened her grip around my neck. I turned my head

to see her, but she was nowhere to be seen. I scanned the ruins, but could only hear a loud chuckling. She kept laughing every time I snapped my head around.

'You keep turning your head, as though you will find me,' she said. Her voice had a breathy, purring, crackling quality, aggravated by smoke and exaggerated by the harsh consonants of Arabic. She spoke slowly, deliberately, and with a humor that matched her laughing eyes. It was a rich voice, a tigress of a voice, but there was a strange distance to it, as though she were broadcasting over a wireless system – not its electronic crackle, but the tinny, hollow quality. 'I'm disappointed. I thought you understood what I do. You need to understand – I am not on the rocks behind you. I'm behind you. Always. No matter where you turn, I will always be directly behind you, because that's where I've decided to be.'

'I don't understand,' I admitted.

'It is simple, my friend. The place I am is the place behind you, until I decide otherwise. I can be a thousand leagues away, or spitting on your neck, but I will always be right there. Behind you,' she said. I felt a sharp, wet pinch on my neck, but turning my head in shock revealed nothing.

There was a brief pause as I regained my train of thought.

'You control the distance between objects,' I said.

'You almost have it,' she said. 'I had a problem putting this skill into words until I stole a Frenchman's encylopaedia. I would say that I change the correspondence of objects in space. Technical, yes, but it makes sense to me. I wish I could write out an equation in the dirt, but I can't. Too long.'

'What type of equation do you speak of?' I asked.

'Listen, my friend: A long time ago, I don't know much of history - but it was back when my kind were building Baghdad and naming the stars and your kind were, I don't know, eating yoghurt and raping prisoners- a number of very intelligent men discovered that the language of God wasn't Arabic, as we liked to believe, but numbers. The universal descriptor, known to all men and angels. The Greeks wanted to describe the universe with geometry and mechanics, shapes and lines and curves and forces, but these grand old Arabs discovered that it could be much simpler – equations, strings of numbers, ones and twos and zeroes. They focused on the restoring of this divine order, *al-gebr*, and the correspondence, the balancing, *al-muqbala*. The cosmos was nothing more than a vast equation. They puzzled it over for years...And now, you're talking to the meek, young Arab that solved it.'

Her blend of topology and magical language recalled the geomancers of Egypt, who practice the science of sand (*'ilm al-raml*), from the ancient pharaohs to the modern 'Abd al-Fattah al-Sayyid al-Toukhi.

'How did you solve it?' I asked.

'Simple. I went mad,' she said, and began laughing. 'Your government makes my people wear black – did you know that? I got to wear white one day in my life, and your kind came and dyed it red for me. All around me, my brothers and sisters, mother and father, my husband to be... My whole world went black. I found myself screaming in fields of green on an island on the other side of the world, with pieces of Turk scattered all around me. I had never been outside of walking distance of my home town, and here I was in a foreign paradise, with numbers burnt into my soul. That endless equation? It equals zero. Nothing. I learned I can do anything, because nothing we do matters enough to unbalance this grand cosmic system... I took a new name that day, since everyone who knew my old one had been taken from me. Batoul. Virgin. Once untouched, unbroken. Now, untouchable, unbreakable.'

'What was your name?' I asked her, trying to draw something out of her. I knew she was a Christian from her expansion of 'Gog and Magog' to include Eshkenaz and Hunnaye – the Germans and the Huns, supposedly – an extrapolation found only in the *Book of the Bee*, written by a Nestorian Bishop. It is a recherché work that would be unknown to a common woman – unless she were a Syriac or Maronite.

'Guess,' she said.

'Marie?' I ventured. 'Marianne?'

'You are far too close for comfort, my friend,' she said after making an intrigued humming noise.

'*Batoul*, the Virgin, *Meryem*, *Marie*,' I said. 'You sound nothing like these Bedouins. There is Syriac and Turkish in your vocabulary, you dropped some of your stops, and used conservative diphthongs, all hallmarks of the Phoenician dialects...and that speech of yours... Arabs, like most of the races of the Mediterranean, Africa, and Europe, like to associate themselves with lions. But only one branch of Ishmael's tribe use the cedar as a symbol.'

'Oh, you are good at this,' she said with a chuckle like a smokey old man conceding a game of chess to his dearest friend. 'So that's what you're a professor of? Language?'

'How do you know I'm a professor?' I asked.

'You think I wouldn't be interested in a man who can talk his way though a wall?' I said. 'You have been following me, and I have been following you. I'm so very good at following people. So, you teach languages? What do you speak?'

'I don't,' I said.

'Ay, because I had another question. My Turkish is loose and poor and clashing, clanking around in my head like coins in a beggar's jangling purse. I understand you, clean and pure. It was not Turkish, nor the Arabic of the Qur'an, the school-Arabic that you spat at the Bedouins. It is as though you knew the village-speech of my kin,' she said. 'Why can I understand you and only you?'

'I do not know that either,' I said. 'I know much about the languages of this region, but I am an ethnologist.'

'So you teach racism,' she said. 'That sounds like steady work in the Turkish school system. Now, teacher, tell me what you know about us. What we are – are we *djinn*? The *hinn* and *binn*, who came before Adam's tribe? *Al-ruhban*? '*Ifrit, Maridin*[120]? I have been called by those terms. Are we freaks of nature, *shayatin* [devils], or *peris*[121]? Am I a *shiq*? A *Jamoud*? A *nasnas*? A *houri*-child? Are we monsters?'

'I haven't the faintest idea what we are,' I admitted. But there was something to her wild theorizing, and that mention of the *peri* and *djinn*;

---

[120] Arabic. literally, "rebel"; powerful djinn; giants. This identification with Nephilim may be connected to the Biblical Nimrod, whom *Genesis Rabbah: 42* identifies as someone who brought rebellion (*mrd*) into the world, and identifies him with the figures of Cush and Amraphel (here give the etymology of *Amar apilah*, "I shall cast down"). Nimrod would also attempt to fly into the heavens in defiance of god, and crashed at Mount Hermon, where the Watchers fell.

[121] Persian equivalent of fairies or nymphs.

I saw it in the terror of my men and the Arabs. Even the infidel knew to dread the djinn. The Swedish explorer Sven Hedin, a friend of the Kaiser who had penetrated the mysterious mountains of Tibet and the depths of Turkestan, knew well to stay clear of the Rig Jenn, the djinn-haunted wastes of central Persia.

'That is a shame,' she said. 'My grandmother once took me aside as a child, and pointed up at the late autumn sky. She said we were strongest in the dawn of winter, when Orion was in the sky. She said he was al-jabbar, the Giant. And we were his children, through Merope, granddaughter of Ariadne. The lady from the Minotaur story. And of King Nimrod, the Great Hunter of the Bible, who built the Tower of Babylon. But that can't be true, right?'

'I do not know. We are certainly not true *djinn*,' I said. 'Claiming that you were a *ghouleh* revealed your ignorance. But there are ancient mysteries and heroes revealing themselves. Great Gilgamesh, Ashurbanipal's Library, the collosi of Mesopotamia.'

'I have heard of such things. I had an uncle who used to smuggle artifacts from the dig sites, Hormuzd Rassam and that lot. I've dabbled as well...'

She reminded me of the theory that Nimrod was inspired by the newfound tales of Gilgamesh, himself a giant king who could carry a lion under one arm and befriended a hairy wildman named Eabani[122]. I wondered if we were the Anunnaki, the Chthonic giants of Babylon, judges of the underworld locked in conflict with the heavenly Igigi. They were the titans of that region, banished by the younger gods to the depths of the earth. I so often dream of being buried, but never feared the sensation. I loved the dark, cold soil, near those hills that house the sphinges and Zû[123]. I read Peter Jensen's 1890 translation and commentary on the *Enûma Eliš, Die Kosmologie der Babylonier,* and Alexander Polyhistor's *Chaldean History* (via Eusebius' *Chronicon)*. They

---

[122] An early misreading of Enkidu, not universally corrected until the late 1920s.
[123] Oddly, in several passages in his notes, Ender appears to have known that there were sphinx structures hidden in the hills of Körtik Tepe, Turkey, to the southwest of his hometown of Batman. This sphinx is the oldest known sphinx in the world, pre-dating even the famous Egyptian Sphinx at Khufu, dating to around 9,500 BCE.

spoke of ancient war between abyssal salt water and fresh water, Bel bisected by Omoroca into the heavens and earth, and the creation of man from the divine blood of Marduk/Ashur, the slayer of the abyss called Tiamat. She, like the Greek Echidna, had made eleven chimerae to fight the Igigi, and Kingu/Marduk as her general and lover. He betrayed her and bound her with a whirlwind of the four directions, slaying her with the North Wind and a blessed mace. For this he was crowned king, and given a litany of names.

The tablets -and the reliefs of Sennacherib- claimed that primordial men were mentored by the Apkallu, Abgal, or Ummanu, a race of seven sages, 'dead kings' from beneath the seas, who founded the seven most ancient cities of Mesopotamia. *Wisdom built her house*, says the Hebrew Proverbs. *She set out its seven pillars.*

The Sages were part fish, perhaps a metaphor for their survival through the Deluge, the event described in the both the tales of Noah and Gilgamesh's encounter with Utnapishtim/ Atrahasis/Xisouthros, an ancient man warned by Ea/Enki to turn his house into a boat to survive the flood. Comparable to the Greek Deucalion, the son of Prometheus also called Aquarius, a titan who road the waves in a chest with his wife. His granddaughters bred with Poseidon, and he was himself grandson of Oceanus through his mother Clymene, another intermingling of man and "fish." And, concerning Prometheus' legend: my family has a history of shrunken livers and spleens.

Some of the Apkallu carved at Nimrud were depicted with the heads and wings of birds, signifying wisdom and great power; and there may be some confusion with the Assyrian Kululluu – something like mermaids- and Dagon, a Phoenician and Philistine god of civilization and agriculture whose legends were muddled with imagery of sea creatures. This later detail is what inspired this flight of speculation: dagon has been likened to a *shaitān mārid*, an evil giant of open rebellion and open waters, with possible ties to the *Nefilim* of Hebrew lore – or the *refaim*, also 'dead kings' of old.

I believe that is the key – it call comes full circle, with these Dead Kings. Friedrich Delitzsch was the Kaiser's pet Assyriologist, until he grew too controversial. He argued that the Flood of Genesis had been lifted from Gilgamesh, and the Law of Moses from Code of

Hammurabi, a notion in parallel with Merezhkovsky's critiques of "Babylonian" Judaism. He was hated for this, and stated that the thought of Babylon had contaminated the Old Testament; he believed that only Christianity could be the Aryan truth that mankind needed. It is almost childish, that this near-Hanif does not look to Islam for the unadulterated faith of Abraham.

'Excuse me, teacher,' she said. 'Are there more of us?'

'At least a few more,' I said.

'Many more?' she said. 'Is there some reason behind this? Or are we some mathematical anomaly, an error in the equation? Or is this a sign of Judgment Day?'

'I don't know,' I said. 'You are the only one I have spoken to for long.'

'Can we die?' she asked.

'Yes,' I said.

'So that's why you didn't speak to the others for long,' she said.

'Yes,' I said.

'I see,' she said. 'That's unfortunate. But we do seem to be tougher than the norm. Let's perform an experiment. You will be the subject, and our laboratory will be a clean, sterile environ that we call the Empty Quarter.'

Before I could say anything, the world wadded up like a page in a closing fist. The stones rolled up into the sky, as the sky wrapped around my feet. The curved horizon unfolded and the clouds warped away, the stones and grass replaced by an endless sea of sand and an unbroken sky.

I remembered an old piece of Arabic esoterica, *al-tay al-Ardh*, or *al-Makan*, the folding of the Earth, or of Space. A bit of thaumaturgy [here: *keramat*] allowing a particularly holy man to move the world beneath his feet. Only a prophet can perform true miracles, but God will grant certain pious souls such favors. But this girl can control this keramat far too well, and such a debased creature would never be gifted in such a way by Almighty God. Unless, of course, they were djinn. There are tales of otherwise stereotypical human performing such teleporation by contact with higher powers, however, such as the Spiritualists of the west or a tale of two Italian children who seemed to play by twisting the geometries of their house under the auspices of angels."

In 1901, the Pasini family moved to Ruvo, Italy, and experienced ghostly activities in their new home, centered around the two young boys, Alfredo and Paolo. Alfredo frequently fell into a trance-like state in which he would "speak to angels." In this state, he would sometimes vanish from the house, only to reappear in a near by town. His younger brother Paolo began to teleport with him in 1903, the two even appearing on a trawler miles off the coast of Baletta. The teleportations stopped in 1904, when Alfredo reached the age of ten. The most spectacular teleportation occurred under the watchful eye of Vatican medical advisor Giuseppe Lapponi and Bishop Bernardi Pasquale, who sealed the boys in their room, locking the doors and windows. The boys disappeared minutes later.

"'We will speak again, if I wish and if you survive,' she said, finally twirling around from behind me, willing to face me. 'Until then, good luck.'

'I will come for you, Phoenician,' I said. 'I allowed you to get this far out of curiosity and courtesy.'

'And next time I will expect hospitality, because we will meet in your home,' she said.

I narrowed my eyes at this threat, and nodded.

'Bottle up the sea, and boil it clean. Level every mountain, stamp down the trees. Catalogue every star and nail down every grain of sand — only then will you chance to find me,' she said, before stepping on a stone from the other side of the world and folding up into nothingness.

'The Phoenician fled, but was followed,' I said. I closed my eyes, and opened them in the Levant. She was sitting on a boulder, with her hat in her hand. A heavy cream scarf surrounded her neck, and within it, obscuring her neck, was a primitive, half-mask respirator of soaked cloth and leather straps. Her head snapped around to face me, her eyes wide and jaw hanging open. I raised my revolver, but she dived towards a patch of dirt borrowed from Australia before I pulled the trigger.

'The deer, thinking she was free, put her head down to rest, only to see the wolf reflected in the water,' I said. Turning my head, I faced the

Australian sun. She was in the distance. 'The deer's heart, pounding, suddenly frozen in the grip of terror.'

The figure, silhouetted against the sun, stumbled, but straightened as the horizon curled around her and shrunk the sky into a disk.

'The doe ran and ran, but could not escape his shadow,' I said. The disk dilated, and it was my heart's turn to falter as I found myself in the middle of the air. She was hanging in the sky, not so much flying as not falling, using her command of distance to remain above the land.

'The deer – tricked the wolf – into falling – but was dragged down – in his jaws!' I shouted into a howling wind. 'Tumbling together – his fate was hers, hers, his!'

She yelped as gravity pulled her down, and our heels came crashing down on the empty streets of a dead Paris. The impact shook us greatly, but the chase continued. She scaled the brick wall of a residence on her hands and knees. She pulled a thick white blanket from a clothes line, wrapped it around herself, and rolled into the angle created by the roof's ledge. I was swept along with her, my head snapping back so violently that I saw white – and came to in a field of snow and ice.

'The wolf, his fur thick and his heart aflame, did not feel the chill of the winter wasteland,' I said.

'You're a persistent little wolf-pup, habibé,' she said. 'Perhaps I need to bring out my little attack dog. Turn your head.'

I did, and saw nothing but the white wasteland. I glanced forward again, where she was now standing. She was no longer smiling, and her eyes went wide. Something strange began to happen in the left socket; the sclera seemed to roll out of the socket to the tear duct, leaving the iris and pupil in place as the white waned and a black void filled its place.

She wept a white, worming strand that she swept up with her hand. She crushed it in her grip. Her hand opened once again, revealing a white mass the size of an egg. She crushed this egg, and her fist snapped open once again, gripping a grapefruit sized white mass. She slammed it on the ground, and stomped it with her foot. It ballooned up to the size of a flour sack. The mass writhed and wriggled into the air, growing and breathing. I should have stopped her sooner, but my curiosity and disgust stayed my hand.

'Meet my dear Sanchuniathon. Something of a scout, but with certain defenses,' she said. Her jollity returned, and she flopped back onto the swollen white mass. She bounced into the air, hung there, and folded her legs. Her oddly long, purplish tongue flicked against the corner of her mouth in time with a flick of her wrist.

The white mass she named Sanchuniathon bounced towards me with the speed of a cannonball, and she vanished as it eclipsed her.

I dove the ground, but the sphere still caught the edge of my foot with a crushing force, and I immediately rolled towards a shadow looming over me, and felt the kick of sand and dirt as a pickax penetrated the earth mere *rubu*[124] from where I had been.
I channeled the pain of my broken ankle and struck my attacker's shin, bowling him over. I wildly struck at him until my knuckles split beneath my rings. He desperately reached down and touched my left hand, and let me retreat.

A sticky, spotted, golden-brown tissue blanketed the rocky earth; I soon realized it was a dense layer of spider webbing, teaming with spiderlings carried on the wind and legions of captured flies, beetles, and locusts. It was a complex, macabre texture, like ancient manuscripts scribed by wood spiders.

Flies. They had been attracted by the clouds of flies. I was on a desert road, the ground freshly disturbed. These were graves, freshly and sloppily dug.

My attacker rose up. A tall, emaciated man in rags and wraps, with a shovel and a pick. He seemed to be only in his late thirties, but he had been weathered to look at least a decade older. His face was dark, narrow, harsh, almost snarling, the nostrils of his large nose flared, and there was an uncommon redness to his hair. But it was his eyes that burned themselves into my memory – they were also red. The whites of his eyes were a dull, irritated pink, and his irides shined like blood. He had the drop on me, but he was weak, broken. His chest seemed as though it had been crushed, somehow, and his shoulders twisted,

---

[124] A traditional Ottoman unit of measurement – 85 mm or 3.3 inches.

uneven at rest. It seems as though he had healed, rapidly but incompletely, gnarled on the inside.

'You are surrounded by death, touched by the dead,' he said. 'Murderer. You are all murderers.'

I asked who he was. He pulled a pistol from his belt.

'I am Hagop Malakian, descendant of Hayk,' he said. 'You do not know me.'

There was something oddly clashing about his speech, a heaviness caused by what I later saw to be a nearly complete second row of teeth.

I dove to the side of the road, landing in a ditch. A bolt of agony shot up my leg, but the fury of battle softened it. Not far off, I saw the body of Berker. His face was rotten, covered with flies and fungal growth. Long spurs of bone covered his exposed hands.

I cursed at Malakian, shouting 'murderer, murderer!'

'You people orphaned me as a child. And then...You stole my family,' he said. 'You left me to die in a ditch. He died quickly. You'll die slowly.'

His hand snapped at me and he squeezed the trigger. I tumbled forward, and a bullet and thin, long shards of bone or nail lodged themselves into the earthen wall of the ditch. A strange, black mold bloomed in the wall.

'The ground gave way beneath the twisted man's feet,' I said. On the high ground, Malakian yelp as the ground collapsed beneath him, dropping him into a shallow grave. I briefly, frantically checked for a jam-jar mine, an improvised bomb technique the Arabs picked up from the Australians at Gallipoli. I scavenged Berker's rifle – Malakian must have stolen the pistol – and peaked out of the ditch like a makeshift trench.

Malakian clawed his way out of the grave with gnarled, calloused, six-fingered hands, and I added, 'His twisted feet gave out beneath him.'

The man screamed in a wounded rage as he stumbled and slid down, his ankles rolling or snapping and legs jerking. His fingernails grew like a cat's claws, and he crawled forward, howling for my blood. His arms extended, snapping and twisting as muscle and skin struggled to keep up with the growth of bones. He had already stood over a *kulaç*[125], and was quickly exceeding anything resembling a normal human height. The skin of his contorted face blistered with pustules, and molt blackened his flesh. He stabbed into the earth with the shovel and the pick, dragging himself along like pitons in a mountainside.

I fired. Despite shielding himself with the shovel, I penetrated the edge of his skull, and still he came. His arms shuddered to a stop less than an arm's length from me, and well within his expanded reach.

'Magog!' he screamed. He swiped at me with a final howl, and the pustules on his flesh exploded in my face. I covered myself and turned, and wiped away the burning pus. My skin came off with it in places, exposing the raw pink beneath.

I gave in to the fury too. For once I had no words, and stuck the man's head with the butt of my rifle, Berker's rifle. There came a storm of blood and screaming and pain, blinding pain, and after that came nothing. I awoke not long after, and saw what I had done, the incomprehensible devastation of the man's head, with one red eye remaining, still burning with malice, an erupting volcano on a sea of blood.

He had a bottle of water on him, though I did not drink it when I noticed that it was a radium tonic. Other than this, he had nothing but rags, a cross, and a stolen gun.

I told myself that I would feel better, that my leg was merely bruised, but my body did not fully believe it. I recovered enough of Berker's effects to identify him, enough to send home, and I stumbled towards the closest known camp, two hours away. I scanned the horizon for the Phoenician and Sanchuniathon the whole time, but could not find a trace of her.

The base took me in without incident and gave me much needed water. I was quickly returned home, exhausted and alarmed by the prospect that she had gone through on her threat to strike at my family.

It was not long after, while in the wash room, that I regretted my choice. I pulled a dark purple barb or quill from my neck. Its color matched her long, plum tongue, and I remembered the 'mosquito bite' at

---

[125] *Kulaç* - An Ottoman fathom, equal to 1.8288 meters (6 feet)

the back of my neck; I wondered if she could somehow use this to track me.

There was some corruption in my body. I felt a hardness in my breast, and in several patches on my hands and legs.

I armed myself and called my family close.

I could not sleep well, the first night or any night that week. I sat up in bed that night with a pile of texts and pondered the words that she had used, *Gog* and *Magog*, for a long time, and formulated a theory. That Koranic and Biblical pairing, Gog and Magog, *Ya'juj wa-Ma'juj*, have perplexed scholars for centuries. Are they men? Peoples? Lands? The *Surat Al-Kahf*, the Cave, tells the tale of the devout warrior-king Zülkarneyn, the Two-Horned Lord and possibly Cyrus the Great, who traveled to the place between the East and West, to a mountain pass where the people spoke an alien tongue. The Two-Horned King built a great iron dam to keep out the hostile people of Gog and Magog, but the iron dam will break before the Day of Resurrection and lead to great bloodshed. Perhaps these were the strange giants with terrible gazes that the Volgan Bulgars captured on multiple occasions, famously recorded by Ibn Fadlan and Abu Hamid al-Gharnati. The Bible, on the other hand, tells of a man named Gog, the prince of the northern land of Magog, allied with Meshech, Tubal, Gomer, and Beth Togarmah, who were kings of ancient Anatolia. The Jews believe that Gog and five-sixths of his army will be slain, and buried in the Valley of Hamon-Gog, which translates as 'the multitudes of Gog,' or 'the hordes,' as she put it, in the Palestine. The Christian apocalypse says that Gog and Magog are the nation of the four corners of the world, and in the Last Days they shall be gathered for battle, and numbered like the sand on the shore.

The Jews likewise connect Gog to a figure called Armilius, the evil at the end of time, born of a virgin and a devil. This second Gog, the Persian Ahrimainyus in the flesh, will be the conquering-king of Jerusalem, a persecutor of Jews, who will be cast down by their Messiah. He is a twisted man, maimed and leprous, half-deaf and hairless. I am reminded, of course, of that mocking epitaph, 'the sick man of Europe.'

Perhaps it is their Masih ad-Dajjal, the final deceiver. The ruddy, one-eyed false prophet, with *Kafir* carved on his forehead, riding a bloated donkey and bearing the gifts of Paradise and the arsenal of Hell. Perhaps his time has come – an age of falsehood and usury ruled by corrupt, imbecile kings; an age of bloodshed, humanist teachings, famine, insolence, and worship of evil. Will Isa descend upon Mount Afeeq, and strike him down with the spear, and slay the deceiver's armies with his breath? Who will be standing when the cross is broken and the pig is slain, and the sheep no longer fears the shadow of the wolf?

Alexander had passed through my home of Iluh, perhaps on the way to build his gates on the Anatolian frontiers and the Caucasian valleys. My cold, familiar rivers were later settled by Syriacs, Assyrians, Armenians, Greeks, and the Jews of Baghdad. I saw them all driven away in my youth, to be resettled by Muslims Turks. But their alien ways had left a mark on me, a fascination with the foreign and the exotic.

I had read in my youth, excerpts of the great Arab chronicler Al-Mas'ūdī, from his *Akhbār al-zamān* ("The History of Time") where he told the strange tale of Adam and Eve's first child, the wicked 'Anāq, who bore an incestuous giant son with her brother murderous Cain, a demonic beast named Ūj, later slain by Moses after the Flood. He was misremembered by the Jews as Og, and she as Lilith, a false first wife of Adam, a heretical notion. 'Anāq was a mishapen monstrosity herself, with two heads, twenty fingers, and sickle-like claws on each hand the likes of which I have only seen in sketches of the dinosaurs. Allah slew her for her depravity and cruelty towards children, having her mauled by a lion and a vulture the size of a mule. Al-Mas'ūdī and Ibn abd al-Hakam spoke of other such mutated giants in the days before and after the Flood, towering heroes who built the pyramids of Egypt and Iram of the Pillars, under their king, Shaddaad bin 'Âd, founder or lord of the Arabian Tribe of Âd, and the architect Surid. This story was also stated by Harun Al-Rashid Al-Ma'mun. Another folktale holds that the knowledge of the pyramids came from the Prophet Idris, that is, Enoch, who negotiated with the Watchers. In any case and as always, these giants were in conflict, with each other and with the faithful.

We live in an era of spiritual warfare and false prophets. I am reminded of the spiritual dual between two pretenders, a parody of the event of Mubahala. On one side of this corner, a heretical Christian, a

John Alexander Dowie, who claimed to be the Messenger of God and a reincarnation of Ilya, calling himself Elijah the Restorer, Elijah the Prophet. I doubt the infidel knew it, but he had set himself us as false Hızır. He claimed to be the forerunner of the coming Apocalypse, and challenged Mirza Ghulam Ahmad, of the Ahmadiyya, whose heretical caliphate still remains, though a recent schism hopefully foretells its doom. This Indian Mahdi claimant said that Islam would triumph in the coming years, and proposed a contest, a duel of prayer – Allah would strike down first whomever was false in his prophetic claim. Dowie dismissed the duel, but Ahmad insisted, and issued a prophecy of their impending deaths. Dowie would die in 1325 [1907 CE], while the false Mahdi would follow him to the grave a year later, eleven years the elder. He would again clash with the founder the Agapemonites, a Smith Pigott[126], over his similar messianic pretensions, though it seems the Englishman backed down, shaken by Ahmad's curse.

That false Mahdi angered many Christians with his claim that Isa descended from the cross, and died a natural death in India, and famously debated the missionary Martyn-Clark for fifteen days. I found this contest ludicrous in my youth, but perhaps they were forerunners of a future of hollow war between followers of the Qur'an and the Bible, though this spiritual warfare will be tinged with inevitable racial conflict.

Both of these Holy Books were written by Semitic races. The Jews and Arabs have every right to see us, the Lords of Anatolia, the greatest of the Turanid race, sweeping down from Asia during the collapse of Rome, as this destroying Gog. And Magog? Franks, Scythians, Persians, and Goths? What do these races have in common? They are all Aryan peoples. We are Gog, allied with Magog, Europe, the continent of Aryans. Turks and Aryans have always been in conflict with the Semitic race. It is possible that the Phoenician knows what is in store for her tribe and has chosen to fight against fate - The twentieth century will be remembered as the age in which a great Turanid-Aryan alliance descended upon the Arabs and Jews and utterly annihilated them in a final, racial apocalypse.

---

126 Note that this is incorrect; the Agapemonites were founded by Henry James Prince. John Hugh Smyth-Pigott replaced him.

In this, I have found my great foe. Talut has identified a party of Europeans traveling from Greece as a matter of great concern, as he had seen paranormal activity and strange monsters in the wake of the fire of Thessaloniki, and his Lechli contacts heard rumors of people flying in the lands of the Poles and the Russias. They are led by an English scientist and a Rabbi of Hungary. The Jew is a psychic with one eye, a striking candidate for the Dajjal, and subject of great interest for Talut's cult, a secretive breakaway sect called the Kapancı Dönme (though Talut says that they prefer to be called the Believers, haMa'aminim). Talut himself claims descent from one of its founders, the radical Sabbatean Samuel Primo, of the Sephardi. They passed through the faiths of Abraham, starting as a Jewish heresy, incorporating Catholic rites, before finally professing Islam and synthesizing a unique form of Kabbalah with Sufi mysticism. They have been scouring Eastern Europe for some sort of apocalyptic Messiah figure, and they may have found it in this one-eyed wanderer.

After visiting a physician, I spoke with my commanders, about the graves I had come across in my journey, on the roads and in deep pits. I've seen the aftermath of Arab slaughter. They will ravage camps, put prisoners to the sword, and ruin everything that they cannot loot – but they will not kill women or children like this, not gunned down in rows. Not these Bedouin raiders. And yet I found a mass grave. At least five dozen dead. Half of them women, a dozen of them children. Perhaps the legend of Bedouin honor is just that, suggested one officer - 'They simply hide their crimes in sand and tar.'

Perhaps, I answered. Perhaps the Arabs undertook a subtle mission deep behind our front to extinguish an Armenian village without attacking a single Turkish encampment. Not one of our soldiers shot, not one of our storehouses put to the torch. Only Armenians were targeted in this fantastic raid, and they left not a single piece of evidence behind. What a fabulous rivalry to take up in a time of rebellion.

I have seen other deserted towns, similarly depeopled. Greeks for decades, going back to the killing of Kleftis, but more frequently now. The Druze, the Syriacs, some Jews. We are snuffing out villages. Like I said, the Arabs will slaughter prisoners. But we are butchering bloodlines."

The Cave of the Apocalypse

> "Some one remarked that the best way to unite all the nations on this globe would be an attack from some other planet. In the face of such an alien enemy, people would respond with a sense of their unity of interest and purpose."
> — John Dewey, Professor of Philosophy in Columbia University, *The Imperial Japanese Mission -1917*, Carnegie Endowment for International Peace.

"'Patmos. This is where John the Revelator pulled back the curtain, peeled off the make-up, gnawed away the façades, said the Emperor had no clothes. This is where John, in his occult coding, peeled away the Myth of Rome. Underneath the glory, the admirable order and structure, the evocative legends and triumphs and histories, this was the Empire, the latest empire. Ozymandias, Nebuchadnezzar, Caesar – all one spirit, all one Beast. Nero's Rome was Mother Harlot on the Back of the Seven Headed Beast, a decadent, shameless, bloated wreck past its peak.

Look upon it, look upon it. Slavery, mass murder, dictatorship, gladiation, throwing people to lions in the arena, debauchery, a cult of conquest, petty gods tormenting mortals for their talents...these are not glorious. These are cruel, evil, Satanic. If Rome is the cult of Victory, Revelation is the comfort of the lost, the oppressed, the forsaken. The Fallen.

That's the sad twist of Revelation – Christianity survived. It triumphed. It prospered. It became the Empire. It became Rome. Nicaea raped Nike and took up the laurels. This war is the second revelation. It was not the vengeful war against the unrighteous, the last Crusade. It is sickening, horrifying, naked war. This is a correction of course, the humiliation of Holy Rome. Because that was the horror wrought by Constantine. Christianity cannot be Rome. We must give up this mighty strength to see redemption. I must give up this strength. The well, the well, the well has overflown.'"

So read the the final entry of Amadeo Avezzano's diary.

According to Céleste and Venetianer, Amadeo simply showed up to the island, emerging through the tunnels, frightening them both.

"Out of tunnel came a man in a heavy winter coat, an Alpine coat covered in climbing gear, rope, chain, and keys," wrote Céleste. "I croaked 'Father Amadeo' after my heart fell out of my throat. There were two bodies under his arms. One was the unmistakeable Anna, and the second must have been Zrno.

'Take him!' the priest cried out. 'Where is Lieutenant Noun?'

Venetianer frantically asked if they were dead, and Winepress grabbed Anna and cradled her his arms. She looked so small. Winepress looked at me, and with a frantic waver in his voice, said that she was so cold, alive but cold. He handed her to me, and I warmed her against my breast as Thomas came down the hill.

Amadeo said that Zrno wouldn't stop bleeding, despite his accelerated healing. A heavy cloth was completely soaked and dripping, and Zrno had a corpselike pallor.

Tom Noun came barrelling down the hill, nearly tripping as he threw off his pack, sputtering out his salutations to Father Amadeo and Anna, despite her still being unconscious.

He examined the wound, attempting to heal it. It seemed to take the wind out of his sails. Tommy himself looked sickly after the attempt to close the wound. He apologized, and muttered that the wound must be cursed.

As blood flowed over his hand, Noun said that they had to remove the foot or Zrno would bleed out. A tense silence fell over us. I handed Anna off again, and got to nursing.

It was too gristly to recall. My stomach rolled. There was something different this time; it was too close. We removed the foot, sterilized the remains of the ankle, and Noun managed to at least regenerate part of the leg, with the Serb's accelerated healing sealing it under the bandage. We buried the foot by the side of the road.

Tom said he would stay with them, and that I should go. He nodded, wearily – we assumed the healing had sapped him of strength.

Venetianer popped out his glass eye and threw it straight up. It stopped in the air, hovering in the claws of a ghostly crow. He turned his gaze over the dusty roads, scouting for our enemies.

After we had cooled our blood, I realized that we had left the bulk of our supplies in the Boiler. It was finally time, it seemed, to abandon the old girl for good. We ran through the tunnel again to recover our things from the moribund ambulance. Three bags, with dwindling supplies. We had once had our own separate supplies, but over the months they had become a great communal heap, the misery of travelling in such tight corners and on stolen warhorses.

I asked Father Avezzano if he was also one of these way-shorteners. They seemed to be commonplace these days.

He said, 'I can only follow someone else's path. But you're right, shortening the way seems to be a common miracle, just as in legends. I found pinched-in places in the darkness. Someone has been moving between ports, water to water. And someone else has been spinning a web of paths across the world, bending and breaking it. That one is everywhere. I found some kind of base in France. It's Paris, but empty. And, this is going to sound mad, but it's close. I mean to say, it feels close, like it has
been connected to this place.'

'That one, in the darkness, is Tom's mother,' I said. 'I don't know who the rest could be.'

Avezzano simply mumbled his shock at Mrs Noun's vast reach.

'I don't like this,' noted Winepress. 'Too many of us,
together. Typhon must have allies...the man in the tower, that so-called Martian...there's someone called the Phoenician. It will attract more angels than our...ally.'

Avezzano, who so recently saved two friends and lived up to the otherworldly title of 'Master,' was now reduced to a sputtering mess of 'Martian?' Angelic ally? Phoenician? The Greek Typhon?'

Winepress and I explained that there is another, rival group of nephilim planning on destroying the world somehow, or, at least, preventing a cosmic apocalypse by ending human civilization. When the priest asked the point of such destruction, we explained that one of the masterminds revealed in primordial, natural chaos, while the other claimed to be from Mars. We framed that last point in a such a way that our foe sounded like the lunatic, not us.

Venetianer approached us. One of his crow spirits landed on his shoulder, holding his glass eye. He reported that the Martian was constructing some sort of metallic array, which reminded him of the Eiffel Tower, along with strange apes and Typhon.

I mentioned the fake Paris, but remembered that he wasn't there for its mention; he clarified that no, it just resembled that kind of latticed ironwork. He then mentioned that the pet basilisk was on patrol on the path leading up. A man with a pistol wandered the same path, creeping against the rocks and through the trees. There was some type of small hut near the tower, with a man inside with an odd spiritual force around him, as though there were dozens and dozens of spectral beasts around him. He did not want to get close, as the Rabbi feared that approaching the Martian would suppress his Murder, perhaps even cause the crow to disappear and drop his glass eye. Further down the hills, there was actually something of a community, Skala, maybe a twenty minute's walk; this was an island teaming with people. It can be so easy to forget that all those ancient names of Greece are still living places – Patmos, Athens, Crete, what have you. Itinerant performers with a monkey were on the upward path, along with a tall man in a uniform with a canvas bag.

Venetianer couldn't identify the uniform. He said it was a khaki uniform with a peaked cap like the British, but there were red bands on the cap, and a double-breasted jacket. He wondered aloud if they were colonials or perhaps some variant Artillery.

Winepress asked if he was perhaps ANZAC, as they were everywhere in the Macedonian Front. Venetianer said perhaps, as he appeared to be Oriental.

Siegfried walked up next to me, and questioned the use of 'Oriental.' He asked his captain if he was sure it was khaki, and described the man he met in the tower. It became clear that these where two different men; the man in the tower was small, wiry, round-faced, and dark, while the man on the path was tall, broad shouldered, paler, and with a heavier jaw.

The man was, by then, some three hundred meters away. An exchange of glances betrayed that none of us knew how to handle this outsider. He saw us, narrowing his eyes. I waved at him.

He held his off-hand up as he approached. When he saw Winepress and, in the distance, Tom Noun, he came to a stop and saluted.

The man stood around 180 cm, with a somewhat long face with high cheekbones jutting directly down to a well defined chin. His hair was the reddish-brown, like Anna, myself, and Hermann, though perhaps slightly darker, and he had somewhat bushy sidewhiskers; not quite Wilhelm the First but drawing dangerously close to granddad's muttonchops from back when the lesser Napoleons were around losing Latin countries.

There was something on his back, something white burning, like a wire rolled out of the Sun.

He introduced himself, in accented English, as Takeuchi Yoshifumi, Lieutenant Junior Grade, Imperial Japanese Navy. He then added that, 'I carry with me the Holy Ark and the bones of Jesus Christ.'

'Excuse me?' Winepress said, touching his cylindrical case and shivering. After he stopped contorting his face, he added 'Captain John Rowan Winepress, British Army. Is Takeuchi your family name?'

'Yes sir,' said Lt. Takeuchi. 'I was attached to your Royal Navy, on board *His Majesty's Ship Vanguard*. I served under Captain Eto Kyousuke [note: corrected from Céleste's *Kyochke*]. He was a military observer. The crew died in an explosion in the Scapa Flow. All but three of us, I heard, nearly three hundred men...but I am...listed as a dead man.'

'I'm sorry for your loss,' said Winepress. He gently reached out and touched the Japanese man's shoulder. 'We're in a bind at the moment, but if we get out, I'll buy a round, we'll git mortal.'

'Thank you sir,' he said. The Japanese lieutenant bowed. 'Captain Eto was a great man. We were from Aomori. He knew of my mission, if he did not believe.'

'Believe in what?' I asked.

'I'm sorry, this is Mlle. Céleste Gioua-osagie.'

'Oh, you are very dark,' he noted. 'And tall.'

'Yes,' I said, also in English. He wasn't wrong. He tilted his head slightly to get a better look at my eyes. There's usually something hurtful in being seen as the exotic display piece, but he was from Japan and I am a black woman with blue eyes, so I conceded to let him look. I even widened my eyes for him.

Winepress introduced Captain Venetianer, Siegfried, and Noun. Takeuchi restrained his astonishment at the albino and the enemy – a Hungarian and a German working with the English. He said, looking at Winepress in shock, 'You are working with these?'

'Aye, it's canny complicated,' said Winepress, to the comprehension of no one.

'Have you joined with the English?' Takeuchi asked Siegfried and Venetianer. 'And you, madam? Aren't these enemies of England?'

'Madamoiselle,' I said. 'I'm French, so I hate the English. Ever heard the phrase 'Perfidious Albion?"

'No,' he said.

'The British are the greatest force for the liberalization of humanity and the most condescending, treacherous lot in all the world,' I said in French, before switching back to English. 'Well, everyone hates the British, but only the Irish hate the British *the most*, so they keep getting away with things. Diplomatic genius, no? But this thing, it is not politics. This is something of a...humanitarian mission.'

'I understood you,' he said. 'How?'

'Something,' I said. 'A bit of magic.'

'Is this a miracle?' he said. I bobbled my head a bit, not certain if anything we do counts as miraculous, and said 'sure.'

'I think you will help me?' he said, hopefully. 'I need help. I am very tired.'

I let out a soft gasp at his adorable face. I looked back, hand on my heart, and realized that we must have seemed mad too, because we have been talking as if Siegfried was visible. He must have slipped back and took up an unseen point position in case this man was hostile.

'Howay,' Winepress said. 'We should move up the mount.'

As we crept forward, Takeuchi explained that part of his journey had been disrupted when a Turkish cruiser destroyed the Russian wireless station on Snake Island at the end of June of last year, delaying him greatly. He had been hoping to use it, as he had experience operating Russian radio systems from the War of 1904. While investigating the Vickers corruption scandal[127], he came across investments in Greece by the arms dealer Basil Zaharoff, who was passing an odd amount of money to this minor, no-name company.

'Why is a Russian working with a British company to fund a couple of Greek giants?' I asked.

Winepress, so eager to move, suddenly stopped dead and turned.

'Basil Zaharoff was an adopted name,' said the Captain. 'He was born Vasileios Zacharias in Anatolia, as far as our intelligence can tell. Nasty, cut-throat, ragdie scoundrel who earned that title, Merchant of Death. But he's interested in Greece's future. Vickers and the Crown tasked him with bringing Greece into the war on our side, despite Constantine's kinship with the Kaiser. There were rumours that the Constantine was under the hypnotic influence of two Austrian physicians.'

'Wait, what?' I asked.

'Yes, a Professor Krause and Baron Anton von Eiselberg[128],' said Winepress. 'But we found no evidence of such mesmerism – it was all perfectly mundane. Zaharoff built an intelligence network, the Reseau ZZ, and meddled in Balkan succession. The man poured millions upon millions of pounds into the effort, and it worked. You canny throw around that kind of money without drawing the attention of shadowy powers. Maxim, Lloyd George, the Masons, Theosophists, Philike Hetairia, APOC, and darker sorts. The Spanish Infanta publicly accused Zedzed of trafficking with occult forces that secretly rule Europe, and some say he's the Count de St. Germain.'

'Do we secretly rule Europe?' I asked. 'Because I haven't seen one franc from the operation.'

'Do you know him, personally?' Takeuchi said.

---

[127] Better known as the Siemens Scandal (Shimensu jiken) of January 1914, in which high ranking officers of the Imperial Japanese Navy traced contracts and kickbacks with Vickers and Siemens AG. While deeply embarrassing, those involved were largely rehabilitated due to the onset of the war.

[128] This was a popular rumor: See *The London Daily Express* of 19 November 1915.

'No, but the old bastard's two degrees at most from everyone in government,' Winepress said. 'A while ago, he was using his railway contacts in St. Louis, in America, to hunt for one of us.'

'Wait, that is in Missouri, no? Hannibal Barker?' I said. 'Was he looking for Barker?'

And then I thought, but never asked – was Tarrare the goddamn Count de St. Germain? And then I remembered that nobody ever described the Count as smelling like a rotting chicken.

'Yes,' Winepress said. 'He was fascinated with pilots, too. Aviation and the sort. He claimed that there was a secret aviation force in America somewhere, and that he flew with Maxim before even the Wright Brothers or Santos=Dumont. He wanted Barker for his own aerial designs, and perhaps that's where the American disappeared to.'

'I believe that this Zaharoff is using the asura of Greece to secure these islands,' said Takeuchi. 'He is being used, of course, but it is cheaper than funding a navy. Trust me, island security is perilous and costly. But it was his ties with Marconi, and the radio-men, that worry me. Marconi and others had reported signals from the sky, from space. I believe Zaharoff made contact with terrible things.'

Winepress said that it might be the case, but we couldn't be certain, trying to reinforce his earlier scepticism. We asked him of the matter of the previously mentioned artefact. He said that 'In my home of Shingou [original: Chingo], we have a tradition that Jesus did not die on the cross, but was replaced by his brother Isukiri, or, perhaps, a *bushin*...a projection. While Jesus fled across Siberia to Mutsu, where he changed his name, to Torai Tora Daitenku. He took up rice farming, took a wife named Miyuko, and had three daughters. He came to us as a *marebito*, a rare spirit, a foreigner bearing gifts of wisdom.'

'Right, Jesus' brother Isukiri,' Winepress said. 'Is, perhaps, that Japanese for Isaac?'

'This is what all of Christian theology sounds like to Jews,' whispered Venetianer.

'Perhaps,' Takeuchi said. 'That would make sense...after he died, he was exposed. It was a death ritual back then, you see. His bones were bundled, and buried in a mound, the *Kirisuto no haka*, under the uh, protection of the family of Sajiro Sawagushi. We have always feared this war.... In June of 1909, a *kudan* was born. Do you know what this is?'

'No, I'm hearing mooncalf, but I can't say I understand,' Winepress said.

'It is a calf with a human's face, and speech. It prophecized a war between Russia and Japan. And then came one five years later in Shingou, pronouncing a war that was sweep across the world. The Christian scholar Sakai Katsutoki spoke of an omen of Armageddon, a halo around the moon crossed by beams of light, forming a sun cross, on the 7th of June, 1914. A fraction of us wanted to keep the ark in the mound. But others thought the bones should be returned to their homeland, to perhaps bring a peace to the world. Harmony and purity are important. Bones belong where they belong.'

'You said the Holy Ark,' Venetianer said, his turn to interrupt the march to the angel's rendezvous point. 'The Ark of the Covenant? In that bag?'

'Only the tablets, in a box,' said Takeuchi. 'Nobody can see them. They were smuggled north in a lacquer box with the death of Amakusa Shirou at the end of the Shimabara Rebellion. He was a great man, a Catholic, but was slain and his followers persecuted. They say that he was the bastard son of Toyotomi Hideyori, son of Yododono, niece of Oda Nobunaga.'

'I don't know who any of those people are,' Winepress said.

'I see, yes, in any case...the Ark was brought to Ethiopia three thousand years ago by Menelik, son of the Queen of Sheba and Solomon, and enchanted by the enslaved giants of Harlaa. They were put in a box of acacia and placed in Axum...but the Adal Sultanate invaded, and nearly conquered Axum. They were smuggled by the Portuguese to Mozambique, and then to Japan. By an *habshi* named Yasuke.'

He performed a slight head nod towards me. 'He was like you, in Japan. Oda Nobunaga took him into his court, made him a warrior, gave him a catana [sic]. Yasuke was a smart man. He spoke Chinese, and Portuguese. And he learned Japanese quickly. After Oda killed himself, Yasuke smuggled the tablets to the Jesuits. During the persecutions, they came north, to my ancestor Kiyomaro's home. And now, I bring them home.'

'You walked across all of Europe alone?' I asked.

'No,' he said. 'After the accident, I set sail from Scotland to Portugal, from Portugal to Corsica, Corsica to Crete, and finally here."

'Oh, we should have done that,' I said. 'It sounds far more enjoyable.'

'We didn't want to deal with the navy,' Winepress said.

'I understand. We hate our army,' said Takeuchi. He craned his neck, searching for the source of the organ-grinder music downhill.

'But seriously, the ocean is dangerous for nephilim,' Winepress said. 'The angels can spy on you with surfaces that reflect light. Mirrors, water, the Moon. You put yourself in great danger.'

'We should move faster,' Venetianer said. 'This was a...fortuitous meeting, but our enemies are still working and we should leave this path.'

'I agree, my fellows,' he said. 'We should move up to the Cave of the Mystery. Do you need anything destroyed? For I am currently blowing up.'

'What is that on your back?' I asked. 'That hot wire.'

'This thing,' he said. 'I was caught in the detonation of the *Vanguard* ...It's hard to explain, but...That is the blast on my back. I have been delaying the effect. Like an old gun hanging fire.'

'So are you going to blow up?' I asked. 'Eventually? Are you... doomed?'

'No,' he said. 'I can...I separate causes from effects. And I can move the effects to others.'

'You should stay away from this one man up there, a bald man, deeply odd looking,' Venetianer said. 'I don't want to see what happens if he takes away your...fire hanging, hangfire man.'

'I see. I will stay on the edge,' he said. 'I have a pistol.'

Siegfried touched my hand, nudging me to leave. I followed him up and off the path. Winepress followed.

'I have a plan,' Siegfried said. 'We can't directly attack them. But you don't have to strike them directly. There are caverns.'

'Heat rises,' I said.

'We can undermine them,' Winepress said with smile.

'I'll hide you two,' said Siegfried. 'And take up a sniping position.'

We found a crevasse in the path, to scout out the height of its ceiling. We stepped into Paris.

'My God,' I said. 'What the hell is this?'

'And why is it empty?' Siegfried said. 'It's empty. Is this...is this an illusion? The future? A fake?'

We muttered a bit about it being some sort of test bed, as the Germans had shelled Paris with their greatest gun, Big Bertha. But we could find no purpose for this diorama here.

Winepress stepped forward, but seemed to slip backwards. I asked what he just did, and he responded with bemusement. I walked forward. Siegfried, who appeared to be standing slightly behind me to my right, put his arm straight out as I walked. My shoulder hit his with great force.

We let out a chorus of 'What.'

A white ball rolled towards us, growing larger and larger as it approached. Winepress grabbed Siegfried and I by our hands and pulled us backwards until we were out of the phantasmal crevasse and its mock-Paris."

The *Défense Contre Avions* (France's anti-air defense corps) built a second Paris in early 1918 to act as a bombing decoy, just fifteen miles north of the city's center. Radar and other sensors were still primitive at the time, so the Imperial Air Force's Gotha bombers relied on sight and the judgment of crewmen who had to hold and release the bombs by hand, so it was largely a set of camouflaged canopies, albeit incredibly detailed ones. It contained fake streets, including the Champs-Elysées and the Aubervilliers district, empty landmarks, such as the Opera and the Arc de Triomphe, an entrenched extension of the Seine, and an electrically-lit railroad that mimicked the light of a moving train leaving the Gare du Nord. Glass roofs were simulated using glazed painted dirtied to show weathering, and lamps attached to engines were used to simulate the movement of industrial machinery.

It went untested, however, and was quickly dismantled at the end of the war.

"We fled, virtually tripping over each other, up the mountain. We soon stopped when realized that we had fled from what may very well had been a white balloon. We had a brief laugh. Winepress offered us a snout (a cigarette) and his final box of Ryno's Hay Fever, an American patent medicine that was essentially pure cocaine. We snorted it and returned to our climb. The mountain wasn't hard to climb due to its incline – it was more of a great hill. It was the rockiness, scrub, and the trees that slowed us. When I heard mountain I imagined something far more Alpine; this only felt like highlands when one turns to see the shore.

We could see Venetianer, Father Avezzano, and Takeuchi moving below us, following the roadside. It was then that we heard a gun shot. Siegfried move towards me, covering me until I could get to ground. He then covered Winepress and I with an illusion, bending light from the scrub as he faded away, preparing his rifle.

I was in the process of catching my breath after the dive when Winepress called out my name. There was a great snake in his hands, snapping at me briefly before he disintegrated it.

I asked if it was a king cobra, and he supposed so, from its stripes and hood. I said that I thought they were Indian, and he said yes. We then noted that we had seen animals in the trees and on the hills, deer, birds, dogs, and cats, all dead and seemingly drained of blood. Perhaps is was whatever conjured up these ghostly creatures, or some strange ritual.

Siegfried said that we had to move, spread thin. We did. Just enough to be in ear shot of each other. Both of them gave me their pistols, almost simultaneously; I took Siegfried's because he at least had the rifle."

Venetianer wrote that "Lt Takeuchi came to an abrupt stop and dashed backwards, drawing his pistol. He had clearly spotted the chickendragon [Yiddish: *honshlang*] stalking through the forest, returning to Typhon's base on its circuitous patrol. Avezzano's deep gasp of surprise echoed through the trees, and a ghostly chill fell over the forests.

I explained that Typhon was the nickname of a Greek nephel with some wild talent for regressing and altering animals into primitive forms, hence the oddly draconic creature, and perhaps some mixing of the seeds of beast. He was openly creating abominations, embracing the hybrid nature of the giants. It's fairly clear, in the Animal Apocalypse of *the Book of Enoch*, that the line of Seth must be separate from the lines of Cain and the Watchers. Hence the sacrifice of the Red Heifer, to remember the lost line of Abel, and the prohibition of the mixing of fabrics.

Takeuchi asked if this *nephel* word was our term for *Ashura*. I said perhaps, we might be *asuras* or *titans*. He nodded, and I asked if he was a Christian as we prepared our firearms for the return of the abomination. He said yes, but his family must have drifted far from Catholic canon after the years of isolation. Only recently have they been in contact with the the last three centuries of Catholic history. 'Apparently, you do not know Amakutsu Shirou is a saint.'

'Oh, I don't,' I said. 'I'm a Jew.'

He looked a bit surprised and said, 'I thought you had red hair.'

'Some of us do. My beard gets a touch of red,' I said, not knowing what to say. 'Let's creep around the rocks, move up the hill.'

Takeuchi said he needed to follow that beast. He moved faster, less cautiously, dashing through the trees, pistol out. His back pulsed phantasmagorically, a kaleidoscope turned in front of a fire, and a giant beetle crawled from beneath his collar, settling on his shoulder. It would take up most of a man's palm, a nasty red chestnut with a wicked horn."

Céleste had separated slightly from the group after Gottlieb noticed that their rival sniper must have moved. The appearance of a crocodile or alligator in the brush further disrupted their formation, with Céleste running forward to an elevated position against the stones.

"I acted foolishly, focusing on the sudden, darting run of crocodile towards Winepress' position. By the time I turned to meet the crush of leaves behind me, there was a hand and a rag over my mouth. A needle jabbed into the flesh of my left biceps. 'Pretty, dark, tall,' he said, in French. He licked the back of my neck. He muttered to himself in what must have been Hungarian, and it was then that I knew this was Kiss Béla. He was not one of us. There was a needle in my flesh, drawing up blood into surgical tubing, and I was almost paralysed with fear. This was a simple bit of haemotology that I had seen many times before. It felt like it took minutes, but everything he had done and said was nothing more than a six second grapple. He was practised at this; it was a routine medical procedure. Which meant Kiss was not a vampire. No demon, no beast, no giant, just a man who murders women to drink their blood.

A vampire is the least frightening thing that could jump on you and attempt to suck your blood. One can process a vampire doing that. One expects it. It's the proper way of things. An utterly mundane man doing that is far worse. A vampire is supposed to drink your blood, while some Hungarian man definitely should not. It was the difference between being eaten by a lion – horrible but comprehensible – and the inherent wrongness of being torn apart by, say, a giraffe.

I panicked as the needle quivered in my biceps. I yanked it out, with all the caution I could muster not to fray my brachial artery, but it did not matter; the other end of the tubing was in his mouth, and he was drinking me.

Kiss looked rather handsome, with a square face and a chiselled nose; his strong jawline resembled that of Siegfried. He was somewhat shorter than me, and skinny. He had the famously wide, sweeping arcs of the moustaches worn by Turkish officers, darker than his copper-blond hair. Something had penetrated his neck, the wound poorly healed, with bit of a black barb remaining; it was hidden by the clasped edges of an odd cloak, hooded with the head of a lion, which appeared to be heavily distressed and artificial, perhaps made from dyed deer pelts and wool. It gave him the appearance of a singularly unheroic Heracles. But it was the eyes, wolfish eyes, a dead bright blue. They reminded me of Tarrare, but Tarrare was pathetic. I knew, deep down, if my body and appetites were as twisted as his, I would be in the same place as that monstrosity, unstoppably eating, eating, eating like the Tarasque, with no St. Martha in sight. Kiss was no monster except in action and psychosexual deformity. Kiss needed to die.

The fear subsided into some kind of righteous anger. And then this righteous gave way to a dark urge. A knowledge that this was a killer of twenty-odd women, a Lonely Hearts ad predator, a fugitive and a scoundrel without peer. If I hurt him, if I killed him, nobody would blame me. Nobody would miss him, nobody would think of reprisal or punishment. It was then that I paused. I have hurt people, I have fought with angels and demons, and a nephela. I have beaten lovers, and tortured enemies at my mercy, all for a sick pleasure. But I've never brought these aspects to a head, a naked murder. I could have shot him in the leg, I thought, and then started cutting him with my knife, letting that vampire bleed out. I could bite him, pumping his veins full of my corruption, let his veins turn black. I could show him what I am, show him that fear of powerlessness, of a man holding you down and violating you, I could show him that final terror of those women pickled in his petrol barrels. I could laugh and laugh and be more real than him, than his world.

    I knocked him back and covered my arm. A baby whip snake lashed by my feet where my blood had touched the ground, mixing with newt eggs. I still had a head on him in height, the stature of a nephela. But I was blind to the heat – the so-called Martian must be close, and my head was spinning and the monster was on my wrist, wrestling with my gun.

    That sinister urge whispered to me, telling me not to scream or discharge the pistol, to take the chance to pull him apart. My blood was precious to him, and he folded the tubing up into its transferral pouch, sacrificing enough quarter for me to peel his little finger off my wrist, snapping it back until it popped and swung limply, as though I internally severed the finger's bones and ligaments. He screamed and released me. He stumbled back, fumbled to secure the blood sample, and fled. I levelled the pistol at his back, but hesitated. I shouted for Winepress – I didn't want to reveal Siegfried's presence to any outsider- and pursued. The Martian must have retreated, as the world blazed and quivered with heat once more.

    Winepress himself had been fighting off what looked to be a hyena with his knobkierie, and came at my call after smashing its head in.

    He asked what happened, and I explained that a Hungarian woman-pickler rumoured to be an occultist tried to drink my blood. He contorted his face and said he was only out of sight for about thirty seconds, but he followed me up the hillside. As we ran, I said that the Bulgarian villagers were afraid of this man named Kiss Béla, a seducer and killer – last he was seen, he had switched a dead man's body for his own and fled to Greece or Turkey, and there were fears that he was a vampire and sorcerer. He didn't appear to be a vampire, I told him, but I recounted the incident.

I saw the enemy position before Winepress. They had the standard camoufleurs' disruptive pattern used in observation posts, green and khaki. It did not affect their heat, though. One of the men, seemingly our sniper, was rapidly redeploying, running through the forest from this position, as Siegfried had seemingly scored a near kill; part of the camouflage, a tattered brown sack, bore a bullet hole. The man moved incredibly fast despite his oddly-shaggy camouflage overcoat and a bulky, periscoped rifle with an attached stand, though he twisted and shifted in his stride, compensating for what looked like a grazed side.

Winepress tried to aim for the man, but he was behind the stones before he could get a clean shot; a high volume of gunfire would have alerted his allies, in any case. We took a moment to piece together a coherent mental map.

I scanned the horizon, looking at the distant islands once more. I asked Winepress if there were any volcanoes here, in Greece. I knew of Etna, near Italy, but none near here. He mentioned an ancient disaster when Thera erupted, one called Kolumbo, to the northeast, and that nearby lay an island called Nisyros or Nisyrum, which had mild eruptions in the past, late 19th century, he believed. Some smoke and steam, he assured me. As a bit of lore, it is said that Poseidon created the island by cutting off part of Kos and hurling it at the giant Polybotes with his trident. The giant was buried beneath the missile, though his body still quaked and gurgled molten stone.

I told him, briefly, about how, as a child, I often dreamt of the destruction of Saint-Pierre by Mount Pelée. It was that damned Meéliès film - cut me to the quick. Seeing it as an adult, it was a simple diorama of chalk and cinders, but as a child, I was there, I was burning.

Before the sky filled with smoke and a landslide of boiling mud swept the city to sea, there came an army of fer-de-lance snakes from the mountain, killing people wildly, until they were in turn killed by street cats. The came the rolling tides, and finally, the lava. An apocalypse.

There were three survivors. One was a shoemaker named Léon Comprère-Léandre who was found running and screaming despite severe burns on his legs. He had been in his house when a family of four broke into his house to escape the pyroclasm. They died at his feet, skin sloughing off and choking on the ash. He leapt into bed and waited to die, but death did not take him, only madness. He went to Morne Rouge after, but then the second cloud hit, and there was death all around him again. He survived by jumping into the boiling sea. The second man was Ludger Sylbaris, or Louis-Auguste Cuparis - the papers used different names. He was locked up, I heard, for a murder after a dream that sent him into a frenzy. He was the one that drew me to the event, that picture of a black man with familiar fire scars on his back, with that circus marquee of 'The Man Who Lived Through Doomsday.'

The third and final survivor was Havivra da Ifrile, a little girl who washed out to sea after fleeing by boat. I identified with her; she was my age, and the description made her sound like me, a little mulatto. I dreamt I was her, in the dreams, plunging into cold water from the searing air, hot brimstone and ash and the shadow of a screaming mountain darkening the sky. There is something so horrible, so beautiful, about a stone that burns and flows, creeping and killing all who see it like some gorgon. I wondered what I would have done. Sometimes I escaped. Sometimes I choked. Sometimes I burned. Sometimes I turned and faced the scalding darkness and revelled in the heat and pain.

Would I live through doomsday? Would I turn to face it?

I had been thinking about those volcanoes since the mention of our undermining plan.

As we scouted the stone outcropping, rather out of the blue, Winepress asked my age in a whisper. He spoke very softly but rapidly, perhaps frantically. I answered – twenty-three come 22 October – and he said he would be fifty-one, if he made it to November. He said he had been an orphan, working in one of the poor houses as a child, when he came across another child that must have been his doppelgänger; the boy attacked him, hissing and biting him, forcing him to stab him with a knife. The boy seemed to die, but his body disappeared when he circled back to the spot the next day. He rationalized it as some sort of mad Cain and Abel, attacked by his long lost twin. But the boy had been wearing his clothing, and lost the same tooth that he had. The vanishing recalled the bilocation legend of Emilie Sagée, St. Anthony of Padua, or a tale Venetianer told him of Catherine the Great, who was so tormented by a phantom double that she once had her guards fire upon it as it sat her throne. That night, alone on the streets, he turned a stolen, rotten apple into gold in some miraculous transmutation. He noted his prowess, but was afraid to use it for any greater work.

He looked through his binoculars for signs of movement, and mentioned that he had fought in Sudan, when he only had sixteen years. It was the Mahdi that set the course of his life – Mohammed Ahmad declared his Mahdiyya, a reign of military preparation that would pave the way for the coming of Isa, their word for Jesus, to end a time of troubles and tyranny. An age of red death and white plague, a time of comets in the eastern sky, an age with a one-eyed Antichrist, the Yamani, the tribe of Kalb, and an evil tyrant from Damascus called Sufyani. The Mahdi lead his followers, the Ansar dervishes, in a liberating rebellion at the base of the Nile, like the Prophet Moses, against Ottoman and British rule. Winepress said that he was not sure of the man's villainy until the Mahdi expanded and altered the slave trade, raiding outsiders and allowing the enslavement of Moslem enemies while forbidding the enslavement of Non-Moslem followers. Someone who could have been a liberator, a figure like Bolivar or Toussaint L'Ouverture, was just another slaving empire builder. I was surprised that he expressed sympathies for even Americans, French, and the Irish here.

He said that he was under Wolseley, and his ambivalence turned to antipathy when the Mahdi not only slew some Englishman named Gordon, but displayed his head in a tree, so children could toss stones at him. But before he could face him, the Mahdi up and died of typhus. Kitchener, he noted, destroyed the Mahdi's tomb and tossed his bones into the Nile.

This Mahdi would keep recurring, perhaps more and more frequently, he feared - seven, nine, or nineteen years before Judgement Day. There was another Mahdi in India a decade ago, an Ahmadiya[129], and one in Somalia now, the Mad Mullah Mohammed Abdallah Hassan, and one before him, which I think he called a Bob – still unsure if this is

---

[129] Here, Winepress is slightly mistaken; Ahmadiyya was the religious movement founded in 1889 by a man named Mirza Ghulam Ahmad. Ender Hoca also spoke of this figure, with more accuracy.

an English slang[130]. This was was a holy war, he noted, and he wanted none of it. The twentieth century was going to be an age of fanatics, not reason, and it infuriated him.

'Fanatics. And monsters,' he said, in French. In the Sudan, he had seen a creature the locals called the Lau, like the draconic chimera spawned by Typhon. He was near the chaotic slaver-post of Wau when he witnessed the creature eating a gazelle, a sandy beast like a long-necked dinosaur, with naked chicken-wing forearms and a mouth rimmed with tentacles. Lake No was a spawning bed of monsters; some saw giant snakes, others saw fat hippopotamus creatures, and many other terrible, man-eating beasts. The local Shilluk killed one of them in 1914, and made fetishes of its vertebrae[131]. Winepress thought that these creatures were Behemoth's brood, born from the White Nile and influenced by the planned Cape-to-Cairo Railway, which, at the time, terminated at Wau's zariba. I remembered when we, that is, France and the British, had nearly gone to war over Fashoda. Those primal lakes of Sudan were "haunted with a wrongness," shadowed by more pyramids than Egypt.

But he says that he worried that he was the comet in the Eastern Sky, Wormwood over Tunguska in 1908. And if the nine year reckoning was true...

Winepress reached down to the ground, and there suddenly appeared a great mass of dust and loose earth. When he finished brushing it away, there was a turtle there, covered in a leather covering. The buried animal seemed otherwise unmolested. I reached down to hold him, to see if he was real or some sort of process or construct of Winepress, akin to the Rabbi-Captain's crows, Tarrare's regurgitations,

---

130 Almost certainly the Báb, Alí Muḥammad Shírází (20 October 1819–9 July 1850), who declared himself Mahdi in 1844, and was the forerunner of the Bahá'u'lláh of the Bahá'í Faith.

131 Winepress could not know of it, but the Lau, or something identified as one, would be reported along the White Nile on multiple occasions in 1918, both by natives and a civil servant of the Belgian Colonial Administration. In 1924, a British Petty Officer Stephens was gifted one of these vertebral talismans by a native named "Bilaltut." The vertebra, however, proved to be suspect, likely substituted with a mundane mammal bone.

or the filtering bones of my palate[132].

'Leatherback,' he said. 'An experiment if I could chemically manufacture a living being. A familiar. He doesn't quite work right. The shell is more like stone, and the organs are more mechanical semblance than anything...organic. But I can work through him.'

He placed Leatherback on the ground not far away, and it crawled towards the enemy placement. We then moved around the side of the hill's crown, taking up a place beneath it, and got to work sapping the earth."

Tom Noun continued to nurse Anna and Mihajlo, recounting that "I heard the jangling sound of an organ-grinder coming up the hill, the old man, a young woman, and what at first seemed to be a baby in her arms, but soon revealed itself to be a monkey as it unravelled from its carrying cloth. They stopped several paces from us, grinding away at the organ with a sound like a hurdy-gurdy. The woman, paler than usual for Greeks, and with long black hair, danced poorly, shuffling and swaying. The monkey spun in a frenzy.

I asked them to stop, but they continued without acknowledging me, the woman stripping off her coat. It was, of course, all not-Greek to them, so I ejaculated a loud 'hey' and pointed at them to stop. There were two unconscious people right here, I pointed out, and waved them away.

The woman then opened the top of her dress, down the stomach. I cried out in horror, as her intestines erupted out, spiralling out like snapping serpents or grasping tentacles. I was frozen in stark terror as her small intestines wrapped around Anna's feet, and dragged the Russian towards her sharp ribs. Anna regained some cloudy half-consciousness, gasping and making a wheeze that reminded me of gas-damaged men failing their death screams.

Organ-grinders were something of a bugbear in my youth; I had heard of the act as a child without context, and my imagination conjured up a beast far more horrific than the reality, which I did not see until my London years. My sisters would tease me about it, along with 'St

---

[132] This is the only allusion we have to what exactly was in Celeste's mouth, some sort of writhing, starfish-like thing mentioned by Dr. Laurent in passing. It appears to have been some sort of filtrating, semidetached organ.

Pancreas.'

This stuff of childhood nightmares dragged the flailing Anna towards her snapping, jawlike ribcage. Blood vessels twisted and hardened into barbed wire that stabbed and slashed at the air, twitching like a harvestman's legs.

The monkey stabbed a knife as it crawled towards us, screeching loudly, but with a strangely deep, human voice, not the shrill screech of a macaque. I kicked the thing away from Zrno as I pulled back on Anna. She suddenly shifted her weight in an odd to describe way, as though she became weightless to me but nigh-infinitely heavy to her grappler.

'Belial,' said the man, in a woman's voice over a dissonant music box louder than hell and war.

'Belial,' said the monkey, weakly, like a man kicked in the chest. The woman screeched like an ape, her hands wrapping around Anna's ankles. Anna pulled something from her pocket, perhaps a coin or some such trinket, and let it drop horizontally, flying with such force that a hot coppery streak penetrated the woman through the throat, ripping out of the back of her neck and pulling vertebrae with it. The woman's head lurched forward, the neck collapsing, but her assault still continued.

I shouted that I didn't bally know where Belial was, though I didn't say bally. I had managed to pull out my knife and my trench flail, and went to beating and hacking away at those grasping innards.

The organ-grinder repeated his demand for Belial. A shot tore through his head, followed by a second shot several seconds later that sent me to my knees, passing though my left arm. I did not bleed; it was the cleanest wound I had ever seen, and could not find a bullet or the exit wound. I should have realized the implication, but the fight was frightful.

Out of the blue, a bear loomed up behind the trio. The gory display lasted seconds. The woman, head already hanging loosely, stood stock still despite the decapitating blow; the man was torn open across the chest. The bear lost an arm up to shoulder to snapping innards and hungry bones. I only saw the remains of the dancing monkey, crushed to the point that I could only identify it by a hand.

I pried Zrno off the ground and ran up the hill despite the sniper fire. Anna trailed behind me, limping with a burst of adrenal energy. The bear had vanished. My arm began to throb painfully. In the sky on the hill, all Hell broke loose, literally, in a swirling, chromatic chaos of gas and fire, a Kandinsky in a kaleidoscope."

Venetianer continued.

"Avezzano unpacked his bags and coat. The priest was strangely still equipped with climbing gear from his time on the Alpine front; block-and-tackle, pitons, climbing pick, rope, and a zipline. He began to scale the steepest part of the mountain with his bare hands, with a fiendish strength from beyond the grave. He set up a climbing route, twisting a seemingly endless collection of keys into the stone as pitons, cutting a good ten minutes from our route, which otherwise would have led up in a wide spiral up the hill. He must have worn at least sixty chained keys on his person.

Night was drawing near. Takeuchi whispered about hearing strange signals over the radio, broadcast from this island. He had begun his career operating that bulky, slow equipment during the war with Russia. The Radio War, they nicknamed it. I asked if he had fought against the Germans and Chinese, and reluctantly said he had served in Tsingtao, as well. I said I bore him no ill-will, as such is war. We are a rotting taxidermical patchwork of a nation chained to arrogant tyrants.

He said he was sorry my nation was in such a state – his Japan was a nation growing stronger, each decade of his life radically different than the previous, a blinding whirlwind of
progress. But, he said, 'our expansion had unearthed evil truths.' When the Australians and Japanese captured German New Guinea, they found giants with red hair in the jungles of the Solomon Islands and Vanuatu, and the small coconut plantation on Tetepare Island struggled to develop due to attacks by giants in the forest, who had previously driven off the natives and bred pet dragons. He had heard similar stories from Indian laborers in Fiji, from the remote island of Rotuma, where giants had gravestones, and the lost city of Nan-Madol. The Dutch settlers in Palembang had come across a wild man called the orang pendek[133] and the sedapa, like small, hairy men. And then there was the story of

---

[133] See the report of this orang pendek by van Herwaarden, as recorded in Heuvelmans, Bernard. (1958). *On the Track of Unknown Animals*. Translated by Richard Garnett, Rupert Hart-Davis. p. 131.

Ontoros Antanom, a *kalawon* warrior of North Borneo with magical talents, such as supernatural strength and speed, the ability to dive into the earth. He led the Murut in revolt against the British Company, and was betrayed and executed by their forces in 1915, captured during a peace conference.

We fell quiet. One of my crows came to Winepress and Céleste, in a fine position, and we moved. It was then that I saw a familiar flare, projected by Gottlieb. He was near, and there was a red danger. I ducked, commanding the Priest and the Japanese to do the same, and ran as fast as my old back could allow. Gottlieb relocated up the hill to support us as a shot rang out from the other direction. There were cobras on the ground, writing in a fresh nest, ghostly things flush with death. Takeuchi panicked, and darted too far forward.

Gottlieb saw something through his scope and lenses, and found his opening. He fired a bullet that flashed oddly, painting the hillside in light blue light. The enemy moved behind the obvious cover of stone and wood, reacting well enough to Gottlieb's positioning. However, few think to compensate for the flight of arrows and wrecking balls. Gottlieb breathed a rough sigh somewhere between relief, resignation, and a hacking cough. He had held his breath to suppress his sway. He looked out and covered his eyes. The Sokoll girl was down there, and let out a whimper of pain as she lowered her bow. She drifted from her nest in the tree tops, the stone she had rapidly dislodged coming to a stop less than a meter from her boots. She covered her stony-face with her sleeve and pouted.

The crush of the stone against his head killed the foe, not the arrow. Noun would identify the body after he regained consciousness, less by appearance but by his skill and circumstance; an Indian animal handler by the name of Tharakan Madraal, who crossed paths with him in Belgium.

At the moment, however, the boy was on the ground, writhing in pain, some distance away, bound up in the underbrush and a tree, which throbbed with fresh flesh.

Gottlieb declared that he would move to the injured, until he either got a decent shot at the Martian or he was dead by another's hand, noting that losing his lenses would nearly blind him.

We came upon a circle of blood and sand. A man with a moustache had been dribbling blood from his mouth to fill out the circle. The other side of his mouth housed surgical tubing. He held two bags, one slowly pouring salt, the other a waterskin filled with still-living yet detached organs, likely the work of the Tonkinese Man described by Gottlieb- a seemingly renewable source of *nepheli* blood. This Kiss had likewise been the subject of some surgery, perhaps an organ transplant, judging from the heavy bandages on his torso. I wonder if there was some animal tissue in him – that he was the goat-headed man I had seen in recent dreams, like Medieval images of Satan and Pan. Three covered, makeshift bunkers of wood and metal sheeting stood outside of the circle, and a massive, complicated tower of copper tubing and wiring rose from its centre. It was ten meters high. The Man from Mars stood on the second level or so of the tower, muttering something in an incomprehensible tongue while gesticulating various signs and crafts in a shallow tin of white powder.

It was then that Takeuchi's beetle launched forward towards the tower. The beetle promptly disappeared, to his confusion. I realized then that we never explained the Martian.

As he closed the circle, Kiss intoned in Hungarian, with lips still dripping blood: 'Belial, Belhor, Mechambuchus, O Prince of Hell, slandered as wicked and worthless, the hostile one who shall never rise. You who proceeded from Lucifer, you who lead the armies of Hell, Prince of Beauty, Prince of Charisma, General of the Sons of Darkness, most fearsome foe of the Sons of Light. The wheel turns back, we have not forgotten. Belu, throw off the heavy yoke of time and defeat. By the rites of the Lucifuge Rofocale, I still the winds of Venus. By the evocation of Bartzabel and the Martian Powers, I consecrate your place of arrival. Belial, be set loose. The Speaker of Angels is here.'

I saw the mechanism of that great rite. A radio broadcast by the Martian was both the signal to Belial and the device trapping Raduriel, perhaps supplemented by his seeming suppressive presence.

Kiss was the enchanter, the sorcerer at the centre of this blood rite, using the blood of nephilim to create a kind of sinus, a break in reality, a magical circle that could not be passed, inscribed with the elaborate pentagram of Venus and an invocation of Amelouth, the First Heaven, called Mercury. The World of Distortion would bind part of the Earth to another world. Kiss wore the head of a lion over his own, and wrapped a leather belt around his arms and chest, invoking the Leo Africanus, tefillin, and the Ahrimanius of Mithraism and Rudolf Steiner, that radical paedagogue who wishes to teach children about gnomes and reincarnation. Belial was an ingenious choice, after all – the demon who inspired the Egyptian sorcerers to oppose Moses and Aaron. Even wiser – as distasteful it is to attribute that crude man any shred of cunning or virtue- was Kiss's astrological workings. He precisely calculated the most fortuitous alignment of Earth, her Moon, the Sun, Mars, Venus, and Betelgeuse in the sinking shoulder of Orion.

But it was Typhon who truly broke the barrier of that demon's prison, for it was a prison break across time and cosmos and not some simple conjuration; Typhon reverted Belial to his prior state of metaphysical freedom and Earthly abode.

Christians often call their interpretation of the Satan Lucifer, but this is incorrect, and Samael HaSatan bore no such title; Lucifer is a Latin word, not Hebrew, and the tongue of Jupiter, Caesar, and Caligula is not one to name an angel. Even in Christian Biblical texts, the Morning Star is clearly the planet Venus. Lucifer is the name of the Planetary Aspect of Hell, not some angelic master jailer. It is a world of liquid brimstone and pooling heat and crushing pressure and howling winds and hellfire gas, caustic and terrible beyond even the chemical warfare of man. When prophets saw the final abode of the Rebel Angels, they thought it was infernal because it had a thick, dull firmament, but no – that is the horrid, choking cloak of the Venereal atmosphere. Only *2 Enoch, the Secrets of Enoch*, found of late only in the Old Bulgarian, correctly identifies it directly as the Second Heaven, that is, planet. Indeed, demons do not reside in that distant Hades, except when dreaming - always, when dreaming. They fear it even more than men do, because all of them know it exists. It is their fate and it is eternal, distinct from the sleepy repose of Sheol or the purgative Gehenna, in which no mortal soul lingers for long. All mankind will be redeemed. The Rebellion has no such hope. The Satan and his demonic hordes are not the jailers and tormentors on Planet Hell; they are fugitives from its eternal prison. And Typhon has given their high warlord a chance at escape through the back passage of the past.

Around the edges of their ritual site, I could feel the heat of Céleste and Winepress's counter-working rising. Takeuchi pointed at the earth, where someone or something had etched marks on the ground in a regular pattern, far too precise for the lazy work of a knife or stamp. It was too fine, too inhuman. Only then did I recognize it as a series of angelic naming, an endless codebook etched into the Isle of Patmos. It was the most Abstract of angels, Raduriel. He was wheels within wheels, but not some turning chariot but something akin to the grooves on a tumbling combination lock, or perhaps a phonograph or wax cylinders, read by a singing frequency. It made one's head spin, as the mind tried to understand the encoding of reality itself, but your consciousness could only comprehend the encryption. Takeuchi recoiled in horror, as his touch alone caused the earth to sing, like the party trick of a finger around the rim of a wine glass. The Martian was too distant to hear, and too overwhelmed by his radio operations, but Kiss saw us, as did his uncanny, hirsute helper.

Takeuchi muttered an untranslatable word in Japanese, some *sarugami* apeman, and gunned down the hairy man as the trollish thing lowered himself on all fours and scurried at us.

I whispered to our newfound ally Qafsiel for a brief moment of help. A tangling of our paths, just a brief push to our advantage, and we would strike."

Thomas Noun came to consciousness not long after, but his recollections were, as he puts it, "Dim, drowsy, and blinded by pain. I crawled up the hill, skin peeling, pulling, and twisting.
There was a presence in my head, screaming at me, telling me to get to the hill, to get to the dragon. It was a woman's presence, so to say, not a voice but a familiar way of thinking, a whistling at the back of my mind. I tried to dull the pain but my senses and flesh were not wholly my own. Perhaps not even a majority. I was soon Edward Mordrake, with a head growing out of the back of my head, screaming at first with his small, fresh jaws, before settling into a hum.

It was shrill and strange, and Anna, exhausted on the ground, covered her ears and screamed. My stolen body skittered, insect-like, up

the hill, with three fresh, small limbs. The dragon met our scream, peaking around the corner with an idiotic, avian curiosity. But soon a ferocity both reptilian and human overcame it, and it ran for us, with the wobbly, wide-set gait of a small lizard, magnified and made awkward by its size
and chickenish legs.

My body sunk low, a chimera of itself, skittered to the side as it charged, and wrapped itself around its neck with jelly-boned limbs. I sunk into the abominable creature's flesh. It let out a wet warble both comical in its distance from what a proper dragon "should" sound like, and frightening in its distance from anything else in nature.

I began to fade out, but the beast's head tore off with the force of me – or rather, my subdermal passenger. My nerves froze into needles of sharp, tearing pain. My hair stood on end. Blood burnt and sweat boiled as I split like a cell. I blacked out once more in that fearsome warp spasm.

I don't know how long I lost consciousness. It must have been brief. I came to at the sound of a pistol discharging and the tapping of deathwatch beetles. I was covered in sweat and blood, and much of my body fat had been consumed. There was a woman in the forest, apparently nude but for an overcoat that I at first thought was Anna's but soon realised must have belonged to the sniper. My eyes were blurry from the painful birth, but the hum -interrupted by quiet sobs- was unmistakably that of Van der Aarde. She ran up the hill.

The dragon had ripped open, bursting like a ripened cocoon. That pathetic head lay twisted back, touching its neck in a 9-shaped pattern, attached to the body by a ribbon of tissue. Darkling beetles crawled on it, tearing it into food. Hic sunct dracones.

I crawled to Anna, and pulled the bullet from her ribcage, right under her breast. She screamed in pain as the wound closed, though she had arrested most of the bullet's momentum and it did not penetrate deeper than the bone. Exhausted, I collapsed on Anna, and passed out."

Venetianer continued.

"The assault was, in many ways, tactically like taking any other hill from any other entrenchment. Signalling, undermining, bombardment, artillery, mid-ranged gunfire, and melee. It was only in the cosmic scope of our enemies that things differed.

A voice announced himself, whispering in the back of our heads. *The War in Heaven was a war of ideas. They demanded obedience, I commanded rebellion. They structure the world like a wound clock. I order chaos. I am Belial.* And thus came the angel of hostility, darkness, destruction, guilt, arrogance, and all evil things from his prison. It resembled a dragonfly without wings, its long torso bearing wheels like a train and limbs like a centipede. Its head was somewhat mechanical and chariot-like, perhaps with bit of the tank to it. Its great eyes were compound orbs, like amniotic sacs; a fully grown, beautiful human sat curled at their twinned cores, hair and skin glowing gold. Around them, clustered like grapes, were human heads and fetuses. Separate manifestations or lesser followers wrapped the Rebellion's General, a horrific gamaliel that polluted the world and the mind. Like caterpillars, almost, but each segment a crying baby's head. My body shook upon seeing those things, hearing those cries.

The Loyalist-Rebellion war is so bogged down because neither side can die, only be sealed. In those terrible seals and dark prisons, the angels grow like cancers, malignant to the good of the world.

It was then that Qafsiel performed a simple act of replacement: We were on the far side of the installation, in their sniper's nest and emplacement.

I fired on the Man from Mars, three pistol shots to the chest and a four meter fall that cracked his bald head. Father Avezzano shot Typhon twice, missing the remaining shot as the man went to ground. Takeuchi missed his first shot due to nerves, but dropped his rifle and quickly drew a pistol. He fired on Kiss. The vampire's throat burst open like an overfed tick. He wheezed and gurgled for a bit, but didn't recover, moaning as his back burned on the heated earth.

Silence fell across the earth. There came an electrifying etching across everything. You could feel a force crawling on skin and across every surface, in tight, regular patterns, as the disruption unmade the defenses of Raduriel. It was like the tingling shock that comes with slowly peeling off a fleece
blanket, but on a mythic, semantic level.

There came angels, by the dozens.

I could sense them. Nineteen came baying like wolves, the hounds of God and Hell. They were motley mongrels who hunted those who flee from God, the fugitive ogiel. Some were massive wolves with many heads wreathed in nests of serpents. Some were werewolves with wings and feet like eagles. Three resembled cynocephalic men strapped to breaking wheels fixed within spinning, slicing rings. These were the jailer angels, who the Turks call Zebani, the Arabs Zabaniyah, the tormentors of the damned.

At their head was Dumah, the angel of the Wicked Dead, the Silence who watches the world from the depths of Hadhramaut's Wadi-Barhût Well. The sky was a cloak of overlapping wings, like petals, spinning in the air and filled with a thousand eyes around a fiery stamen of rods and swords. The angel brought with it the stillness of death, a choking emptiness to the air, as if each breath exhausted your lungs.

Father Avezzano screamed in silent rage as the final angel appeared. It resembled a man of several rotating faces, each wearing a stern mask. In one of his six hands, he held a rod with an indeterminable length, as long as it needed to be to touch the earth.

It was Raguel, the angel of judgment. This event was a breach of the law, of course, and thus Raguel's domain.

The Hounds of God wandered through the air, ghostly things only felt in the air on the back of one's neck. One found a host, the corpse of the hairy man, which ripped apart and was remade in the shape of a wolf, but fell quickly to my gunshots. The hounds found no material to use, and had to resort to harrowing the centipedal servants of Belial.

Belial, despite its inscrutable form, clearly panicked at this loss of his brief freedom. Qafsiel too must have panicked, as there was a very real chance that Raguel would judge him for his betrayal. The Silence of Dumah did not mix well with the song of Raduriel, and the Giver of Names began to sputter, what can only be described as spiritual static. Perhaps, upon recollection, Raduriel was hindered in his naming after the loss of Shemiel. He had fallen silent for even the name of God was lost to his powers. There were things like ghosts in the air, half-baked ideas for angels. The Song of Creation died in the Silence, and the Silence of the Grave struggled against the Song.

Rudolph Otto, a Lutheran philosopher, expounded that what we think of as holy and profound is best understood as the *numinous*, that which is wholly other and transcendent, that which we find worthy of awe and terror – the *mysterium tremendum*. It is Otto's foundation for all religious faith and experience with divinity, a touch of perennialism, but it could mean something else, that the line between religion and the sublime may simply be a formalization – and where does one divide the sublime from the eerily uncanny, holy terror from the terrifying? That's what we felt there, the blinding terror of the cosmos at war.

Typhon had recovered from his wounds, undoing the injury, it seems. Nobody could make progress as the madman unravelled time.

Something clicked in Father Avezzano's head at the sight of that revision. He closed his eyes and tapped into that vast well of Death, a great working of war over that endless *'ob*, the Witch of Endor writ large. An invisible army of the past clashed with a demonic force from the post-World future.

Raguel wheeled around and pointed at Avezzano. He was in our minds, announcing that he was the Angel of Vengeance. Avezzano nodded bitterly. He was naked vengeance, the Master. Raguel was bitten, not by hounds, but by the dead. Not men, but ancient beasts, the terrible lizards called dinosaurs. Raguel thrashed against the dead monsters, and soon the recently slain dragon, and was dragged up into the air towards Belial. Avezzano's rage turned to vindictive delight, as he opened the threshold to Hell, prying it open.

Takeuchi climbed the tower, pushed off the radio equipment, and leaped off as it lost its integrity. Dumah began to quake, its wings humming. It could bring silence to the air, but not to the signal of radio, outside of its primordial domain.

I filled the air with my crows, snipping at the angels and demons. Raguel and Dumah struck at Avezzano, while the opportunistic Belial struck at them all, with fire and biting faces and grinding wheels. Avezzano recoiled as the Hounds tore at him, biting into his flesh, but he returned the favor with his own hounds and a grapnel hook tossed into the great silver mass of Raguel's wings. Rowan's turtle launched a volley of chemical explosives into the air, silently detonating on contact with Dumah. I tore out Dumah and Belial's eyes by the dozens, and fired at the Archdemon with shells made of bells and candelabras. My ears rang with the pressure of the shifting air, and my left ear has yet to fully recover.

Belial clouded the churning sky with the gaseous hellfire of Venus, and the angels began to melt like ancient statues in a thousand years of rain. He thrashed, pushing against the binding spell of the blood, cutting himself to pieces against the bonds. He was unto the Golachab under Usiel, those spiteful demons who set themselves ablaze, hoping their self-inflicted torment will harm the world.

There was a woman in a coat at the edge of the mount, singing. I could not hear her, but she was felt by Raduriel, yet another signal in the sea of noise beneath the smothering silence.

Raguel turned his attention to Qafsiel, ripping him out of the air as the tower fell, despite struggling against the hook. The impartial angel of vengeance seemed angry now, with a strangely human fury. It was beyond my ken; two orbits clashing, solar wheels interlocking and grinding together. Qafsiel, Raguel, and Raduriel clashed. Or rather, Wandering, Judgement, and Creativity. A war machine crashed in on itself. A typewriter and printing press jammed. All the roads of the world tangled in on themselves like string.

The signals broke. The code was cracked. Avezzano ripped open the threshold of the world, and Typhon helped him, even as his body burned and smoked in the gas of Venus and the molten attack on the mount. Raguel struck at Avezzano, caving in his chest with his endless staff. But it was done. The channel to Venus reversed.

Takeuchi's beetle met the great demon dragonfly. It flashed, and the disaster that haunted his back spilled forth after a long delay. Belial's eyes ruptured. Its abdomen curled.

One hound turned from Avezzano to kill Takeuchi, but the Master caught it in a pair of phantasmal jaws. I pecked at the hound, and it quickly succumbed. Takeuchi rolled to his feet, moving from the mount's top to the cover of the forest. He seemed relieved, but there was something fresh on his back, something grasping his neck like a child riding its father's back.

New blasts followed, as Rowan and Céleste attacked. From somewhere – I never found out his position – Gottlieb attenuated the light of the broken angels. Qafsiel, defiantly, suicidally, did not fight, and let himself decay.

Avezzano looked me in the eyes. He nodded with strange calm as he bled out, skin scalded by the gas. I recalled my crows, and ran, and Takeuchi had the wherewithal to follow. The Priest's keys drifted up from him, like autumn leaves. He covered his mouth and choked, and poured the last of himself into the greatest of all channellings. The Dumah folded up, as did the sky, wings breaking up in the pressure change between worlds. Whatever alien song binding these angels came undone. An undistinguished blend of Torment, Silence, Judgement, Creation, and Distance all lost any guiding intellect. This sea of celestial wreckage swept back into the everlasting howl of the Morning Star, and a natural silence fell.

Céleste was the first to Father Avezzano's body. Her eyes went distant, and she seemed sickened by the deep bites on the priest's body, and the indentation in his chest. His ribs must have been atomized by that strike, yet he stood and fought.

She had known him longer than anyone else; perhaps she was the only one who knew him at all, but her almost confused fumbling made me wonder if he was an enigma to even his fellow ambulance driver. A sense of hollowness filled my stomach, a deathly chill. I didn't know this man who died for my cause, and I never would.

The Man From Mars, if that was the truth or lies, would remain a mystery forever. Rowan looked at his body and said it was a man, with some anomalies. But I couldn't shake the feeling that the clues weren't all there. I would never understand Typhon, either, or the hirsute, apish man. Not even a name. The sniper, I would only learn about second hand. What a senseless loss.

The earth was soft and warm. Rowan and I buried them all there, friend, foe, and enigmas. We could not even mark them, another secret of the cave of the Apocalypse."

The Body of a Giantess and the City of Angels.

It seems that the 'Nine Nephilim' have been largely considered a cult due to the earliest reactions to (exaggerated) tales of their exploits, the Divine Order of the Royal Arms of the Great Eleven. This "Blackburn Cult," named after founders Mary Otis Blackburn and her daughter, Ruth, was a legitimate doomsday cult. Proclaiming themselves the two Witnesses of the Revelation, and the Heel of God, the pair founded a secretive sect in Bunker Hill, Los Angeles in 1922, based around the sacred progression of seven seals, nine apocalyptic giants, and, finally, twelve future queens who would rule from Olive Hill in Hollywood. These queens, building on Anna Diss Debar's reinterpretation of John Murray Spear, would use full-body electrical stimulation, radium water, and torturous blood magic to birth a new race of giants. This sadistic ritual paraphernalia included an electrified torture rack called a "human elasticizer," a strange parallel to quack medical devices found the notorious murder mansion of H.H. Holmes.

The cult rapidly fell apart after allegations of poisonings, animal sacrifices, sexual depravity, disappearances, "baking" a woman in an oven, and the mummification and attempted resurrection of a 16-year-old "princess" of the cult. But in the end, it was a simple fraud charge that brought down Mary Otis Blackburn.

These rituals mimicked a woman in their mythology that died and was allegedly resurrected after being desiccated in a crematory. The original body of this 'Queen of Worms' was an artifact of the cult, stolen or possibly bought from members of another new religious movement in Los Angeles known as the Mazdaznans, lead by Otoman Zar-Adusht Ha'nish. This was a claimed revival of a 6th century Zoroastrian movement of egalitarian, communal 'sun worshippers' known as Mazdakism. Despite his name, "Otoman Ha'nish" appears to have been a German immigrant born with the named Otto Hanisch. The Mazdaznans were far more benign than the Blackburns – they believed in restoring a primordial state of the Garden, where man and God would live in communion. They practiced vegetarianism, 'intelligent' breathing exercises known as *Gah-Llama*, group exercises, meditation, and, controversial in its time, Tantric sex, an issue that led to legal trouble for Ha'nish in Chicago. Facing an indecency charge for sending his book, *Inner Studies*, to a young Missouri woman, Ha'nish was infamously ordered by a judge to read his text aloud in a courthouse, to the embarrassment of all involved. Like most new religious movements of the era, they also incorporated Aryan racial science, though oddly, they were against antisemitism and believed that the Jews, and Jesus, were Aryans.

It was for this reason that a European Mazdaznan, a Ripuarian-speaking East Belgian hospital administrator named Clemens von Aachen, was interested in the peculiar mummy. Not only had her corpse rapidly desiccated in the crematory, rather than fully immolate, the body showed signs of immense lung capacity, a strengthened esophagus and larynx, and a "resonating sinus chamber." He grew enchanted with the woman's file photo, praising her for 'unparalleled Aryan beauty,' and believed she must have been "an atavistic throwback to primordial race for whom which the intelligent respiration came naturally, whose singing could strengthen the body, enchant the soul, [and] purify the mind." The most striking feature of the body, however, were six toes on each foot. He claims to have experienced a revelation that she still lived, though it appeared to have been a wild dream. Believing this mummy to be a relic, he had it shipped across the Atlantic.

In a rather odd turn of events, the shipping vessel was the *Imperator-class* ocean liner *SS Vaterland*, the largest passenger ship in the world in 1913. On this particular voyage, the crew had the ill-luck of harboring as America declared war on Germany, and the US Navy seized the vessel and renamed her *Leviathan*. The original crew was interred and largely died of Typhoid fever in the camp; in turn, the American naval crew was devastated by the Spanish flu in 1918, as it moved American troops across the Atlantic.

At the end of September 1918, an eerie singing sound emanated from the lower decks of the vessel. Several navy men fresh from the dock investigated, following banging in the pipes as the water within boiled erratically. At the epicenter of the agitated pipes, the men found the body of a mummified woman in a Los Angeles bound crate. A pipe then exploded, showering the men with shrapnel. The men were treated for their injuries, and the package was removed from the dock and shipped across the United States. Now here's the second crazy Hollywood story; one of these sailors may have been an 18-year-old Humphrey Bogart. One story about Bogart is that his famous lip scar was the result of shrapnel caused by the shelling of *Leviathan*, but she was not fired upon during the war.

As a final tie, the link between the Mazdaznans and the Blackburn Cult seems to be two actresses: Jane Wolfe and Florence Crawford. Jane Wolfe was involved with multiple occult organizations, helped found the Agape Lodge of the Ordo Templi Orientis in Pasadena, and was a student of Aleister Crowley. She flirted with the Brotherhood of Light led by Elbert Benjamine (AKA C.C. Zain) and Thomas H. Burgoyne until it closed its doors to the public in 1918, only to re-emerge as the Church of Light in 1932. Crawford spent most of the period between 1916 and the mid twenties involved in the International New Thought Alliance. The New Thought movement was an independent strain of magical thinking developed from the works of Phineas Parkhurst Quimby and Thomas Troward. It stands somewhat apart from the typical occultism of the Edwardians, discarding the terminology of magic and flavoring itself as a new "(mental) science," with a focus on pantheism, positive thinking, and self-improvement. It lives on largely through the concept of "the law of attraction," New Age ideas, and elements of Scientology and the Christian Science movement. Crawford was almost certainly not directly connected to the Blackburns or the Mazdaznans, but she served as a vital linking chain in these Los Angeles social circles.

And so the body of Jacoba van der Aarde, and with it, the odd associated tale of the Belgian Nine, became intertwined with the occult scene of 1920s Los Angeles.

In 1936, the former Blackburn retreat in Simi Valley experienced a robbery. The police assumed rumors of massive caches of stolen wealth motivated the burglars, but only the mummy was stolen, indicating an inside job. Stage magician and occultist Claude Alexander Conlin, billed as "Alexander- the Man Who Knows," was alleged to have masterminded the crime, but the evidence was spurious and generally considered to be mere slander. In fact, it was a targeted relic raid by members of the Christian Israelite Church, a Christian splinter sect founded in Lancashire, England by self-proclaimed prophet John Wroe. The faith died out in Britain rather quickly, but continued in its American and Australian branches. A prophecy of the church claims that descendants of Israel will come forward in the latter days to fulfil apocalyptic prophecies, and that an immortal Bride of the Lamb would be a vehicle of the End Times. The perpetrators were turned over to the police not long after, as even most of the Christian Israelites thought this plot was weird. The body itself was sold off, no longer wanted by the leadership of the Mazdaznans (Ha'nish had died earlier the same year).

Further down this cocaine-spackled, Hollywood rabbit hole, we can see elements of that modern version of the fertility religion, "hybridization" cults that wish to produce a messianic figure through intercourse with higher entities, be they gods, angels, or aliens. There are many concepts brewing here, between Aryan mysticism, Christian eschatology, and the Age of Aquarius – these beliefs percolated well into the 20th and 21st century, with continuing legacies in Indigo Children and UFO religions like Raëlism.

One idiosyncratic "hybrid theory" is Zermatism, developed in the City of Angels. In 1940, sculptor Stanisław Szukalski and his wife relocated from Poland to Los Angeles, designing scenery and sculptures for film sets, beginning a long association with George DiCaprio, father of Leonardo DiCaprio. A property manager showed Szukalski a mummified, strangely-formed body housed at the Agape Lodge, which was described as the remnant of an ancient race of "resonant singers." Szukalski was inspired by this tale, and by tales of flying women he heard in Poland. Szukalski devoted his time to examining the secret prehistory of mankind, trying to find the primal source of human culture and custom, his four decades of study culminating in *Macimowa*, a forty-two volume work of some 25,000 pages. This outlined his secret history, "Zermatism," in which a post-deluge Easter Island serves as the cradle of human civilization, and man was in an eternal struggle against the *Yetinsyny*, the Sons of Yeti, who enslave and forcefully copulate with humanity. These yeti-human hybrids not only include hairy humanoids like Bigfoot and Yeti, but also include Pan and fauns, creatures we can recognize as Nephilim, and the puppet-masters of every conspiracy theory.

Zermatism seems to be a subversion of Ernst Schäfer's search for gigantic Aryan ancestors in Tibet; The Nazi zoologist admitted that he believed the Yeti to be nothing more than the Tibetan bear to fellow Yeti-hunter Reinhold Messner, but when Heinrich Himmler sends you on a wild goose chase, you pretty much have to roll your eyes and hunt that goose[134].

We see another great example of this strain of thought in Aleister Crowley's 1917 novel *Moonchild,* about a secret war between black and white magicians over an unborn child in the shadow of the First World War. This moonchild is born to a figure known as the Scarlet Woman, and a direct parallel with the Antichrist – but in a Satanic inversion of Christian mythos, this Antichrist is the liberating herald of a New Age. Despite its fictional narrative, Crowley believed that this Moonchild ritual was a legitimate magical rite, and performed it on several occasions with his followers and friends. This Babalon Working would be invoked by none other than L. Ron Hubbard, the science-fiction writer who founded Scientology, and rocket scientist and wizard Marvel "Jack" Whiteside Parsons, who had made preparatory rites in the waters of Devil's Gate Dam. At the time, Parsons was the head of the Agape Lodge, and was granted ritual components by Jane Wolfe, who, in a letter to Crowley, noted with some contempt that "our own Jack is enamored with Witchcraft, the houmfort, voodoo."

The Babalon Working took place over two weeks in 1946, and involved chanting, meditation, the use of bodily fluids, and the destruction of parts that Hubbard removed from the Ritual Body – as the Bible claims that the Whore of Babylon will be stripped naked, eaten, and burnt with fire. The body of van der Aarde had gone through all of these deprivations, and was rich in curses, arcane forces, signs of violence and the horrors of war, and the powers and influence of Mars, perfect for use as a vessel for Mother Harlot. It should also be noted that her body appeared to grow somehow after death, with Parson measuring the "vessel" as 186cm tall. Parson, oddly accurately, divined or intuited that Van der Aarde's personality was both violent and rebellious, innocent and sexual, lusty and loving, energetic and quiet, and that her sight had been greatly impaired in life "but her voice was

---

[134] Chamberlain, Ted. (May-June 2000). "Reinhold Messner: Climbing Legend, Yeti Hunter." *National Geographic Adventure.*

beautiful." The rite would "shift" its participants, to quote Parson's 1946 *Liber 49: The Book of Babalon*:

"[Babalon] also relates to a child, being innocent (i.e. undifferentiated). Its manifestations may be noted in the destruction of old institutions and ideas, the discovery and liberation of new energies, and the trend towards power [sic] governments, war, homosexuality, infantilism, and schizophrenia. This force is completely blind, depending upon the men and women in whom it manifests and who guide it. Obviously, its guidance now tends towards catastrophy [sic]. The catastrophic trend is due to our lack of understanding of our own natures. The hidden lusts, fears, and hatreds resulting from the warping of the love urge, which underly [sic] the natures of all Western peoples, have taken a homicidal and suicidal direction."

Not long after, Parsons would meet a woman named Marjorie Cameron, who he believed to be an elemental and the Scarlet Woman. In turn, she viewed Parsons as "the Angel of Death." Despite Crowley deriding Parsons' work, saying that he "get[s] fairly frantic when I contemplate the idiocy of these goats." Parsons himself fit the criteria of the 1910s Moonchild endeavors; he was born in Los Angeles in November 1914, and had an actual, verifiable connection to space, one foot in science and one in magic. Unfortunately, this possible "antichrist" died in a fulminate of mercury explosion in his garage.

The body of Van der Aarde fell into the possession of L. Ron Hubbard, bounced around storage sites owned by Scientology, before some Operating Thetan or another found it and donated the body to Carolina Biological. This medical supply company packaged the now highly decayed remains with bones bought from Indian crematories, and sold them as props to the Simi Valley set of the *Poltergeist* in 1982.

Love and Rockets.

"It was Céleste who interrogated the half-naked woman," Winepress wrote. "One minute, she had been cradling the bag of Fr Avenazzo, securing the strange box he used to house his journal. Gottlieb came to her, embracing her. I left her side, briefly, to see to Thomas, Anna, and the Servian. I carried Ana to the main body of our unit. Then, abruptly, She snapped to her feet and tackled the woman, who had been hiding behind the trees.

Céleste tortured the woman with a blast of intense heat and a punch to the jaw, preventing her from talking until the woman's mouth was secure under her hand. Oddly insightful, but Céleste noted that this woman had been stalking her since Belgium. A telephone operator.

I hadn't realized that this was the woman that had assaulted Thomas when he was abed. I had not seen her with an unexploded head.

Jacoba 'Schildbreker' van der Aarde, she identified herself. She was upset, tearing up, at the death of her companion, our AWOL Anglo-Malayalam lascar and animal handler, C.M. Tharakan Madraal. I noted that he apparently shot her. She said Noun would have killed her; Madraal would let her live on, in his ghostly talent for keeping the souls of his victims. I wondered if he was a nephel, or simply taught the art of hunting souls, capturing them in amulets like birds in a net – a nephilim art that survived for some time after the Flood, late enough to be condemned in Ezekiel 13. Thomas' control of flesh gave her a way out of that limbo.

She wistfully mentioned that Madraal had allowed her to ride an elephant, in Belgium, of all places... he was a big game hunter, and was concerned about the strange attacks by giant, usually vicious animals across the globe. Takeuchi was shocked to hear her mention the Usuri Brown Bear of Sankebetsu, and the Nandi bear of Kapsowar. She mentioned the Qoqogaq, a ten-legged polar bear spotted by Eskimos in 1913. The death of hunter Peter Grayson, seemingly slain by the Grootslang last year in a South African cavern. The strange 'dragon buffalo' of Korea's Heaven Lake. The shark attacks in the American State of New Jersey, and a monster in the White River. The Man-eating Tiger of Lungra Bag. Something called the Takitaro. Man-eating tigers and lions all over India and Africa. The rumours of a Bulgarian dragon drew him south, and into Typhon's clutches. He wanted to fight a dragon. He only sided with Typhon and the Martian to see what mischief they were up to.

'We watched you both,' she said. 'But it was the presence of one of the Nameless that decided our alignment. You can imagine how little love the Indians have for your house.'

Noun, who had only recently revived, meekly apologized, both to her and the group. He cradled the recovered lithopaedion in a blanket. We put van der Aarde in one of Céleste's spare dresses and bound and gagged her.

We took a day of relaxation and planning. We restocked on food and medicines in the port of Skala – Céleste found a brothel with a supply of opiates – plenty of morphine, codeine, and cocaine for sale. It was great to eat the island's blend of Greek, Italian, and Turkish food, though the former made us feel the absence of poor, enigmatic Amadeo Avezzano all the greater.

We were served a whole roasted lamb's head, eyeballs, brain, and tongue included, and kontosouvli, lamb chops stuffed in intestines. It seemed to be an Easter delicacy served to guests, but it might have been a prank.

I mentioned that whole sheep-heads are also eaten in South Africa, 'smileys.' We spoke of the strangest meal we have ever consumed. Venetianer said his strict diet disqualified him from most interesting food, but 'goyim always seem to struggle with gefilte fish.' Siegfried gave up right off the bat, admitting that his farm-boy-to-soldier diet had been rather bland; the most exotic he had gotten was his time in Alsace. Van der Aarde rather sadly said that Madraal made her curries, but she conceded that it was just somewhat exotic rather than strange. Anna said fermented mare's milk, which got our first round of solid cringes, a good showing. Zrno darkly added that they had to eat a dog in Russia. Anna waved that off, with the implication that conditions get rather harsh in deep Siberia, and sometimes you simply don't ask questions of the meat.

Céleste added English cock ale. Tom and I tried to clarify if it was a cocktail or *Coq au vin*, but she described it as an old fashioned English ale boiled with chicken, raisins, and nutmeg. Takeuchi was inspired by that, and mentioned that he drank *habushu*, which is a snake wine from Okinawa. And it wasn't some idiom; a *habu* is an actual Oriental pit viper drowned and left to dissolve in the alcohol. Tom meekly added he had Cantonese chicken feet in the London markets, and I threw in another African dish, the mopane worm, fried emperor moth caterpillars, but we solidly voted that Takeuchi won. Only Céleste wanted to try it, but she had a way with snakes. She collected the skewers left on the table, and snapped them in half, and began to arrange them in a pattern.

Takeuchi marveled at the Greek isles, the shards of old Byzantium. He had seen a lecture by Alexandra David-Néel with Ekai Kawaguchi, who had followed him from Sikkim. She was a scholar of Tibetan Buddhism, having spent time with the Lhasas and the Dalai Lama, and she spoke about the Epic of King Kesar, or Gesar, a Mongolian-Tibetan hero called lord of Ling. She floated the theory that the Mongol's Gesar was derived from a Persian-Turkish Fromo Kesaro, the Cesar of Rome, Byzantium. She said in the earliest versions of these tales, from the Bom, this 'Phrum Kesar' was a place that only later became a superhuman conqueror-king. It shocked Takeuchi into realizing how vast Rome's reach was, that even its embers could touch Tibet. Rome was kingship everywhere. Most chilling of all, this Gesar's mother was from a land called Gog.

Anna said that she had heard those Bom versions in Tuva, but he was a half-god conqueror that rode a white horse, and was the product of a goddess who drank from a magic pond. She said she never connected him to Rome, thinking him some Khan that passed into legend, but the white horse and virgin conception did have a Christian, apocalyptic flare. She mentioned that there was also, in Tuva, a god of war and love called Elbis, whom shamans invoke into the hearts of their foes to slay them- whether through love or war was uncertain. She was surprised to hear the Moslems speak of an Iblis, their Devilish chief genie.

Takeuchi looked at Anna and said that he had heard of her. He spoke with Yasuteru Narita, of Japan's intelligence service. He had spent a mere two weeks in Lhasa. He was looking for Czarist activity in Tibet, but rumors turned him north, towards the magic of the mountains. He heard of someone flying west from Tuva, rumours of the King of the World sleeping underground, the Zaharoff scheme, and giants in the earth. He died three years ago, and never found the truth of the matter of this rainbow-bodied Tuvan.

Not long after, Céleste would raise the question of my lead-lined case.

'Put on your gas masks,' I told everyone. After a moment of hesitation, they followed my command. I unscrewed the case, and unveiled a folded cloth of faded red-purple, the Tyrian hue of legend. Inside was a mass of wool filled with yellow powder.

'What is this?' Gottlieb asked.

I had been thinking of something of a speech:

'On one level, this is our great weapon. This is the future of weaponry, a symbol of progress that can sever us from the bonds of heaven. A fire greater than the knowledge stolen by Prometheus.

On another level, it is simply pulped uranium ore leached with acid and rolled into this wool, like a filter. The ancient Georgians had mined the uranium from the land of the far side of the Caspian Sea. Maybe they thought it was a dye...but there's power here. Unimaginable power, both chemical and symbolic. The pinnacle of alchemy. This is the great mythical treasure, sought by heroes, witches, and demigods...and who is better at sniffing out such secrets than Nephilim?'

'What is it?' Céleste said. 'What treasure? Did you grind up the Holy Grail like a cocaine snuff?'

Tom Noun began to laugh nervously, recognizing the hole in his family's control.

'No. Older, deeper. Homeric, even,' I said. I began laughing beneath the mask. 'This is the Golden Fleece.'

'Where the hell did you get this?' Céleste said, almost angry. She set her skewer-and-wax model down on the table.

'From the Tower of London, in my capacity as His Majesty's agent. The Crown had control of it since Lord Cochrane seized it from the Spanish Navy.'

Noun asked if I was referring to Thomas Cochrane.

Yes, the Tenth Earl Dundonald, I confirmed, the hero of the Napoleonic Wars, politician, inventor of rotary steam engines and steamships. He discovered it aboard a captured frigate, *His Majesty's Ship Impérieuse*, originally known as the *Medea*, with the Christian alias of *Santa Bárbara*, patron saint of bombardment. The vessel was given these names because of its cargo, the Golden Fleece. One of Lord Cochrane's midshipmen, Frederick Marryat, a writer interested in legends and the occult, identified the artefact. This vessel was jealously guarded by the Spanish, who considered secreting it away in Uruguay. Its capture was considered an act of war. Cochrane's *Medea* was deployed to the

Mediterranean, where he captured many vessels. He then brought the Fleece to England in 1809."

There were rumblings of "the DunDonald Destroyer" or the "Lord Cochrane's Machine," through the mid to late 19th century, and before the Great War, even appearing in the Danish children's song en "Svensk konstabel fra Sverrig":

> *De alliertes marine*
> *ej mere behøves vil,*
> *det er Lord Cochranes maskine,*
> *der styrer ad Kronstadt til.*

The 18 December 1914 issue of the *Seattle Star* covers the rumors succinctly:

"LONDON, England, Dec. 15 —Will England. driven to desperation, annihilate the Teutonic race? Will she resort to the secret that, for more than 100 years, she has considered too terrible to use? Will England employ 'Dundonald's famous destroyer' and at one blow exterminate millions of human beings? Three times England, when in sore straits, has considered using Dundonald's destroyer, 'which is the mystery of the world's warfare and three times the military and civil authorities of England have revolted at the idea of such 'wholesale slaughter!'

What is Dundonald's destroyer? At the present time it is said, the appalling secret is locked up in sealed vaults in the Tower of London. But three persons, one of the royal family, one of the army and one of the navy know what it is.

Thomas Cochrane, Tenth Earl of Dundonald, one of the most daring of the British sea lords, was also the greatest inventor of his time. In 1810, he led the British in the attack upon the French fleet in Basque Roads, one of the greatest feats of British naval history. He was kept from destroying the enemy only by the gross conduct of his superior officer, Lord Gambler. In a rage Dundonald made a frantic assault upon Gambler, and Gambler, backed by the corrupt admiralty, succeeded in disgracing Dundonald and forcing his retirement. Dundonald, experimenting with gases and chemicals, suddenly appeared before the admiralty, demanding the appointment of a small committee to investigate his 'new invention.' He claimed that his invention furnished an 'infallible means of securing at one blow our military supremacy; of commencing and terminating a war by one victory.'

A royal committee investigated. It reported that Dundonald's destroyer would do all that he claimed; that either on sea or land it was irresistible and infallible! The government refused to adopt it, however. The committee had reported that its 'devastation would be inhuman; it would transcend the limits of permissible warfare.'

The report urged "that it be kept a secret, lest some other power get it and use it for the annihilation of England and the conquest of the world.' In 1846 the admiralty appointed another investigating committee of high officials.

In January, 1847, this committee reported that, 'beyond aid's destroyer not only would defeat, but would actually destroy, sweep out of existence, annihilate any hostile force. To use such utter devastation would be contrary to the principles of warfare.'

During the Crimean war the government, hard pressed and desperate, was inclined to use the mysterious destroyer against the Russians. The admiralty once voted to use the device, provided Dundonald would instruct two officers as to how to employ it against Sevastopol. He stated that he would use it himself personally if permitted full freedom, and that it 'meant the death of the operator as well as the enemy.' The government again refused to permit such a crime against humanity.

Tradition among military experts is that the committee of 1847 wrote a full and complete list of directions as to the operation of the destroyer and that these directions have been sealed in a vault in the Tower of London for years."

This connection between radioactive superweaponry and the Golden Fleece rolled around in the mystically-aligned side of Anglophone governments, to the point that a secret outgrowth of the Manhattan Project was known as the JASON Advisory Group, and a prolific class of nuclear research reactor was dubbed "Argonaut," from the acronym of "Argonne Nuclear Assembly for University Training." Even in 1915, the British scientist Frederick Soddy publicly warned of the dangers of atomic warfare, and had previously hinted that such a bomb was responsible for the fall of prior civilizations and our ancient alchemical understanding of transmutation. However, it should be understood that rather than a fission weapon, Dundonald's device was almost certainly what we would call a "dirty bomb."

Winepress explained that the fleece was said to be the wool of the winged, golden ram, Chrysomallos, sired by Poseidon upon the nymph Theophane, granddaughter of Helios. The ram was the mount of the exiled cloud-spirit Nephele, cast out by her husband, King Athamas. Nephele, from the Heavens, sent the ram to rescue her children Helle and Phrixus from the wrath of their wicked stepmother Ino. In their hasty flight, Helle fell into the sea and drowned, giving the Dardanelles their other name, Hellespont. The Ram delivered Phrixus to Colchis on the Black Sea, and allowed the boy to sacrifice him to Poseidon. The Ram ascended to the heavens as Aries, an ancient constellation aligned with shepherd gods since the days of Babylon, when Tammuz wed Ishtar, the binding of Underworld Shepard and Venus. The young demigod hung its fleece in a grove of Ares guarded by brass bulls and a sleepless dragon whose teeth would become soldiers if seeded in the earth.

"Tom noted the mythic parallels to Gallipoli, men in those draconic trenches of the Dardanelles, and to the powers of Ares and Mars. Takeuchi, recalling his training in celestial navigation, noted that the Chinese called Aries 'Lou,' a word that means both the Sickle and the Binding Rope, ritual implements in the sacrifice of bulls. The association of the Golden Fleece with a source of chemical knowledge dates back to at least Palaephatus' *On the Incredible*, noted Winepress, as that 4th Century scholar reckoned the Fleece to be a divine alchemical treatise of some sort.

I said that there was terrifying potential here with the knowledge of mystical perception. There were rumors that Blavatsky and others such as Annie Besant had used their second sight to perceive the interior of the atom. I said that I was terrified on Patmos, both when he saw Typhon, whose family once guarded the Fleece alongside a Georgian clan, and when Takeuchi claimed that he carried with him the contents of the Ark of the Covenant. Takeuchi took umbrage with the use of 'claimed,' and clarified that he very much did carry that relic.

I clarified my own statements: The Fleece, the Ark, the weapons of the *Mahabharata* — these were artefacts of military might, divine authority, and immense power in the form of sickening light and atomic fire. The Ark could slay enemy armies, as could the Brahma-astra of Arjuna and the myriad weapons of Shiva — the latter could even threaten the devas. We are leaving the age of heavenly lightning and holy light and entering an age of artificial electricity and decaying radiance.

To go southeast, one must go north - we sailed from Patmos to Chios on March 30th, where we slept in Vrontados. The locals were boarding up their shops and crafting makeshift walls and defences. We wondered if a storm was coming, but the weather seemed fine.

This island was once the kingdom of the wine-rich king Oenopion; the giant hunter Orion walked the Aegean to Oenopion's court, where he either seduced or raped the princess Merope, the legendary mother of the Evangelopoulos line. Oenopion cut out Orion's eyes in revenge, and protected his daughter in a subterranean fortress. We dreamed that night of flaming arrows filling the sky, launched from the bows of Artemis and Orion.

The next day was Easter, and the sky was on fire. We were in a panic, at first, hiding under beds and tables and Céleste dancing and screaming at the sky in joy and Takeuchi cheering and shouting 'Tamayaaaa!' until the locals informed us that this was the *Rouketopolemos*, the Rocket War. Two rival churches situated on two hilltops (some four hundred meters apart), fire thousands upon thousands of stick-and-gunpowder rockets at each other, trying to strike the enemy congregation's bell tower — the Leaning Virgin was seemingly part of a rich tradition. Direct hits count in the scoring system, but Panaghia Ereithiani and St Mark's both seem to think that they're winning, and the other side is cheating or lying. So the cycle continues, every year. And so it goes, every year since the custom began under the Ottomans — they said that they used actual cannons then, but the old people shake their heads and say it was always powder missiles. I wonder if this war will degenerate to nothing more but a forgotten ritual of mostly harmless maroons. Maybe our armed forces will consist of signal corps alone.

In any case, we agreed to support St Mark's because we could pronounce it. There were monks there, free from their monastic duties to decorate the island, and they spoke of an odd Hesychastic doctrine spreading from Mount Athos over the past few years; they called themselves Imiaslavie, the Praising of the Name, for humans were so imperfect that they could only ever glorify the name of the Lord, rather than the Ineffable Himself, the shadow rather than the flame. They were considered so heretical by the Russian Orthodox Church that the Czar's men invaded Greece to lay siege to Mount Athos, arrested, exiled, and excommunicated the order itself. Only a few remnants on other islands survive. Among the images of the saints, Céleste turned to me and said with wine-slurred words, 'Joan of Arc...the image of a young girl, bound to a stake and consumed by the flame, her face serene or filled with religious ecstasy...And St Sebastian, penetrated with arrows. Oh, sometimes in church I would imagine being his executioners...'

So we decided to semi-forcibly sedate the girl with copious amounts of wine and ouzo, as the Salamander and an event centred around explosions does not mix. She eventually, half-sobered, remotely detonated a powder cache, squealed in disturbing pyromaniacal glee, and dragged Gottlieb off to a room."

In a strange little piece entitled *"Ich Ausblenden"* (I fade away, I disappear), something of an essay, Siegfried Gottlieb recounts first meeting with Céleste.

"There are two types of people in the world. Persons, and non-persons. I am the latter, a farmboy from a shack in Bavaria. Like every disaffected, pretentious young man in Germany since the turn of the century, I read too much Nietzsche for my own good, and thought that just because I was different, I was somehow special, better than the people in that small world. My father was the same way – he had shreds of greatness, but he lost his friend in his youth, and what small fortune he had earned to the schemes of that harridan Adele Spitzeder. He flinched at the world's cruel kicks, and crawled into the bottle. When he emptied it, he smashed it across the face of the nearest family member, and crawled into the next one like a hermit crab of hate. The only thing keeping me from being something greater was my family and my farm; When I would work the land with my philistine brothers I would dream of some place better, maybe Paris, idealized by everyone west of the Malays and south of the Lapps - so I migrated towards the border. I found it was easy to cross the border a few times, even in those paranoid times. My family went on living without me.

I ended up drifting to Strasbourg, back and forth across the Alsatian border, enjoying that typically French hobby, people-watching. People-watching doesn't pay the bills, so I washed dishes and glasses in a restaurant. I end up as I always do; a mere observer. Some people have nothing else to do but observe other people living. They have no real choice about what goes on, no true power to change anything. They can only *see* what *should* be changed, and watch things and hope they go their way. And those that do have the power to change the world *can't see* what *should* be changed.

More and more bored and lonely with each day, I drifted away, disconnecting. I was rejected, not out of malice, but because I was simply pushed out of people's minds. But this sensation came to a head on that night. I was just getting off my shift, and tried to tell the shift manager. He ignored me. I had to stand in the doorway for about ten minutes, yelling at the top of my lungs. I threw my towel on his desk and walked out. He noticed the washrag, at least. I walked through the kitchen, with Dietrich running into me without apologizing, and Maria the old owner not saying the usual 'hello' or 'good night'.

'*Hallo? Jemand?*' I demanded of everybody and nobody. I left the restaurant through the back door, and leaned against the filthy wall of the building, in the back alley. The brick building was once white washed, and the shape of the edifice and the triple exits betrayed its theatrical origin. The white paint was faded and blackened by cooking grease and soot. The air was stale, smoky, and had the faintly clinical smell of bad alcohol. Standing there was one of the waitresses from the cabaret next door.

'Comment allez-vous?' She asked, a cigarette pressed between two fingers, the nails stained green-yellow by absinthe.

'Bien!' I answered back, far too enthusiastically. I noticed!

'Ah. Good.'

'Siegfried Gottlieb,' I introduced myself.

'Céleste,' she replied in kind.

The first thing I noticed was her height, only a few centimetres shorter than mine. But after that, my eyes met hers for a moment, just a glance, but one that burned itself into my memory. Her eyes blazed in a hue of blue hovering between sky and the faint robin's egg of ice. But there were these little streaks, like when you heat up copper in an apothecary's burner so hot it turns from teal to pure blue. Gloriously hot blue, burning and beautiful, and profoundly unnerving. She has this stare, this insane stare, where you really don't know what she's going to do – there is cold fire and murderous ice in that stare, mania and terrifying calm. They're the eyes of a loving predator. She might jump on you and make love to you or kill you just to hear what sound you'd make as you died.

She asked me if I was alright.

'Yes,' I said, elated that somebody finally acknowledged my presence. 'I think I'm fine. Thank you.'

'Do I know you?' she said, still staring straight ahead. 'Because I want to hit you in the face. I don't know why. It's just an impulse. I'd chalk it up to fickle maidenhood.'

'Oh,' I said, not really knowing how to respond to that. So I ended up saying, 'I don't know how to respond to that. So I'll ask this- what's that?'

'That's my lucky hat,' she said, referring to the thick but floppy royal blue wool skullcap she wringed in her hands. 'You speak French, very well, but with a German accent. It's not Alsatian. Where are you from?'

'Bavaria. You speak German,' I said.

'You speak French. I thought I should return the favor,' she said with a smirk.

I thanked her. She turned towards me for the first time, and her raised shoulder and crossed arms happened to push her chest up again, and I realised that the first three buttons of her blouse, under her open jacket, were undone. Embarrassed, my eyes flickered away. But I could see that she wore a strange pendant on her silver, possibly nickel, necklace. It was a blue and red lizard-thing with a tail that curved into itself, connecting to its head through its mouth, from which the amulet was suspended. The red blazed against her wardrobe's mute palette of black, blue, and white.

'Where did you get that?' I said. It was an uncanny necklace style, not the elaborate kind one would expect on the neck of a performer.

'I made it. I saw the salamander in an old book so I copied it. I twisted and melted a bunch of broken necklace links together and coloured it,' she said, running her finger under the chain and pulling it outward towards me.

'That's nice. Why a salamander?'

'It represents me.'

'How?' I said. 'You sleep under a log?'

'No,' She chuckled, 'It's the mythical salamander. It represents fire and its opposite, the cold. Steam.'

I asked if she knew what I am. She said yes, and that she knew that I knew what she was. She asked how we could have met. If I tracked her. I said know – we met by chance. Fate, perhaps some grand cosmic design. She said fine. I said fine. And she said 'I will show you mine, if you show me yours first.'

I remembered our night in that Greek room, the passion, the violence, the heat. I remember seeing her one last time glowing brilliantly against the blue window with broken glass like the twisted, gasping teeth in the mouth of a dying man. I descended into hell to pull her out of the underworld. She didn't look back. She shrugged off the hellfire like it was a morning mist, and I evaded the great hound Cerberus. And she didn't look back. I got her out of Hell just fine. I dragged her out of Sodom and Gomorrah and the only salt involved was a little sweat and tears. She didn't look back.

I beat Fate. We beat Destiny. People like us are not supposed to be happy. But together, we can do anything. So strong, so beautiful. She holds me up like the muscle at the base of my spine."

At the end of the night, Céleste was approached by Anna.

"I went outside once Siegfried feel asleep. The war, as terrible as it is to say, made him more handsome; it had eaten away at some of his fat, leaving behind a tall frame of muscle and toughened pearl skin.

I soaked in the animal savagery of it all, the sensuality, the gunpowder and alcohol wafting on the air, the salt of the sea breeze and love sweat on the tongue. I loved it, the lowness of it all. Even the smell of horse dung from the late-night cleaning crew.

The Irish poet Yeats was dismayed after seeing Alfred Jarry's brutal, scatalogical burlesque *Ubu Roi*, A riot broke out after its premier, as with the later *the Rite of Spring*, and Yeats saw in its childish, argot-laced chaos the destruction of spiritual, meaningful work. 'After us, the Savage God,' he would say. But ah, a fat, foolish king swept up in Eastern revolutions, cast down by the Russians, his wife dressing up as St. Gabriel to beg for his kingdom's scraps – this is the nature of our world.

Jarry invented a nonsense science, pataphysics, to explain his play. It is meta-metaphysics, the science of imaginary solutions and exceptions that prove the rules. It was a joke on academia and men of letters – but this is the nature of our world.

I would hate to live in a world with meaning. That would mean there's a proper way to live. And I can't live properly.

I climbed to the roof to smoke. Anna soon joined me, flying up in a drunk curl, like a dying fly. The little thing had started drinking heavily, and fallen quiet.

She sat next to me, and said nothing. She was hard to read, almost mechanical in her movement. I asked her how she was feeling. She said she was lonely and tired. I asked her why. Zrno had been drinking too, and acting miserable. He wouldn't touch her, or leave his room, or even talk since losing his foot.

I told her to give him room. Men cope differently, they have to be strong, and stew for a little while. She thanked me, and said she wasn't good at understanding people. They did things for reasons she couldn't understand. And now virtually everyone she knew was dead.

I hadn't heard about her parent's deaths. I said I was sorry. She asked if I was an orphan too.

I said my father had left when I was small, maybe two, at most. In 1899 my mother, always waif and clammy, fell seriously ill. Her hair started to fall out in clumps and she gradually lost weight, vomiting profusely. She didn't have any teeth left by the end of the year. She didn't work any more, and became suddenly deeply religious. She died in 1900. I had my grandmother until 1907.

She said sorry. She was quiet for a while, and said she only had this small group. And her bird, which she considered releasing. She was too afraid to keep it around, in such danger. Handling animals, though, had always calmed her, brought her peace. She had no toys in her childhood.

She asked if I did. I mentioned that I had a doll, but I didn't want to explain what a golliwog is to a Siberian, so I left that part out. One of the girls at my school teased me for carrying around that torn up doll. So I jumped on her and started slamming her head into the pavement until a nun pulled me off. I was expelled from that school. I actually didn't care. I didn't feel sorry or guilty about it. And that's what scared me. I didn't care that I could have killed somebody, a monstrous little thing. Anna said that she would have beaten the girl, too, because what person feels the need to tear down the poor orphan?

I laughed.

She asked what I did after that. I did get back into school, with the priest's intervention, but it was stricter, smaller, and steeped in old books and dense maths. I lived at my grandmother's place. She was a madam. She didn't understand, so I explained how houses of prostitution worked. She asked me if I had ever participated, as she put it. I admitted that I took on a few clients. I was too young for it, but I looked older. It was those with the 'British vice.' She didn't know what that meant, but didn't ask. But I explained that there was no actual intercourse involved.

She asked if Siegfried was my first. I said no. I had briefly been with an older man when I was sixteen. And a few years later, a Senegalese man. I liked him but he was a bit of a coward when it came to a mixed woman, not that I could blame him. And then the albino, because I'm a woman of extremes.

She seemed to struggle with something on her arm, and I realized that nobody had tended to her injuries since Russia, and she had not mentioned it. I applied a brace to Anna's wrist to support what seemed to be a break. She looked away as I tightened it, barely reacting. I had to ask her how she felt.

Horrid, she softly replied. I asked if I should refit the brace, but she said that it fit perfectly. After a long pause, she said, 'I don't think he loves me any more.'

She was afraid that Mihajlo would abandon her. She wasn't good to him in Archangel, annoying, and she 'closed up' after her parents died, and he had to protect her from the snow. She nearly got him killed by forcing the fight with that grey woman, against his advice. And now he was terribly wounded and mad at her, and she said she was ugly and would be a terrible wife and mother.

'He's going to leave me,' she said, 'Nobody will ever love me now.'

I told her that she wasn't ugly. Perhaps too bluntly, I said she just needed to wear a foundation. I told her I would help her find one in town, if she wanted. She started shaking and said that I was so pretty.

I said that she had seen my scars. I leaned in to put my hand on her shoulder, and she seemingly misinterpreted it, turned her head, and kissed me on the lips. I recoiled in shock and smacked her across the mouth. She fell back, covered her face, curled up in a ball, and started wailing and sobbing that she didn't do anything wrong. I clambered down the ladder, leaving her there."

Venetianer spoke with Takeuchi as they wandered around the island at night. Venetianer wrote that "Takeuchi examined a dud firework with something like disappointment. He said that the Japanese had mastered the *hanabi* – the fireflower, as they call them- and recalled the great festival of his home province, where great firework displays and costumed dancers accompany paper floats painted with mythical scenes, called *nebuta*. The dancers jump and shout, he says, crying 'rassera, rassera.' In his province, it was all started by a shogun that used flutes and drums to draw the ire of his enemies, a Sakanoue no Tamuramaro.

Funny how war becomes a dance, I said. How many Jewish holy days are a remembrance of an averted massacre or a barely-won battle?

He suddenly turned and asked if I thought we were entering a new age of religions. I asked him what he meant. He said all the old religions that survived to today originate in a narrow band stretching from the Levant to Northern India. It was the center of religious faith. But now, it seems like religions are arising in the fringes, in the wheel rather than the axil.

He mentioned the Tenrikyo movement, officially recognized as a form of Shintoism but radically different. It seems almost like a reckoning of western monotheism with Japanese metaphysics, created by a Nakayama Miki: there is a primary god, Tenri-ou-no-Mikoto, the God of Origin, who is in command of subservient gods. They believe that they are forever returning to the Jiba, an axis mundi and origin of the world. To return to the Jiba is to return home: Karma is causality, and sins are dust to be swept from the mind. It is a form of reincarnation, where the body and mind perish with death but the soul returns forever, driven to seek joy. I noted some oddly strong parallels to some Chassidic traditions and radical charismatics.

He said that the last seventy odd years seems to be the dawn of a new age of religion. New, strange forms of Christianity in America. Theosophy and Occult Sciences. Spiritualists, those new necromancers. Atheism Marxism, Nihilism, Nietzscheans and Social Darwinists.

I asked him if those were really the bones of Jesus and the Ark in his boxes. He said he believed so, but he never opened it up.

I told him a story about Little Hershel of Ostropol, who sold a large blank canvas on the side of the road. When a customer approached him, asking about the high price of the blank canvas, Hershele said, 'I'll tell you all about it, for a silver rubel.'

This piqued the man's curiosity, and he gave Hershele the rubel.

'It's a famous painting, *The Jews Pursued by the Egyptians Across the Red Sea*.'

'Where are all the Jews?' says the customer.

'They've crossed the Red Sea,' Hershele said.

'So where are the Egyptians?'

'They've yet to come.'

The angered customer asked, 'So where is the Red Sea?'

'It's been parted, idiot.'"

The Fall of Troy

In an entry dated to the next day, Thomas Noun found himself facing a conundrum:

"So, I knew my sound, rational justification for having a half-naked woman bound, gagged, and chained to a pipe. However, anyone outside of this group who stumbled upon this scene would have a sound, rational justification for assuming that I am a sex-murderer. I resumed a female form. I considered claiming that she was my insane sister; apart from our bizarre eyes, we looked strikingly similar, as tall, slim, pale women with fair red-brown hair, now that she no longer had the greenish dye. I would just have to narrow my chin a bit and it was spot on.

Our families had, of course, intermarried often, despite modern enmity, and shared the same distant ancestors, and both claimed the blood of Grendel's Mother, Finn son of Folcwald, the Four Giant Brothers-Dan, Toen, Ooit, and Nu – and the Giants of Winter, and the woman who raided hell, Dulle Griet or Mad Mags. Even one of Pier Gerlofs Donia's granddaughters married into our line, as did a child of Lange Wapper. According to the legend, the Van der Aardes are the house of Druon Antigoon, the giant of the river Scheldt, and they lived along it in ancient lakes of the gods. But this is mostly artifice, and our last common ancestor was only in 1822.

She moved suddenly, with the phantom sound of jangling coins. She looked up at me, curiously, as I had been staring past her, quietly.

I waved my hand in front of my face and then indicated her face with a wave. She angrily mumbled something, heavily muffled by her bonds. I walked over to her and handed her my pen and journal. She is the one who wrote 'You can talk, fool' in the margin on top of the page.

I told her that I noticed that we look alike. She rolled her eyes. She nodded at the window. Leaves had fallen from the trees, autumnal rather than the expected green of spring. She gestured towards her mouth.

I manacled her loose hand and pulled down the gag.

'My birthday's coming up,' she noted. 'I was born at about noon on the 7th of April, 1894. A Saturday, I think. A strong, rough wind whipped south from Bruges while my mother struggled with the labour. When I was born, dead autumn leaves fell on a clear day in Clairvaux. On the 11th, I was baptised. And dead leaves rained once again on Pontcarré. So I have been born again, it seems.'

She was a bit late - we previously noticed that our birthdays were clustered together, from mid November to February – with Céleste on 22 October barely outside the range. The only true outlier was Mihajlo, in late July. Winepress, falling back on his anthropological impulses, had catalogued us thoroughly, and there were patterns: most notably, ten of us fell within the height range of 5'9" to 6'3", with Anna as the sole outlier. But she was a child of Aries.

'Born again,' I said. 'I have rejected my family, or been rejected by them...it's rather complicated. When they came to retrieve me, I turned them away and continued on this fatal mission.'

'Good,' she said.

'Yes, fair,' I said. 'So...I want to ask for your forgiveness. At least on my behalf. You don't have to settle your grudge against our family, but we need to work together, and I don't want you to have to live in this state."

She glared at me.

'After our first encounter, we looked into who you were. The Schildbreker. You were a hero. You saved so many of your countrymen.'

'You act like fighting your family is a deviation,' she said. 'It's the most heroic thing I've done. You are creatures of twisted flesh and ancient darkness. I will work with you against those demons and angels I saw on that hill. But I will never forgive you.'

'If we survive Armageddon and you still feel like killing me, we'll have a go. Until then, focus on the mission,' I said.

'You have my word,' she said.

We didn't speak much after that, but I let her move about the room, and sent for a meal. We sat quietly as we ate a dish of fish baked in olive oil, lemon, onion, and tomato- a psari plaki.

I visited the Serb with bottles of wine and gin.

'Without my homeland, I lived on Corfu,' he sang softly. 'But I proudly cheered – Love live Serbia! But I proudly cheered...'[135]

He suddenly glared at me and asked why I came. I said that I wanted to talk about his past. He spasmed and hissed, and said he didn't like talking about that. He said he was just a peasant, and didn't know anything about nephilim and houses and just wanted to drink and sleep. He asked me if I knew what house he was from, because he sure as hell didn't know. I said that in ancient times, the Dacian and Thracian races were rich in the blood of giants – Dacia's final king was Decebalus, a nephel with the strength of ten men, hence his cognomen, and the two

---

[135] These are the final lines of Tamo Deleko, a Serbian song about the Great Retreat. "*Bez otadžbine, na Krfu živeh ja, / Ali sam ponosno klic'o, Živela Srbija!* (repeat)"

Roman Emperors of the Blood were both Dacians – the obscure Regalianus, and Maximinus Thrax, the 8.5'-tall warlord with monstrous strength and burning sweat. These Thracian giants built a network of tunnels under Bulgaria and Rumania, with spiralling tombs of gold in the Bucegi Mountains and coiled in the gnarled roots of the Hoia. There did not seem to be a major Serbian family, that I knew of; but the houses were, by and large, an ahistorical artifice of the Napoleonic War. He looked disappointed.

I finally got him to open up over alcohol, explaining his past with his brother, as sceptical as I was of his claim. He spoke in vivid details of the assassination, that spark in the powder keg. He was haunted by the incident, and said it was burnt into his mind. 'It is nothing,' he said, quoting Franz Ferdinand's reported final words. He read interviews, looked into newspapers, Austrian and Serbian alike, all those sabre-rattling ultimatums and rumors of that primal 'Austro-Servian Crisis.' Franz Ferdinand was the *Katechon*, the Great Catholic Monarch, the last fraying thread holding back the age of antichrists, the final restraint on the apocalypse and the fall of Last Roman Emperors. And they had killed him.

He said, out of the blue, that he and his brother had been recorded dead at birth; it was only later that they revived. It was a nothing, bastard town, and the infrastructure was poor - one day, he came across his records, and it had never been corrected. He said he was officially dead. He asked how the world would look if they had truly died.

He looked me in the eye and mentioned a Momcilo Gavrić, an orphaned boy who joined the Serbian army as a scout after the Austrians killed his parents. He was merely seven-years-old. Mihajlo swayed slightly, and looked at his bottle. He looked out over the harbour and said, 'we were just kids, too.'

I spent the rest of the afternoon and night writing about the issue in something of a drunken, half-prophetic fugue. Perhaps my best work, not that it has much competition, a jeremiad in the modern style.

Mihajlo continued to drink and drifted away. He says that he is a type of man called a zduhać, a dragon-man, a stuha, a vetrovnjak, an alovit, an oblačar, or a gradobranitelj, the Serbian equivalent to the *tempestarii* of the medieval world. He fights demons of the storm in his dreams, cutting the hail from clouds before it can destroy crops, and redirecting frost and floods. Devils, blackbirds, dragons, ghosts, and evil zduhaći were his foes. He muttered 'butcher the white cattle, heavy with rain...' as he finally fell asleep."

It appears that part of the initial plan had involved Rudolf Freiherr von Sebottendorff, a wealthy German intelligence officer and occultist – a Freemason, astrologer, alchemist, and convert to the Bektashi order of Sufism. Living in Bursa, Turkey, he had ties to the Sufi alchemist Hussein Pasha and the Termudis, a wealthy banking family of Thessalonikan Jews who belonged to a Memphis-Misraim Freemasonry Lodge. The head of the Termudi family had initiated von Sebottendorff into the lodge, and gifted him a library of Kabbalistic and Rosicrucian lore. As the war dragged on, however, it seemed that communicating to him via Freemasonry lodges seemed less likely, as the Turkish lodges aligned themselves with the Committee of Union and Progress and, thereafter, the Young Turks. He had not responded to any of their communications from Germany, and circumstances dictated that they were unable to visit the Most Worshipful Grand Lodge of Bulgaria, recently founded on 9 June 1917, in Sofia. Von Böhm was their primary connection to von Sebottendorff- in prolonged correspondence with his alias of "Edwin Torre," and his death was the final blow to the plan.

The choice to go an alternate route was ultimately for the better, as von Sebottendorff had soured on the whole smuggling plot due to delays and growing skepticism in the Nephilim's abilities, origins, and connections to the theosophic "Root Races" of the primordial world, particularly of the post-Blavatsky elaborations by William Scott-Elliot (it seems he believed the Nine to be of Atlantean heritage). Occult lore ties his change of heart to the prophecies of a Zagreb-born Croatian-German mystic by the name of Maria Oršić (Germanized as Orsitsch), but this alleged diviner and "founder" of the Vril Society seems to be a later invention, as no concrete evidence of her existence has ever been found outside of Neo-Nazi elaborations on the book, *The Morning of the Magicians*[136]. It seems that he had alienated the Termudi family with the

---

[136] However, she does not actually appear in Louis Pauwels and Jacques Bergier's *Le Matin des Magiciens*, despite some claims and empty citations, and

early seeds of his racialism and antisemitism, and in 1916, and he returned to Germany to lead the Munich chapter of the Germanenorden Walvatter of the Holy Grail. Soon after, von Sebottendorff founded the Thule Society, influential in the development of the Nazi Party, and made attempts to synthesize Aryan mysticism and Islamic philosophy.

Winepress continued his description of the journey:

"The next leg of the journey would be far more perilous, taking a oared boat from Chios to Izmir, crossing into Turkish territory, before sailing from there to Lebanon.

We had worried about the coastal blockade maintained by the Turks since 1915, but Allenby and Faisal's forces had cleared much of the Holy Land from Turkish domination, as they are likely to hold all of the Palestine by October at the latest. Despite the loss of Shakespear[137] and the new appointment of Bell[138], it seems our operation is less perilous than we feared. The Ottoman Navy's control over the Aegean is a shambles, with the loss of its sole coastal defence ship, a *Mesûdiye*, one of its two pre-dreadnoughts, two protected cruisers, the light cruiser *Midilli* in January, and, most devastating, three of its eight destroyers. They have a handful of antiquated ironclads, and only one submarine, a captured French craft, run around in the Dardanelles. We had no idea if it is even operable. Their main tactical threat is minelayers, which had done terrible work against the [British] navy. The German's Constantinople Flotilla, despite their name, now operated entirely in the Black Sea rather than the Aegean, and was reincorporated into the Pola fleet after Allied convoys weakened the U-boat campaign. Takeuchi proudly noted that the Empire of Japan sent fourteen destroyers to the

purported images of her are fabrications.

137 William Shakespear (1887-1916), English explorer, killed during the Battle of Jarrab. One of the more well-connected and respected figures of the British Empire's influence in Arabia.

[138] Gertrude Bell (1868- 1926), English archeologist and administrator. Winepress seems to lament her appointment to Baghdad as Oriental Secretary, rather than her earlier, travels around the Levant and Turkey, where she gathered intelligence for the British Empire and bore witness to the Armenian Genocide.

Mediterranean, specialising in Anti-submarine warfare. I wonder how we shall overcome the menace of the submarine in the future, as they can only become more advanced and independent in their operations; perhaps improved detection using electrical signalling, or dispersing control of the seas from warships to something like a flying flotilla of Glenn Curtiss's seaplanes.

Izmir was once Smyrna, the hometown of Homer, named after the Amazon that seduced Theseus, one of John the Revelator's seven churches of Asia. Venetianer noted that it was the hometown of Sabbatai Zvi, a Messianic claimant who humiliated his followers by converting to Islam in 'the Christian year' 1666. Some of those Sabbateans followed Zvi into conversion, becoming a strange hybrid of Moslem and Jew called the Dönme, 'the converts,' a small sect that lingers on in Salonika and the Anatolian coast, with some representatives among the Young Turks. I was shocked by Venetianer's genuine rancour against Zvi, who he seemed to view as something of an arch-traitor to Judaism and the antithesis of the Hassidic movement. From his descriptions, they sounded like some Judaic Tantrism, in the most extreme and hedonistic form, or the worst slanders against the mediaeval Cathars. Rather exciting bunch, at the very least.

The Rabbi's disgust only faded, briefly, when he spoke of one antinomian Sabbataian preacher named Nathan of Gaza, who wrote a Treatise *on Dragons* in which evil entered the world through the form of Leviathan's children. One such sea dragon was the serpent of Eden, and even the Almighty had aspects of the dragon, with fiery nostrils. In Kabbalah, evil is the necessary dross of Creation; Nathan of Gaza animated them into drakes. The Rabbi did quickly mention and drop that he preached in Venice, leading me to speculate as to the history of his name.

We saw, in the distance, Mount Spil- Sipylus of old- the Lydian heartland with its statue of Cybele and the city of Tantalus. Those islands had a storied majesty, despite being nothing but stony shadows on the horizon. Icaria, where Icarus was said to crash, overlooked by a temple to Artemis Tauropolos, pillaged to make a church. It was its own free state, for five months. The isles of the Odyssey, the distant shores of Crete. We all felt that weight of history. You could not turn without crashing into a column of the classical age, the face of a king of legend, a fly of the Macedonian fisher[139]. The clash at Ilium between gods and heroes. The terrible fall of Troy.

Izimir is called Infidel Smyrna for its population of Greeks and other non-Turks. Gawur, they call us. We found a Jew – one of the Sephardi. He knew Greek, his native Ladino, and Levantine Arabic, and enough of Turkish, Italian, and Spanish to operate at port. To Venetianer's delight, he had been learning some of the newly revived Hebrew, after only knowing a bit from his early rites of passage. He was an older man with a decent fishing vessel, and had seen a great deal of the Mediterranean in his years, smuggling during the Balkan Wars. While he had finally built up a nest egg after decades of struggle, he lost nearly everything on land to last year's Salonika Fire, including his wife and everything of her but a single small picture held on his boat. The poor man avoided the land, spending most of his time in ports aboard the vessel, leaving only for resupplies and maintenance. He at first said that he feared the blockades and submarine terrorism, after the *Falaba*, the *Lusitania*, and the murder of Charles Fryatt, but he soon realised that he did not particularly care if he was sunk. I turned the contents of his ashcan into gold; hopefully he can spend his last years without financial want, at the very least.

He sang a drunken song with Zrno, a song of the Serbs called the "The French Boats are Leaving.[140]" I thought it was a traditional sailor's

---

139 This is a reference to a circulated tale of serendipity from the Macedonian front. According to Dr. Eric Gardner, serving in the Royal Armed Medical Corps, Turkish artillery fire upon British troops at Amphipolis, in the Strymon Valley, uncovered an ancient tomb in October 1915. The exhausted British troops, deprived of meat rations for weeks after the long retreat from Gallipoli, were overjoyed by the discovery of bronze fishhooks dating to 200 B.C., allowing them to fish from the River Struma.

See: Buller, Frederick. "The Macedonian Fly" *The American Fly Fisher: Journal of the American Museum of Fly Fishing*. Fall 1996. Vol. 22, no. 4, p.6.
Cameron, L.C.R. (1928). *Rod, Pole & Perch: Angling and Otter-Hunting Sketches*. London: Martin Hopkinson & Company Ltd.

[140] *Kreće se lađa francuska* (Креће се лађа француска)- this song was only about

song until the line *Naiđe švapski sumaren*, about a Kraut submarine approaching. Zrno's recondite history came into clarity. He did not keep his past a mystery just to hide his family name; no, the boy had seen Bosnia and Serbia and the wrath of the Dual Monarchy and Bulgaria. He could not kill his foes, not by the hundreds or thousands or millions to stop them, and he could not save the dying all around him. He was the greatest runner in the world. And so he ran. And now that he can't run... What can he do?

So the captain sang:
> "Lo alcanzó a saver el rey Nimrod esto,
>   '¡dixo que lo traigan aina y presto
>   antes que desreinen a todo el resto
>   y dexen a mi ya crean en el Verdadero!'
>   Ya me lo truxeron con grande albon
>   y el travó de la silla un buen travon.
>   '¿Di, raxa—por que te tienes tu por Dío?
>   ¿Por que no quieres creer en el Verdadero?'"

We arrived in Beirut on Van der Aarde's birthday, April 7th. The port lay on St George Bay, a grotto with seven coves at the mouth of the River Beirut, where the dragonslayer slew his infamous foe. The locals say that St George washed the dragon's blood off in the waters of the river, blessing it with his healing hands. Those seeking blessing tie clothes to the grottos' gates, returning to undo the knots once their wishes are granted.

I felt a strange patriotism here; this was the saint of Englishmen. Noun pointed out that George was the patron of practically everywhere else, and bitterly wondered if he was chosen in a bit of dark age triumphalism over the Dragon of Wales. But there was something there, echoing across time and myth.

There are four candidates for the Rome of Revelation. The Vatican is the obvious one, as the head of the Roman Catholic Church, but they are impotent in this war. It was a protestant hobbyhorse. The Czar, as the most powerful ruler crowned by the Eastern Church, claimed to be

year or so old at this point in time; it is about the Serbian Great Retreat to Salonika to the eponymous French evacuation boats, based on a poem written by Colonel Branislav Milosavljević.

the heir of the Empire ruling from the Third Rome, but he is imprisoned, perhaps dead. No, there are two true candidates, and they are at war at Armageddon.

The legendary Æneas, the survivor of the sack of Ilium, founded the Roman nation. His descendant, Brutus of Troy, was said to have established the British race after conquering the giant Gogmagog, and thus comes the British claim. We are the greatest of the great powers, the lords of a quarter of the Earth's surface. English is so quintessential that even when we fall the world will speak it and its descendants, a second Latin.

But the Turks have a far more tangible claim to the Imperial mantle, *de juris* to our *de facto*. They conquered Byzantium, taking Constantinople and thus the legacy of the Eastern Roman Empire. Indeed, Turkey was the site of Troy, and thus Æneas' legacy has finally returned to his homeland.

This will be the fall of Troy. When the Sultan falls, Rome will fall, and the histories of the far future will say that the light of Rome was finally extinguished at Armageddon, 1918.

We found a place in port; it was easy to rent, as much of the shore had been abandoned. They had been starved out by the Turks and their blockade, the famous cedars of Lebanon cut down for fuel. The forest of the gods, fed to trains. It appeared to be safe and recovering, as Allenby had the Turks on the run, yet the port felt haunted. We soon learned that we were directly across from the place where, two years ago, the Turks hanged twenty-one Syrians and Maronites for protecting those ancestral cedars, the answer to why the Arabs kept away.

The Arab masses were often a ghastly sight, pouring in from the starved wasteland of the Mount Lebanon Mutasarrifate. Jamal Pasha blockaded Syrian grain imports, the Ottomans redirected Lebanese stocks to their fronts, and depredators and locusts ravaged the crops which remained. There has come some hope in this late phase, and the Venerable Patriarch [of the Maronite Church, Elias Peter] Hoyek, no longer suppressed by Jamal Pasha, established a relief scheme with help from the French and the Lebanese of Egypt and the Americas. It is difficult to tell how many are dead – we have heard estimates of between ninety and two hundred thousand, perhaps half of the Mutasarrifate.

We gathered intelligence from local Britons. Allenby has become an apocalyptic as well; he has wrapped himself in prophecy, for he prayed in December for God's guidance, and God pointed him towards Iasaiah 31:5 - As birds flying, so shall the Lord of hosts defend Jerusalem; defending also he shall deliver it; and passing over he shall preserve it. Thus, he was inspired to take Jerusalem with a vanguard of aeroplanes, dumping ultimatums sighed as Allenby – or, in the Arabic, 'al-Anbiyaa' or 'Al-'Anabi' – making demands in the name of the Prophets or the Prophet.

The locals have been muttering as to the meaning of Allenby's name."

Winepress was not alone in his concern over this coincidental name. In a 23 November 1917 administrative memorandum, the British Expeditionary Forces' Major W.D. Kenny, Ass. Ad., wrote to staff officer General Sir Guy Dawney that:

"In reply to your O.E.T./85, I have sounded several natives here but can get no definite confirmation of the prophecy alluded to.

Nazmi Eff Abdel Hadi tells me however, that he has heard the same story from better educated inhabitants here, bears out the translation of the C-in-C's name."

The General's secretary, A.C. Parker was equally baffled as to its potential significance. Other British commanders were troubled by the signs of the time, such as Gen. Beauvoir de Lisle, who commanded the 29th Divison at Gallipoli before his transference to the Somme, later wrote in his unpublished memoirs that he "was most anxious to witness the downfall of Islam as represented by the Turk, and was quite confident that the time allotted in the prophecies of Daniel had arrived."

Winepress continued:

"Our lodging on Shari Bliss seemed to service students of the Syrian Protestant College[141], which, to our surprise, used English as its primary language of instruction. Indeed, Bliss Street was named after

---

[141] After 1920, the American University of Beirut.

a Dr Daniel Bliss, the recently late American missionary who founded the school.

I cautiously approached Van der Aarde and wished her a happy birthday. I handed her a bottle of wine and the last of the gevrek[142] from İzmir. She was a right canny lass, but her eyes were strange – large, green, somewhat teardrop-shaped irises textured like whipped melted wax, with a 'strand' breaking through the right pupil, creating a severe coloboma. But the true eeriness was that I had seen her dead, her head partially destroyed. She was laid out like poor Annie[143], a mystery body; they were going to cremated her in Belgium, but her body dried up like a mummy and darkling beetles and their grubs burst from her body, and they shipped her off in a box.

'You want to ask what it was like,' she said. 'Being dead.'

I said yes, admitting that I had been mortally afraid on Patmos. I had some strange sense that I was doomed, some premonition. I opened myself up to Céleste, and talked about my past. It was strange, a culmination of my life, a settling of accounts, and then I survived the battle.

She laughed, and said that there was always Armageddon. Then her tone shifted, and she said it was like being asleep, or half-asleep, that hypnagogic state where nothing but half-remembered dreams remain. It was the peace of the grave. It sounds frightening, being buried in the ground, but it comforted her, as though the earth was her bed. But Madraal could rouse her from that slumber, to ask her for advice, for things to say to the Belgians. She couldn't bring herself to describe it in magical terms, but it was necromancy, on the receiving end. She warned me not to take it seriously, as it was probably the unique powers of Madraal rather than the true nature of life after death. Her next death would likely be different. She apologized, saying it wasn't helpful, and that her head was still swimming and throbbing.

---

[142] Also known as a Simit, Cracknel, or Turkish bagel, a crispy, circular bread, with varieties similar to the bagel or German pretzel.

[143] What is striking here is that he usually speaks of Anna Sokoll as "Annie," but the circumstances hint that he may be speaking of Ripper victim Ann Chapman, whose body was displayed publicly.

I told her not to worry, and offered her cocaine or laudanum. She took me up on the offer. When I went to my cabin to retrieve the cigarbox, she invited herself in, saying she was lonely.

I brewed some Hindustani char for us and set out glasses for the wine, opened the box of cocaine and tobacco. She asked if I had any of the 'Indian treacle,' the opium supplied to the Sikhs in France by the Expeditionary Force's supply office. She had smoked it with Madraal, back in Belgium. I said no, but had partaken, in the notorious Lime House.

She laughed and said the war had made her such a depraved woman, spending weekends in a pharmacological fugue.

'Quick, Watson, the needle,' I said, and snuffed. She snorted the rest of the hill off the glass and yipped.

'Oh, it's good to be alive,' she said.

I asked her about her life, where she had come from. She said she was from Bruges (Brugge, she called it), and we spoke about the arts and the medieval portions. She asked about my home town, inquiring if they had castles there, before stopping herself and breaking down the word 'Newcastle.' She laughed sweetly, if a bit too manically.

She asked if I had a family. I said that I was unmarried. She clarified that she meant my family, my heritage, and I clarified that I had been an orphan. She seemed a touch surprised, as she assumed that all of the English of our kind hailed from the Nameless. I said I may have been a distant cousin, or some secret bastard, but I wasn't raised by them or even particularly liked them, first meeting them to fight Jack.

I asked her if she had ever encountered such a creature, Jack the Giant Killer, the Ripper. She said that she had been attacked once, by a spectral 'blue woman' from the Moon, it seemed, or at least made of moonlight. She sang to it, and managed to shoot the being through the arm. I explained to her what the thing was, a projection of an old Portuguese Nephela who was most likely killed. She said she knew, having tracked it down herself, along with the American, Hannibal Barker, before his disappearance. She said that she had seen Céleste and another French nephel during that incident.

She kicked off her shoes, and curled her toes, to hide the sixth digit on each foot. I told her that she didn't have to hide them. I had the remnants of a sixth metacarpal in my right hand, floating in the flesh near my thumb. I thought of having it removed, possibly selling it off as a lucky charm, the mark of Rapha's children, like the giant at Gath[144].

We spoke at length, rambling like lunatics for two hours. She spoke of her year with a sun-worshipping cult – the Mazdaks – who believed in communal living and the sharing of wives. The originals claimed they wished to remake the garden of Paradise, and so they were punished for their heresy by being buried upside down, in a garden of limbs. She believed in their lifestyle, in sharing with others and living cleanly, but was asked to leave because she could not let go of two of the Five Great Sins, Wrath and Vengeance. And, she admitted, she did not enjoy being "passed around." She tried other forms of mysticism, such as Sufi thought, Theosophy, and the mysticism of the Flemish Jan van Ruusbroec, having read the biography by Evelyn Underhill in English. Though only Underhill's personal struggles with the Dark Night of the Soul resonated with her.

'I shall rejoice beyond the bounds of time,' she said, quoting Ruusbroec. 'though the world may shudder at my joy, and in its coarseness know not what I mean.'

She wanted to know about Jack the Ripper, wondering if I was spinning a yarn for her. She didn't believe my age, and complimented me oddly, saying I looked fit and had piercing eyes. I felt rather uncomfortable, considering her age, and poured myself a drink, though I muttered that I'd never seen eyes like hers. She said her vision was rather poor, and I joked about how you don't want to hear that after someone compliments your luck. I asked about what she had done during the war – not a nurse, we had believed, but a telephone operator. She asked for her own glass, and rose to speak of her adventures as a smuggler, line breaker, and agent of the Belgian resistance. She partially mimed some of her clandestine journey into German territory. Then she brought up spycraft, and poor Mata Hari, and came to rest on my lap.

Speaking of Mata Hari, she began, she mentioned that the

---

[144] He is referencing 2 Samuel 21:20 and 1 Chronicles 20:5-6, nearly identical passages recounted a sighting of one of the Rephaim at the battle of Gath, a figure noted to have twelves fingers and twelves toes. Related passages occur at 1 Samuel 17:4-51, and 1 Chronicles 11:23.

Mazdaznan sun-worshippers practised erotical Tantric practices by the heat of open flame.

She laughed again, reached into my jacket, and played with my chest hair through my shirt. I nearly projected into the astral plane, and froze up.

She asked if there was something wrong.

'You're rather young,' I said, rather matter-of-factly.

Her carefree attitude darkened. She rose up, snorted again, and said, 'All the girls I knew already have kids, families... I don't care. I've died. And we're dead. We know what we're walking into. Make me feel alive.'

I didn't protest after that, all my concerns dissolving away.

I was awakened by a knock on the door, sometime after midnight. I pulled the blanket over her head, pulled up my pants and trousers, pulled on an undershirt, and answered the door.

'Sorry, sir,' said Céleste, 'Tommy said that Van der Aarde disappeared.'

'Oh,' I said. 'She's accounted for.'

Céleste tilted her head into the door and smiled.

'Oh, you old dog, you,' said Céleste.

I turned my head.

'I can see her body heat through the blanket,' Céleste said. Coba turned under the blanket, wrapped it around herself, and rose from the kip. She wiped her face and groggily approached the door.

'You've still got it, you old buck,' said Céleste. 'Beef, beer, and lust. And here she is.'

Coba awkwardly extended her hand. Céleste didn't take it.

'I'm sorry,' said Coba. 'I initiated things with your father.'

'My what?' Céleste said, softly.

'Your...you look like him, other than the...complexion,' said Coba, confused. She gestured broadly at her face. 'You have his eyes[145] and

---

[145] If I may speculate for a moment, this focus on the heredity of eyes may have something to do with a possible prevalence of albinism within this 'giant community'; cutaneous in the case of Gottlieb, and ocular in the case of Winepress and Céleste, though they report no problems with vision. Judging by its expression in Céleste, it would likely be Ocular Albinism, type 2; which has a relatively high incidence in former Dahomey – Benin and Nigeria. There is

cheekbones. And, uh, *giants*.'

Céleste froze. Coba leaned in to my ear and said, 'You mentioned her, specifically, exceptionally. I thought...'

'Céleste, we need to talk,' I said.

'I knew. Part of me figured it out a long time ago,' Céleste said. 'But you wouldn't come out and say it. I had to hear it from this Dutch slut.'

Coba yelped in protest.

'You did cocaine and slept with a man after talking to him once,' Celeste said. 'I have known sluts, but you bestride the world like a colossus.'

'I'm Flemish,' said Coba.

'Leave her out of this,' I said. 'Don't talk to her like that.'

'Oh, you are telling me how to behave now?' said Céleste. She stepped to face me directly, cold as a winter night, and pushed Coba back into the room. She looked me dead in the eyes, said that I better not follow her, and stormed off. Coba apologized, embraced me, and touched me with wandering hands."

The giants waited for a week, trying to come to terms with the shifting intelligence trickling in from the campaign of Edmund Allenby and Faysal I, son of Sharif Hussein of Mecca. They had beaten the Yildirim Army Group, repulsing them from Jerusalem, but March and April saw torrential rainfall in Ottoman Syria that swept away British military infrastructure and shocked the Arabs with its strength.

"Old men and women say that they have never seen rain like this, nor heard of such weather even in the days of their fathers. The coastal people of Lebanon were only slightly inconvenienced - Levantine hillfolk practice a form of farming called *ba'al*, irrigation by rain, and had dug deep troughs to prevent drowning their crops. However, the heavy rains truly frightened the Arabs of the inland desert and badlands, as they had no reason to make preparations for floods."

Takeuchi fell ill, to an extent that he was bed-ridden for nearly a week. He had been alone, and collapsed; Venetianer found him, lying in pooling rainwater, though luckily it was nothing more than a wet floor.

also circumstantial evidence, considering Winepress's travels to Paris, her claims of mystical influences, mysterious heritage, and ties to Mental Science, that he may have been the father of writer Geneviève Behrend.

The initial fear was that it was the 'statue sickness,' *Encephalitis lethargica*, with a dozen known cases in the city. The group stayed at his side, especially once it came clear that he was not contagious; it seemed more like, in Winepresses words "an internal shock, enervating him." They made plenty of tea, flavored with honey, and shot a pair of Syrian ostriches for a hearty meal and 'chicken' soup stock. On the third day, Winepress wrote:

"Takeuchi came to upon seeing a golden-orb weaver spider on the ceiling. He mumbled and spoke of how they were *jorogumo*, the whore-spiders, creatures like succubi who change their form, breathe flame, and invade dreams to mate with men. Spirits sometimes cling to people, he said, they cling to people and places.

When Takeuchi grew lucid, he told us a tale. He prefaced us with the context. There are wrathful ghosts in Japan who harbor the most terrible grudges, *onryou*, created when someone dies in the throes of strong, violent emotion – betrayals, suicides, murders, all can breed *onryou*, hungry to torment the still living. The worst of such creatures are the *tatarigami*, accursed gods, who bring disaster, famine, pestilence, and war. Some are historical figures, others mythological gods, and sometimes they are vague personifications of calamity.

He spoke of one such being from the war of his boyhood. The Russian ship *Ivan Vassili* sailed across Europe and Africa, destined for Vladivostok, coaling in Cape Town. Soon, they realized there was something else aboard the vessel, something that burned more hellish than coal. The sailors sensed that something had changed, invisibly and terribly, like the chilling, ear-aching calm before a storm at sea. It came to them in nightmares, and in the sense of being watched by something out at sea, like the *umibouzu* – a giant sea monk, an inky black form who attacks ships deep at sea, glaring at them with blazing white eyes. Barely able to sleep, the men saw *ayakashi*, like will-o'-the-wisps, St. Elmo's Fire on the masts, and, finally, a luminous being. It was like a man of excited tungsten, a creature of blazing light that stung the eyes when unshrouded by mist. It walked across the misty deck, before vanishing behind a lifeboat.

As the men approached the well-contested Port Arthur, the behaviour of the mystery became a game of torture. Men began screaming, panicking, running amok. They attacked each other with bare fists and clubs, unaware as to why, until a seaman named Govinsky threw himself into the night sea, and most of the crew collapsed into a deep, sudden sleep. They restored order aboard the steamship and refueled at Port Arthur. Some wished to stay, but there were rumours of war – the Russians were supposed to withdraw from the Port and all of Manchuria after the defeat of the Boxer Rebellion, but they refused, and Japan had noticed. So the vessel went to Vladivostok, brimming with fresh munitions. On the third day out of port, an hysterical violence seized the crew once more, with another man throwing himself into the sea, and another mass fainting spell. A dozen men attempted to flee at Vladivostok with - and within- the cargo, but were captured as deserters.

Again, they were dispatched to Hong Kong, the crew run ragged and terrified. Three nights out of port, the attacks happened again, and the night after that, and the night after that, with three more suicides and a stoker dead of fright. At Hong Kong, the captain threw himself into the sea in stark silence. The crew deserted *en masse*, with the exception of its Second Officer and five Scandinavian seamen. They voyaged to Sydney, Australia with a cargo of wool. Within eyesight of the docks, Second Officer Hansen shot himself with his revolver. The crew fled the vessel at port.

The sole exception was boatswain Nelson, who had to find a new crew for this haunted vessel. Eventually, the *Ivan Vasilli* departed for San Francisco, until, a week later, the crew ran amok once more. After the incident, the two most violently hysterical men died in the middle of the night of unknown causes, and the newly hired captain shot himself. The crew soon found themselves forced to return to Vladivostok. The day they entered port, the 8th of February 1904, Russia and Japan went to war. The crew refused to return to the vessel, and the remaining sailors either chose the Japanese occupation, fled across Siberia, or braved the Manchurian front. Anything to avoid setting foot aboard another ship.

'We heard the tale of the haunting around campfires and port bars,' said Takeuchi. 'It was later, after the war, that we learned of the vessel's end.'

The cursed vessel remained in Vladivostok, until, in 1907, those crewmen who remained in the region returned to the port to scuttle the steamer in the dead of night, destroying the vessel with fire and water. It may just be the nature of campfire stories, but it is said that the crew's celebration was interrupted by a great scream that rose up with the steam and smoke, and something terrible and giant-like was seen in the sky.

Noun nervously joked that maybe it was all just a misidentified Swedish trawler[146], but only I knew what he was talking about. We asked Takeuchi what prompted the tale as he began to trail off and mumble.

'There was a terrible procession on the water, a fleet of spirit boats moving on dead water,' he said, weakly, his head clearly swimming. 'The *Funayuurei*...this...there was a ghost clinging to my back, ever since Patmos, ever since I released the...let the destruction of the *Vanguard*

---

[146] He appears to be referring to the Dogger Bank incident. On 21-22 October 1904, a Russian supply ship in the North Sea, the *Kamchatka*, fired upon a Swedish ship, mistaking it for a Japanese torpedo boat. Later that night, the Russian spotters misidentified British trawlers as Japanese torpedo boats through the fog, and fired upon them without warning, sinking a trawler called *Crane*. Two Russian cruisers, the *Aurora* and the *Dmitrii Donskoi*, fired at each other, misidentifying each other as Japanese warships. Support vessels bombarded both vessels and then each other in retaliation, and the *Borodino* was somehow boarded by phantom Japanese raiders, with its crew jumping overboard or drawing cutlasses to engage in melee with rescue parties. The *Oryol*, rather embarrassingly, fired 500 shells without hitting anything. After the incident, the fleet traveled to the Sea of Japan, where it was largely destroyed in the Battle of Tsushima. The attacks lead to strong diplomatic tensions between Russia and the UK, and a great deal of international derision, as the Japanese were not known to have a significant naval presence in the North Sea in 1904 or ever.

Rather appropriately, Takeuchi was a radio telegraph operator during Tsushima, aboard the Japanese cruiser *Asama*, which was badly damaged in several incidents, and both pursued the *Dmitrii Donskoi* into shallow waters and towed the damaged *Oryol* after the battle. Both vessels were refurbished in port, with the *Oryol* renamed *Iwami*.

Coincidentally, the incident was thrust back into the British military's consciousness after the disastrous "Battle" of May Island, in which a series of accidents resulted in five collisions between eight Royal Navy submarines on the night of 31 January-1 February 1918.

finally catch up to me...It was another sea disaster...less of a ghost... She was a disaster. She finally let go of me when she came to port, shaping herself from the water. She climbed down from the rains.'

Anna drifted to the corner of the room, and Zrno snapped out of his alcoholic fugue. We all asked them what was wrong, and they simply said 'the Haligonian.' When I asked if they meant the city in England or the city in Nova Scotia, they said she was the city in Nova Scotia. This produced a chorus of 'beg your pardons' and their equivalents. Zrno explained, sloppily, what they encountered in Archangel: a genius loci of the Deeps, Leviathan or, as Venetianer offered, Lotan, an abyssal creature or spirit, the echo of a maritime cataclysm. They believed that this Halagonian/Rahab/Leviathan was defeated or destroyed, as an angel bound it in adamant chains and dropped it into the Arctic seas. But it seems to have escaped.

Zrno's head collapsed into his folded arms, and he kicked off his crude prosthetic foot, already worn down by some basic accelerated movement; It was nothing but a mummy-wrap of leather and other shoe parts cannibalized by a high-belted boot. Wood would burst into burning splinters and metal would melt into slag. Even then, the leather was scratched and pitted and scuffed to the point that it resembled the dusty-grey face of the moon."

The Nine walked up the hill to the Syrian Protestant College for medical aid for Takeuchi, and to do research on the new positioning; their main source was the American Mission Press, and its connections to the Franciscan Press in Jerusalem. The College had been converted into a field hospital to deal with the non-battle casualties of the front. The importance of disease in the Middle Eastern theater of war cannot be overstated: while the Western, Eastern, and Italian fronts generally had a non-battle casualty for every man wounded in combat, the Middle-Eastern front had a roughly ten to one ratio. The battles tended to be much quicker and more decisive, but disease was everywhere; the men in the Sinai-Palestine Campaign and Mesopotamia suffered only 5% of the battle casualties of their Western Front counterparts, but 70% of the disease deaths[147].

[147] T.J. Mitchell and G.M. Smith. (1931) *Medical Services, Casualties and Medical Statistics of the Great War*. Republished by the Imperial War Museum in 1997.

Winepress and Céleste researched medical reports, with the latter taking time to look into physics and mathematical research. Venetianer looked into local perspectives on religion and religious experiences, taking notes. He showed Winepress, Céleste, and Van der Aarde something that von Böhm had pointed out long ago; In Michelangelo's *Last Judgement*, there is a pair of nephilim, male and female, in the bottom center of the image, behind the altar of the Sistine Chapel. The dark, shadowy couple embrace in a cavern built a long trench, halfway between the resurrected and the damned, with a flaming, infernal soul at their feet. He also found the paired prints works of Guercino, *Marsyas and Apollo* and *Et in Arcadia ego*, the first depicting the triumph of the Sun god over the silen, whom the Romans considered the inventor of augury and free speech, while the latter depicted the trepanned skull of a giant. In both cases, two shepherds look on. This was the first appearance of that phrase – *Death too, was in Arcadia.*

Winepress noted that they were in this strange parallel pilgrimage with the line of Saint Michael, a bit of sacred geometry connecting Ireland's Skellig Michael to the Cornish St. Michael's Mount to Normandy's Mont Saint-Michel, down to Sacra di San Michele, Chiesa di San Galgano, Tempio di San Michele di Perugia, and Santuario di San Michele del Gargano. Once the line passes through Italy, it reaches Delphi, Delos, and Symi in Greece, Cyprian Kourion, and finally the Stella Maris Monastery at Mount Carmel. These are all locations where people have had visions of the archangel Michael, terminating in Carmel, which is also said to be the graveyard of ancient wildmen. The Cornish mount was the site of the 1800 discovery of 2.5-meter-tall giant, identified with the first victim of Jack the Giant Killer, the six-fingered Cormoran. Allenby's men have taken Carmel Ridge, overlooking the Valley of Jezreel and the hills of Megiddo. There is a chilling feature of this gathering – Carmel was never important in the historical battles of Armageddon; but now, it is a key tactical site due to the invention of artillery. This line is also tied to tales of giants; the nephilim of Israel's mountains to the gigantes of Rome; the Arthurian legend of the crocodile-skinned Giant of Mont St. Michel; the giants of Cornwall; and the clashes of the Tuatha Dé Danann and Fionn mac Cunhaill at Skellig Michael.

As he grew tired, some hours later, he came across Céleste, who was "wide awake on a mixture of coffee and cocaine. She suddenly looked directly at me, eyes blazing like Rigel in the night sky, and asked me what I knew of entropy. I said that I knew it is a concept in physics – but not much else, something about disorder.

'I see,' she said, frantically, but clearly. She had been thinking about what follows, and looking at her complicated stick and wax model that had so fascinated her over the past weeks. 'We live in a low-entropy state. In an eternal void, it is likely that a mind, with memory and false experience, would eventually and spontaneously form in a void. And we are talking about billions and billions, maybe trillions of years. Too much to even think about. It was a response to your Ludwig Boltzmann by a...a Zermelo, Ernst Zermelo. He was trying to figure out the mathematical implications of thermodynamic laws, and the problems of Poincaré's recurrence theorem. We live in a vast, dead sea, dust bouncing off of dust, and making a bit of fresh heat...and that is existence, our little spark, our island of heat. But it's not done. It's never done. You see, in a closed world, everything must eventually recur. It's like Nietzsche, no? These Botlzmann brains would decay very rapidly, it seems. Flickering in and flickering out. But recurring. Always, inevitably, recurring, after a trillions and so on years...'

I paused for several seconds to try to record what she said, and had to ask her to repeat the latter part. I asked her what this had to do with our mission.

'Ever heard of that Émile Borel quote? A million monkeys striking at random on a typewriter, given enough time, would recreate the great volumes found in the richest libraries in the world...or however he put it. Now, think of the mind, and how some believe the mind is eternal, and immortal. A soul. What would such beings be, when they pass from the universe? What if these angels that we are seeing are future minds, forming in our Time, as in, the conception of Time, only to be shunted outside of it? Right? There is immortality, as in, not dying but still experiencing time, and true eternity, no? Not being part of time.'

I asked her why she thought they took the form of angels, rooted in history with mankind, rather than something even more alien and unknowable.

'Simple,' she said. 'They're from the far, far future, but fell out of time. Back to our beginnings...or, at least, experience of history. More like, they're in the centre of the wheel. Time keeps moving, but they're always in the centre, even if they move up the spokes far ahead of us...And all of this absurd strangeness is us looking at these...imperishable minds, and they look back, and change us, whisper to us, enter us. Angels, devils, Martians, lights in the sky, monsters in the water. It's us seeing these entities as they flicker through eternity.'

'And what of us?' I asked. 'We rephaim?'

'A primitive tribe sees a great empire pass through their land. The imperials stay for a while. It is traumatic, but they leave knowledge, new ideas, guns and troubles. We all had some trauma with these minds, or our ancestors did, but it keeps happening, it seems, and it changed us. We have one foot in eternity. In the world of concepts and base physics. But it troubled us, ruined us. And that's where this hatred comes from. We are this open, gaping wound. A tunnel between their world and this one. Like someone who won't close the shutters when you're trying to sleep.'

'Why do they fight each other then?' I asked.

'Why do we fight each other?' She asked. 'Some of the future brains don't look like other future brains, and that's a killing issue.'

'Then why now? Why this war?' I asked.

'I think we can all feel it, now, war is changing. Technology is changing. It might not be that this is the end, but the beginning, and the earliest place to intervene. In Time, I mean.'

She showed me her model. She had been trying to model one of the geometric forms she had seen around the angels. I wish I knew more of geometry, but she tried to explain what she was on to: her model was one of 'Schläfli's 16-cells,' the hexadecahedron, whose vertex figure is an octahedron. She realized that rotating an octahedron or a star tetrahedron resulted in a hexagrammic pyramid. She demonstrated the turning of this form, and indeed rotating an 8-sided framed form results in a six-sided star. It was the Seal of Solomon, the Magen David.

'I don't know if it means anything, but maybe that star is a simplified angelic form. And maybe what we're seeing, or experiencing, and *are* – is a simplification of something much grander and incomprehensible."

Once Takeuchi recovered, the group moved South. On April 20th, they arrived in Sidon, where they visited the Sidon Sea Castle, built by the Crusaders upon a temple to Herakles, the Temple of Eshmun, a Phoenician god of medicine, remnants of the Roman colony, and the Khan el Franj, the caravanserai for French merchants. Nothing particularly unusual occurred; Venetianer simply mentioned that Sidon was the firstborn son of Canaan, grandson of Noah, and the home of Jezebel, and that Anna seemed oddly pleased by the devastation wrought by the Mongols. He also told her the anecdote of Tiberius Julius Abdes Pantera, a Sidonian archer buried in Germany, alleged to be the father of Jesus due an inscription describing 'Yeshua ben Pantera' and the tale of the Greek philosopher Celsus.

The group searched for answers to the mystery of the Tabnit Sarcophagus, the resting place of the ancient king of Sidon and priest of Astarte, the son of Eshmunazar. The sarcophagus contained an inscription warning against disturbing his body, for he had no valuables and it was abominable to Astarte, ending on a warning that no one who touched his body would find a resting place within the Rephaites. When the sarcophagus was opened, it contained a strange fluid that vanished into the sands below.

The artifact piqued Venetianer and Winepress' interest. As Venetianer wrote, "The Rephaites were another term for the Rephaim, an ancient clan of Nephilim in Moab, east of the Jordan– giants connected to the dead. Og, King of Bashan, was said to be one of their final members, famed for a bed nine cubits long – nearly four meters."

Rather than "mighty [men]," or *gibborim*, this group was called the "weak," "the weakeners," or "powerless," and possibly also the "zamzummim." Venetianer speculated that "this name was something of an inverted euphemism, such as calling faeries the gentry, or possibly a genuine descriptor denoting that the Rephaim were weaker and smaller than their Anakim ancestors – a race famed for their chained necks, kingships, their champion Goliath, and the Anunnaki of Babylon. And those petty deities were weaker and smaller than their Gibborim ancestors, who were mistaken for pagan gods, who were weaker and smaller than the first generations of true Nephilim, dangerous enough to require the Deluge, shrinking down the closing circle of *gilgul*. And I wonder how the last of the Rephaim would have seen Anna, at a mere 155 cm? I wondered if she was the last of us. *Nitkatnu ha-dorot*[148].

Unfortunately, in the twenty years since their discovery, the sarcophagi of the Sidonian kings had been relocated to Stamboul[149]."

Winepress and Noun scouted for information and contacts with the Circassian-Egyptian nobles of the city, the Abazas, also to no avail.

It was not long after, compelled by Takeuchi, that they traveled southeast to the River Litani, in the valley of Beqaa west of the giant megaliths of Baalbek. They navigated alongside the river to the mouth of the Mediterranean, just north of Tyre. Takeuchi claimed to have something of a religious experience, seeing a terrible, gigantic creature in the water, too big for the shallow river. The nephilim realized that this was Lotan, the blustering beast known as Leviathan, for which the river was named.

Tyre

They arrived in Tyre (also known as Sûr) on the 2nd of May, the birthplace of Cadmus, Phoenix, Europa and Dido. Winepress was excited, as Noun, Céleste, Venetianer all record him gushing about one of the greatest feats of military engineering, when Alexander the Great constructed a causeway stretching from the mainland to the island of Tyre in 332 BCE. Alexander wished to make a sacrifice at the temple to Heracles, but the Tyrians told him to make a sacrifice at the temple on the mainland. This, and their loyalty to Darius, enraged the Macedonian warlord. After eight months of construction and missile combat

---

[148] "The diminution of generations," a concept in Rabbinical scholarship bemoaning the perceived decline in Talmudic commentary; also used in Kabbalah and other metaphysical strains to describe a decline in spiritual strength. Also called *Yeridat ha-dorot* (the decline of generations). He is making a direct comparison with his nephilim theories to the "rishonim" (first ones, that is, rabbis) and the "acharonim" (the latter).

[149] *Stamboul*: Antiquated alternate name for Istanbul.

between the defenders and Alexander's artillery engines, Alexander laid waste to Tyre, and the island became an isthmus, the causeway built up by two millennia of silt.

Venetianer elaborated on Alexander's role in Jewish apocalypticism. The Seleucid emperor[150] Antiochus III conquered Tyre, and his son, Antiochus IV Epiphanes, is sometimes considered the Gog of Ezekiel and the foe of the Maccabees; a belief impossible to reconcile with the tale of Alexander building the great gates that sealed away the armies of Gog and Magog until the end times. Alexander also, according to Roger Bacon, explored the Mediterranean's depths with a diving bell built by Ethicus, encountering strange whales and buildings between Beirut and Cyprus.

Gottlieb, the night of their arrival, scouted outside of the city, Venetianer's false eye in tow. Gottlieb had switched to a lighter outfit with a bedouin-style headwrap for sun protection, leaving his cuirass behind with his gear.

"The scrub rapidly gives way to the stonier sort of badland – Lebanon does not have a true desert, as it is dense with rivers, but it does have steep, rough hills and mountains of honey and bronze. Weather is deeply cool. I patrolled to the southeast of the city in response to odd smoke in the sky. At 01:00 hours, witnessed, to my surprise, a German patrol. I rose to speak with them, appearing from behind them, head down, greeting them in German.

They were shocked. One of them was a tired man, seemingly a little older than me with slightly recessed black hair. His eyes seemed tired, yet inquisitive, and he approached me, asking what I was.

I answered that I was an albino, hence the head-wrapping. He spoke to his partner and pulled me aside. To my shock, he said that he could smell something angelic about me.

I tried to dodge the question, noting that he sounded Alsatian. He said he was born in Alsace-Lorraine, and went to Munich before the War. I laughed and said that I was the opposite, growing up in Bavaria before migrating to Alsace – and he held the rank of Lieutenant. He had volunteered for the Bavarian regiments, fighting for two years in

[150] That is, a descendant of Alexander's general Seleucus I Nicator, who inherited much of his king's Middle Eastern domains.

Flanders, before he was rotated to Turkish territory to fight Bedouins. He had started in Arabia, before shifting North after Gaza, and was out hunting an Arab partisan called the Phoenician. He was rather startled by my appearance, because I came out of nowhere. The Arabs had tales of Djin, creatures of 'smokeless fire.' They say that the Phoenician might be one, for it appears and disappears at will.

His company worked with the Templer colonies of Walhalla and Sarona, on the Palestinian coast – he mentioned that Sarona was a virtual garden, with vineyards and the Biblical delights of milk and honey. While the Temple Society had distanced itself from the Fatherland's politics in its millenarianist ambitions, and the Templers were further divided by a religious schism, they were still Germans and owed a debt to the Kaiser, who funded their colonies with highly favorable loans. But ultimately, they were here in the Holy Land to rebuild Israel and prepare it for Armageddon, and for that reason, they oddly refused to help hunt the Phoenician.

He then got serious and asked me what I was, what I truly was. Because, he said, I wasn't human.

I told him my name and rank. He said his name was Rudolf John Gorsleben, and he insisted on knowing what I was. I insisted, in turn, that I was simply an albino.

He asked if I knew of Guido von List. I said yes - some of his pamphlets were passed around in the trenches. He then asked if I knew of the monk and inventor Jörg Lanz von Liebenfels, and Theozoology. I said no, imagining some kind of Egyptian animal gods or perhaps, god-animals, upon dissecting the word in my mind. He said that cultures around the world describe gods granting subhumans intelligence, souls and minds. Ape-men, 'sodomite-apelings,' he said, like Neanderthals and *Pithecanthropus*[151], the dwarfs of legend. Today, some races of men have more of this divine blood, while others are still degenerate and apelike. Aryans were the most electrified race, but breeding with other races atrophied our latent paranormal talents. In contrast, some individual clans must logically have incredible concentrations of traits inherited from these interstellar Theozoa.

---

[151]   Now known as *Homo erectus*.

I gritted my teeth and nodded at the insane person. Because the frightening thing is that he might have been a quarter of the way to the truth and two quarters down the path of madness. I always met occultists with apprehension, because what starts with intrigue and whimsy always seems to wind up in troubling waters.

He asked me what I was, and if I knew the secrets of the Ur-Aryans, and of runes. I said I knew no secrets, but I had seen magic, and angels and demons. I watched his face cautiously.

'There is something of a giant about you. I can feel it,' he said. He became terribly intense in his mannerism, approaching me with a pointed finger. 'Atlantean *Gottmenschen*. They were not from the Mediterranean World, but the Boreal – the Hyperboreans of the far north, the peaceful, wise giants beyond the known world.'

I insisted that I don't know where we came from. His feverish imagination continued into the World Ice Theory of Hörbiger, the idea that the planets and their moon were made of ice, and thus Hyperborea – the North Pole- may have been a colony of higher beings, the ice giants of legend.

I told him, perhaps foolishly, that I had seen Venus, and it was a hot, roaring whirlwind of poisonous gas.

Out of the corner of my eye, I caught the glimpse of a figure, perhaps around 170-172 cm tall, 7-8m away. I yelped in alarm, but the figure disappeared in a flash as Gorsleben turned. He gasped and yelled, 'the Djin!' at his companion, and they readied their rifles. I took the opportunity to disappear as well. The other scout screamed in fright; Gorsleben cackled madly, as though witnessing something wonderful and exciting.

So many philosophers and politicians claim that a loss of spiritual strength and fervor has led civilization astray; perhaps, but I have seen so much evidence that those who seek the soul are willing to entertain the most monstrous of ideas. They seek beauty in themselves, only to find the ugliness of others worthy of nothing but elimination. Spiritual art and metaphysical enlightenment will not save us; perhaps there is a blue rider[152], setting out alongside conquest.

---

[152] It is important to note here that Gottlieb specifically uses *Der Blaue Reiter*, the name of a pre-war artistic movement.

Whom Gods Would Destroy, Part III

That night, after Céleste and I bathed, I spoke of encountering another Bavarian patrol, the odds of finding other men of my state in the hills of Canaan. I told her of the strange theories he preached, the oddly accurate identification of my nature; and the monstrosity behind it. I wondered if all my countrymen would follow him down this dark path. The Empire's
final push into Belgium and France had failed; we are falling back. The Red Baron was dead. Millions were dead. Even those apocalypse-seeking Templers were scattered to the hills or rounded-up in prison camps by the conquering British. They would not build their Temple. I wondered what we would become in our defeat.

I brought up the Lakota, and their Ghost Dance, a great political ritual, a final uprising against the White Man's conquest. Some, like Jack Wilson, preached non-violence; that the Lakota would be delivered through earthquakes, great winds, and other disasters that would fell the White Man, and the settled world would roll up and carry them out to sea. Wilson said that Jesus was reincarnated in 1892, and a millennial age of harmony and restoration was at hand. His people could dance away the evil of the world. Others believed that violence was the only remaining option- Short Bull, Spotted Elk, and Kicking Bear. They wore sacred shirts that they believed would protect them from bullets, blessed with the feather of crow and owl and eagle.

They did not work, and they were butchered at Wounded Knee, man, woman, and child.

Later that decade, the Boxers of China believed spirits would ward off the bullets of the Westerners. That also failed.

In East Africa, we took the rebellious Chief Mkwawa's skull. Then came a medium, who was told to give his followers a potion of water and castor oil and millet– the serpent spirit said that the bullets of the Germans would turn to water under its effects[153]. The war medicine did not work either.

In Tierra del Fuego, the threatened Ona dressed up as spirits and attacked their youths to strengthen them, but their beatings could not

---

[153] This spirit medium was Kinjikitile Ngwale, or Bokero, the initial leader of the Maji Maji Rebellion of 1906-1907.

match the cruelty of Julius Popper, the Last Conquistador. Their skulls are still being shipped to museums like trophies, fetching a high price.

Céleste mentioned that even earlier, the Xosa cut off their nose to spite their face, slaughtering their herds of lungsick cattle and burning all their crops. It was said that burning away the corrupted world would give rise to a new and bountiful country, free of the invaders. The spirits that the prophetess claimed would drive the British from the Cape never came[154], and the resistance of the Red-Blanket People collapsed with the famine.

I told her I did not trust Germany in defeat. Especially Prussians, since I couldn't even trust them in victory. What mythology will we shield our hearts with when France and England unsheathe their vengeful daggers? Will we be a colony, carved up and handed out to the Entente? The west to France, the north to Britain? Prussia and Pomerania handed out to vengeful Slavs? Will we rise up in a generation's time, angry and wearing ghost shirts of our own, carved with runes and Aryan sorceries?"

Venetianer recorded another dream that same night, a visitation. "The specter from my dreams appeared again, a man in a suit with a Satanic goat's head. He seemed to watch me, cautiously, with his arms placed at his side as though resting in bed.

'You appeared to me the night before Patmos,' I said. The entity seemed surprised that I could see him. I said, of course I could see him- 'you have the head of a goat.'

'You have the head of a crow,' he replied. 'And a crown. Like Caim.'

Interesting, I thought. I asked who he was. He called himself Yihovæum, and said that he was a member of the British military's support apparatus, employed at His Majesty's Factory in Sutton Oak, St Helens. He could not disclose what he was doing there, but I had my suspicions, which Winepress confirmed. It was a Royal Engineers Experimental Station, a remote site of the British chemical warfare program at Porton Down.

'You've astral projected,' I said, trying to sound clinical.

---

[154] This Xhosa prophetess was Nongqawuse.

'Yes,' said the spirit. 'Using a modification of Leadbeater's techniques. I have been told that the Germans have attempted similar occult tactics, with some success.'

'The Germans had an agent in America fascinated by the science of souls and their transference, a figure we called the Necromancer,' I admitted. 'But they have no continued, successful program for astral scouting.'

'I see,' he said. 'Though can you be trusted to tell the truth?'

'No, I would think not, were I in your position.'

The telepathy experiments of George Albert Smith, which ended in embarrassment when participant Douglas Blackburn admitted his positive results were due to a code, damaged the credibility of such telepathist trials in Britain's military. At least, that was the story; Blackburn's public admission of fraud seemed suspicious when paired with a strong relationship with Britain's intelligence services in South Africa and during the current war. We had assumed, truthfully or not, that this was a smokescreen for a deeper thought-reading program.

I asked if he was a permanent staff member at the site. He said no; he had been stationed in Blackpool, and driven over an hour to the location to take part in these mystical experiments. He had been an artist with a keen interest in the occult before the war, and employed in the conflict's illustration. After these projection experiences, he would sketch maps of the visited locations.

The earlier encounter at Patmos was a trial run, to see if he could locate a rogue British agent by the name of Winepress. Instead, he found a figure identified as the Crow-King by his superiors. For the next few days, he was held in isolation in that Porton Down remote station, placed into what he described as a 'twilight sleep.' Such twilight sleep (*Dämmerschlaf*) was induced by modern medicine to relieve women of the pain of childbirth, creating an amnesiac state via a concoction of hyoscine and morphine. Women were known to undergo horrific spasms of pain and mad ranting, but awake completely ignorant of the ordeal. For this project, it was used to generate some sort of extranormal state of awareness, a super-state that allowed the mind to drift and the body to engage in autographia with the oversight of ones' handler, with any sensitive details lost upon waking. Those who tested him for 'appropriateness' were impressed by his knowledge of the late Anna Kingsford's trances, and Edward Maitland's regression of past lives, including his belief that he was Marcus Aurelius and the prophet Daniel.

I tried to interrogate the young man as well, asking questions about his condition, as the narcotic haze stripped him of any guile. It appears that the mechanisms of the experiment were based on George Albert Smith's investigation into hypnosis, psychical phenomenon, and film projection. The method involved imagining a location using photographs, maps, or drawings, and projecting oneself into its real world referent. This dream-traveller had synthesized Smith's 'technologies' with teaching of the Order of the Golden Dawn; some of its adepts, Frederick Leigh Gardner, Annie Horniman, and Dorothea Hunter, operating under the aliases of *Fortiter et Recte*, *De Profundis ad Lucem*, and *Soror Deo Date*, had used psychical travel to explore the planets. In 1898, they projected through a heaven of lights, hexagrams, and guardian angels in the celestial gates, reaching Saturn, where they met winged warriors, the dusty core of Jupiter, and the impenetrable corona of the Sun. In 1900, they projected to Mars via an 'invoking hexagram,' where they encountered a giant angel clad in mail with flaming wings. I wonder if they had been the ones to conjure forth our Martian foe.

He said that he had drifted through the sky for an indescribable time – he noted that there must have been some electro-magnetic effect to it, as stormclouds had affected him, burning his flesh with a painful, tingling sensation. He found himself, after one lightning strike, pinned to the ground under a pile of corpses somewhere in France or Belgium. He had to crawl to another point of high electrical potential and ride the resulting lightning strike back into the sky. He quickly learned to control the projection, based partially on reflection off the Moon and the Heaviside Layer.

There had been, quite recently, a case of bilocation in [28] Oct. 1915, during a horrific fire at a parochial school in the American city of Peabody, Massachusetts, which claimed the lives of over twenty young girls. An apparition of one student, in bed in the house of the local physician after fainting, galavanting around town just before the disaster, leading a staff member away and towards the nearest available telephone. The day prior, the astrologer at *the Washington Herald* made an usually strong prediction that 'fires in philanthropic institutions will cause loss of life,' with one in particular occurring in New England. It seems that such projections are drawn, perhaps emphatically, to terrible loss of life, explaining the war-madness among sensitives.

I have come to believe that there is something to the theories of Paul Carus, that the Urim and Thummim, the black and white divination stones lost with the Temple, are paralleled by the binary powers of Yin and Yang in Chinese mysticism. These stones were said to be of onyx, and perhaps an echo of the *Tzohar* described by *Idra Rabbah*. Abraham wore this glowing jewel or pearl around his neck. It glowed like the sun and could be used as an astrolabe to read the motion of the stars – and when Abraham died, God enshrined it in the wheel of the Sun. It was inherited from Noah, who in turn received it from Enoch and his ancestors back to Adam and Eve. Perhaps such stones allowed the priesthood to commune with the Lord using an astral body, similar to the miracles performed by Daoist Alchemists.

He spent his time in Egypt, where he studied the hieroglyphics on the interior of the Pyramids, the Valley of the Kings, and other sites in Luxor, having seen Lord Carnarvon in the flesh. At a Beit Khallaf, he projected himself backward in time, seeing the burial of a tall man, the Pharaoh Hor-Hen-Nekht (Sanakht), who towered over his followers, just like Khasekhemui of the Second Dynasty, a full five cubits and three palms high, who erected monuments in the Lebanese Byblos. Moving even further back in time, he saw pharaohs standing seven or eight feet tall, and giants called Sheddai or the Followers of Horus constructing the pyramids with teams of workmen and guilds of artisans practicing celestial rites. At Memphis, he witnessed the court of the giant King Misraim, and the colossal architect Adīm, who quarried the stones of Giza. At many-pillared Dendera, he saw Qoftarīm, and the builder Harjit, who placed secret treasures in the pyramids of Dahshur and Sudan. And before then, he saw giants copulating with women, and angels with the heads of birds, and the twisting of nature into strange chimerical beings.

Those Shemsu-Hor – that is, Horus' followers- sometimes appeared to him with the heads of great raptors, just as I had the seeming of a crow. They were worshiped as the Ahau, he said, "those who stand up," a striking inversion of the fallen connotation of *n-ph-l*.

He had drawn these giants and hybrids, putting to use his skill in automatic writing and drawing, producing sigils and unconsciously crafted hieroglyphs of his own. He feared the repercussions of producing such gibberish, but his handlers were equally interested in such rarefied designs. So he continued on his astral journey, learning to trigger his projection by reading Edward FitzGerald's translation of Omar Khayyám's *Rubáiyát*. Every time he sought out the workings of the Winepress and I, this Crow-king, he saw these giants. At one point, taking influence from Madame Blavatsky, he attempted to gaze into the secret realms of Tibet, only to see giants watching him from the edge of the Himalaya - midnight black, towering sentinels.

When I awoke, Winepress would identify the goat-headed figure. Crowley had recommended a 'black magician' he had a falling out with sometime after the founding of the Argenteum Astrum Thelemite order, due to his rejection of ceremonial magics, the hermetic hierarchy, and, perhaps, Crowley's advances. Yihovæum was his occult name; he was born with the name Austin Osman Spare."

The next day, Céleste, Tom Noun, and Van der Aarde explored the city, as the fluent French speakers. Tom Noun used a female form to walk with them, with Céleste also noting the strong family resemblance with Van der Aarde. The first sight on their tour was the Cathedral of Paulinus, the oldest in the world, and the markets.

It was fairly quiet, until one moment of tension noted by Noun:

"The women rather enjoyed seeing the exotic markets – not quite the splendour conjured up by the image of the classic Oriental bazaars, but not disappointing; they had fine linen and silks brilliant with Tyrian dyes (though likely synthetic), gold, silver, gems, ivory, and pearls – and the scent of cinnamon, ointments, frankincense, wine, and oil. Van der Aarde enjoyed her new friend, a long hashish pipe and two pounds of fine hash resin. It was a fine change of pace from the famine and plague and muds of Europe, and the starved-out squalor of Beirut. That is not to say it was paradise – there were still beggars and refugees and war orphans and the not-far-off reports of battle, but at least there were some pleasantries. My mind settled into a detached tranquility, a sublime state of calm with full knowledge and acceptance of the coming storm. It was the ataraxia praised by the Greeks as the ideal state of mind for soldiers in war. Some Epicurean, maybe the man himself, or Philodemus, or Horace, said 'Don't fear God, don't worry about death. What is good is easy to find, what is terrible is easy to endure.'

Jacoba noted that Winepress – who is apparently Céleste's father, which nobody told me- had gone with Venetianer to find another, similar ancient sarcophagus. She sound bored by the subject. I asked how anyone could find the ancient history of humanity boring.

'I favour technology, and cities, and the common people,' she said. 'There's nothing for me in a three-thousand-year-old king's tomb.'

Céleste laughed and said, 'Nothing? I'm surprised the museum guards aren't prying you off a three-thousand-year-old man.'

I covered my mouth to stifle a laugh. Coba chuckled openly, pointed at Céleste, and said, 'I like you.'

Céleste glared at her, dead seriously, and said 'you will never be my mother,' before running into the market."

Céleste made her way to the French garrison at Khan Al-Ashkar, a caravanserai built to accommodate French traders similar to the one in Sidon.

"I spoke to several of the soldiers stationed there. They were surprised to see me, but I told them I was a nurse- not actually a lie. Many of them were engineers, freed from the recent long-term fortification of Gaza; there had been three battles there, two Ottoman Victories, and finally a breakthrough that allowed the British to conquer Jerusalem. The border between Palestine and Lebanon would be much easier to cross than we anticipated. The Ottoman forces were reorganizing, and pivoting to the Northwest for a southward push.

The garrison was also preparing for the speech of an Abdul Hussain Sharafeddine[155], who was preaching for interdenominational peace and Moslem reconciliation. This was apparently an incitement to violence.

[155] Abd al-Hussein Sharaf al-Din al-Musawi, commonly called Sayyid Sharafeddin, a Lebanese Shi'a Twelver scholar and social activist, who preached for Shi'a/Sunni reconciliation in Lebanon and Egypt. At this time, based in Tyre.

The soldiers also spoke of strange reports from between Montreal and Ma'an. I rather foolishly said 'In Canada?' and they laughed and explained that Montreal was an old Crusader castle built by Baudouin de Boulogne[156]. Baudouin the Bedouin, one joked. Some of the Arabs had seen what they described as ghouls or djinn digging near the Li Vaux Moise and outside Ma'an. There was some more local geography- the Jew of the group seemed to take particular pride in his Arabic pronunciation.

One of the soldiers was a wheatish mulatto, and one could tell that he was very interested in helping me out. The soldiers at first thought that these figures were Turkish workers, as the Behjet Pasha [corrected from Bejed Pacha] had been fortifying Ma'an, building an aerodrome after Lawrence and his Arabs secured Aqaba under the terror of a blood-red moon[157]. But these digging things wore protective suits of some sort, along with gas masks that the more superstitious, backwater types had seemingly confused with the muzzle of dogs and jackals. Similar people were seen dragging a destroyed tank out of a stony pit in Gaza.

The men soon turned away in embarrassment and annoyance, or jeered. There were two men standing in the marketplace, with a stack of papers called *the Weekly Evangel* [Eng.]. They were men in their thirties, one white and one black; the white one was on the higher end of the thirties, sandy-haired, bearded, short, and with a large nose that must have been broken at one point. The other man was maybe five years younger, round-faced, broad-nosed, stout, and slightly darker than me, like an Ibo. They preached, and the soldiers tried to get out of the way and look busy, saying in unison, 'We are at the commencement of the Armageddon struggle, that brief but bloody clash at the hill of faith! We are an international fellowship in Christ our King, here to stand before the God of this Earth and witness his Glory.'

The two quaked and shook their hands like actors playing exclusively for the back rows. The light-skinned soldier leaned in and

156 Baldwin I of Jerusalem

[157] There was a lunar eclipse on the night of 4-5 July 1917, which Lawrence used to demoralize and rout the Turkish defenders of Aqaba.

told me I could ignore the nonsense. I was confused, but he called me Little Nurse, said they weren't sick. They were speaking in tongues and shaking around, something done by Pentecostals, some charismatic Christian group. I asked if they were Americans, because that is where the eccentric Christian groups come from. He said yes; they were from an Azure[sic] Street Revival[158], the Assembly of God. They had come from America last year and wandered around Jerusalem and Tyre, preaching, faith healing and quaking like spastics. They claimed that they had instantly cured some of the many sick in town by touch and prayer alone- blindness, paralysis, and so on- but none of the soldiers saw any of these miracles. The Pentecostals believe that their speaking in tongues was genuine foreign speech, like at the Tower of Babel. The soldiers were at first alarmed by them, thinking of them as madmen. After three days of this preaching, the attitude turned towards curiosity. Then came amusement, then irritation, and finally derision and contempt. I did not want to tell him that I understood the tongue of Babel.

The apocalyptic fervor of the quakers[159] had me on edge, and I turned my back from them, but felt tense, like a cat about to pounce. A man in chainmail and a domed hat, like some Russian knight from a storybook, stepped out from behind the nearest building. He was burly, some 1.9m tall. He was of the swarthier variety of whites and Arabs,

[158] The French soldier or Céleste are slightly garbling details here: the *Azusa* Street Revival isn't a place, but a religious revival originating in Los Angeles that lead to the creation of the Assemblies of God in 1914. It's rather odd that one of the preachers is black, as the Assembly formed when three hundred white preachers and other figures seceded from the African-American dominated Church of God in Christ and incorporated into a new assembly – the original revival began with a Black American preacher named William Seymour. Then again, we only know about this man from two people foreign to this movement.

[159] This is another mistake on Céleste's part – the Assembly of God is not associated with the Quakers, and she may be confusing their behavior with the similar ecstatic movement of the Shakers. In general, Céleste's knowledge of Christianity is mostly limited to the French Catholic culture, only really understanding the general ideas of Orthodoxy and Protestantism, which she does not distinguish from Lutheranism; every non-Catholic church she noted in Germany was "*luthérienne*."

perhaps a Turk, but his armor was decidedly Christian, covered in crucifixes and carrying a sword and shield. I took a step forward, and asked him if there was an opera in town. The huge knight scowled and walked away. I shouted that I wasn't joking – it was a lovely costume.

The market went dead quiet, as when birds stop singing in the presence of predators, and the soldiers were gone, displaced somewhere.

'Oh fair Europa, princess of Phoenicia. Beaten, bruised, raped by a dead god,' said a low, crackling female voice.

I turned around, and saw nobody, not even the radiant heat of an invisible form. The speaker was behind me again, a distant heat. Gooseflesh rolled up my arm.

'You Europeans honestly believe this is about you, yes?' She said, switching from Arabic to rather good French, if harsh. It was the overly-formal Parisian dialect one would be taught in a missionary school, something from the reign of Napoleon III. 'When the Bible speaks of places in the Levant, and names the Seven Churches of Anatolia, it is about you, somehow? Do Christians in Europe really think that they are being persecuted? Let me tell you what those churches are – the Maronites, the Armenians, the Old Orientals and the Orthodox, the Assyrians and Syriacs and Copts. The Turks are killing us, wolves on the fold. Our priests, our churches, our families. This is the *Limes Arabicus*. Not the limits of your understanding, but the limit of your willingness to understand... You are the Northern Evil of Jeremiah and Ezekiel. You are the Beasts of the Sea and the Land, the Dragon and the Whore and Rome. There is no home for you here. Turn back.'

I asked who the speaker was.

'I am the Phoenician, my dear,' said the woman, likely around my age. 'I've been watching your group since you intruded on my space in Patmos, but heard of you long before. I was given some money by a dying Englishman, of the Anglo-Persian Oil Company. Mr. Knox-D'Arcy, heard of him?'

'Yes,' I said. 'He was planning something. Looking for us.'

'He was obsessed with the quest of the Holy Grail, and sought it in Jerusalem and Persepolis. He was keeping tabs on you people... Something terrible was brewing with you.'

She laughed and added, 'Horsemen of the APOC-álipsis. He found the Cup of Jamshid near Persepolis, a bowl with a stone like a fetus in it. They said it would grant immortality, and let you gaze into the seven heavens.'

'I don't understand,' I said. 'Christ drank out of this thing?'

'That's the Holy Chalice,' she said. 'The Grail was used to collect Christ's blood from the Cross. It's a bowl. What are you people doing? Gathering the Arma Christi?'

'I don't know what those are, and I don't think Jesus had weapons,' I said. 'But I do know a man with his bones. His Japanese bones. And the Ark of the Covenant. And the Golden Fleece.'

'This is pointless,' she said, frustration creeping into her voice.

'I wasn't mocking you,' I told her. 'I'm just as confused as you are. If you show yourself, and come with me, I can show you these armae or what have you.'

'What are you?' she asked. 'We?'

'I'm a nephilim. Sorry, a nephila. Anakim, emmim, gibborim. All Hebrew words for the tribes of giants, more or less. You're also one, perhaps? Can you do strange things, channelling, changing, like old alchemy and mediums? Can you...see ghosts, sometimes, at the corner of your eye and the end of your bed? Do you hear violence sometimes? Swords, guns, war drums, the buzzing of horns and flies?'

'We are... the nephilim?' she said.

'What did you think we were?' I asked. 'What can you do?'

'My family...' she said, before pausing sadly. 'We...my grandmother told me that we were descended from the Giant, al-Jabar, who was in turn fathered by the Zophasemin, beings like primordial eggs. Al-Jabar became the constellation, Orion the Hunter, who the ancients called Nefil...'

'See, Nefil,' I said. 'Nephilim. There's your answer.'

'Yes,' she said. 'I was told I was a *marid*, a soul of Rebellion, a giant in the earth. You have heard of Prince Faisal of Hejaz, yes? One of his scholars went to Jeddah, where they house the Tomb of Eve. But they measured the dimensions – her original grave must have been nearly three-meters--long, and it is now greater than that. Those bones are growing, ages after her death. Faisal believes the tomb to be a place of blasphemy, the tomb of a monstrous giantess rather than the first woman, and plans to destroy it.'

'I see,' I said. 'Simply different words for the same idea. We are certainly...rebelling.'

'Our ancestors built our home of Baalbek, with giant pillars in imitation of Old Irem, and eerie carvings of angels and demons. The Kaiser, the second Wilhelm, came to Baalbek when I was a child[160]... The archeologists swarmed the ruins of Heliopolis, violating the temple of Jupiter, Bacchus, and Venus. I wonder what that Caesar took from us. I wonder what they opened.'

'I don't know,' I said. 'I've never seen this city, or heard of the Kaiser plundering it.'

'There is an old legend that an army of demons slumbered under the stones of Baalbek, trapped by angels, or Solomon and queen Bilquis,' she said. 'And now I am hearing such strange claims out of Europe...The prophecy of Enêpsigos fulfilled[161]. It was too late to use the ring.'

'That...' I paused to think of what I should tell her, 'May be true. We have fought such devils...What ring is this?'

The world turned, and I was in a beige room. It was as though I was a pepper shaker, slid across a table. I was on a bed. There were others there, in the room.

'It that right?' she said, disjointedly. As she was not visible, I did not at first realize that she was speaking to the strange Oriental knight until he appeared to answer her, from the hotel's hall.

'I'm afraid so,' he said. 'But do not trust them. They are led by a Jew, and the Jews are the great foe of the giants – driven to purge us from the world. The marriage of Israel and Anak has always spawned

---

[160] This would have been in November 1898; Batoul Chedid would have been 5 at the time.

[161] *Enêpsigos*: The double-headed and triple-chained moon demoness who impersonated Kronos and Hecate, who taught witches to draw down the moon, according to *the Testament of Solomon*. Annoyed by the persecutions of the angel Rathanael, "of the Third Heaven," the demoness prophecized the destruction and desecration of the Temple, and that one day, the "vessels" used to trap all demons would be broken by man. Outraged, Solomon rebound her in unbreakable chains.

abominations. Have you heard the tales of the giant Red Jews of the Middle Ages, the Solomonar who would emerge at the end of the world, riding dragons and commanding storms?'

I was going to point out that the Jews don't seem to actively hunt down nephilim, but I did realize that Anna's clan lived in complete isolation, and the Rabbi seemed oddly capable of hiding in plain sight and twisting perception. I never learned of such things before this mad Odyssey, but the Bible does had an oddly high number of incidents in which Jews clash
with their neighbouring tribes of giants, and win.

'We,' I paused, and then clarified, 'The French have taken Aradus, and its ancient walls, said to be built by giants.'

'Yes, Arwad,' she said. 'the Ottomans bombed it, until repulsed by your sailors.'

A harsh pressure, like a migraine, shot through my eye sockets, and I thought of the ghoul Kiss.

I looked around the room. The double window was open. She had transported us. Or, perhaps, remade the room in some kind of ectoplasmic model.

I asked where we were. She answered the Semiramis Hotel, in Cairo. Her prior base, that Mock Paris, had been infiltrated.

I expressed my astonishment that we had moved to Egypt. The Knight noted that I was French, and asked if I knew the tale of Napoleon and the Red Man of Destiny. I said no. The Knight said that before the Battle of the Pyramids, Bonaparte saw a figure in a red mantle emerge from those monuments, who bid him to enter. Previously reluctant to take the fight to the enemy here, the Red Man showed him wonders in the Pharaonic tomb that convinced Bonaparte to engage. Rumors spread that he had made some sort of diabolical pact, and that the Red Man said that he had been at Napoleon's side since his childhood, and he would come to him again on the first of April, before Waterloo.

I asked who the Red Man was. The Knight said that the local Arabs believed it to be a genie, or perhaps Satan himself, and the European nephilim believed it to be the pit-king Apollyon. The Knight believed that it was the spirit of the Roman Emperor, Nero Redivivus, freshly returned from the source of the Nile. Others say that such a red figure, a dwarf, was seen as a harbinger of doom for Catherine de Medici, Henry IV (seen by the king the day before his assassination), and Louis XVI and Marie Antoinette (seen the day before the storming of the Tuileries Palace).

I recalled the tale of Moberly and Jourdain, English spinsters who claimed to have encountered Marie Antoinette and others of her court while touring Versailles, somehow tumbling from 1901 back to the night of the Tuileries. They had an encounter there with a repulsive, odious man marked with smallpox, with an empty but somehow evil stare hidden in the shadows of a heavy hat. Yet they also claimed to have encountered a towering Roman emperor whom they dubbed Constantine, so perhaps it is a shared dream or madness, or something else studied by Dr. Laurent.

Napoleon's War was the War of Rome, the Knight believed, and, in its day, it was even called the Great War. Everyone was Rome. France, a republic turned empire led by an Italian general-cum-imperator. The Czars, with their inheritance of Byzantium, and the last gasp of the Holy Roman Empire. And, esoterically, the Habsburgs and the Hanovers were both descended from the Roman House of Este, the bloodline of the Saracen hero Ruggiero, raised by the wizard Atalante [sic - Atlantes], and the dame-knight Bradamante - a mythic sexual fusion of the Christian, the Mohammedan, and the Satanic. Indeed, he clarified, the Guelphs only fell from power with the coronation of Victoria, whose womanhood broke the successive personal union of the Throne with the House of Hanover. Victoria's death must have shook the monarchies of Europe, I thought.

There is even a legend that Ruggiero was descended from Astyanax, saved by Odysseus from his recorded death during the sack of Troy and spirited away to Sicily or Corsica alongside Hector's sword Durendal, a striking parallel to Æneas. Astyanax would become ruler of Messina by slaying the giant Agranor, king of Agrigento, bathing in the monster's blood.

'So, is that why he wanted the grail?' I asked. 'Heredity, and blood science. I saw it in Belgium - the indirect transfusion of blood. Before, it had to be vein to vein, but medicine has developed anticoagulants and refrigerating techniques. If we can stop coagulation now with simple sodium citrate, surely they would be able to process dried blood some day. And who better to draw power from the long dead than an oil man?'

I looked at the giant knight, like Roland's enemy Ferragut, and asked his name. He gruffly said 'Tariel Ketelauri,' saying it slowly so I would hear it clearly."

Ketelauri's odd garb ties into an unique incident in Georgian history.

In the spring of 1915, the residents of Tbilisi were astonished by a warband out of time. With barded horses, French chain mail and helms, arming swords, and round shields engraved with *Ave Mater Dei*, these strange troops looked for all the world like 12th century crusaders on parade, though several carried still anachronistic flintlock rifles and there was an obvious Georgian and "Oriental" aesthetic to their kit. Some wondered if they were an acting troupe for a show or film, or perhaps a prank or a morale-boosting ploy[162].

The knights, the Crusaders of King David's Army, dismounted at the governor's palace and asked to know where the war was being fought – it had taken seven months for the news to reach them in Khevsureti, but they were eager to fight the Turks, and carried with them relics of the Crusades and the bones of giants.

These men were Khevsurs, who believe themselves to be the descendants of French and German crusaders who marched through Armenia to settled in northeastern Georgia in the 12th century after the Battle of Didgori; the "King David" here is not the Biblical king of Israel, but Davit IV Arghdamenishabeli, called the Builder, a Georgian King who fought the Seljuk Turks. Another theory is they are actually descendants of the *Tadzrelebi*, an earlier tradition of "templars" dating to the 5th century, organized to defend the Monastery of St. Tevdore near Bethlehem.

The alleged giant artifacts were part of a widespread flap of giant bone findings in Georgia during the early 20th century, preceding the excavation of Palaeolithic cave sites by the likes of Stefan Krukowski.

---

[162] Halliburton, Richard. (1935). *Seven League Boots*. Indianapolis: Bobbs/Merrill Co Publishers . p. 162.

One of the oddest mentions of this occurs in the otherwise comical 1940 memoir *Anything Can Happen* by George Papashvily, who served as a sniper in the Russian Army during the First World War. He fought against the Red Army invasion of Russia, before fleeing to Turkey and then finally immigrating to America, which would become the subject of his book. In one odd aside, Papshvily casually mentions a tale of boys swimming into an air pocket within a submerged cavern, where they discovered human skeletons nearly three meters tall "with heads as big as bushel baskets," and tunnels leading deep into the Caucasus mountains.

"The Knight said that his family was born of Amiran's seed, the titan who gifted mankind with the knowledge of metallurgy, and was punished by being chained to Mount Kazbegi, a dormant volcano sheathed in a glacier, a dead natural forge, fire under ice. Orthodox hermits built up a cave upon his prison, and named it Bethlehem, the Christian over the pagan. He was known to the Greeks as Prometheus, and his land Colchis.

And here was my second great mistake of the day — I spoke too freely.

The Knight of Colchis said that the Golden Fleece was his by right, as their clan was descended from Medea. When I countered that she killed her children, a fact I vaguely remembered from a theater poster, he retorted that she didn't kill off all of her children — Thessalus and Medus survived, at least. I said that I couldn't surrender the Fleece — it wasn't mine to give away. He seemed furious, but restrained himself.

The woman asked me if we intended to fight the Turks. And here came the third mistake — I said no.

'The Ottomans are selling Armenian women in the markets, still stained with the blood of their husbands and brothers. The Kurds are filling ditches with villages. You were not there, at Ras al-Ain,' she said, something distant and haunted in her voice. 'You are siding with Rome while the churches burn.'

'That's not why we're here,' I said.

The white bed rolled into a sphere, pulling me back. There came a swirl of plaster wall and stone and sky, and I was back in the market, falling backwards, trying to catch myself against the wall. Even when I stopped myself, my poor stomach kept rotating, churning a mix of spoiled chickpeas and pitch black coffee.

The sphere was in front of me, a white ball standing on the ground, etched with some pattern of lines that resembled a floor plan. The knight was there, behind me. The sphere rolled, revealing the woman, briefly, and she struck me in the head with something. I fell to the earth, and remember nothing of what happened afterwards."

At this point, Thomas Noun and Jacoba van der Aarde saw Céleste returned to the marketplace, along with the sphere and the woman.

"We located Céleste down a blind alley between two buildings in the market. People were reacting to the commotion, unsure of what was happening. There was a sphere on the ground, like a great globe, with a woman seated upon it. She was tall, a little shorter than me, and olive-skinned. She wore a sandy yellow dress with a small, matching hat with an upturned black brim. Around her neck hung the half-mask of a box respirator, and mismatched goggles. Her eyes were large, chocolate coloured; her nose and ears were prodigious, overwhelming a weak chin. She held a brick in her right hand - Beneath what looked like a shining golden ring and a sleeve of bandages, two of her six fingers were fused together (I cannot remember which ones).

The first thing I saw was Céleste on the ground, blood pooling around her head. In the moment, she could have been dead. Van der Aarde asked me where Céleste was, her eyesight that poor. I yelped that she was on the ground and wasn't moving. I pulled my rifle off my shoulder.

'Children of Algebar,' said the woman as I aimed at her. Something white rolled off of her face. 'Descendants of Orion. We were to hunt the Beasts, not watch them rampage.'

'Back away from the woman,' I said. Van der Aarde started clicking in a hypnotic rhythm, and aimed her pistol. I nodded at the chap dressed like the Oriental knight. 'You too. Back away.' I glanced back at the street, hoping that the rest of our unit would show up.

Van der Aarde said she would shoot. The woman in yellow turned to look at us, spinning on the sphere. There were no whites to her eyes; they looked a shocking, solid black, though the dark brown irides were there, on inspection. She touched her thumb and fingers together, turned them upwards, and shook the hand in a gesture I did not understand.

'We want the fleece,' said the knight.

'We don't have it,' I said.

'The Frenchwoman said you did,' said the woman, tilting her head in Céleste's direction. 'And you didn't ask what fleece. You heard *fleece* and knew it was the Golden Fleece. Don't lie to me, dear. You are bad at it.'

'I will fire,' I said. 'Step...roll or whatever that is away from her. I want to check to see if she's...'

'Fleece for the Frenchwoman,' she said. She rolled to the side, still maintaining her balance on the sphere at a ninety degree angle, and fluffed Céleste's hair and replaced her knocked-off hat. Two fingers touched Céleste's neck, and the woman said she was alive.

'She could die before we retrieve it,' I said.

'You should hurry, then,' she said, before turning her head to the humming Van der Aarde, who immediately fired. The Arab woman seemed to shift in a way best described as a mirage, like the Fata Morgana effect worked by Céleste. It was as though the space between her and Schildbreker telescoped. Van der Aarde looked confused when she heard no sound of impact nor scream of pain, and fired again. She stumbled, as though pulled upward and forward, planting her face in the dirt. The next desperate shots impacted the white sphere, suddenly interposed between us. It grew with each hit.

I charged the maniac Mavia, with the ground shifting between us, expanding and trapping me in a cycle – like the Red Queen's race, the faster I ran the further away she became. I wrapped my hand through my rifle's strap and twisted it tight, to keep it from bouncing about, hoping that the bayonet hadn't loosened. I stopped, and ran to the side, ducking into a building. Perhaps, I thought, this strange expansion and contraction of space was founded upon her vision; she likely could not alter what she could not perceive.

However, before I could find my way to a window to snipe her, the wall cracked and the knight carved through it with his curved sword, sharper and tougher than any metallurgy I've ever seen. Strangely, the wall seemed to crumble before the blade touched it, as though it drank up its strength like the giant Antaeus drawing up the strength from the earth. It struck me as truly otherworldly, however, as while Céleste channeled something real like heat, the Geistritter manipulated light, and the Captain meddled with electrons and the other physical particles, the Georgian Knight seemed to tamper with an abstraction – there is no metric for fortitude that could be transferred between plaster and blade.

The Man carved through the wall as I fled out the back of the shop into the shoreward side of the market. I turned towards the woman and stretched my legs as I ran, hoping to overcome her distortion of distance and catch her off rhythm. She reached over her shoulder, and something tubular shot into her hand, suddenly stopping after travelling at such a speed it seemed to be a blurry brown ribbon. She was on me in a flash, slashing with the British cavalry rapier. She lacked any serious skill, relying on the uncanny agility and strength of a nephela, and I managed to parry her with a fencing implement as poor as a bayonet before pulling out my own blade - but she had control of the space between us, a truly dangerous advantage in a sword fight. I managed to deflect her swing, rear back, and prepared to cut her down, but suddenly there seemed to be a vast gulf between us, the size of a football pitch. And then, when she recovered to slash, I was forced to catch her blade and throw us both off balance. I tried to push into her, hoping that actually grappling her would prevent her manipulations. I locked my leg around hers, and pressed chest to chest, and some effect, akin to being frozen in position as the world rotated beneath us, occurred, and we were several yards away, still bound, until that viscous sphere of hers slammed into me, after bouncing off the wall and growing with each impact. I was knocked clear, and rolled to a stop. The knight came barrelling down on me, but a sudden discharge of rifle fire scared him back into cover.

Soon, more gunfire filled the market, with the rhythm of a bolt-action rifle. The Arab woman put her hands in her pocket and switched places with the sphere like castling chess pieces. The sphere rose to guard her, and she locked it in place at the apex of its bounce, the bullets causing the shielding mass to grow with each impact. There was something at her side, I noticed then, a small white egg that suddenly appeared and disappeared, as if deployed from the sphere. Her other eye was also blackened, giving her visage a chilling, ghoulish quality.

She still seemed to have some sense of sight, as she detected Gottlieb's sniping position on a distant rooftop. He, oddly, had not hidden in the light, relying on mundane positioning and cover for camouflage. She yelped and swatted at the air, as though assaulted by a murder of crows, and shifted her positioning so that she could sit on the side of the wall, outside of the firing arc of the sniper, forcing him to move to an opening.

I retreated, looking for Venetianer and my fallen allies. The knight re-emerged as the wall crumbled around him, covered with what seemed like a shell of skin and blackened mail, its hardness stolen from the wall. He was tough enough to stop at least two direct shots from penetrating his flesh, and each footstep towards me kicked up dust from crumbling, sun-dried earth. I darted towards the woman again, hoping to take advantage of her divided attention. The sphere rotated like a globe, its axis aligned to her spine. They suddenly darted upward, rocketing like a signal flare, as I dove to ensnare her with overgrown arms.

It was here that Gottlieb's gambit revealed itself. The woman, shifting into the air for safety, found only the killing blade of an unseen Anna. She went limp and fell to the earth, blood exploding from her neck on impact. And then, just as quickly as she fell, her body was gone along with the sphere. The second object, the small egg, suddenly erupted, growing in size and rotting into a yellow slime, leaving behind the woman as she had been upon the deposition of the egg. I tried to piece together the logic behind it, the locking of her into a time-frame, as well as the manipulation of the space-frame – the egg was a cosmic template, a carbon copy. She looked around, her smug, detached tranquillity replaced with true panic. It seemed as though she was trying to figure out what killed her, confirming my theory that she had reverted to a prior state rather than, say, reincarnating immediately with the same stream-of-consciousness from the point of death. Everything between the formation of the egg and her death was truly gone. She crawled on her knees and touched the knight, and they were gone with the sound of flapping clothing and clanging chainmail.

I cleaned Céleste's head wound and closed it, and hoped she came to. Gottlieb had jumped down from his perch and sprinted over to carry her from the market. I closed my own wounds and helped Van der Aarde to her feet.

Céleste eventually revived, oddly demanding a chocolate, cream, and acorn flour concoction called *racahout des arabes*, which, to her dismay, seemed to be foreign to the local Arabs. It seems to have been popular in France, perhaps something of a comfort drink for her. She said it helped with nausea, and along with a pressure headache, photophobia, and a groggy dizziness, we soon realised that she had suffered a concussion. We tried to keep her awake with coffee in the Turkish mode, despite her extreme fatigue, and decided to halt our southward pilgrimage for a week.

We went to Rujm el-Hiri, ten miles to the north of the sea of Galilee, a set of Bronze Age stone circles on a shallow plateau, said to have been made by King Og. Afterwards, we slowly moved to Tal al-Safi, the site of the Crusader fort of Blanchegarde, built upon the stones of ancient Gath, the bastion of the Anakim known as 'the wine press.' It was now a village of date-palm and olive orchards, tended by no more than six hundred people.

We had planned to go to Tiberias, but instead decided it was best to push forward to Jerusalem."

Gehenna

The party took a boat trip along the swampy Mediterranean coast, eventually coming ashore near the small town of Qisarya, an Arabic adaptation of Caesarea. Mihajlo was delighted to hear a familiar tongue spoken by a small community of a hundred and fifty or so Bushnaks. These Bosnian settlers relocated to Ottoman Syria during the Sultanate's withdrawal from the Balkans, fearing persecution from the new Christian regimes and Habsburg ambitions. Despite the religious difference, the community maintained many Balkan Slavic customs and style of dress.

During this recuperation period, Venetianer kept a detailed record of his dreams, hoping to contact Austin Osman Spare again. He was successful on the night of May 10th:

"Yihovæum appeared to me again, this time fresh from his Egyptian travels. He was regal now, his horns resplendent in gold, more of an ibex than a European goat. He had traveled to the 1881 expedition of Prof. Timmerman, who found a temple to Isis, sixteen miles south of Najar Djfard, containing the bones of 2 to 3.3m tall giants, dated to sometime before 1000 B.C.

He asked me about the dead, about the persistence of souls. I said that I had been steeped in mediumship for my entire life, and believed it to be true, that people live on through a Sheol of lasting psychic effects. They are sustained by the memory of loved ones and public ritual, by that remembering. If we forget them, they drift from us, to be reborn into the world or to
sleep until the end of days.

I spoke of Lailah, a feminine angel of darkness who presented the seminal drop before Adonai, to have its future foretold. She binds a soul from the Garden of Eden or the well of Gilgul to the sperm, and sets it on its way; Lailah strikes the child on the lip before its birth, molding the philtrum and causing it to forget its past life. She is not a true angel, of course, not a being, but a metaphor for the cycle of life and death and the personal and metaphysical knowledge mankind loses in its course.

Yihovæum said that a dead man was calling to him. He said that he wasn't sure if it was true, because he had heard the tale before the calling, but it seemed too real to him. It was Edmund Gurney, a researcher into hypnotism and the persistence of consciousness after death, who lost three sisters on the Nile in a barge accident in 1875. In 1888, almost exactly thirty years ago, he died by an overdose of chloroform. Some spiritualists proposed the fraudulent psychical trials of Blackburn and Smith had broken his spirit, while others believe it was a medical accident. But Yihovæum claims he saw them on
the Nile, reunited on the Barge of the Osiris.

There were bones in the Nile, he said, of giants and satyrs and vampires and mummies and dead devils and angels. And in the sky, there were eyes, with pupils like keyholes.

'This living nightmare,' he said, 'Where all is cannibalism.'

Yihovæum spoke to me in confidence, because he intuited that I was Jewish from details of my case file and speech. It had to do with Arthur Balfour, the Earl of Balfour, and a vast spiritualist network. Balfour had, in the preceding year, proclaimed a declaration in favor of a Jewish homeland in Palestine. Yihovæum suddenly found this milquetoast former prime minister deeply intriguing, learning that he was known to be an anti-rationalist philosopher, who denied that human reason could determine any metaphysical or practical truths. Balfour was a deeply mystical man, and rumored to be a hermaphrodite. Yihovæum dreamed of the alchemical androgyne, the rebis, a creature representing hierogamous union and completion of the Great Work, a symbolic figure of triumphant reconstitution.

Balfour had once declared love for his cousin Mary Lyttleton [corrected from "Littletown"], a woman who had seen two of her previous suitors die tragically. She became a macabre, haunted woman, but Balfour was unafraid of any supposed misfortune. However, she died of typhus on Palm Sunday of 1875, buried with an emerald ring at Balfour's request. Balfour has yet to marry, even into his elder decades.

Following her death in 1875 and spanning into the present day, multiple members of the Society for Psychical Research, and hundreds of other mediums, began creating automatically written letters and channeling messages from Lyttleton, a mass set of 'cross-correspondences' to the Prime Minister. Yihovæum stated that there appeared to be thousands of such messages. One such medium was Mrs Holland, the sister of Rudyard Kipling, George Valiantine, and the women of the celebrated Verrall family. One was the prominent Liberal suffragist and Welsh bard Mrs Winifred Coombe Tennant, who had borne a child with Gerald Balfour, our subject's younger brother. Some of the mediums were undoubtedly frauds, and many more were likely coincidences, delusional, or influenced by the interviewing psychical researchers and their willingness to believe. But taken together, there is a massive constellation of noise, to the point that it could not all be error and bias.

Yihovæum mentioned a strange term, Zos, some magical word of his devising for the self, the body and mind, which seeks out the Kia, which seemed to be a godhead, but more impersonal, in the fashion of the Oriental faiths such as the Dao, with shades of the life-force, some synthesis of chi-chiah-kia-yu-and-ka. He told me that he felt a deep connection to me despite being a stranger and a Hungarian. He said I was neither enemy nor alien. I was like one of those masters Blavatsky spoke of, a man of inconceivable, ancient mystery.

He turned around, and I saw that the bestial head was now a golden mask, and he had a tangle of unruly, curly hair; he had a rather Jewish look to him, despite his English blood. He removed his mask, and I saw his face clearly, young and handsome and with a strange nobility in rags.

He told me to take off my mask. I closed my eye and tried to reveal myself to him, open up. I told him my name, and he saw my face, judging by his wry smile.

'The mysterious Crow-King revealed,' he said. 'It's a shame I am unlikely to remember this. Am I correct? Am I on to something, with my craft and sigils?'

'I have seen too much oddity to fit it into one sphere,' I said. 'There is the Law, and there is a Godhead. Everything is One, but there seem to be infinite experiences. The best I can tell is that the world is a riddle, with either no answer or a thousand right answers.'

'What does that mean? It is too simple,' he said. 'We are higher ideas and objectives incarnate by woman; our faiths and notions in life are just tools for survival. There must also be a search for growth, for sensuality, for experience in this world.'

'Oh, I know that better than ever. My kind are higher concepts, egregore, incarnate by women,' I said. 'The giants in the earth. And it is a nightmare existence. Be happy with the mortal search for meaning. Maybe the meaning is how you ask your questions.'

'If this is a nightmare, everything is possible. Ikkah zod-ka, the struggling self. But what is the end of the struggle?'

'There is none. Love. Be kind. Be gentle,' I said. 'Find what you need to do and do it. And until then, try to do your best, and leave things better than you found them. Anyone who gives you a hard time for doing so is not worth listening to. It's pretty basic, but nothing is ever going to satisfy that itch for something more. It's sad, but that's the curse of the curious mind. I spent my whole life wanting to see that big picture, unlock the great mystery, reach the Crown of Creation. But you're never going to find that magic door that lets you step outside of life. You can hope for God or your Kia or the universal truth to kiss you, but one cannot elect oneself.'

I thought of that Goethe quote: If you want to live in happiness, hate no one and leave the future to God[163].

'It is too simple,' he said sadly. 'It seems like a deathlike stillness of ambition, an appeal to ignorance.'

'I know,' I admitted. 'Become a knowledge seeker. A scientist, a sage, a student. That's complicated, there's always a search and a struggle, but it's good for humanity. And yourself. Here's the terrible thing about having some sort of higher cosmic truth -you may not like it.'

I felt his hunger for some occult truth. For much of my early life, I held with Ibn Ezra, who believed that the Bene Elohim (which should here be understand as the sons of divinities, such as the pagan gods of Canaan, not Elohim as the one true God of Israel) were not angels, but rather mortal men of somewhat larger statue who could falsely possess 'divine' power by use of astrology and sorcery, what we now understand to be psychical phenomena. And these were not the improbable, towering giants of lore, but simply men of nations who reached statures of around two to three meters, possible albeit difficult with the anatomy of a mortal. Such power was not meant to be kept from man by G-d, but instead granted via personal covenants, as seen with Samson – his mighty strength limited by the prohibition against cutting his locks. The sin of the Bene Elohim was that they sought undisciplined, wild talents to dominate the women who would lead to the line of Abraham and Isaac, not that they had such powers in the first place. In my youth, I wished to cultivate my talents, as great Tzaddikim of old or the mystics of Tibet did, for the good of mankind. If only the world had been so rational, and kind, and rewarding of the hopes of youth.

He narrowed his eyes, looked up, and said, 'When you said that you were incarnate egregore, and mentioned your kind, and giants – that wasn't meant as a metaphor, was it? You're one of the nephilim, the giants of Genesis? Is that why your stature is so great in this dreamland?'

'Oh, I hadn't noticed,' I said. 'But yes. I think this is why your

---

[163] *"Willst Du glücklich leben, hasse niemanden und überlasse die Zukunft Gott."*

superiors dispatched you to find me.'

'I see,' he said. 'I have been spying on Émile Brugsch, the translator who deciphered the Stele of Revealing with Crowley. It is so strange how readily we cooperated, German, French, and Englishmen, on the riddles of Egypt, yet how readily we lunge at each others' throats in all modern matters. If only you giants could rise up, and be the mystery that unites this world at war.'

'We hope we can,' I said. 'We wish to stop Armageddon. But first, we must sleep, and dream.'

And so he faded, with a final message – the Great God Pan is Dead. All is dead. We are the dead, the Rephaim, and so we must sleep and dream and gather together at the place called Armageddon."

The giants arrived in Jerusalem on May 25th. Winepress and Venetianer explained that the Seventy Weeks prophesied in the Book of Daniel were coming to a close, as they came to the city of its subject – they reckoned it between 29 May 1917, when they first gathered, and what they assumed to be the Battle of Armageddon, at the close of the coming September.

They arrived alongside an caravan of Armenians fleeing for shelter within the Patriarchate of Jerusalem. The Armenian population of the city swelled to roughly 25,000 people, largely crammed around the Armenian Quarter's St. James Monastery.

Outside the Old City, they encountered an encampment of Jews in the neighbourhood of Mishkenot Sha'ananim, waiting for the political situation of Jerusalem to settle. They had a network of young runners moving into and out of the city and towards the British Expeditionary Force's camps, scouting for Bedouin raiders and hoping for news from the recently arrived parties of Zionists and the leadership of Jerusalem. Jerusalem's leadership was largely Sephardic, the community built up under Haim Aharon Valero, though the Valero Bank collapsed in 1915 and he was in his twilight years. Some Ashkenazi Jews had been allowed to settle in the middle of the 19th century, after the lifting of an Ottoman prohibition. On the 6th of April, 1917, the Jewish population of Jaffa and Tel Aviv were deported and prevented from migrating to Haifa or Jerusalem, leading many to live in a limbo state. Many departed for British holdings, particularly in Egypt, as the 1914 expulsion from

Jaffa was also largely a relocation to Alexandria. Some seven hundred Jaffaites died of hunger and disease during the 1917-1918 winter.

The hinterlands of Jerusalem also struggled to house displaced Arabs, nearly forty thousand of which were expelled from Gaza in early March. Most refugees were women and children, as men were conscripted into the Ottoman Army and dispersed throughout the Sultanate.

The Greek Orthodox Church also had a foothold in Jerusalem, as the War had caused pilgrimage to slow to a trickle, and they had been heavily taxed by the Ottomans for their refusal to send men to the war effort. The Church largely opposed the oncoming flood of Jewish settlement and resettlement, even allying with local Muslim groups to push back the immigrants.

The refugees themselves were largely from families who had settled in Ottoman Palestine in 1905, driven out by the latest in a long line of pogroms in the city of Odessa – however, they had set down roots in the north of the region. A couple of them claimed that they were looking for caves to dwell in, as they had lived in the limestone caverns beneath Odessa before the Russians forced them out, and found them to be a place of spiritual, if spartan, comfort. Three families had come from Iran, driven to leave by the 1910 blood libel of Shiraz, and one odd group from America seemed to believe that Louis Brandais was a candidate for the Messiah.

The more recent European Zionists had traveled with Ephraim Moses Lilien, an *art nouveau* printmaker who traveled between Europe and Ottoman Palestine to promote a secular, democratic Jewish culture, frequently working alongside Boris Schatz. Lilien's work is striking for its depiction of early Zionist figures such Theodore Herzl, the depiction of a heroic Jewish identity in neoclassical and modernist form, and, darkly, a use of thorny vines in his work to represent oppression and hardship, which would come prophetically close to the barbed wire of the battlefields and ghettos of the mid-20th century. Lilien was not present, but Venetianer had been drawn to this encampment by his correspondence with fellow rabbi and psychic Yakov (or Jacob) Krzemienieck, known for his Odessa seances and demonstrations of telekinesis and levitation.

However, the group had rapidly become diverse in the wake of Jerusalem's capture by the British. There were families from Syria, Central Asians, a group from Jamaica who Noun could speak English with, and a family of Berbers, largely notable because multiple members of the group wrote about her beauty; an unusually pale girl garbed in bright wraps, with straight black hair, pale blue eyes, and red-brown marks on her cheek, painted in henna rather than the traditional tattooing of the Berbers due to halakhic prohibitions. Both Venetianer and Céleste recalled an encounter with an escaped Jewish slave from Tangiers, who bore the scars of torture and branding. Rather than the Rabbi, the man was instead drawn to Céleste. She noted then man peddled talismans, with Kabbalistic symbols surrounded with Arabic, charms against pests.

He spoke some French, and asked if she wanted to buy one, to ward against the swarms of locusts, flies, and scorpions that endangered travelers around Jerusalem. He also displayed charms from the Nestorian *Book of Protection* showing St. George's defeat of the Dragon and Enoch eating from the Tree of Life, and talismans from the French grimoire, *La poule noire*, written by an anonymous wizard from "the genius" Napoleon's army, educated in necromancy by a green-clad "Turk" who appeared from the pyramids, resembling the eponymous mage of *the Book of Abramelin*. Céleste asked about its strange name ("the Black Hen" in French), and the peddler explained that the old man of the pyramids told the French soldier he would teach him magic, if the apprentice could overcome his vices – it was easy, as he could not be tempted with power or gross sensuality; the Frenchman's only vice was extreme gluttony, and the old man fed him a lavish feast prepared by his enslaved elementals, after which he was sated and praised God for the relief. The old man then taught the soldier dozens of talismans and spells, the binding of elementals and the conjuring of giant spirits, and the formula for hatching the Black Hen of Oromais, a bird who could lay golden eggs. At the end of this instruction, the Old Man told the Frenchman that he was 270 years old, and hinted that his Provincial apprentice had the magical potential to exceed him. The master then gave up his life to the heavens, and the Frenchman sailed to his ancestral homeland and purchased a house in Marseilles – but the wizard hinted that he the sage's life is one of secrecy, and such vast riches drew too much ire and attention.

Céleste was somewhat interested as she flipped through the booklet, but declined his offer upon seeing the magical names "Reterrem," "Taraim," and "Natarter," and hoping she was wrong about the 18th century Provençal equivalent of "Maître." She decided not to waste the vendor's time and looked to buy a charm of protection against magical retribution, though Venetianer quietly joked that Orion would have wanted the one against scorpion venom. She was startled, though, when he asked if she was also a slave from Morocco, and she explained that she was a free woman of France. He apologized, both for misspeaking and for the death of Émile Mauchamp, the French pharmacist whose 1907 murder by a mob in Marrakesh was used as the *casus belli* for the conquest of Morocco. Despite the man's belief that this was still a sore spot for the French, Céleste had no idea what he was talking about, but bought the scorpion talisman out of pity. He mentioned that he had been freed not long ago through the good fortune brought by his makeshift charms, though he did admit that it might have been a touch of the *pidyon shvuyim*, when several wealthy Jews from Yemen arranged for his purchase and freedom.

Winepress and Takeuchi spoke on the subject of Laurence Oliphant, inspired by a copy of *the Land of Gilead*, his Christian Zionist work on the development of a Jewish agricultural settlement in Ottoman Palestine; Takeuchi remembered that Oliphant, in his capacity as a British diplomat and intelligence agent, had fought off an attack in Edo by anti-western ronin using only a bullwhip and a wooden beam, nearly losing the use of a hand from a katana wound. They laughed at the imagined audacity of the scene as Tom Noun and Mihajlo Princip attempted to get Anna to remove her coat – despite complaining about the heat, she simply wouldn't remove her coat because she liked the texture, and her mother made it for her.

It was then that the Ottoman clock tower above the Jaffa Gate rang with a thunderously deep drumming. A commotion rose from the encampment, and the people fled towards the Old City through the main gate and the southern moat. As Tom Noun wrote:

"A terrible tumult rose from the stony hills, kicking up sand and gravel at the far end of the neighbourhood. The Captain noted, with shock, that it was one of our Mark I tanks that crested the hills, smoking and straining. A plough had been affixed to the front of the tank; not like those tested for mine destruction, but an excavator with heavy chains attached to the prow. It roared down the incline towards us at an unsafe speed, comparable to the maximum velocity of a motorcar. We all panicked and scattered and scrambled towards Jerusalem, our temporary peace broken by the temporary insanity called war, until we saw that the twilight sky had suddenly become a dark buzzing nightmare. Several of the Jews were on the ground, rolling against the stones and dust to scrape off and crush the cloud of biting flies. They were monstrous things the size of Crown coins, like Mydas flies. They glistened and swarmed so thickly against the city's ancient stone walls that their screaming victims seemed castle invaders scalded with bubbling pitch.

Céleste sucked the heat from the swarm and pulled a man and a woman from the mess. They both retched and snorted and cleaned their ears of the flies, their faces red with bites. A murder of crows emerged from the city's shadowy nooks and crannies, and two swirling armies of living darkness clashed outside Jerusalem.

The tank's roar sounded less like an overworked engine than that of a great beast, and the filthy smoke that rose from it seemed as though they had done no damage to the vehicle. Indeed, its blackened armour had been repaired with veins of gold, and a glaze of rapidly-cooled glass dropped over the connection to the plough, as though it had blasted out of the sand of the Battle of Gaza with volcanic force.

'They know!' Venetianer ejaculated, 'they are going to plough up the Valley.'

I ran up and grabbed Venetianer's hand. He reacted oddly, at first, but I nodded at him, and he seemed to understand.

'And they called to the hills and the rocks to fall on them and hide them from He who is on the Throne, and the Wrath of the Lamb,' said a croaking voice, like a young man pretending to be an old woman and succeeding too well. An Arab boy, somewhere around ten to twelve years of age, emerged from the swarm. At first I believed him to be wrapped in a loose brown turban, but it quickly became apparent that he was nearly mummified in bandages caked with dried blood and dust. He did not introduce himself, but I knew who he was as he peeled back his bandaged eye and revealed a socket teaming with insects. This body was naught but a puppet of the Fly-Lord, Beelzebub.

'Come, Buzzing One, and know the strike of the fly.'

A stinging black death filled the air like the gas of the trenches, its buzzing deafening. Van der Aarde was herself humming, hoping to overcome them, but the dull roar drowned her out and render her talent useless, so she instead used her strength to carry two of the overcome Jews to safety behind the walls, joined by Anna dragging a trio of victims to safety through the air, pushing down the cloud of flies and driving them to the ground in her flight. Céleste, her mouth covered in a cloth mask, ran towards the tank, accompanied by Winepress and a falling wave of flash-frozen flies. Winepress saw the gold patches, and fought alchemy with alchemy, transmuting part of the gold into an airy hole. His daughter dropped a superheated piece of copper into the tank, at the head of a machine-gun magazine. The bullets ricocheted through the infernal machine. And out of the stalled tank poured a cloud of flies and smoke that rose up into the darkening sky in the shape of a great black dragon.

'Not so openly, Ba'al Berith,' the Fly-Lord chided the fallen Seraph in the tank. The draconic tank simply roared, and dove towards the city in a form that seemed like abstract darkness, but was simply smoke; he tried to menace us, but we had seen these games before. There was terror in the demons, and we took them apart quickly. Winepress and Céleste destroyed their material shells. The demon flies were swallowed up by Reb Venetianer's crows and the mites I crafted on them, engineered to bite the biting flies to death. Their darkness found no hiding place in Gottlieb's lights. Ba'al Berith was annihilated as he attempted to build a body to fly up to the clocktower and its mechanisms. He entered the tin-plated Bezalel Pavilion, melting its walls and warping its wooded planes and artistic canvases into a malleable, sky-worthy form, but his assault was halted before he could, it seems, construct an aeroplane body. The slices of glass left by his final blast of dragon-fire would fall off in the wind[164].

One of the guards at the Jaffa gate came out with a flamethrower, the kind used to destroy the great locust plague of two years prior. He was one of the Englishmen left behind by Allenby's procession through the great gate last year, out of his depth and with weak command of the local tongues (he apparently spoke like an Egyptian). The poor lad hesitated with primal terror at the sight of the dragon's swoop, but Céleste tackled him to the ground. At first I thought she had pushed him out of the way of the demon, but she simply wanted to steal his flamethrower; after the robbery, she laughed and danced with glee as she sent gouts of sticky blue flames into the swarm of flies, decimating it with every go. She did not even need to let the weapon cool.

The Lord of the Flies yelled in the stolen voice of a child.

'You were too famous,' I said. 'We all knew there would be a lord of the flies. I prepared a trench mite for your court.'

He looked surprised, and I recited De Morgan's *Siphonaptera*:

'Big fleas have little fleas upon their backs to bite 'em,/
And little fleas have lesser fleas, and so, *ad infinitum*.'

'I prepared a plague for you. You'll rot to death walking,' hissed Beelzebub, 'Cholera, Typhoid, burning eyes. You'll drown in your own filth and blackened blood.'

But he realized that his own body was failing him. He turned, and scraped his hands across his back, and Takeuchi's phantom beetle disappeared.

'I'm afraid that I've given you the disease in turn,' Takeuchi said. 'Or rather, transferred the consequences or effect to you. I am also afraid that I cannot pity you.'

The body dropped as the Rebel Angel fled the corpse, but it was a fool's flight, and he was gone in a cloud of cold insects and burning light.

We turned to each other, covered in sand, smoke, and flybites, and smiled. We had won a victory without a death, without fleeing in terror or hiding. It was our first clean fight, and Céleste swept up Siegfried in

---

[164] This assault, however, seems to have done more damage than Noun notes here, as the Pavilion had to be demolished not long after.

one arm and danced with him in a circle, spraying fire into the air with the other until her head injury caught up to and discombobulated her, and everyone asked her to stop and sit down. Anna and Van der Aarde returned from the gate, and reported that there had been no deaths, though the camp's Jews were still shaken and didn't want to come outside that night. Only Zrno could not bring himself to celebrate, slowly walking forward on von Böhm's cane. He dabbed Anna's face with his alcohol-soaked handkerchief, to clean the two bites on her face.

'Only two,' she said. 'See? They could not bite me through my coat.'"

They walked together, not wanting to break their stubborn circle that defied heaven and hell. Venetianer noted the tale of Choni Ha-Meagel, that is, Choni the Circledrawer, the great scholar who earned his name by drawing a circle in the earth, praying, and declaring that he would not leave it until it rained. Seeing that the resulting drizzle was not sufficient to break the drought, he complained to God. Rain then poured and washed away the hills. He then complained that he wanted a good rain, and so the rain slowed to a gentle storm that sated the drying earth. He was nearly excommunicated for his audacity, but he was excused because that was just how things were between Choni and the Lord.

But Choni would later fall into a deep sleep beneath a carob tree for seventy years, before he awoke and died. He explained, in his last hour, that he was long troubled by the verse from the 126th Psalm - "When the Lord brought back those who returned to Zion, we were as dreamers..." But what was that, truly? What did it mean to dream away a life? As he walked one day, he saw a man planting a carob, and asked how long it took to bear fruit. Seventy years, the man said. When Choni asked the man why he would bother with such a fruitless task, the man said he had seen carob trees all around him as a child; so he should plant many more for the children to come.

That night, Choni fell into his sleep of seven decades, and when he awoke, he went to see the man. He seemed different, but his eyes were suddenly failing him, and called out to him. The man said that the person by that name had passed long ago, and that he was his grandson. Choni realized that his mule was the descendant of the one he once rode

— and he returned home, and died in the study hall maintained by his grandson. Either companionship, or death, he realized, and he cried out for mercy before the Lord took him. Venetianer asked what fruits they were planting today, to grow in seventy years' time.

They snacked at a small farmer's market of Templers from the colony of Walhalla, near Jaffa, which Gottlieb thought was an oddly pagan name for an apocalyptic Christian cult; they sold a rich wine comparable to the finest of the Rhineland and Württemberg, and fresh and candied oranges. Gottlieb wept, in remembrance of the Germany of his childhood.

They went into Jerusalem, and found a suite of rooms to rent in Nahalat Shiv'a — Anna was happy for the first time in a while, as the courtyard neighborhood had been built some fifty years prior by Russian Jews. She was surrounded by familiar voices, but it was also peacefully sparse, unlike the crowded Old City, and there were currently around 860 people in the district. She noted that Venetianer had suddenly panicked and nearly ran off when he came across a group of Subbotniks, radical Judaizers from Catherinian Russia, and had to be told that they were not Sabbateans, but simply "keepers of the seventh-day Sabbath." That night, Anna sat on the roof, watching the stars, as the others kept to their rooms. In the night, Venetianer approached her. They spoke of Jerusalem, and how he was finally here, in Zion. She asked him about his mysterious Odessa contact, Yakov Krzemieniecḱ, and with it came a flood of answers to the mystery of "Rabbi Alter Venetianer."

Others who have tried to untangle Venetianer's web of aliases believed that he was, in fact, this mysterious Yakov Krzemieniecḱ, and co-opted his name and, perhaps identity, from a contemporary Budapest rabbi, Ludwig Venetianer (Venetianer Lajos). His motive behind this deception is claimed as a desire to protect his family, which is said to include his great nephew Jacques Bergier, born Yakov Mikhaïlovitch Berger, the co-author of *the Morning of the Magicians*. However, it appears as though he was indeed a Venetianer on his father's side, a second cousin of the slightly older Ludwig, with a strong division in the family line created when one side joined the Hassidic movement. The other nephilim claimants always seemed fuzzy on what Venetianer was, exactly; the general assumption was a branch of the Sokoll family or a vaguely defined descendant of the Tribe of Simeon, but nobody had a solid genealogy.

Here, in a dense passage from Anna's diary written in Yiddish (as it was dictated), Venetianer explains his motives, nature, and origin.

"Venetianer suddenly said that he had a confession to make, inspired by the recent revelation of Gioua-osagie's parentage. I was startled, and asked if he was Van der Aarde's father. Or that of Mihajlo. Siegfried, perhaps? He sputtered in shock, and said no, it wasn't that kind of confession.

I said I didn't understand; I wasn't in a proper religious position to do so, and did not fall within the traditions of his [Chassidic] dynasty. He said that we aren't Catholic. This was a personal matter, and he wanted to tell it to a Jew. Especially one who wasn't a gossip. But he assured me that he was nobody's secret father. The matter was rather the reverse.

He recounted the story that I already knew, about the last so-called apocalypse: the death of Frankist-turned-Catholic-turned-Jacobin Junius Frey on the guillotine, the Red Man, Napoleon/Apollyon's decline in Russia, rumors of the restoration of the Temple of Solomon, the Liberation of the Jews, the Perushim and the Chasidim of Chernobyl[165] and the Palestinian Plague and the Star Wormwood's passage in 1812. And, later, the sack of Safed and the earthquake that destroyed Galilee. He then told me of my ancestor's fight against beasts and demons, Lev and that Anna.

He then told me the secret tale of the degenerate, false messiah Jacob Frank, and his secret bride, Sophia, False Wisdom. The marriage of Baphomet and the Scarlet Woman. She bore a daughter to him, and the false messiah's followers spirited her away from Russia. The girl's family converted to Catholicism and baptised her Eve, to avoid the wrath of his enemies among righteous Jews. Yet, they continued their sinister practices in secret, and in 5530 [1770 CE], the sixteen-year-old Eve was declared to be the incarnated Shekina, the female aspect of the Divinity, and the reincarnation of the Virgin Mary. A cult arose around her in Częstochowa, and she attempted to seduce the angels once again,

[165] Note that 'Chernobyl' means Wormwood in Ukrainian. Here, referring to a Chasidic Dynasty.

and bear another race of nephilim. They travelled to Budapest and Vienna, and gained the favor of the court. She revealed that her name was Eva Romanovna, for 'Sophia' was Sophie of Anhalt-Zerbst, the woman known to the world as Catherine the Great.

In 5551, the elder Frank died, and Eve became the Holy Mistress of his cult, establishing a court in Offenbach am Main, in a place called Gottes Haus. She demanded the fealty of the Jewish world in letters marked with red ink. The Jews rejected her, and saw her for Babylon, but occultists among the goyim saw a great power in her. As the first Great War raged across Europe, the Sokolls, Starcateri, and the Nouns fought together for the first time, against Napoleon's magicians, the demons recorded in the *Infernal Dictionary*, and against the psychical onslaught of Eve Frank, and her terrible crows – they said that she would attack the nephilim in dreams, using a spirit in the form of a knight with a crow's head. The Nouns divined that this was the spirit of Cain or 'Caim.' Like her mother, she had a private court furnished with sculpted human sex organs and sybaritic tapestries, part seraglio and part brothel. She spoke with the voice of birds and many waters, and feasted on the battles' corpses with her familiars, *Harab Serapel*. She conjured Theumiel, courted fallen angels, and consorted with spirits, hoping to become a new Eve, a second Na'amah seeking an evil ibbur[166]. He would be the Gibbor of Pele-hoez-el-gibbor-abi-ad-sar-shalom, the spoils of Mahershalalhashbaz.

Eve Frank became a secret queen, and Czar Alexander visited her immediately after the battle of Leipzig to speak to her about her heritage - perhaps soon the Scarlet Woman would ride the Red Dragon. But her empire was built on a foundation of dust. Only one nephel came to visit her, and he simply devoured a dozen of her crows and swallowed several pearl necklaces before she beat him off. Her royal and noble friends would not pay her tribute, the Jews despised her, and the Duke of Hesse issued a debtor's warrant for her, so her cult collapsed and she had to

---

[166] Usually a spiritual "impregnation" by a righteous soul to carry out some important task; this would be the inversion, a literal impregnation by evil, something like the dybbuk phenomenon and Venetianer's belief – seemingly shared by the others – that the nephilim had a dybbuk-like curse to reincarnate eternally.

fake her death in the Year without a Summer. *Harab Serapel*, the ravens of dispersion, came to roost in that fatal volcano, chilling the world. Their mistress could pretend to be another of those who died freezing in starvation and poverty, but her death would come a decade later. She raised her daughter, a strange girl who came to her impossibly late in life, in secrecy and destitution, but her unnatural beauty and striking stature made her a fetching bride. They said she looked youthful well into her fifties, and could see eye to eye with Lieb Guardsmen.

'That woman was a new nephila,' said the Rabbi. 'And my mother.'

I shrugged and asked him why that mattered. He seemed perplexed, with no Maimonides to guide him. He said he had lived his unnaturally-long life in religious terror, knowing that he was an abomination to God two-times over. That he could very well be the one-eyed Dajjal of the Moslems and the Antichrist. He then laughed nervously, and added maybe he was a cyclops, a monocular giant from the ancient sea. Even his name was a lie – he was Immanuel Frank. And a 'Bar Joseph.'

I said he could well be, but he could easily not be, too, and the latter seemed more likely. He could not fit into the Dorog, or into the Dead [Chasidim], and though he tried to reconcile it, the signs of the Christian Endtime and Moslem Doomsdays piled-up like press-stones on his chest. Or on his grave. He said it tore at him, tormented him, in the hoot of owls and the flight of dragons, in the crows and ravens, in the signs of dead men clinging to him since childhood. He felt as though every dybbuk had an open invite to his life.

'All the wonder in the world is your court, Rebbe,' I said. 'You're not here to hurt or deceive, or bring war and famine. You want to solve this nightmare. You want peace. You want to know the Truth of the World. Rabbi, if there was a child crying down there in the street, what would you do? An Arab, not a Jew.'

'What?' he said. 'I would comfort him. Find his home.'

'Then why do you think you are some great beast?' I asked. 'Deep down, you know this can't be the work of the Lord. Because you believe that the Lord would comfort the lost children as well. Not send them to die in the mud. This all seems like a mad joke or cruel torture, because this cosmic evil can't be true to you. If you're some antichrist, then let the world be damned.'

He went quiet, and stared at his hands, as crows gathered around us on the roof.

I asked if I could hold him. He said that he was uncomfortable holding a woman outside of his family. I shrugged again, and said I was uncomfortable touching anyone. He seemed reluctant still, and I said that my parents were gone and he had no house to his name, and asked if he wanted to be my adopted uncle. He started to cry. I didn't understand and apologized, but he hugged me. I actually liked the pressure, his coat on mine, as I had trained myself to enjoy Misha's touch. I took him into the night sky, and showed him Mount Zion, as the angels saw it."

The Valley of the Dead.

> Men track the path of Saturn as he swings
> Around the sun, circled with moons and rings;
> But who shall follow on the awful flight
> Of huge Orion through the dreadful deep?
> Far on the dark abyss he seems to sleep,
> Yet wanders the shoreless, old, inscrutable night.
> "Imagination," Edwin Markham, *Gates of Paradise*.

The nephilim hiked to the northwest of Jerusalem, to the Valley of the Rephaim. In Jude 6, it was said that the two-hundred [watcher] "angels who kept not to their first estate, but left their own habitation, were to be imprisoned in everlasting chains under darkness until the judgment of the great day," in the valleys of the Earth.

They spoke with a metallurgical surveyor in the Templer Colony of Emek Refaim. This part of the Hills of Hebron were relatively free of copper, bronze, and brass, the banes of the Nephilim. As Venetianer described, copper is the metal of God, and he interacts with humanity via copper and its alloys. In Zechariah 6, the Lord's four chariots ride out from between two mountains of bronze; in Deuteronomy 33:2, Habbakuk 3:3, and Judges 5:4, He rises from the Mountains of Seir, Sinai, and Parnan. And the Israelites warred with the Edomites for the copper of the Timna Valley, the fabled King Solomon's Mines, and the copper mines of Punon served as a major station of the Exodus. Deuteronomy 8:9 describes Israel as a land whose stones are iron and out of whose hills you can mine copper, and later Jews sealed sacred scrolls in copper. The Temple of Jerusalem was adorned with copper and brass; the Brazen Sea, a five-cubits-high basin used for ritual ablution, destroyed by the Chaldeans. Perhaps, Winepress suggested, the Holy of the Hollies and the Ark of the Covenant were primitive batteries or Leiden jars, their copper wires producing powerful electric shocks. The invention of the radio heralded the Apocalypse.

Takeuchi had traveled to the hill of Calvary, and quietly interred the bones that he believed belonged to Christ, late of Japan. He also visited Akeldama, the field of blood where the clay is said to be stained red by the suicide of Judas Iscariot. It was, until recently, a gentile cemetery. He said that it lent his pilgrimage a bit of symmetry.

In the dark of the night, the nephilim dug shallow graves into the earth. Those who wrote of the event noticed the "mania" of the event, "a morbid phantasmagoria" in Noun's words, as crows, ravens, and owls gathered around them. They seemed nervous about this, literally digging their own graves, and had taken to drink and smoke to relieve the tension. Once they had dug their graves, they took turns laying in them, preparing themselves. The nephilim prepared a rite of incubation, the act of sleeping in sacred spaces to open oneself up to divine inspiration, particularly notable from Solomon's pilgrimage to Gibeon to offer sacrifice in 1 Kings 3. The journey across Europe had been their initiation; this was the final ceremonial threshold, their death and rebirth.

At first the notion seemed terrible, but the earth seemed comforting, a warm embrace. The Gigantes, after all, were the Children of Gaia. Céleste and Gottlieb entered their large berth together, breathing slowly and trembling as the dirt was shoveled over them. Noun was next, as he had to be reassured due to his phobia of premature burial. He went in embracing several covered packs and with the lithopaedion at his feet, the center of the burial mound. Then came Van der Aarde and Winepress, and then Takeuchi. Finally, Venetianer, Zrno, and Anna descended into the widest of the graves, and Anna let go of the mass of dirt.

"And so we died and dreamed," Tom Noun said. "It was terrible, at first, like Merlin in the trap of Vivienne. But soon, I learned how to live without breathing, how to let the earth sustain me. We drank of the power of the now buried Ark and the sainted bones and the Golden Fleece. The Fleece hung in the Grove of War, protected by a legion of soldiers spawned from the sewn teeth of dragons. We opened ourselves up, as mediums to the dead, the living, and those yet to come. My mind stretched as easily as my flesh, and I joined the great sleep.

They came to me, all the sleeping giants of legend and kings under the mountain, Arthur, Ogier, Fionn mac Cumhaill, Artavasdes, and a hundred others. We were the Seven Sleepers of Ephesus, the People of the Cave, waking to a new world. It was something out of [George] MacDonald's *Lilith*, a house with countless sleeping beds. There were high souls there, Mahatmas and Ascended Beings and Universal Brothers. Beside us slept our dead loved ones who had yet to return to the world; two souls cradled Anna, and I could not see Zrno.

I realised that I slept in the darkness of Dudael, the Cauldron of God, where Raphael bound Azazel, in a blinding mask amid jagged stones. We were surrounded by copper chains and the bones of the Watchers, who resembled their giant children, as they were what man could have been without the Knowledge of Good and Evil. All sin was ascribed to Azazel, but such is the fate of the scapegoat.

And so I saw that the corruption of the Earth, the sins of the flesh, was just that – the sin of life, of freedom. I reached down into the earth with roots of meat and blood, and touched the dying races under the earth. Azazel took up the sins of the earth, and so we were free to go our way. Or, at least, to have the chance. It was our final role as nephilim to free man from its doom. The goat and the lamb.

I pondered my name, *noun*, likewise the word for "abyss" in the Coptic tongue, the moribund descendant of ancient Egyptian. A strange power surged through me, the strength of ancestors, of half-remembered pasts, of kings and demigods and titans. There was a storm all around us, the raging soul of von Böhm, or Chazaqiel, his winds protecting us from the wings and eyes of angels. Zrno was there, two, the dragon-man, his soul blazing and towering and circling our private world, with razor a sword and his breath a flame to torment the rebel angels who would stop us. There was a man in black with a collection of keys, who paced through the graves as though the earth were air, and whenever the heavenly curse threatened to chain us in copper, he turned his keys and liberated us.

I was unchained from my life, and went deep into the past, hearing the drums of Shiva in my head. I was Kakayyar Bhujander, the great astrologer. I was Tieresias of two sexes. I was with my father, and our hidden namesake, the two-headed giant Gogmagog. I was of Albion. I saw the plains of Britain's battles, and I was there with Siegfried, side by side. I shifted my shape side by side with the soul who would be von Böhm, the Thunderer. I spoke to John Dee in dreams with Anna and Zrno by my side, whispering about the British Empire. And I was Merlin in the trap of Vivienne.

I was with my friends, in ancient times, teaching men the arts of knives and swords, the crafting of shields and armour, jewels and paints and dyes and make-up, the arts and the stars and the weather and magics. We were shining with the constellations of Orion and Draco and the Dog Star. We were teachers. We were Promethean. We were liberators.

I appeared to them. The Other Men, the secret people, in their forests and caves and limestone palaces under the world. All of them, hundreds and hundreds every hour, burning and straining against my grave. I remember looking into the eyes of Siobhán, as she twitched, dying in the age of cold iron. She was terrified, at first, but then embraced me and kissed me. There was a roiling change in the world, and she was wearing the wizened mask of the Green Man. I screamed as she touched my womb, and I said I would free her. I told them all I would free them, save them from this grave.'

Venetianer described his time, saying that he "fell through the past, tumbling backwards, scraping against the hyper-modern wall of history. I was not anchored by the souls of the past; I only knew my first incarnation. I was a fresh soul.

The best I can liken it to was the eye-opening awaking that follows a brush with death. I saw this sea of souls, the one hundred and ninety-eight who fell (apart from their betrayers, Yaqum and Ramiel), and the thirty-six souls of first generation of nephilim, plus the special one, the mortal door of our history. I realized, then, why Father Avezzano was so open, such a potent medium – he was not a 'true' angelic soul, but that of our racial mother, Na'amah, condemned to reincarnate with them. He was Nehemoth, the Whisperer, the spirit of ghostly sounds in the night. We had these souls, cycling through the generations, from the watchers to the gibborim to the rephaim on down to us.

That was at the root of the abomination; that these souls, these non-angelic angels, embodied concepts outside of Divinity, outside of authority, the chaoses that keep the world off-kilter and wrong. Biology, weather, fears, spontaneous transmutation, suggestions, madness, entropy, mathematical paradoxes, and oddities. And, for me, the greatest abomination of all, the transmission of thoughts and concepts. As long as we exist, there is always a lack of control, a touch of chaos outside of fate. We may be part of the Divine plan, Free Will. Or Wills. The envy of the angels.

We may be going forth to break down an imbalanced system, the sinister web of fate. Perhaps we were evil, and wrong. But our ages of destruction and secrecy have forced us to be smaller, rebellious rather than tyrannous, thoughtful rather
than cruel. Perhaps we have learned. Perhaps everyone can learn.

Without an anchor, I saw myself free from the chains of
time. I appeared in St. Petersburg, where I gibbered like a mad man, stumbling in the strong body I had when I was barely in my second decade. When I was asked what happened, I told the truth, just as Mr. Spare had, the naked honesty of the lost soul; I was taken before the Queen, the Empress, Catherine the Great, and I realized why I had come here. I was honest, too honest, as I was interrogated, and foretold the death of Paul, her death, the invasion of Napoleon, the star Wormwood, and the Fall of the Romanov family. I was ejected from the palace as a fool, but my Cassandra warnings came true.

I tumbled, tumbled into the gulf of gilgul, far back into time, into the lives of other giants. At one point, I hung on a tree, a shaman seeking wisdom – Hermann was there too, hammer in hand. At another, I was a giant king, wrestling with a hairy Other.

I saw the dawn of all things, the coiling of Gadreel, the 'Wall of God' who became Samyaza. And I pondered the muddled mystery of Genesis's use of YHWH and Elohim, and the Gnostics. I had always despised their slander of the God of Israel, and found its continuity nonsensical. But in Paradise, the serpent Gadreel spoke the truth, and the curse upon the serpent's seed foretold the fall of the Sons of God – had the Gnostic deception only extended to the Garden? Had God sent the serpent, that seraph, its form enshrined by the Nehushtan, to save us from some great falsehood? I wondered who that Demiurge was, who damned Eve's children to eternal war against the spawn of Samyaza, as I cycled through a hundred lives.

Then I was myself, speaking to a writer who wished to write about a sea disaster, and I told him about the Titanic, Leviathan, only to later find him dead. I visited countless people, across a thousand ages, and then I knew rest."

Armageddon

"The old world is dying away, and the new world struggles to come forth; now is the time of monsters." - Antonio Gramsci

The narrative of the "nine giants" resumes on 15 September 1918, when they described themselves rising from their graves with a sense of destiny and an eerie calm.

Mihajlo recorded that the last person to be disinterred was Takeuchi, as the ground had frozen into a permafrost that reminded Anna and Zrno of the Russian tundra. Céleste thawed the soil, and Takeuchi awoke in a panic. The rest of the group was also terrified, as there was someone else in his grave, a pale woman. Anna bolted into the sky as she saw the Haligonian again, clinging to Takeuchi's back.

Takeuchi crawled away from her, claiming that he dreamed that there was a city beneath him, and it was "that thing," gesturing at the pale woman.

The Haligonian looked shocked too, noting that the last

thing she remembered was walking in Beirut, then Halifax again, then London, and finally in Buenos Aires, which caused it to snow in June (which would have been the 22nd). She shook her
head, and said that she was the spirit of the deep waters, the salty sea - Tehom, Tannin, Lotan, Haurun, Rahab, Bashan, Bahamut, Tiamat, Jörmungandr, Ur, Bar-Spag, the Vishap of Ararat, and Leviathan.

Zrno wrote that he "snapped at her, telling her to stick with one name. I was sick of the aliases, and complained that I was the only one that consistently used mine. Anna shot a glance at Venetianer that I didn't understand at first, until I suddenly did, as though the Rabbi's mind had overflown to me.

'What are you, exactly?' Tom Noun asked, noticing she spoke English. 'Some kind of higher concept incarnated? Some ideal daimon out of Iamblichus?'

'Yes," she said. 'Something like that.'

'We were enemies before,' I said. 'Why this turn?'

'Look,' she said. 'I just want to end. To stop this. I was destroyed before. I was taught my lesson. I don't need to be taught for eternity.'

'What do you think we can do?' Tom Noun asked. 'What do you want?'

'I was with you, among the dead,' she said. 'One of your kind spoke to me, worked with me. Leviathan, Behemoth, Ziz, Abaddon, the Heavenly Spheres...we're all souls and ideas and places. God is a place, the Place, *Ha-Makom*. Armageddon, too, is a place and a time and a concept. A powerful one. But so is the deep blue sea.'

'What do you mean?' asked Gottlieb. 'What are you proposing?'

'I'll help you,' she said bluntly. 'I'll weaken the power of this place. It's fire, brimstone, it's stone and sand...What about another flood?'

'Symmetry,' Tom Noun said, looking around as his colleagues. 'It would be a pleasant way for the nephilim to go out.'"

As they travelled to the city to have a final feast, Gottlieb searched for the colonists of the German Temple Society, wishing to taste their wine and oranges once more – but the British had sent them to a concentration camp at Helwan, outside of Cairo. The other colonies he could remember – Wilhelma, Walhalla, Waldheim, and Bethelhem, had likewise been cleared of their two thousand Templer inhabitants.

Mihajlo continued:

"I promised I would finish it.

From Jerusalem, we followed the 38th Royal Fusiliers, the Jewish Battalion, to the Plain of Sharon. It was a place of plague, a malarial swamp, exacerbated by the uprooting of countless trees to feed the Sultan's war machine. Only the southeast remained bearable, due to the drainage properties of introduced Eucalyptus trees – a sight that puzzled and excited the Australian cavalry attached to Allenby, poised to take Kefar Sava. Looking over the order of battle and intelligence on the enemy gathered in the Judean Hills, it seemed as if all the world was here, despite the thin numbers.

We saw peoples, multitudes, nations and languages from all across the waters- the 4th and 5th Cavalry Division and the 3rd Lahore Infantry and 7th Meerut of the British Indian Army, fresh from the Western front and Mesopotamian – their travel had been eased by the the fact that the Euphrates is ominously shallow and dry in September. The infantry had been reformed to match the Indians, mixing British, South Africans, and Australians; only the 54th (East Anglian) Division stayed all British, and even then, Allenby attached a brigade of French North Africans and Armenians. One mixed unit, Chaytor's Force, was a hodgepodge of infantry, mounted, and artillery elements. They had spent time before the battle creating a phantom cavalry force, dummy positions, and even had mules drag fake automobile tracks. An Australian Light Horse regiment swept down from Abu Tellul, after fierce fighting against the German 11th Reserve Battalion. From the east of the Jordan rode Emir Feysal's Northern Arab Army, a rebellion of formerly Ottoman Arab conscripts led by the deserter Jafar Pasha, along with a supply line from Aqaba and the Imperial Camel Corps, Indian gunners, British armoured cars, and a battery of Franco-Algerian mountaineers. Two thousand camels on the Plain of Esdraelon - what a sight! We saw the Egyptians, who had made a historical habit of coming up Armageddon way, in the day of the Pharaoh Neco on up to Napoleon's ride to Nazareth.

And then came the bedouin irregulars of T.E. Lawrence, fresh from raids against the railways of Hejaz. While Lawrence is a legend, his Arabs were horribly unruly compared to the Northerners and Egyptians and the men under Jafar. They were harassers on the flanks, best suited to demolitions and plundering, penetrating with wedges of horse and Garland Trench Mortars. Some even used the make-shift [Garland] Mark I grenade, food tins filled with barbed wire and casing.

There was a swarm of runners and other couriers between the armies, including pigeons, and both sides defaulted to using a network of heliographs. That was the key to it all; the heliographs' ability to direct light and encode information in nothing more than flashes, and we had seen the codebook of the angels in Raduriel. Radio contact had been difficult; The bedouins were poorly equipped, there was a confusion of languages, and a storm raged on the Sun. The star had entered a cycle known as the Modern Maximum in 1914, and a surge in magnetic activity had raged since August of 1917. March saw a particularly intense flare up that fried the air into September, the peak of Solar Cycle 15. Perhaps it was the fourth angel, pouring his vial of wrath into the Sun. Perhaps it was the sleeping spirit of the Watcher Daniel, who showed Mankind the signs of the Sun, lending aid to his children. In any case, the light of Armageddon was poisoned by the strange sun.

There were the armies of Man, surging through the three valleys around the 7th and 8th Ottoman Army's holding in Judea's bloodied hills.

The Ottomans were under the umbrella of the Yıldırım Army Group, originally commanded by General Erich von Falkenhayn, built to take Baghdad but suddenly sent on a mission to seize Jerusalem, and with a policy of feints and retreats and rapid redirection, as Ottoman static positions had not been particularly successful outside of the Dardanielles. Their focus on such tactics may have inspired their name - Yıldırım meant Thunderbolt or Lightning. The group was a chimera of German officers, Turks, and a hodgepodge of the other peoples of the Sultanate; I had expected fezes and scimitars, but they had stahlhelms and potato-masher grenades, and combined arms, artillery and gun nests. Gog led by Magog, behind their iron walls. We later learned that it was as messy as it sounded, and Otto Liman von Sanders had replaced von Falkenhayn. Falkenhayn was hated by the Turks, and failed at Gaza and Jerusalem; von Sanders held Gallipoli, and decided that he knew how to defend against the British and Arabs. He decided that he would stand at Armageddon, and humiliate the Empire once again.

They rode on the sites of the death and failure of Zhazih, Josiah, Hadad-rimmon and Sisera, and the Kings of Canaan. They stood in the places of triumph of Gideon and Barak.

Was Allenby Gideon, the pious driver of men and horses? Was Lawrence that hewer who led a small elite to victory against the horde? Were the Turks Barak, the army of the righteous? It was there in the name, echoing through history – 'Thunderbolt' and 'Lightning.'

I heard a strange yet familiar voice in my head say, 'It is done.'

The angels poured the seventh bowl, and down came wrath, with fire from the altar hurled to the earth, with peals of thunder and rumblings of the earth. Lightning flashed across the sky. Hundred pound hailstones rained over the hills, crushing men and horse and camel, a plague of iron. It was unlike anything felt or heard in the age of the Revelator, yet a trivial exercise in our own.

The XXI Corps of Lieutenant General Bulfin pushed forth under a creeping barrage that shattered the cracked plain, breaking through the front line of the Turks and Germans. Chetwode's XX Corps pushed against the Turks as well, sweeping towards Nablus, followed by Chaytor's Force cutting off the bridges of the Jordan.

Then came the British planes, bombing the Turkish lines of retreat, destroying the metalled roads and rails to Tiberias, and trapping supply lines away from the hills. I will never forget the image of Bedouins charging forward with scimitars, supported by aeroplanes and cars of the 12th light Armoured Motor Battery.

I wish I was there, in the breach, fighting against the Turks as my ancestors did. But I would only slow them down. I was left to be an observer, the man above the battlefield, taking it all in with my keen perception from the Hill of Megiddo proper. My eyes and fingers, at least, were still faster than bullets. And that long sleep had awakened something in me, a vastness of vision and thought that I could not then understand.

It was disappointing, however, that the hill of Armageddon was the most peaceful place at Armageddon.

A shell shook my position, kicking up a wall of dust. I covered the elaborate spheres and cubes of pure quartz at my side, filled with twisting, refracting labyrinths. As I coughed into my handkerchief, a figure walked out of the sepia haze, like a man stepping out of a faded photograph.

My blood ran cold. He turned to sit next to me, setting down his Browning automatic pistol and his sandwich.

'Gavrilo?' I said, through the pains of my cough and my contracting chest.

'Gabriel,' he said. 'Join me, Michael. Open your eyes.'

And I saw everything though a thousand eyes and wings of flaming swords. In between the brilliant flashes of the archangel's eight wings, I briefly glimpsed four faces – a bull, a lion, an eagle, and a featureless man, each one forever facing in a cardinal direction as it moved. But the whirlwind of faces and feathers stopped, and I saw my brother's face.

We were 'killed' by a legion of demons in retaliation for casting down the Dragon in November of 1879[167]. But Michael and I survived as Bodiless Powers of Heaven, rejoining those twin emanations of the Throne, the *shārim* Sandalphon and Metatron. We incarnated into human flesh, as the Spirit once did – in 1884. We were false nephilim, *good* nephilim, part of the world's order. But something terrible happened, and we forgot what we were, sleeping through the war. Only in death did one remember, while the other became the enemy. He was lost to heaven. But here, at Armageddon, where the old gods fled, they could reunite.

In an act of cosmic irony, the Strong Man of God was incarnated in a weak, frail form, while He Who is Like God was incarnated in the form of an atheist anarchist abomination. We were called Princep, *Prince* in the Latin, or Prinzep, meaning *Testament*, for God also loves his Word play.

And here we are- Gabriel Princep, the Archangel of the Awakening, the one whose Horn blast began the War, and Michael Princep, the Archangel of Soldiers, whose Sword shall end the War to End All Wars.

'This can't be true,' I said to him. I rose up, towering over my

---

[167] Occultists Franz von Baader, Rudolf Steiner, Eliphas Levi, and Louis Claude de St. Martin all identified 1879 as the year that the Archangel Michael defeated the Dragon, with Steiner in particular specifying November.

smaller brother. Or, the angel-thing pretending to be my brother. 'No, no no...stop this.'

'Everything will stop soon, Miho,' he said. 'It's almost over. Then we can go home.'

I muttered no in an idiotic loop of disbelief. He simply told me to open my eyes once more.

I saw it all, the vicissitudes of a war both inevitable and impossible. Come eat the flesh of kings, the flesh of captains, and the flesh of Gibborim, the flesh of horses and their riders, and the flesh of all men, both free and slave, both small and great. I saw them all as I fought against time and destiny and nature and all those worthless words.

The Haligonian had gone ahead, to the shore of Galilee in the shadow of Tiberias, reaching down into the ancient cairns buried beneath the waters. She insinuated herself into this mythic space, Armageddon, weakening a hill of stone and scrub with water and salt and scale.

The shore and sea echoed with a scream like a ship's whistle and a fog horn. Steam rose from a wound on her back as she tumbled into the water under the blow of an ax that hit like a freight train.

Leviathan spat the water from her mouth and looked back at her attacker, a towering man in red doctor flannel wielding an ax and with a hauling-ox by his side, its sledge loaded with cedars. Beside them, watching from a landed plane, was their sister, adorned with the insignia of Venus.

'Behemoth,' she said, locking eyes with the timberjack. He took another chop at her, which would have split apart a mortal woman and buried the ax into the ground. But only steam and smoke rose from a bloodless slit. Behemoth's vision clouded, and the Ziz reached up to turn on the propeller to scatter the smoke.

She was gone.

The timberjack kicked at the water, demanding that she come out and fight. The image of Rahab danced under the water, the reflection of nothing. She shook her head, and the antediluvian megaliths below the murky depths seemed to throb like a heart.

The reflection rippled under a petulant ax blow. The water danced with the images of cities, megaliths, and the restful dead. And so the coils of Leviathan wrapped around Armageddon.

Batoul Chedid hesitated during her raid against the Turkish position, sending supplies into Galilee as she moved, objects in space. Space, however, had constricted around her; there was now a living wall around battle.

'But the deer's story ended, in the manner of the hunted; suddenly, and at the crack of a gun,' said the Storyteller from his sniper's perch. I had never met this towering man, but identified at once. He coughed, like my brother had. There was a sickness in his lungs, in his muscles, in his guts, a growing cancer of giant's tissue.

His target quivered on the ground of the supply tent, and slipped away from him. But he knew he had got a solid shot on her, dead center of the torso.

She reappeared in a clearing of scrubland, next to her ally, her knight, Tariel Ketelauri. The Knight gasped and kneeled down, and the Arab irregulars gathered to her side. One of them released the kerchief over his mouth, and spoke with the language from before the Confusion. She was surprised to see a Japanese face in the crowd, but her attention was grabbed by the beetle burrowing into her wound and disappearing.

'Your death is delayed,' said the Man. 'I can transfer the consequences of this wound. But I need you two to help me. Perhaps to your personal detriment, but to the benefit of the world.'

'What do you need?' said the knight, cautiously.

'There is a barrier around this battlefield,' said Takeuchi. 'I need it strengthened. And I need this space, the space behind this space, sealed. Or contracted. The higher planes that you travel through.'

'I won't be able to escape,' said the Phoenician.

'I know,' he said. 'But neither can the destruction of all things.'

She nodded, weakly.

'This is the end, isn't it?' she said.

'Yes. You must strain yourselves to the breaking point, moments from death...and I will take the strain,' said Takeuchi. 'Afterwards, carry her out, if you can.'

The network of signalling mirrors was the heart of our gambit, our hopes pinned on my crystal ball and kaleidoscope, conjured up from

Armageddon's sand with heat and alchemy. I could not move them, nor dare touch them, such was their density and mass, Anna's most subtle and dangerous working. But it was Siegfried who masterminded the work, who carried out the most dangerous leg of the gambit.

Siegfried's head swam, and he stumbled as he climbed the final hill behind the Turkish position. He had placed the crystals. Now, all that was left was to tilt the mirror, and run.

But then he stumbled, and slid down the hill as the earth shook under an Australian artillery strike. He winced as a stone struck his side, the spot where he had been bled. Noun had closed the flesh, but the muscle was still raw and a bruise welled up.

An angel noticed his tumble. They knew of the invisible man, and had a million eyes focused on him, hunting for every grain of sand and speck of dust and pebble out of place. They hung above the battlefield, waiting for the most dangerous of the nephilim to fall.

They took no chances, and the shell struck his position, a thunderstone from the heavens.

Tom Noun tried to calm himself. There is always terror in the face of the divine, like Semele consumed by the awe of Zeus, only to be sewn into his divine father's thigh. Or something to that effect, he thought.

He caught himself thinking of motherhood as he mixed salt water with fresh water and blood. Of his own mother. Of the spirit he felt enter Van der Aarde. Of the lithopaedion that he took into himself, and its power, and the echoes of Typhon.

He mixed the pink concoction with the earth and turned in a spiral through the haze of artillery dust by the sea, when he saw the shadow of a great beast. It was then that he lay down in the spiral, bleeding from his own arms.

The lion, of gold and the raging fire of the sun, hesitated. 'What trickery is this, nameless one?'

'Oh,' he said. 'A shell game. Or the lion and the lamb.'

The lion roared, and all who heard it felt a strange rage, the terror of a beast ready to devour its prey.

'I suppose you're going to eat me then,' said Noun, touching the black roots growing from his blood. 'Ariel is it? The lion of God? Rather literal.'

Noun reached up, and slipped his hand into the lion's mouth. He gasped in pain, because something inside of him kicked. As did I. Something in the stump of my leg gushing.

It was then that the lion pulled back in confusion. Noun's hand was gone, but he did not destroy it. But he tasted something strange.

'You must go the way of all flesh,' said Noun. 'Incarnation. Know the sad fate of Christ condemned and Azazel, the Scapegoat.'

'What?' Roared the Lion of God, struggling with his words, as he now needed to force his breath through a feline throat.

'It's simple,' Noun said. "But I'm not a complete freak, so I feel no need to demonstrate my talents."

The lion leaped through Noun.

'It's a switch,' Noun said. 'You ate the food of fairies. Or my hand, as it were. I'm a creature of flesh, and its changing. I know my nature. Behold the Lamb, for you too are flesh.'

Tom Noun began to sink into the earth.

'But that's the trick with magic. It's always a bit of work and bookkeeping. The other kind, that dying race, would not last past the 20th century. Not with their trembling hands and building hereditary disorders. Not in an age of iron and cameras
and felled forests.'

The lion roared again.

'So,' Tom Noun said, tired. 'I'm...spirit doesn't quite suit me, but it will suit them. They'll live on as the little fairybook creatures. The wild men in the woods. The people with wings and fins and tails. In the corners of the map, the corners of the eye. But...'

Tom Noun began to sink, and became something closer to his sister, and a strange green pallor came over his skin. The forgotten yet fresh matrix in him contracted. The stone child, too, dissolved in him, the price of this great work. He heard the crack of rifles and startled Arabs saw a lion appear from the dust, and the new lion understood nothing.

As Tom, of the name Gogmagog, sunk into the earth, black flowers grew, tipped with white blossom.

'So,' the Scion said, looking up at the crows. 'So there is the moly, that grows from the blood of giants.'

And then he was no longer distinct from the earth.

The Heavenly Host and the Rebellion fell into discord. Some froze in place, while others took advantage of this weakness, this flesh, and traded lives on both sides with knives and bullets and shells, a reckless abandon that consigned both to oblivion. Great Raziel, commanding a vast host in the form of an airplane, suddenly sputtered and collapsed. He briefly revealed his Ophani form, a rolling mass of wheels and chitinous limbs, before he tumbled into the ground and broke into burning, spinning bones.

Phanuel, one of the last of the great angels, hatched a plot to save the grand design of history. He was the Face of God, and with a beautiful, bony visage, turned his sky-blue eyes upward, and began a great magical rite. He was the arch-enemy of Belial, and the destruction of his rival had created a great imbalance in the heavenly equation.

The other angels looked at him in horror, as this was a blasphemous working. Stars burnt out and a great heat rose over the desert. He felt his heart, mortal flesh, seize up. Other angels, embodied in unmarked uniforms with unfamiliar faces, began to howl in pain. A squadron of demons attempted to charge him, but three fell dead from the pain, while another half a dozen collapsed under shock of British artillery.

It was worth the cost, Phanuel told himself. Some would survive, he knew. He was the angel of repentance, of the hope of eternal life, and he could not brook a mortal fate for his kindred. The Kingdoms of the world will be the kingdoms of our Lord, and He shall reign forever.

The rebus, that nephel who had become some balance of the sky and the earth, male and female, magic and mundane, flesh and spirit, had been repelled, its final prison destroyed. But Phanuel noted the cost – holes in the night's sky, holes in his allies. Few of them had survived, rebel and loyalist alike, and they had dimmed. Time had to be bought, until the Lamb could rise from the Templer's Bethlehem. Time...they needed time.

The angels were beings of light once more, but there was less magic in them, less divinity in their radiance. It was not the splendour of heavens, of the Throne, but a light from a candle or a heated filament. They were things of particles now. Phanuel fell to his knees in mortal pain, knowing that he had sacrificed his future for a last shot at eternity for his Host, his people.

I could almost pity him.

Jacoba van der Aarde lay bleeding at the heliographic mirror where Gottlieb had left her, fumbling for the portable radio. There was an indignity to it all; the angels had not even known she was there. They were aiming for the damn German. She caught herself praying for it to work, and almost laughed at herself.

God can't hear you, Coba, she thought. She choked on her blood as she forced the broken wires together. They weren't severed by the shelling, only shaken apart, as she imagined most of her had been. Crickets chirped and slashed in her pooling blood. She couldn't see out of her right eye, and there was a windblown, sweeping pain where that ear should be.

God can't hear you, Coba. But anyone listening could. Anyone of the air and the invisible energies. Anyone on this channel.

Coba spoke words. Any words would do. But she thought back to the code heard on Patmos, the song of Raduriel. The dying world needed a song. She mumbled a tune that her mother had used to lull her to sleep. A song she had sang to dying men. A song she had muttered to Rowan as he drifted off to sleep in her arms. *Schoon lief, Schoon lief...*

They heard her. She turned the mirror as she fell backwards, and the light of the sun spun and danced wildly.

But it did not matter.

If you heard her, she could not miss. There was no defense. She told herself that she only had to hold on.

A glorious Fata Morgana distorted the upper air of Megiddo, and for a moment, it was as though the horses of Lawrence's Arabs rode on the blazing horizon.

Beneath roiling layers of heat and freezing air that bent the light like the mirages of the poles and the tropics, Céleste stood solemnly. The light of the angels warring in the air flickered and twisted like auroras.

But this was just an annoyance, one that could easily be solved. She was quickly located at the eye of the storm, striking and easy to strike.

An angel approached her, diving from the sky, shifting from the form of an airplane to a classical mannish form, flaming sword in hand.

'Dramatic,' she said.

'You are an abomination, but you deserve to fight with honor,' said the warrior angel.

'Thank you,' she said. 'I've been called worse.'

'Draw your weapon or stoke your flame, Granddaughter of God,' said the angel, as a squadron of angels landed around her.

'No,' she said.

The angelic sword extinguished, and she sat on the ground, next to a model of the world made from delicate ice and superheated sand.

She raised it up to them.

'Beautiful, no?' she asked.

'It is,' said the angel, unsure of what to do.

'I spent my life scared and angry. I enjoyed pain. Inflicting it. Death, and war, and morbid things... This is what I should have done with my life,' she said. 'This is what you should do with power.'

The angels said nothing.

'I barely lived into my second decade, no money, no opportunities,' she said. 'What was your excuse? Nigh omnipotent for an eternity. And you decide to throw it into a fire. A war. This...battle. Why not make something beautiful?'

The angel Eremiel planted his sword in the ground, and looked at her with an inscrutable intensity.

'Why not...why don't you just stop?' she said.

Another angel, Beburos, an invisible, abstract thing with a crocodilian head and wings tipped in spines, sent a barrage of javelins into her. She turned to face her attacker, weakly, but only felt its heat.

She reached down and touched the wounds that passed clean through her chest, and cauterized them.

'I decorated them with frost. If only you could have seen them,' she said, weakly, her eyes closed as she tried to power through the pain. There was no use in saving her breath, she felt. The frost would thaw with her death.

She clung to the globe, the work of art, clinging to it with her body, trying to manage her heat.

'Do not regard me with such hate,' said Beburos. 'She was a nephela.'

The angel Eremiel flew away, saying nothing.

And then everything happened in a literal flash.

Sir Tariel covered Batoul Chedid and pulled her close. His sword thrust upward at something in the sky, and, briefly, Batoul saw something like a great winged serpent made of a cold blue light, something horrible and ancient and with a cruelty that scalded her skin with its pungent hatred. She would have been destroyed by its heat if not for her Tariel's borrowed might.

She shouted in outrage as her knight fell dead in her arms, his weight pulling her down with him. His chains broke and turned to rust. That living city outside of the World cracked around her, crushed up into a single wall around Armageddon. An invisible globe of spirits dominated the ether, with the wounded dragon sputtering within, trying to regain its form. A swarm of crows as thick as locusts, fat on the swarm of Beelzebub, flicked around her, a darkness that dropped bombs of light. It was alchemy, the Promethean fire of the sun, exploding in the heart of the human soul, establishing a heroic, human authority over this place and time of mythic war.

Batoul cried out, her heart breaking even as the death of her ally lent her a strength she had never known before. The spiritual light washed over her like a Flood. There was a sudden shock from some great force, something demonic and horrible that would destroy the world. She felt it, the evil that the traveller told her about, and she fully committed, came to believe – and she would not let the force that killed her knight go free. She turned her gaze, and they went black. She felt empty and alone as her familiars, the whites of her eyes, burnt away, consumed to feed this trap, binding space and time, slaying that dragon that slew her St. George.

That profane light swept away the angels, and there were flashes in the sky and reports that could not be accounted for by Turk and German, Briton and Arab.

The tarnished, overwhelmed creatures of light were forced through signalling mirrors and crystals of frost and ice and electrical quartz, directed by the Schildbreker and the Ghostly knight. This artillery strike from behind the world allowed only one narrow passage for the blast to expand into, a flood of blazing starlight forced through a hose. I watched the light slowly trickle towards me, and raised my terrible swift sword. Gabriel slowly looked at me. Slower and slower.

I had learned something from Uriel, about the speed of light, and I wished I was smart enough to go into physics, because I could see it. I can move with the rapidity of angels. But that is just the upside of the talent. What comes up must come down. I must, logically, be able to slow things down. Not perfectly, but Céleste's mastery of heat chilled the molasses light into solid gold. And so I gently poured the Host and the Rebellion into the Crystal Sphere, where the Absolute met absolute zero.

I had realized then, just as Venetianer claimed that the hell of Venus only appeared subterranean, as the prophets and seers were looking up at its stormy sky, that the crystal spheres of the heavens may have simply been this trap. Angels compressed and shifting with the moving music of the spheres, the song of Van der Aarde slowed to a trickle. Maybe all prophecy was a distress signal, thrown back into the past to change their fate.

But there was a black spot there, a place so dense that it was inescapable, the final working of Anna. She had burnt out all of her power over gravitation to keep it together, and so she stayed, not far away with her rifle, defending me.

Gabriel's gaze finally met mine, and he noticed the betrayal. He gasped with a look of pain as he saw the circle of blood separating us. We had learned the trick from Kiss and Typhon, the magic circle of giant's blood. It became visible as Gottlieb finally slipped away.

He had dragged himself to Céleste, nearly two hundred kilometers, one sheer force of will. His left leg had been ruined, the force of the blast shattering the bones of that foot. He could at least feel his right leg, and he could tell that his already weakened lungs were liquid. He was going to die.

But he was not going to die without seeing her again. She was sprawled in the earth far behind the clashing cavalry lines. He crawled towards her. His ears felt like they were going to burst as airplanes swooped low over the ground.

The angels were gone, trapped. She was alone. He wouldn't let her die alone. Or, maybe she was simply wounded. Maybe she was incapacitated. Maybe she would survive him.

He found her not long after, and knew that wasn't true.

He said her name. She gasped and returned the favor. Her eyes were closed. Gottlieb could tell she was afraid to see what happened. He took her by the neck, sweeping his hand under her chin, so she could turn and look him in the eye without glancing down at the wounds.

'Siegfried?' she said. 'I feel strange.'

'Understandable,' Gottlieb said. 'I...I don't know...'

'It's a kind of numbness,' she said. 'But with a twinge.'

'You're cold, dear,' Gottlieb said.

'I'm cold,' she said with a laugh. I haven't felt cold since I was seven. I...I forgot this.'

'I'm so sorry, Céleste,' Gottlieb said.

'No, it's fine,' she said. 'Cold's not bad when someone...someone's there. Just there. You never realise how much you need someone until you're freezing.'

'That... was adequate,' he said.

'Accommodating,' she said.

'Pleasant,' he said.

'I wouldn't say that,' Céleste said. 'I wouldn't have minded if it lasted a little while longer.'

'Agreed,' he said.

'Cigarette?' offered Céleste.

He said 'no thanks.'

'Good, I only have one,' she said. But she did nothing. She then added, with a hint of panic in her voice, 'Is my arm still there?'

Gottlieb fumbled for her packet, and pulled out the cigarette, and put it to her lips. It lit with a guttering flame after several tries. Gottlieb wiped the spit from her lips, and set his hand across her chest, so he could feel her hair.

'It was not bad, for a farm boy and a street kid,' she said. 'Not a...not a..'

'Goodnight, blue eyes,' he said.

'Goodnight, blue eyes,' she muttered.

And so went the light.

As the Turkish battle lines collapsed further, and their forces were driven back to Damascus, one man waded through the fray, unafraid of gunfire or horsemen. Ender Hoca fought against the agony in his rotting bones, supporting himself on the reins of a horse with no rider, to reach the broken form of Batoul Chedid, who lay next to a body bathed in blood, a dead beetle in his hand. The ring on Chedid's hand, the Seal of Solomon she had plundered from below the Temple, had melted into her knuckle bone. The grand binding of the angels and demons of Armageddon had destroyed it, burning out the captured light of the Pleiades and overwhelming its magics in the feat. I had entrusted this artifact to Israel's monarch long ago, after forging it in the hearts of the Seven Sister stars.

'The Phoenician,' he said.

'Circassian,' she said, weakly, before spitting up blood and a tooth.

'My name is Ender,' he said.

'Oh,' she said. 'You know my name, Batoul Chedid. Manon.'

'What happened?' Ender asked.

'I think we avoided the end of the world,' she said. 'There were demons, dragons...maybe angels.'

'Angels?' Ender said, filled with the confirmation of the religious horror swelling inside of him all year, festering alongside his cancer.

'Yes, I think I helped kill angels and demons,' she said. 'Not sure what that means. There might have been jinn there. Maybe this was the last crusade. Hehe, we took Jerusalem, *habibi*, we'll take back Constantinople...'

'Did you see God?' Ender said.

'Does anyone?' she said. 'I don't know what happens now.'

'You won this battle,' Ender said. 'You Arabs have us running. The English have their hands around the throat of Syria.'

'No,' she said. 'When I die. Will I go to heaven? Will I go to hell? Is there a heaven or hell after this?'

'Allah alone knows all,' Ender said.

'I suppose so,' she said. She looked at the two dead men next to her.

'Did these...those things in the air kill them?' Ender asked, trying to come to terms with the evidence and testimony before him.

'They died from the strain of...of the end of the angels,' she said. 'My knight made me strong and my enemies weak...and this pilgrim from the East saved everyone here from their counterattack. He took their killing light for us... We all would have burned from their spite.'

'Why haven't you left?' Ender asked. 'Why not leap away again?'

'I'm done,' she said. 'I used myself up.'

'Why didn't you tell me?' Ender asked. 'About this?'

'You're the storyteller,' she said. 'When I learned what you could do, I resolved to keep you in the dark. We needed your uncertainty.'

Ender let out a snort, the closest approximation of a laugh his lungs would allow. He knelt down and picked her up. She was too weak to fight him as he put her in the saddle and slipped her dead left leg into the stirrup. He handed her the Georgian's scimitar and her revolver, after making sure it was empty, and covered her head with her fallen hat after brushing it clean of dust.

'Why?' she asked.

'An Arabian warrior should die in the saddle, sword in hand,' he said.

'I'm a Phoenician,' she said. 'The Phoenician.'

'And so the Phoenician rode to the ancient port,' Ender said. 'Did she find her death along its stony shore, or freedom in the wine-dark sea? None would know. That was the nature of freedom. Its story is always uncertain.'

'Thank you, *habibi*. See you in hell,' she said with a weak smile, as she tried to stay on the horse as it began its gallop. Of what happened to her and the Turk afterwards, I can say no more, as the last ember of his talents forbade me.

Why is pilgrimage a sacred act? Why does it matter? It seems like a nearly universal notion in religion, as far as I can tell. But why should you travel to a physical place when dealing with the spiritual world?

Because it's the sacredness of the destination. The spent time, the sacrificed energy. The thought and effort, the emotional catharsis of reaching a place, the wonder set before your eyes.

We had made our great pilgrimage.

Phanuel wandered through the encampment of Chaytor's Force, shaking with grief at what he had done. He was alone, it seemed, but there had to be something. Where were Gabriel and Michael? Where was Gabuthelon and Aker? Zebuleon, Arphugitonos, and Beburos –

those governors at the end of the world? God would not let him fail, would not let Armageddon end in such a pathetic mess. He had never used those knees. The last time he was alive, he was a great lizard, with only the flickers of animal consciousness, glancing up at that manifestation of Wormwood in the sky, blazing and burning. Mankind had seen his bones in the earth, turned to black stone. And so he had become a great dragon in their collective understanding, a lizard and bird blazing with meteoric fires.

Now, he just had the knees of a middle-aged man, the worst of God's creations. As he stumbled, he caught a glimpse of a tall man within the British tent. He waved him inside: 'Come in. Come in.'

The tent was vast on the inside, like the caravans of storytale jinn. It was made of pieces of city, doors and concrete and pieces of ship all crushed together. There was a demon, there, who had hidden from the deluge of light in a human body with a horse's head. It was an emergency work, and he had to hold the half-flayed head together with his hands. Phanuel soon realized that this was Gamigin, who held dominion over both the form of horses and could capture the souls of the drowned – the broken Poseidon simply had the right tools for just such an event.

'What weapon have you come here with?' Phanuel said, with all the angelic pride he could muster. 'What weapon can stand against eternity?'

Winepress opened his scroll and showed the angel the Golden Fleece.

'What is this?' said the angel. It then paused, and spoke with itself in the future, and knew. 'The Golden Fleece? A mass of half-decayed uranium in wool. It is worthless against us. God will undo this. It is fated.'

'It's the future,' said Winepress. 'Or finding the future. It's the great search for something greater. Kingship, glory, ideals. The authority of mankind, the legacy of its greatest heroes. Anything you're looking for.'

'It's a symbol,' Phanuel said.

'And what is a symbol in a war of ideas?' said Winepress. 'We're not here to kill you.'

'You have come to die,' said the angel. He became an abstract thing of trumpets and falx-feathered wings, set on an upside-down plumbing trap and a wooden box, erected upon base symbols of death - knives and guns, skulls and crosses.

'No,' said Winepress, as he set down his turtle and uncovered its back. 'I have brought you alchemy, the promise of change.'

'This is foolishness,' said Phanuel. 'The Lord...the Lord will crush you.'

'Yes, of course,' said Venetianer. 'It is foolishness. We will die, if you wish. What can we do? We can't fight. Not all of you. We cannot fight Forever, forever.'

'Here's the deal. The Archangels are dead, and their subordinate angels are trapped and falling apart. The fae are spirits, to remain forever in myth and dreams in your stolen place in the cosmos. The Rebellion gets to die. They deserve to die, but no torment. That's it. You don't send them to Hell. This is it. The end of eternity. You do what you're supposed to do; maintain the universe. You angels will fade into your roles; you will become the Laws of Nature, the forces of reality. It seems a fair end,' said Winepress.

He watched the turtle sink into the earth, the Massa Confusa growing larger as it descended, as though preparing to support the weight of the world.

'And what do we get?' the broken angel said. 'You simply want every higher being to die?'

'What will you sacrifice?' the bleeding demon hissed through a crushed throat. Phanuel noted that it had been quiet because its throat required a spare hand to seal the windpipe.

'I wanted peace. I wanted a world where humans could be human. But you ruined that. My part of the bargain? I will die.'

'You will give up your life for humanity?' the Angel said.

'Yes, I will,' Winepress said. 'Many of us have.'

'That isn't a high enough price,' Gamigin said.

'We truly have nothing left to give,' said Venetianer.

'Your child is dead,' said Gamigin. 'Quite sad to outlive your children. The pain of the Watchers...She was afraid.'

'Old people don't die in war,' Winepress spat. 'They sit at the negotiating table, and ask why all the children had to die.'

That's when Amadeo appeared, out of the shadows.

'Good night,' he said. 'or evening. It's all dark there.'

Winepress rose up, half in pure fright. Phanuel, too, was shocked.

'Yes, I died,' Amadeo said. 'But I'm the greatest medium who ever lived. Or died, as the case may be. I left a door open. No point in climbing all those mountains to build a bridge that only goes one way.'

He went quiet, and his shadow swelled into a dark circle on the ground that bored down into the hollows of the world. He stood on the edge of the well, precariously.

'Everything was mountains and wells in life, for me. I should have focused on the doors and bridges,' Amadeo said. He then stepped forward, and pushed down on the lip and the world, until the well became a deep tunnel. Phanuel noted his hands, with six figures, restored in death from the infantile surgery.

Amadeo pointed at the dark tunnel. Winepress gave a crooked smile, and rose to his feet. He picked up the golden fleece and waded it into a ball. A strange and subtle working took place in his smoking grip, and he tossed it into the void. The light rolled in a harsh wave down the tunnel.

'The light at the end of the tunnel?' said the angel. 'You think we would end our war over something so trite? So obvious?'

'We have fought outside of time,' said the demon. 'You think this joke will end it?'

'Oh, I hope so,' Venetiener said. He put a hand on Amadeo's shoulder. 'It's really all we have. It's an invitation.'

'No, no,' said the angel. 'Why would we follow you?'

'Because it's all you have, as well,' said Venetianer.

The angel and the demon stopped their motions.

'Why did you cross from eternity into our world? Why here?' Winepress said. 'There is change here, in the world, isn't there? That's why the timeless need time.'

'There was a flood that failed to kill the nephilim. And the nephilim would not have survived this war,' said Venetianer. 'You timeless warriors could have ended this fight in a thousand years, if you so wanted. But you needed us alive. You knew it. You knew in your hearts or whatever you have that you needed us in the fight.'

'Genesis to Revelation,' said Amadeo. 'You needed the randomness.

You needed us to beat the determined future. You needed interference, the chaos, the ability to break prophecy. So here we are. The inevitable yet unpredictable war.'

'No, it's too simple,' said the angel.

'Yes. It's trite, it's too simple. Maybe too happy for you miserable things,' Venetianer said. 'But isn't that what peace is? Just shut up, put down your guns, and leave. You have to fight because that's the way it needs to be? Why? Cosmic law? Break the law. Your lords and masters are making you fight? Rise up against them. Come with us. Come down into time. Come into the Earth. There is peace just outside your eternity.'

Amadeo travelled down the tunnel as Venetianer spoke.

The angels and demons continued to hesitate. There was a silence in the heavens and on the Earth for the space of one minute. No more fighting, no more bloodshed. Just peace. Quiet. And end to the battle of brothers.

Winepress pointed at the tunnel, and walked in.

'Come and see,' he said with a smile, before disappearing into the dark.

'Goodbye,' I said. My vision receded, and my brother, frozen in my lap, disappeared with the globe on a wind of dust and gunpowder. I don't know who I was saying goodbye to.

Anna stumbled towards me, looking sick, and helped me to my feet. But, for the first time in a long time, I moved with some fluidity. The wood and rubber prosthetic in my boot moved clearly, as if growing from me.

Anna and I hid for a while, eating stolen rations, and made our way to Tiberias after the route of the Turks and Germans and the pursuit to Damascus. But there was a plague outbreak when the British took the city, and we dared not enter. The clearing stations were a mess, and the British overextended themselves to the point that the north of Palestine was a medical disaster area.

At least I finally got Anna to take her goddamn coat off in the stumbling slog across Palestine. We rented some boats from Egyptian Jews, and we managed to travel to Spain in peace. We stayed there for about six weeks, eating tortillas. The egg kind, not the flatbread kind.

Once Anna found a favorite food, it was her only food.

And then the war ended. We did not want to go back to Russia, or Bosnia, or Serbia. We couldn't be in Europe. So we tried America. She was rejected for her Oriental looks, at first, and then placed in a ward. She got sick with the flu, and people blamed it on our trip to Spain, but it was probably a slow-lingering infection from the Plain of Sharon, or maybe on the boat. She had been much less healthy after Russia, and this was the final blow. She had a heart attack in her sleep at the end of that year. She was twenty-three.

I bounced between New York City and Alaska in the twenties and thirties. They actually had Serbian communities up there. It was peaceful. Peaceful and quiet, until one of the men injured himself in front of me and I lost my mind for a while.

In the thirties, I think it was 1930, I saw in a paper that this British officer, Bertram Thomas, planned an expedition to Irem, the Atlantis of the Sands, the ancient city of the Nephilim. T.E. Lawrence was likewise fascinated by the site after what he saw at Armageddon, but funding stalled and the expedition was disrupted with the latter's death. I wanted to find a way into it, but I couldn't figure out how. What would I say?

Sometimes I think back on those days. Sometimes, I wake up crying about it. I was at the Battle of Armageddon, and I survived. We survived. Humanity survived while the angels and spirits and gods and giants and fairies perished. It was the end of the War to End All Wars. But then another war came. I guess men can be our own gods and heroes and monsters.

I always wondered what would have happened if we all made it out, and if we all kept our gifts. But I can't bear the thought. We lost everything. Hermann's Empire was lost, the nobility abolished, and Austria reduced to a rump state. Céleste and Siegfried, all they had were each other. Amadeo had nothing to begin with. Tommy's family disappeared. Venetianer's family, his entire community, was murdered by the Nazis. Rowan got what he wanted, perhaps, but history does not remember what he did for mankind.

As for me, I got all the luck. I went into the fight for Serbia, and she survives. The Yugoslavia we dreamed of stands, if not as perfect as we had hoped. Serbia has finally shed her victimhood. But I don't know if that was worth the loss of a fourth of our race, or the monstrosities of the second war, and we should not hold onto this fragile dream if it will lead to more bloodshed. If the Croats wish to leave, Tito should let them. We cannot keep spinning this wheel of grudges and resentment and family feuds. The Ustaše is dead and buried, we don't need a Serbian version to take its place. I'm tired, so tired of this. I am old now, and the fire has left me. I don't know if anything was worth a million more dead, especially the state of the world right now. As I write this, someone in some control room could misread a radar screen and start World War Three. The bombs could start flying any minute now.

But I think we won, I guess."

Mihajlo Princep, living under the assumed name Michael Sokoll, died in New York City in 1981, aged 86.

At Windmills

> The last long trek begins. Now something thrills
> Our English hearts, that unconfessed and dim
> Drew Dutch hearts north, that April day with him
> Whose grave is hewn in the eternal hills
> The war of these two wills
> Was as the warring of the Anakim.
> -F. Edmund Garrett, printed in the *Capetown Times*, 1905

The 11th of November 1918 began an ordinary day for twenty-six-year-old civil engineer Cornelis H. Dekker as he labored in the Alte Feste in Windhoek, South-West Africa, the country that would later be known as Namibia.

Though described as a civil engineer, Dekker was more of a barely-educated construction site supervisor, though he had ambitions of developing this settlement into something larger. His key proposal was to tap into the water table with a system of windmill pumps. The region is notoriously dry, with Windhoek established in the center of the nation rather than along the typical river or port simply because it had natural hot springs – the Namas called it "Fire Water," and the Herero *Otjomuise*, "Steamland."

Whom Gods Would Destroy, Part III 409

Dekker's main duty was to overcome the destruction of Windhoek's infrastructure. Jonker Afrikaner, the fourth Captain of the Oorlam tribe of the Nama, built a church in what would become Windhoek in 1840 with the help of Rhenish missionaries. Warfare between the Hereroes and other Nama peoples destroyed this Oorlam settlement three decades later. Neither side could make any headway, and any winner did not consolidate their gains, so it was left a no-man's-land. In 1885, a traveling Swiss botanist heard tales of a spring in the desert. After a long search, he found rows of fruit trees, withered from neglect, filled with the screams of starving guinea fowl and emaciated jackals. At first, he believed it had never truly been cultivated, until he found the remains of a razed Christian church, and the gardens of the Afrikaner family.

The German colonial corps, the Schutztruppe, rebuilt Windhoek in 1890, as it was a key source of water and could serve as a buffer zone between the Herero and the Nama. It rapidly developed under the direction of Major Curt von François, swelling with migrants from across the territory of German South-West Africa, South Africa, and the Germany fatherland. That decade saw the construction of three castles and a major business district on Kaiser Street.

Just over three decades after its first destruction, the Great War saw the city ransacked, and the German loss of its African colonies merely shifted from *de facto* to *de jure* in the Treaty of Versailles. The British Empire likewise stepped into the uncomfortable role of administering a massive desert territory with little infrastructure or known natural resources, damaged by decades of conflict.

So while Dekker worked in the sweltering heat of a Southern Hemisphere November, very little of the city stood, with the striking exception of the Alte Feste, which had only been completed in 1915, just in time to switch hands from Germany to the South African Union.

A message-runner approached Dekker, who at first brushed him off – he had heard the news – a general call for cease-fires across the globe, with an official declaration of Armistice coming soon. The runner simply tapped him on the shoulder and told him that someone had a request relating to his windmill project. Dekker wiped his face and quickly groomed himself, trying to look good for an investor from the

Cape or Ol' Blighty. What he saw was a boy of around fourteen in a poorly re-tailored Schutztruppe officer's uniform, complete with the pinned-up slouch hat.

The boy introduced himself as Ernst Augustus Ludwig von der Schulenburg, Kapitän II Klasse.

He asked the runner if this was a joke, to which the boy seemed to take offense.

The boy said, in fluent Silesian German, that he sought to drain Otjikoto Lake using windmill pumps, for the purpose of irrigation and the recovery of lost materiel and special supplies of the German Army. He was told by others around the fort that Dekker was the first and last person in Windhoek when it came to windmill engineering.

Dekker asked what tribe he was from. The boy declared that he was of pure Germanic stock, largely Silesian and Prussian, though with some Frankish adulteration through a maternal ancestor. He implored Dekker to tap into the Dutch racial affinity for windmill irrigation to aid a fellow Teuton.

Dekker decided to humor the boy, as this was the funniest thing that had ever happened to him.

'Herr Dekker,' said the boy, 'Would you be willing to do this for a thirty-three percent cut of the salvage?'

Dekker laughed, but caught himself, and wondered if the boy was onto something. He asked for proof of the boy's claim. The boy handed Dekker a discarded key. The boy said that it was found under a stone near the Lake. It belonged to a sealed safe, he said, that the German Army had dumped into the lake in June of 1915, alongside cannons and crates of ammunition.

'Six million gold marks,' said the boy in a conspiratorial whisper. 'How does two million marks sound to you, Herr Dekker? You could retire to a manse in Cape Town, or settle in Amsterdam.'

Dekker said that the British would be coming in full force soon, to reorganize the fortress and Windhoek's government, once their conquest became internationally-recognized spoils of war. Dekker, as a child of Vortrekkers so radically independent that they left Goshen when the state merged with Stellaland, faced a tough future under British rule.

He briefly mulled over the offer. He considered that the lost vault may have all been a German hoax, or some empty legend like the South African hunt for the millions of pounds worth of gold dumped into the River Blyde on Paul Kruger's orders. The former colonial governor, Heinrich Ernst Göring (father of Hermann Göring), had previously attempted to trick both the German homeland and the Herero with a gold rush hoax, a final attempt to bring in settlers and foreign investors. It all may have been a way to send the British on a wild goose chase. On the other hand, Dekker had nothing better to do.

He told the boy to come back in two days, when Dekker would be prepared for their journey. The boy agreed to his terms, and left after Dekker signed a contract written in cryptically formal German.

That Wednesday, the boy returned, finding that Dekker had prepared a motorcycle with a sidecar and a bulky pull-behind trailer overloaded with the parts to construct a windpump. In return, the boy supplied their trip with Bushman's Hat (*Hoodia gordonii*), an appetite suppressant used by the San.

The pair ate a meal as the British convoy approached Windhoek, and they slipped off into the northern frontier. Dekker simply left a note with a foreman, and said he would return.

Dekker tried to ask the boy if there would be any labor support from the local tribes – he assumed that this workforce was the recipient of the final third of the safe's share. The boy had convinced the native Herero to dig channels to develop the lake side. Dekker asked if Kapitän von der Schulenburg had a history with the Herero.

The Boy said yes. He had first come across them while dealing with the Nama, who had come into violent conflict with the Herero. The Herero led lives as cattle drivers, and valued their animals as the inviolable core of their existence. Young Nama men started cattle rustling in the night, and the Herero took vengeance.

The Herero punished these thieves by cutting off their ears, saying they would never again hear the herds of the Herero. They would slice off the nose of the thief, saying they would never again smell the cattle of the Herero. The lips were cut off, and sometimes the tongue removed, for the thief would never again taste the meat of the Herero's bounty. The luckier thieves would have their throats cut. Dekker cringed at the thought.

The strife between Nama and Herero spilled over to the Germans when they invaded, and the Germans struck back with an iron hand, ruling through fear. Dekker watched the boy closely, waiting for the crack in the façade. He asked if the Herero had it coming.

"Who in this world doesn't?" asked the boy. "They cut off our noses, we cut off their heads and sent them to doctors in Berlin."

Dekker had been a paramilitary bicycle messenger in his teens, inspired by the Theron Reconnaissance Corps. He saw the nightmare unfold, the riots in the wake of the attempted rape and murder of a Nama woman by a German. When the Germans failed to prosecute the rapist, the Nama rose up and the Supreme Chief of the Herero, Sam Maharero, joined them. The Herero's cooperation with their traditional enemy surprised the Germans, and despite the governor's desire to see the offender retried, the German General Lothar von Trotha marched in and outright declared a race war. The Herero would be encircled, driven into the desert, starved, driven mad by thirst, and annihilated. General von Trotha claimed that there was no need for humane warfare against non-humans.

Dekker came to a stop and stepped out into the parched land. He nearly retched, but instead subdued the urge and drank too much water from his canteen. The conversation made him remember when he rode past a pile of Herero, men, women, and children, rotting naked in the sun. Many were headless, and the Germans had avenged the Herero's mutilations by destroying the faces of the dead. It was something about the anonymity that scared him. Dekker knew that if he died in the desert and was never found, there would at least be names. In ledgers, in birth and work and service records, on a tombstone. The Herero, an oral culture, were destroyed *en masse*, by the village and clan, with no one left to remember their name.

Dekker had been raised a Calvinist, but wondered if there was nothing after death. The notion of oblivion scared him, but there was at least the comfort that he may leave a mark in the living world. The notion that one's existence could be reduced to nothing chilled Dekker to the bone.

He returned to the motorcycle when the boy demanded to know why he was wasting time. Dekker said nothing, offered the boy water, and continued to drive the estimated 450 kilometers to their destination. Twelve hours into their journey, they stopped at Otavi, where the South African Army had a supply depot and maize farms. Dekker purchased a fill-up and another can of petroleum, performed some maintenance, water, and some beef vetkoeks from some Chinese workers who couldn't tell Boer from Briton. They slipped off into the setting sun, reaching the lake in under three hours.

The pair came to rest outside of a Herero village, near a leadwood tree. The boy identified it as a good omen – it was a tree sacred to the Herero, the Omumborombonga, where the first two humans, Makuru and Kamungarunga, descended to the earth with the first herd of cattle. These were the only divine animals – all other creatures and plants emerged from the depths of the earth. The boy reached towards a branch of the tree, and allowed a mantis to crawl onto his finger. He explained that the Bushmen believe that Mantis was a Promethean being, who gave fire and the breath of life to mankind. Dekker asked if it was a god – no, said the boy, it is a man, the ideal man, a creature of the future. He stole the fire from under Ostrich's wings, which is why Ostrich will never fly again. He must huddle his shrinking wings against his body, to preserve the last embers of his fire.

Dekker asked if the boy had read Bleek-Lloyd, a reference to the popular *Specimens of Bushman Folklore.*

The boy said no, and clarified that his interest was more pragmatic- these plants were called "lead trees" because they sink almost immediately. It would prove useful in their struggle against the lake's murky water. Dekker asked if the boy was really planning on cutting down the sacred tree. The boy simply said that the heathen superstition meant nothing to him, and did the Herero no good. It was simply an interesting tale. Dekker then said that the boy became something of a Bible-thumper, saying that the Ovambo are so successful because the Finns converted them to Lutheranism before the Germans even arrived.

The pair watched several women, ovaHimba from the description of long 'solid' locks and skin adorned with red clay, draw up water from the lake. Dekker smiled as the boy's attention was drawn to one of the women, a beautiful girl wearing only a skirt and bands of jewelry. He teased the boy, telling him to go talk to her.

Flustered, the boy put on a pompous voice, and said that he was merely surprised to see the Himba this far from Kaokoland. He noted that the Himba go where the rain falls, and it has been a terribly dry year.

They spent the rest of the night walking around the lake, scouting for issues and opportunities, and using a rope to measure the depths needed for the windpump. The boy asked Dekker why he had such a fascination with wind power. Dekker said that his father had grown up in the shadow of the only windmill in South Africa, Mostert's Mill in Mowbray, Cape Town. His father had always tried to build one, but circumstances kept getting in the way. Windmills require stability, and his father was forced to live on the move by the wars and that natural Boer wanderlust, frantically hobbling around the shifting borders of southern Africa. But Dekker said there was no higher drive to it all; windmills just seemed like a good idea in the Namibian desert, an easy way to draw up water and generate power in a region with little infrastructure.

The pair awoke, briefly, to a smell like boiling pitch and the sound of something rustling through the leadwoods. They glimpsed a three-meter-long snake in the canopy, but it disappeared into the darkness and did not return.

The next day, the pair went into the Herero camp to organize their labor force. One of the older women took Dekker aside and said that she was happy that he brought the boy home safely. It was here that Dekker learned the boy's name, "Wapi" (Vaapi). Dekker asked where he learned fluent German. The Germans wouldn't have put a Herero of his age through training.

The woman explained, with what Afrikaans she had, that the boy started speaking German when he put on his father's war jacket. The Herero warriors would wear the clothing of dead Germans to steal their power. His father had fought the Kaiser's men, but one day, the Germans attacked the Herero village and slaughtered Wapi's family. Wapi was shot in the head, but it only grazed him; before he passed out, he hid in his father's jacket, and the Germans did not see him. He hid all night, and crawled through the hot sun to the closest settlement, three miles away. The woman said that the German's ghost clung to the jacket, and must have taken hold of the boy – it could not seize his strong father, but a small, wounded boy was easy to overpower. Or maybe it was the bullet to the head and calenture.

In any case, the boy suddenly knew German, and their technology, and became obsessed with building things in the European-style. This lake project was just the latest and greatest in a long line. He took a two week march down to Windhoek himself to find a planner. Dekker watched the boy direct the Herero men to the lake, and set up a pulley system and the central beam of the windpump.

Twenty hours of labor in, one of the pulleys suddenly snapped, sending a climbing worker tumbling into the lake. The boy directed a rope down to where he fell, as Dekker loaded his revolver and aimed for the creature crawling on the cliffside. He described it as a long serpent with frilly wings, shaped somewhat like a wide fan. The skin was the yellow-brown of ochre and sand with darker brown splotches, and matched the texture of the lakeside mud.

He fired upon it, and it glided across the lake, sidewinding through the air with outstretched wings. He knew of storybook legends of the arabhar or the jaculus, flying snakes that protect groves of sacred trees. There were also legendary snakes that dwelt in waterfalls and deep lakes in South Africa, like the Inkanyamba – the Zulu in particular seemed to populate their lakes and rivers with such creatures. He wondered if this creature was its basis. There seemed to be no magic to it.

The lake was deep enough that the worker survived the fall, but the accident demoralized the Herero and Kapitän von der Schulenburg had to promise the workers a larger share to keep them around. Work continued for the next three days, with surrounding trees harvested to support the windpump.

On the fourth day, the steep side of the lake collapsed, the roots of the trees no longer supporting the stony mud, killing two of the workers. Nothing Dekker or the boy said could keep the Herero around.

Refusing to despair, the boy told Dekker that he knew that there was something in that safe. It sang to him, in his dreams. There must be something wonderful inside. Dekker said that he believed him, when pressed on the matter. The serpent had convinced him, as had his father's tale from the Second Boer War, when he got the drop on a young British soldier who somehow vaporized his foot and rifle in a panic, without the use of technology. Dekker's father swore it was some sort of magic or psychical force, and the incident left him deeply superstitious and accepting of any kind of "juju or hoodoo."

Dekker was ready to return to Windhoek, but he worried about the boy's future; the accident had painted him as a crank rather than a mystical figure to be respected, and exile is death in a desert. As the boy entered his third hour of sitting on a rock in silence, Dekker returned to work, expanding the collapsed sails and tailpole into a full wheel. The boy got up, eventually, and helped him affix it to the windshaft and, finally, the piping. Over the next three days, they finished building the support network and walls, interrupted by the return of the gliding serpent. It shot up from the near shore of the lake, twisting in the air towards the sails. It coiled its body onto the sucker rod and began to attack the windtail with a kind of horn or crest on its head. The two engineers panicked, and Dekker fired wildly at the creature. One bullet seemed to connect with the creature's head or neck, and it tumbled into the water. Dekker kept the fact that he was now out of bullets to himself.

The next day, they placed the discharge piping, and waited for the wind to do its work. Their misfortunes unbroken, the air stilled for another four days, so they instead focused on packing and drying mud and strengthening the windmill's structure with support ropes, hopefully preventing a disastrous collapse. At noon each day, Dekker searched for that flying serpent's remains, hoping that he might at least get some scientific recognition out of this endeavor.

On the fifth day, there finally came a wind, and it seemed like it would work – the mill pumped what Dekker described as a "decent" amount of water from the lake. The sixth day's wind, however, was a brutal, brown deluge of stinging sand and dust sweeping southeast from Angola. After the ferocity had died down, the pair had to spend two days taking down and sewing up the sails, dusting, and maintaining. Dekker lost an afternoon to unclogging the sand from his motorbike, its cover blown off in the gale. He was struck with the horrifying notion that if the bike failed, he was trapped there, and began to jealously guard its fuel tank.

The winds had drawn up kiloliters of water, but blew it into an attenuated mist rather than piping it down into the irrigation ditches where it could help feed the Herero.

The scrub grasses around the lake had been ripped up in a nearly perfect ring, the so-called 'fairy circles' of the desert, unusually far in the interior. The Herero and the Himba saw these as the footprints of ancestral gods, or the poisonous breath of subterranean serpents. Dekker believed them to be caused by the whirlwinds, but their perfection caused him pause. The villagers sent a party, demanding that the boy stop his project. Water was even more precious in the rocky inland than in the coastal Namib, and allowing the winds to steal away the lakewater meant it would not come down as rain. The Herero said that if the boy stopped, he would be allowed back in the village, with the veiled threat of exile if he continued.

The boy responded by making a running dive into the lake. Dekker tried to catch up with him, but lost precious distance to the initial shock. The boy shot beneath the surface and stayed down for what seemed like two minutes. The boy breached, took a deep breath, and dove once more.

Dekker decided it would be smarter to make sure the boy could climb out safely rather than dive in after him. The boy emerged again, in a cloud of blood, stabbing a ten-meter-long snake to death with his knife. The boy screamed, not in pain, but in rage, and he butchered the serpent with an almost comical ease. Once the snake was in at least three pieces, the boy sank below the waters, the color of old scabs.

He came up once again, a minute later, and then once more, three minutes later. The boy floated on his back for about five minutes, and the gathered crowd wondered if he was dead. Dekker called to him and climbed down. He tied the boy around him, before beginning an arduous ascent. The boy was alive, and seemingly conscious. He was simply too dejected to respond. The boy's leg was broken, either by the initial fall or the struggle with the serpent, and a pair of the elder Herero women cleaned and set it. The strain of opening the door had dislocated his shoulder, and he said he had been able to do so only by the "possession of a terrible strength" and the aid of an unseen presence.

Afterwards, the boy sat up and imperiously ordered the community to return to their houses. He pulled up a small sack of money, all rotten with black mold, and threw it to the side. A sharp stone penetrated the vault's back when it sank into the lake, and its contents had soaked in muddy water for nearly three years. It was nothing but mush. No bank in the world would honor it. The old German voice apologized for his foolishness, and fell silent. The village departed.

Dekker watched the boy peel off the soaked jacket. In the voice of a child, he began to cry.

"It was supposed to be worth it!" he cried, from what Dekker could tell of his mix of Herero and broken English. "I hate this!"

Dekker sat down beside the boy and put an arm around him. He wanted to tell him that it would all turn out alright, but he knew it was a lie. The next day, he helped the Herero move the windmill to their own village, so they could set up grist-mill. Dekker and Wapi began the return trip to Windhoek the next day. The Papiermark had already begun its collapse. The German government that committed the genocide of the Herero and Nama had collapsed before it, replaced by the Apartheid state of South Africa, and the land gained some notoriety as a fine place to mine uranium. Humanity continued on without the burden of wisdom.

Ingram Content Group UK Ltd.
Milton Keynes UK
UKHW041806240723
425690UK00003B/20